24 DEC 2012

GREEN GIRLS

Also by Michael Kimball and available from Headline Feature

Undone
Mouth to Mouth

GREEN GIRLS

Michael Kimball

HEADLINE
FEATURE

First published in Great Britain in 2001
by HEADLINE BOOK PUBLISHING

A HEADLINE FEATURE book

10 9 8 7 6 5 4 3 2 1

British Library Cataloguing in Publication Data

Kimball, Michael
Green girls
1.Suspense fiction
I.Title
813.5'4[F]

ISBN 0 7472 2311 4 (hardback)
ISBN 0 7472 7268 9 (trade paperback)

Typeset by
Letterpart Limited, Reigate, Surrey

Printed and bound in Great Britain by
Mackays of Chatham PLC, Chatham, Kent

HEADLINE BOOK PUBLISHING
A division of Hodder Headline
338 Euston Road
LONDON NW1 3BH

www.headline.co.uk
www.hodderheadline.com

For my daughter Sarah

Thank You

Richard Callahan
Brian Chernack
Kevin Farley
Chris Fahy
Jodi Frechette
Nancy Graham
Rick Hautala
Phil Jones
Chuck Landry
Paul Mann
Bo Marks
Art Mayers
Alan Philbrook
Nessa and Pete Reifsnyder
Brenda Reimels
Linda Richmond
. . . for reading early drafts and being honest with your opinions

Special thanks to Richard Callahan and Jodi Frechette, for multiple readings and keen insight
Bert Allen, for showing me around the Piscataqua River Bridge
Michael Dow, for your carpentry expertise
John Mercurio, for your racing expertise
Bo Marks, John Pelletier, and Pamela Ames, for your legal expertise
Todd Lyon, for hypnotizing me
Chris and Laurie Simpson, for introducing me to the Secret Garden
Howie Nielsen, for your knowledge of birds
Alan Ereira and the BBC, for your videotape about the Kogi Indians, titled *From the Heart of the World, The Elder Brothers Warning* (ISBN 1-56176-247-4)
Howard Morhaim, my literary agent, for making me get it right
Stephen King, forever, for giving me my break
Bill Massey, my editor, for your patience and good editing
Glenna Kimball, for years and years of your love

Note: Although character names were borrowed from friends, personalities, relationships and events are totally fictional.

In the beginning, there was blackness.
Only the sea.
In the beginning no sun, no moon, no people.
In the beginning there were no animals, no plants.
Only the sea.

The sea was the Mother.
The Mother was not the people.
She was not anything.
Nothing at all.
She was when she was, darkly.
She was memory and potential.
She was Aluna.

Kogi Shaman

One by one he subdued his father's trees
By riding them down over and over again
Until he took the stiffness out of them . . .

Robert Frost, *Birches*

PROLOGUE

A great time to figure things out. The young man and his heart plummeting from the top of the bridge, his mind scattered in the ocean wind. A girl falls beside him, reaching for the sky, the two of them silent, weightless, floating like fairies, balanced against the crescent moon.

The way time slows down, as the trussed steel of the bridge whispers past, the young man not only can smell the river that rises to meet him, he has time to consider how a particular mustiness tinges the odour.

It's metabolism, the reason time slows down. Hummingbirds, for example, have such a high metabolic rate, they perceive human movement in slow motion. To a fruit fly, we are statues; their day on earth lasts a lifetime.

In humans, fear increases metabolism . . . which is why the victim of a car wreck will describe the accident as though it happened in slow-motion. Extreme fear causes extreme time stall. What is the limit? It's long been acknowledged that some people who fall to their deaths actually die of heart failure before they land. Perhaps they die of old age.

In the 4.03 seconds it takes to fall 250 feet, from the top of the Piscataqua River Bridge to the water, a man with an active mind can do a lot of thinking. Not that Jacob William Winter is plummeting to his death and watching his life pass before him. Because he is not.

He is simply seeing how things came to be.

PART ONE

CHAPTER ONE

'**M**y wife didn't bail me?'
'She refused,' said the lawyer, unlatching his briefcase. 'She did bring your car, though, and by the looks of it, threw all your possessions in the backseat.' He pulled out a manila folder and set it on the table in front of him. 'You were bailed by a woman named Alix Callahan.'

Jacob didn't recognize the name at first. All his possessions?

The lawyer gave him a look. 'I assume she's a friend.'

'Alix Callahan?' Jacob said. 'There was an Alix Callahan in school with me, fifteen years ago. But we were definitely not friends. Why is she bailing me?'

'Maybe she's had a change of heart,' the lawyer said, then snapped on his tape recorder and said in a work-weary way, 'Okay, tell me what happened.'

'I had a difference of opinion with my psychiatrist,' Jacob said. 'That's what I've been told.'

'You hit him with a radio,' the lawyer said, 'then proceeded to tear your house apart.'

'I don't remember,' Jacob said. He could see his car outside the courthouse window – a cardboard box shoved up against the rear window. After two nights in the York County Jail, all he wanted was to leave, go home and talk to Laura. 'What do you mean, all my possessions?'

'Clothes, computer, bathroom things.'

'My clothes?'

The attorney leaned back in his chair, taking care to straighten the pleat of his wrinkled trousers, waiting for Jacob to get it through his head: Laura didn't want him coming home.

He'd barely slept since he was locked up, pacing and pacing and needing to talk to her, needing to know. During his first night, he even

5

tried to bend the bars. It was incomprehensible, the chain of events that had led him here, and how everything he'd believed in – his family, his home, his life – everything . . . Was it really gone?

Now another part of his brain churned with this new information, the woman who had paid his bail. At UNH, Alix Callahan had been a notorious undergrad – lesbian-activist slash poet slash rain-forest-activist. Jacob Winter had been a star-pitcher slash architecture student who finally quit school at the end of his junior year, when he got his first book published, a small press phenomenon called *John*, that slid onto the *Times'* bestseller list where it remained for seven weeks before slipping off into obscurity, along with Jacob himself.

'Mr Winter, I have eight other cases today,' said the lawyer.

Jacob shook his head helplessly. 'I have no memory. I'm sorry.'

'That's not the way it works,' the lawyer said. 'With them, you can't remember. With me, you have total recall.' He spoke in a superior, if somewhat careful way. Men, in particular, tended to be careful around Jacob. Six-two and two-ten, he was solidly proportioned and handsome in a Nordic way – square jaw and heavy brow over hazel green eyes, a mess of brown hair on his head. Even when he smiled, it seemed a muscular function.

Now, lifting his eyes to the plaster ceiling as though it were a movie screen, he paused to let the wave of disbelief pass over him. Up till now, Jacob Winter had prided himself on living a scrupulous life. Mayflower descendant, distinguished author, furniture maker, Little League coach, unequivocally faithful to his wife Laura, devoted to their son Max; a tireless worker, did not cheat at sports, did not cheat on taxes, had never cheated another person in business, and had managed through a gift of language to avoid – with one or two exceptions – ever causing offense to anyone, even those in need. Yet here he was, in a room with a public defender, trying to recall two minutes of oblivion that would forever change his life.

Over the past thirty-six hours, Jacob had replayed the episode relentlessly: coming home from the Red Sox game with his son Max, seeing Price Ashworth's green sports car in the driveway – a new BMW Z3 Roadster.

He told the lawyer everything as it replayed: Max running into the house, Jacob stopping at the Roadster to feel the hood, then walking into the kitchen. He can smell the dinner before he sees it, actually its aftermath on the kitchen table: two red lobster shells on their good Italian stoneware, the garganelli-mussel soup on the stove, the half-eaten loaf of Italian bread on a cutting board, the empty wine bottle.

He remembers every detail. The matching bowls of olive oil and grated Parmesan.

Even if Jacob wanted to abandon the film, he could not. The same scenes kept looping over and over in his mind.

'Looks like someone had a nice dinner,' Max says, taking an ice cream bar out of the freezer.

Jacob thinks he can hear the Red Sox game playing. But the kitchen radio is turned off. And they have no television.

It's impossible to forget this much: It's the way he steps into the hallway . . . then stops when he sees his bedroom door is closed. It's the way he turns back to the kitchen.

'Maxie, why don't you go down to the field and play,' he says to his son, with a quiet tightness he hopes Max won't detect.

'Play what?' Max's mouth full of ice cream.

Jacob holds onto the doorway, his stomach clenched. 'Okay, Champ?'

Max complies, but only after giving his dad a quizzical frown.

It's the way Jacob stands there with his eyes shut, listening while the boy's footsteps tumble down the porch steps. Then the way he turns and floats to the door in absolute silence, while his head churns with noise. Last week he came home from baseball practice to find Laura sitting on the couch with a bowl of popcorn, talking on the telephone with Price. He thought it odd, since she's worked for Price for twelve years, spends forty hours a week with him. She explained that Price was thinking about moving his practice and was seeking her advice. Jacob didn't question her. Laura is his wife of twelve years, Price Ashworth his former psychiatrist. Jacob tries not to speculate.

But now he watches himself, the way he opens the door, just a crack, as if he's afraid of disturbing them. It's too dark to see anything – the shades are drawn – except the two sets of eyes regarding him from the bed, dark and darting, the eyes of squirrels.

'Keep going.'

Jacob stared dizzily at the table. 'I hit him,' he said with a shrug, as if he wasn't sure.

'And?'

'I must have. With the radio. I don't know.'

'You gave the man a concussion. The radio's smashed. Your house looks like a tornado went through.'

'I've tried to remember—'

'You swung a radio,' the attorney said, with a shrug of his own. 'Dr Ashworth's head was in its path. What don't you remember?' He had

7

photos in his hand. 'Looks like some very nice furniture – which I understand you made yourself?'

Jacob wouldn't take the photos. His mind was engaged: Had he been too self-absorbed? Too caught up in his work?

'For the record, your wife is also claiming memory loss.' The lawyer moved his brow in an almost sarcastic way. 'And Dr Ashworth has declined to press charges – which ultimately doesn't matter. It's felony assault.'

'I don't understand,' Jacob said. The low sun through the window blinded him.

'State of Maine versus Jacob Winter. With felonies, it's the state that charges you.' Setting a bottle of pills on the table, he said, 'Dr Ashworth brought these for you. He came with your wife when she brought your car. The desk sergeant said you refused to take the medication.'

'I don't need them,' Jacob said.

The attorney examined the bottle. 'Haldol,' he said. 'It's an anti-psychotic, is that right?'

'I was diagnosed as having an overactive imagination,' Jacob told him. 'Twelve years ago. My mother had died, and I was distraught. I don't need to be medicated.'

'I see,' the lawyer said. 'You are aware that aggravated assault carries a potential ten-year prison sentence—? "My client can't remember" is not a defense I want to bring before the court.'

Jacob turned his head to the window again, waiting for the tremor in his chest to subside. All his questions – How did it happen? What had he done to turn her away? How long had it been going on? – suddenly replaced by reality: Prison. And the raw terror of being separated from his son. He turned back to his attorney. 'Maybe it'll come to me. It won't now. May I go home?'

'Of course not.'

Jacob's heart stopped.

'Restraining orders,' the lawyer explained, and he pulled a document out of his folder. 'Under no circumstances are you to make contact with, or go anywhere near, your wife. Or Dr Ashworth.'

'How can I talk to Laura?' Jacob said.

'You can't.'

'I've got to talk to her.'

The attorney shook his head, wide-eyed. 'Under no circumstances.' He enunciated each syllable. 'You are not to telephone your wife, write her a letter, send her an email. If you see her on the street, turn your head and go the other way. No contact.'

'What about Max, my son?' Jacob said, standing.

'Take your seat, Mr Winter.'

'He needs to see me.'

The lawyer raised his brow as he studied Jacob, waiting for him to sit. Jacob took a big breath, then complied. He brought his fingers to his head. He felt like he was suffocating. 'Can we at least open a window?'

'We're almost done,' the lawyer said indifferently. 'Visitation arrangements with your son will have to be worked out between your wife's attorney and myself.'

'I'm trying to make you understand,' Jacob said. 'Max has problems. He needs consistency in his life.'

The lawyer jotted something in his legal pad. 'I'll see what I can arrange,' he said, while Jacob asked himself for the thousandth time: *How did I drive her away?*

The lawyer pulled Jacob's car keys out of the folder and slid them across the table. 'Also, your wife left two messages,' he said as he removed a paper clip from a piece of note paper. 'A Chief Adler called.'

'I'm a part-time dispatcher at the Kittery Fire Station,' Jacob explained.

The attorney said, 'You've been suspended without pay, pending outcome of the case.'

Jacob took another breath. He decided that he'd hire his own lawyer and find some way of paying him, maybe trade for furniture.

'And a Donny Donnelly?'

'He's my coach,' Jacob said, looking up with dread anticipation. 'I manage my boy's baseball team.'

'Mr Donnelly will be taking over the team,' the lawyer said. 'The league voted.'

Jacob got back to his feet, unwilling to hear any more. This time the attorney stood with him, not about to argue. 'Call me when you get settled, and we'll arrange a time to talk,' he said, then picked up the bottle of Haldol and tossed it to Jacob.

'What's this?'

'*That?*' replied the lawyer, 'is step number one in convincing the DA's Office that you feel remorse for your actions and you're sincere about seeing that it never happens again.'

Jacob paused. He could feel the blood pounding up into his head. He set the pills on the table, very gently.

The lawyer gave him a look. 'I also want you to get a steady job as soon as possible – and suitable living arrangements. From here on, you need to be the model of stability.'

'Thank you,' Jacob said, opening the door to leave.

'One more thing. She wanted you to have this.'

Jacob's heart gave a hopeful tug. 'Laura?'

'Right.' The lawyer handed him a business card, colored green. 'No, your old schoolmate. Alix Callahan.'

As soon as Jacob was able, he broke the law. Pulling up in front of his house – Laura's car wasn't there – he didn't even have time to turn off the key before the front door burst open and Max came running . . . limping, actually. He already had his baseball uniform on – SPEED-WAY TAVERN – and Jacob's heart swelled. He didn't know how he was going to manage this conversation.

'Mom went to the store for some things, you coming in?' Max said, stopping at Jacob's window – which meant that Laura had evidently told Max about the restraining order.

'Not right now,' Jacob said. 'What happened to your foot?'

'Nothing.'

Jacob could see his ankle was bandaged and his glasses had been glued together at the bridge. He reached out and tugged the brim of Maxie's cap. 'Let's take a ride.'

'How was summer school?' Jacob said, after they had driven a half mile.

'Lousy.'

'Stick to your behavior plan?'

'I guess.'

Normally Jacob would be there when Max got off the school bus, full of chatter about the day, while they had popcorn or peanuts or a bowl of fruit together. 'How many hours did you play computer games this afternoon?'

'I reached the seventh level,' Max said nonchalantly. 'Bet I'm the only one in this town. Probably the whole state of Maine.'

'I wouldn't be surprised,' Jacob said. 'How'd you hurt your leg?'

'Fell.'

'Broke your glasses too.'

'Yeah.'

'Doing something crazy?'

Max shrugged, waiting for the real conversation to start.

Jacob pulled the car into Seapoint Beach and shut off the engine. The two of them sat and listened to the waves for a minute. Finally Jacob began. 'Max, you know how we always try to be honest with each other?'

'I got something for you,' Max broke in. 'When Mom was packing your things.' He dug in his pocket and came out with the purple ribbon and brass-plated medallion. *Bravery, Gallantry, Honor.* Max turned it over and read aloud: ' "To Jacob William Winter, from the Firefighters Association, Town of Kittery, Maine." '

'Want it?' Jacob said.

'It's your medal,' Max said. 'Keep it, it's cool.' He opened the glove box and tossed it inside.

'Maxie, I did something wrong.'

Jacob stopped, reconsidered. The boy didn't deserve this, he thought angrily.

'What I'm trying to tell you is, I hurt somebody.'

'You hit Doctor A with the radio, that's what Luke Fecto said.' Luke Fecto, son of Phil Fecto, the detective who had arrested Jacob. Luke was also on the baseball team, one of the no-talent jackals who tried to distinguish themselves by ridiculing Max.

'I'm not sure what happened,' Jacob told him. 'I did lose my temper. Dr A was injured. And I got arrested.'

'Luke said that's why the police won't let you come home – because you blew your mind.'

Jacob shook his head. 'Luke Fecto doesn't know his rear end from a hole in the ground. Did Mom talk to you about it?'

'She said that Doctor A fell off his bike, and you got arrested for speeding.' Max rolled his eyes.

Jacob said, 'Well, I guess Mom was trying to protect us both.'

Max gave him a look. 'I thought we weren't supposed to lie to each other.'

Jacob remembered something his father said to him once: *Sometimes a little lie is the only way to show your love.* In fact, it was the very last thing his father said to him – and it was bullshit then, same as now. He put his hand on his son's shoulder and could feel the heat rising off his young body.

'Maxie, you know how sometimes people have emergencies, like their house catches on fire, or their cellar floods?' This is what Jacob had rehearsed. 'Well, Mom and I have had an emergency in our marriage, and for a little while I'm going to be staying someplace else.'

'Mom already told me that,' Max said, staring down at his baseball shoes. 'Why can't I go with you?'

'I'm going to be right down the road,' Jacob told him. 'You and I are going to spend lots of time together, just like we always have.' Stay focused, Jacob told himself, as he swallowed back the lump in his throat. 'Maxie, Mom and I love you very much, and we're both making

11

sure we do the right thing for you. Right now the right thing for you is to stay with Mom until we work things out.'

'But what did she do?' Max said, looking up at him, his voice getting smaller. 'I could hear you yelling and breaking everything.'

Jacob couldn't meet his eyes. And he thought things had already gotten as bad as they could get. He shook his head. 'I was wrong,' he said. 'I did a stupid thing.'

'But I don't want to stay with her.'

'Maxie, this was my fault,' Jacob told him. 'Mom's a wonderful person and a wonderful mother. She loves you and she'd do anything for you. Anything. You know that, right?'

He waited for his son to look at him, but Max was picking at his ankle bandage. It was true, what Jacob was saying. Laura had once gotten them all evicted from a year-round oceanfront cottage because the owners, officers in the local Boy Scout organization, had terminated Max's membership for climbing a forty-foot pine and hanging the troop flag at the top. Not that he shouldn't have been disciplined for the daredevil stunt – Laura punished Max herself: took away his computer privileges and grounded him for a week – but they all seemed so happy to get rid of him. So she marched next door and threw his uniform into their barbecue pit. Laura had loved that little house. But she protected Max like a mother bear.

'Come on,' Jacob said, rubbing the back of Max's head. 'I'd better get you back so you don't miss your game.'

Max gave him a look. 'You mean "we," don't you?'

Jacob sighed.

The boy turned away again. Jacob started the car and pulled onto the road.

'Max, I have to take a break from coaching the team,' he said, 'just until we work things out. I guess Mom and I will have to take turns going to your games. Tonight can be her turn.'

Max watched the houses go past. Jacob saw him wipe a tear from his eye, and he felt the ache rising in his chest again. 'You can pretend I'm there, okay?' he said. 'You know what I'd tell you to do.'

'Lay off the high, hard stuff,' Max droned.

'That's right,' Jacob told him. 'Your heart wants a home run, but your head tells you you've got a much better chance of getting a single. Which are you gonna listen to?'

Max kept the back of his head to his dad. Jacob let him have some time, and quiet. Coming into their neighborhood, seeing Laura's car in the driveway, he pulled in front of the neighbor's house, keeping his eyes on the windows, trying to get a glimpse of her. Then the side door opened and she was there, wearing jeans and a plain white shirt, looking achingly beautiful. But the way she stared – first at Jacob, as if she were in pain – then at his car, as if she were taking down his license plate – like a stranger. Then she went back in the house.

Jacob's heart sank into his lap.

'Are you guys getting divorced?'

'What?' Jacob gave Max a puzzled look, as if he'd asked if it was going to snow. 'Maxie, you're jumping to conclusions. It's like I tell you with your baseball, don't let your emotions take over for your brain.'

But the way Max scrutinized him through those magnifying lenses. 'Mom was on the phone today, talking quietly so I wouldn't hear,' he said. 'Afterwards, I hit redial, and a lawyer's office answered.'

Speaking of high, hard ones. Jacob had no ready answer.

Awaiting his response, Max turned to stare out his window, as though waiting for a doctor to stick him with a needle. The question was inevitable; also one that Jacob himself did not know the answer to. He stared out at his hollow house, his insides melting. The truth of the matter was something he had not been able to admit, even to himself: Whether the marriage survived or not, the life they had known – all three of them – was over.

'Maxie, do me a favor,' he said to his son. 'Let Mom and me worry about the adult stuff, okay? We'll figure things out. What you need to worry about is your swing.'

'I know,' Max said wearily, reaching for the door handle, while Jacob reached for his shoulder and felt it slide through his fingers.

'Maxie?'

Max looked back, his eyes watering.

'I want you to remember,' Jacob said, and he made the same vow to himself: 'Your head, not your heart.'

CHAPTER TWO

The shadows stretched lazily across the road when Jacob finally checked into E-Z Acres, a string of one-room cottages off old Route One. The rent was reasonable enough, $300 a week, with a telephone, stove and tiny refrigerator. No TV. No pets. He got his boxes, bags, laptop and printer out of the car, set them on the floor, then distributed his clothes on the bed: his underwear, his khaki work pants, his blue work shirts, his team jersey – SPEEDWAY TAVERN. He folded the clothes and assembled them in the bureau. He hung his pants and his two dress shirts in the tiny closet. He brought the bag of toilet articles – Laura had thoughtfully packed his toothbrush, razor, deodorant, soap, and another bottle of Haldol – into the bathroom, where he organized the things in the medicine cabinet and flushed the pills down the toilet, along with his small medal of valor: *Bravery, Gallantry, Honor.*

Then he lay down on the hard bed, hoping to read, or maybe sleep for a few minutes. But his mind was racing too fast, so he took his notepad out of his pocket and made himself a schedule: 7:30 GROCERIES. 8:00 DINNER. 8:30 READ. 10:00 BED.

This is how Jacob contains his mind – with order, not medication.

Tomorrow. 6:00 WALK, NEWSPAPER. 7:00 SHOWER, BREAK-FAST. 8:00 JOB. 9:00 CALL LAWYER, ARRANGE TO SEE MAX.

In his books – and he hasn't written anything in several months – he describes objects, he explains functions. He does not create characters. He does not invent stories. He reads only non-interpretive nonfiction; currently, *The Arms Bazaar*, an out-of-print book that documents the history of international weapons trade since the industrial revolution.

He does not indulge himself with fantasies, does not speculate. When he makes love to Laura, he is always present with her, and her alone. The furniture he builds is classic in design, always practical. He employs the golden section – that is, a dimensional ratio of three

14

to five – because such relationships are aesthetically pleasing. His furniture is rectangular, the wood painstakingly selected and finished to a natural luster, and his tools – he uses only hand tools – are always sharp. He puts them back in their place at the end of every work session, and always sweeps his shop. The work is meditative, contemplative, it grounds him. It contains his mind.

But now he was forbidden to use his shop; and too agitated to sleep, or read; forbidden to talk with Laura; forbidden to attend Max's baseball game. So maybe he'd take a long walk on the beach. Of course, what he really needed was to see Laura – ask her the thousand questions he had – but he knew that making contact with her could get him thrown back in jail.

He thought about Alix Callahan – in fact, she hadn't been out of his mind all afternoon – wondering again and again what she wanted with him. Having no plausible explanation, he thought that perhaps if he knew why this woman had reached out of the past to help him, then maybe he could begin to understand the reasons for Laura's infidelity.

Then he was back in his car, determined to find out.

GREEN GIRLS, the business card read. EXOTIC GROWERS.

According to the little map on the card, her place was located on the Portsmouth bank of the Piscataqua River, in the shadow of the I-95 bridge – also called the High-Level Bridge. Because Jacob didn't like heights, he took the Memorial Bridge over the river, one of two lower lift-bridges that connected Maine to New Hampshire.

As luck would have it, the gate arm swung down just as he reached the middle. As the roadway rose up in front of him, he watched a two-masted sailboat float past, heading to the marina. He looked in that direction, where the green, arched bridge towered over the river – and a familiar weightlessness went through him. He looked away.

They'd been in three classes together, he and Alix Callahan – Creative Writing, Modern Poetry, Shakespeare. Even in a school the size of UNH, she'd made a name for herself. Jacob first heard about her lesbianism in the spring of his sophomore year, in the locker room. Fueled by the lack of evidence to the contrary – namely, she'd never been seen with a guy – Jacob's baseball teammates concluded that it had to be true. Not that any of them would have cared, except that Alix Callahan was about as disarming as a girl that age could possibly be: confident, cool, mysterious. All that Jacob knew of her was that she never spoke to anyone, male or female, unless she was asked to read her poetry – which was usually of the fiery feminist kind.

15

Michael Kimball

First time he ever heard the word cunt uttered by a woman – and it wasn't used derisively; rather, as an object of affection – it came from Alix Callahan's lips. As soon as she'd said it, Jacob felt his face flush, and she caught him, and kept her eyes nailed to him while she read the rest of the poem, as though she were reciting just for him – or accusing him of something. That was the last time she ever looked at him.

No matter. From that moment on, Jacob could barely look at her, either, without imagining this tall, aloof, brilliant girl making love to her roommate, a tattooed, fierce-eyed redhead named Emily Packwood, who sang in an all-girl power-punk band called Tongue in Groove, and who singlehandedly drove Jacob's teammates to distraction, debating the fairness of such a foxy thing wearing those skimpy leather skirts – the fairness and, after all, the downright honesty. Although Jacob didn't take part in such conversations, the locker room consensus was that Miss Packwood was simply riding the lesbian bandwagon and in time would come to her senses. That is, until she was seen tongue-kissing Alix Callahan publicly and repeatedly at an REM concert, at which point the team was suddenly faced with a twin revelation: that Alix's roommate the previous year, a long-haired freshman beauty named Whitney, had also been sleeping with the poetess.

A car horn blasted, shaking Jacob from his reverie. The gate arm was up, the roadway down, and traffic was moving again. He crossed into Portsmouth and worked his way through Market Square, rich with the fragrance of restaurants and crowded with tourists, then westward alongside the river. Just beyond the on-ramp to the High-Level bridge, he made a right turn through a cozy neighborhood of small, brick houses. As the steelwork arch rose up into view over the river, the road swung underneath the approach span and left the neighborhood behind, white pines growing on both sides. Then, glinting out of a sudden clearing on the river side, the glass appeared, reflecting the red sun. GREEN GIRLS – EXOTIC GROWERS.

Less like a flower shop than an unruly, renovated home, the structure looked like it might have once been a two-family tenement. A wooden sign hung above the front door, and a full dormer faced the street. Attached to the back of the building, Jacob could make out an enormous greenhouse, filled with wild and lush greenery, and stretching back indefinitely. He wondered if it had been a solarium salvaged from some luxury hotel, or perhaps a defunct orangery – definitely not part of the original structure, nor anything that belonged in Portsmouth, New Hampshire. In fact, he thought he could see a slender palm tree pressed against the glass.

16

Jacob pulled his car into a small worn area in the uncut lawn. The only other car parked there, presumably Alix's, was a ten-year-old green Volvo wagon with GREEN GIRLS – EXOTIC GROWERS stenciled on the door. Not a prospering business, he thought.

He walked up the flagstone walk and rang the bell, then waited two or three minutes before the door popped open and Alix Callahan stood in front of him, barefoot on the slate floor. She was tall, as he remembered her, and she gave him a pleasant look, not exactly a smile. He couldn't picture her smiling. Behind her, flowers and leafy plants hung from the ceiling, clung to walls, and exploded full-blown from pots on the floor.

'I guess you know who I am,' Jacob said, his glance unintentionally drawn to a gnarled, plum-shaped scar on her right cheek.

'Come on up,' she replied, and when he'd turned back after closing the door, she was already climbing a circular iron stairway behind the checkout counter. He looked around the dusky showroom and noticed, on the opposite wall, glass doors leading out to the greenhouse, with signs reading NO ADMITTANCE. Squeezing behind the counter, Jacob ducked into the staircase and started climbing, wondering again: What in the world did this woman want with him?

At the top of the stairs he emerged in a white room filled with hanging plants, potted plants, a terrarium. A stereo system sat on a table, with two loudspeakers propped on either side, and a black leather love seat on the opposite wall, facing them. Rustic pine shelves had been constructed on a third wall, filled from floor to ceiling with CDs, tapes and record albums. Laura loved music, he thought. Ray Charles. Bob Marley. Luciano Pavarotti. In April, three months ago, they'd gone to a Bonnie Raitt concert in Portland, and afterwards went for a walk on the Promenade, hand in hand. Had she already been involved with Price?

'In here,' Alix called, from the next room.

Jacob ducked through the doorway into a kitchen that was staggeringly hot and humid, and bathed in green light. The outside wall consisted entirely of sliding glass doors that looked down on the glassed-in jungle. Alix sat at an oak table backed to the opening, her head framed by the fronds of a strapping young palm. Other trees and vines climbed and clustered behind her, sprung with flowers of vibrant reds and yellows.

'Coconuts in Portsmouth?' Jacob said.

'It's a rainforest,' she said, closing a laptop computer. Her hair was chopped just below her jaw, the way it had been in college, but not as

17

tidy. Hay-colored and parted unevenly over her left eye, it looked as though she had pushed a hairbrush through it once, maybe a week ago. In the brighter light, the scar on her cheek looked like a dog had bitten her. A large bottle of red wine sat by her elbow, and a half-filled tumbler. 'Want some?'

'No,' he said, 'thanks.'

She did not invite Jacob to sit – which was fine with him. Something about perching at the edge of a twelve-foot drop . . . But when she lifted the bottle to fill her glass, he spotted his book on the table. *John*, a 300-page ode to the toilet on a train he had ridden from San Francisco to Boston, following his mother's funeral.

'I can't stay,' he told her. 'I just stopped by to thank you.'

'You could have called.'

'Actually, I wanted to ask you—'

'Uh-huh?' She slouched boyishly in her chair, studying him with a bemused glint that told him she was well-aware of the power she held over him – this knowledge – and seemed to delight in it.

'Well, why you helped me,' he said. 'I mean, as far as you know, I was just some baseball jock who wrote a stupid book and got lucky.'

She said, 'I didn't know you played baseball.'

Jacob chuckled. Clearly, she hadn't lost her withering charm – but suddenly she seemed troubled by something she saw out in her garden.

Jacob saw it too. The girl came out of the greenery like a jaguar, wearing dark sunglasses that seemed to lock on him immediately – and he was struck by her beauty. Jet-black hair hung around her face, which was tanned and oval-shaped. She was young, her shoulders bare and brown, and she held Jacob's eye until he looked away, then she retreated back into the foliage. He remembered the first time he saw Laura, in Price Ashworth's office. She was Price's receptionist, just out of college, and her eyes—

'That's July,' Alix said. 'She's mad at me.'

'*July?*' The way he said it, as though it were the name of some beach bunny, he was returning her barb.

'It wasn't my money,' Alix told him. 'Someone paid me to bail you.'

'Who?'

'Someone who wants to remain anonymous.'

Then that was the end of it. Or was it? The way she continued studying him, Jacob thought there might be something else she wasn't telling him. 'In other words, you're just the gopher,' he said, deliberately pushing her buttons, looking for an opening.

'Just the gopher,' she agreed, and poured more wine. 'Sure you don't want a glass?'

Jacob smiled, declining. 'I guess I should go,' he said, 'that is, unless you have any other secrets.'

She swallowed a sip of wine. 'I know the DA who's going to prosecute you.'

'Okay,' Jacob said, feeling like he was finally gaining some control of the situation. She definitely did not want him to go, at least not yet. But why?

'Her name is Susan Evangeline,' Alix said. 'She's going to crucify you and take everything you have.'

'Everything I own fits in my car,' he told her.

'Including your son?'

He stood rooted to her floor. A couple of inches above his head a skylight was opened, presumably to let out the heat, but it did little good. Sweat rolled down his cheek.

'What do you know about me?' he said, studying Alix Callahan very carefully. 'Or my son?'

'I know a lawyer who can help you,' Alix began – then her eyes darted.

It was the black-haired girl again, standing in a doorway of what appeared to be a pantry. Even in the relative darkness of the small room, Jacob was struck again by her beauty. Her arms were velvety with moisture, her legs and feet bare, and caked with mud to her ankles. A brown dress hung lightly on her shoulders by ribbon straps, clung to high breasts and ended at the tops of her thighs.

'This is Jacob Winter, an old friend of mine,' Alix said to her. 'He used to be a writer.'

The girl seemed to glare at him for a second, then she spun away from them both and went to the refrigerator, bent low and came up with half a lime. Ignoring Alix, she turned and gave Jacob another look while she stuck the lime between her lips and sucked on the fruit. Steam came out of the refrigerator and enveloped her body.

'Did you write poetry?' she asked Jacob.

'No,' he answered, although literary journals used to describe his books as epic poems.

'Good,' said the girl, as she sucked pensively on the fruit.

'July, shut the fucking door,' Alix said with a long-suffering sigh.

The girl left the room.

Jacob walked around the island and closed the refrigerator, and suddenly music started, loud and bright and Irish, racing fiddles and hornpipes, and a riotous hand drum pouring down from speakers set high on the kitchen cupboards. Then a female voice came in, breathy

19

and haunting, and singing in Gaelic.

He moved closer to Alix so he wouldn't be overheard. 'Correct me if I'm wrong,' he said, prodding again, 'but have you ever been involved with anyone who didn't look like they stepped out of a Victoria's Secret catalogue?'

Alix gave a dismissive smirk, but something in her eye told Jacob she'd been stung by his remark. 'Don't make a mess,' she said.

Realizing that she was speaking to July, he turned to see the girl standing at the island, pouring rum into a green glass pitcher. By the sullen glance that passed over him, he suspected she had heard what he'd said.

'Actually, I recruited July from the other side,' Alix explained with a glint, while the lush, percussive music pounded out over their heads.

Jacob glanced back at July, who gave him a sensual peek as she sliced the lime into wedges. No longer wearing her sunglasses, she had the eyes of a fawn. Then he noticed her hand. Her index finger was missing.

'Come down to the garden, we can't talk here,' Alix said, standing so abruptly that her chair toppled backwards and fell out the open door. With the loud music, they never heard it hit the ground.

She led him into the pantry, where a second set of circular stairs led down to the rear of the flower shop. Through an open glass door they stepped into a startling eruption of green, South American plants pushing out of the New Hampshire soil, a wild grappling of color, broadleaf and blossom filling every inch of the humid, glassed-in sky.

'So, this lawyer you know,' he said.

'Shh,' she told him, entering the middle of three dirt paths. Jacob followed. While leathery, fanlike leaves slapped off their legs, the big house disappeared behind the greenery.

'How do you get a rainforest in New England?' he asked.

'I have a few people, birders mostly, who bring me seeds and cuttings,' Alix explained. 'Eight different heliconias, more than forty anthurium.' From low branches hung small wooden boxes that housed flowers, their woody roots spidering down, exposed. 'Vanda orchids,' she said, lightly brushing her long fingers over one as she passed. 'Their roots collect the moisture from the air.'

Then she stopped and looked behind them. 'Willard Zabriski is his name,' she said. 'He served three terms in the Maine Senate. He's the best lawyer on the seacoast. He can beat Susan Evangeline.'

Jacob was about to say he couldn't afford any lawyer, let alone the best.

'He's already been paid,' Alix said, preempting him. 'He's expecting your call.'

'Paid,' Jacob said. 'By the same person who paid my bail?'

'That's right.' She started walking again, as if the conversation was over. Then why was she heading deeper into the garden?

'How do you know Laura?' he asked, catching up to her.

'Your wife? Never met her,' Alix said. 'Watch your step.' She pointed to the right, where a yellow frog, little more than an inch long, clung to the stalk of a leafy plant. 'Poison dart frog,' she explained. 'Also called *Phyllobates terribilis*. It's the most toxic animal in the world.'

Jacob stopped. With the low-cut moccasins he wore, he might as well have been barefoot.

'July breeds them,' Alix explained, and as she moved toward the frog, it leaped off the path into thicker foliage. 'In certain parts of South America, the Choco Indians still treat their blow-pipe arrows with the skin secretions of the *terribilis*.'

Jacob looked around his feet. 'Is that where July's from, South America?'

'One frog produces enough poison to kill twenty thousand mice. Or ten humans.'

'Why does she raise poison frogs?'

'You sound interested,' Alix said, as another Irish jig danced over their heads.

'You seem to think I should be,' he replied. 'But you still haven't told me how you recruited her. Or is that another one of your secrets?'

Alix stopped beside a small thatch-roofed hut climbing with flowering vines. 'When I met July, she was in the process of leaving her husband. I helped her.'

'And this has something to do with your bailing me out?'

Alix turned, made eye contact. It was a full, decisive expression, or else a warning look, punctuated by the sudden rustle of leaves behind them.

He turned and saw July standing among the ferns holding two tall glasses in her hands. The drinks were cherry red, with wedges of lime floating. She seemed to be staring at him again – with her dark sunglasses, it was hard to tell.

'I could only carry two,' she said, as she came forward and handed Jacob one of the glasses. Then she took the straw of the other into her lips and slowly sucked up the liquid while she stared at him. If she wasn't flirting with him, then she was doing a good impression of someone who was.

'Why don't you take this one, I don't drink,' he said, handing his glass to Alix. 'Besides, I haven't even unpacked.'

'Sure you won't stay for dinner?' Alix offered, which came as no surprise. Jacob knew she wasn't through dangling information in front of him – whatever her intentions were.

'Stay,' July told him, 'I'll make you one with no rum.'

'Where are you unpacking?' Alix asked.

'Some rental cottages on Old Route One,' he said.

'Unpack later,' July told him. Jacob noticed the quick glance Alix shot her. Clearly, the women were not getting along, and it seemed to Jacob that he might have located Alix's weakness: jealousy.

'Are you sure you don't mind?' he asked her, having no intention of leaving, at least not until he learned what else she was keeping from him. The way she was drinking, he thought it wouldn't take long.

'Why would I mind? I invited you,' she replied, then said to July, 'Wash your feet before you come back in.' Snapping through the fan leaves, she walked off.

Jacob turned to follow, but July grabbed his shirt, held him back until Alix had turned the corner. 'I need to tell you something,' she murmured. This close together, he could smell a keen acridity rising out of her sun dress. Then she released him and began walking deeper into the garden, as though expecting him to follow. He did, but carefully. The ground was warm and oozing, and he watched around his feet for frogs.

'They're more afraid of you than you are of them,' July said, looking back at him with a teasing turn of her hip. Then, barefoot, she ducked underneath a shawl of deep red blossoms. A few feet ahead of her, the rainforest abruptly flattened against the glass wall. Through tiny breaks in the foliage, he could see the bridge towering up in the reddening sky. The cars passing over already had their headlights on.

July went toward the corner of the greenhouse, where Jacob saw a natural wading pool that was about six feet around, with an orange beach towel spread on its flat, grassy rim. On the towel lay a pair of skimpy lime-green briefs and an empty green drinking glass. Jacob wondered if she had been sunbathing when he'd arrived . . . but didn't have time to put on her underwear?

'Hold this,' she said, handing her drink and sunglasses to him – and he was momentarily captivated by the contradictions of her face. There was such youthful softness to her features, such delicate symmetry. Yet in her eyes – deep brown and almond-shaped – Jacob saw someone disarmingly knowledgeable. She lifted the hem of her dress and stepped down into the water. Mud moved lazily off her feet and was swept away. It was an underground brook, he realized, that continued underneath the glass enclosure and ran down to the river.

'How long have you known Alix?' he asked.

'A few years,' July said, as she lifted a foot onto the rim, then bent and began washing it with her hands. Jacob watched the top of her dress fall away, briefly exposing a plump breast. She looked up, caught him.'Were you lovers in college?'

'Alix and I? Hardly.'

She studied him for a moment, then bent over to wash her other foot, once again exposing herself to him, the soft flutter of her flesh.

He averted his eyes. 'It's just that someone gave her money to pay my bail—'

'You got arrested?' July said, looking up at him. 'For what?'

Now Jacob understood – he was not the only one Alix had power over. It was obvious that July had no idea why he was here, either. 'It's not important,' he said. 'I just wanted to know who to thank.'

Reaching for Jacob's hand, she climbed out of the pool. 'You shouldn't have come,' she said quietly.

'What do you mean?'

Suddenly the music stopped. The look she gave him was keen with caution. She grabbed the towel, spilling her panties into the water. Quickly drying her ankles and feet, she said in a whisper, 'We'd better go back.' As if they'd done something wrong.

Indeed, Jacob felt as if they had.

It took about five minutes for Jacob to realize his mistake in staying for dinner. The problem was not in his strategy – the tension he had fomented between the women was palpable, evidenced by the prickly silence at the table while they ate Alix's rainforest salad – but despite his plan to exploit Alix's jealousy as she dulled her defenses with drink, he was just too tired to be effective, his rebellious mind constantly wandering back to Laura, a picnic they'd had recently, their daily beach walks, and all the quiet nights and mornings they'd made love while Max lay sleeping.

Yes, Laura was emotionally complex, but what woman wasn't? She was also emotionally honest – or so he'd believed – and that had remained the core of his love for her: She did not hide her feelings; he did not need to interpret her. He had never known, nor even glimpsed, a part of her personality that would pretend love once she'd lost it. So the question remained: When had she stopped loving him?

'Jacob wrote *John* after his mother's death,' Alix broke in finally, with a gesture toward the island, where she'd left his book. 'It's about a toilet on a train.'

July turned to him. 'Then the toilet,' she said, 'is a metaphor for loss?'

'I just wrote what I saw,' he said, hoping they'd talk about something else – though he was impressed by her perception.

She watched him as if awaiting a better answer, but he had none, so he took another drink of the non-alcoholic punch she had made for him. Beneath its syrupy sweetness, he could taste bitter herbs and earthy vegetation. He masked the taste by eating a red blossom from Alix's salad, which wasn't much better.

'I just figured out why there isn't a single person in any of his books,' she said to July.

'No people, really?' July's gaze still hadn't left him, and he knew it was getting to Alix.

'Same reason he doesn't drink,' Alix said. 'Control.'

Jacob grunted, not about to concede the point, not about to debate, either.

'Look at the evidence,' Alix said. 'The author's mother kills herself, and he writes a book in which we learn the history of trains, the history of mobile toilets, and what happens to human waste on railroad ties. In this book, he vows permanent estrangement from his father, who has the audacity to be homosexual, and describes his mother's addiction to alcohol and pain killers, and her subsequent suicide, in such clinical terms you'd think you were reading a medical journal. It's such brilliant self-delusion: The author trying to convince the world he feels no pain.' She gave Jacob a look. 'Which is precisely what makes the book so devastating.'

'I guess that's what's called a win-win situation,' he said. 'I got published, and you got to feel superior.'

'You're not published any more,' Alix came back, with no hesitation.

'I don't know why you're being so mean,' July said. 'You're the one who bailed him out of jail.'

Silence returned to the table. Now he could also feel Alix's eyes on him.

'I do have to admit,' she said, 'something about his writing is extremely sensual. The fire in Baltimore? I'm not sure if it's that he treats violence sexually or sex violently. You'd appreciate it.' Which was a dig at both of them.

July turned back to him. 'Did you always dream of being a writer?'

'Space explorer,' he answered, glad for the change in subject. 'Red Sox pitcher. Actually, when I was a boy, I used to dream about rescuing

Michelle D'Entrement.' He wondered where that memory came from, or why he'd brought it up.

Alix said, 'Who's Michelle D'Entrement?'

'A girl in my class,' he explained. 'I used to have to save her life all the time – aliens, terrorists, sorcerers. I'd rescue her, and she'd melt in my arms.' He turned the question to Alix. 'How about some of your fantasies?'

'Same thing,' she said with a glimmer. 'Rescuing all the cute, helpless girls.' She looked pointedly at July, who got up and walked out of the room. 'Oh, July—'

After a few seconds, the cello music stopped. In the uncomfortable silence that followed, Jacob said quietly, 'Speaking of control.'

Alix fixed him with a searing glance.

'I'm very tired,' he said. 'If you have something to tell me, why don't you just tell me, so I can leave.'

'Fine,' she replied. 'Something is missing in your life.'

'*My* life?'

'You're not going to find it here.'

Music exploded from the speakers, making a retort impossible, not that he had one. It was another Irish girl singing in layered, breathy harmonies over a galloping Celtic beat. Alix closed her eyes in a pained way, then July returned to the table with a wooden bowl from which she filled Jacob's plate with fruits, oysters, artichoke hearts, all smothered in a yellow curry paste. She set the bowl in front of Alix, who served herself, saying, 'Don't be polite. Dig in. July's a good cook.'

Having barely eaten in three days, Jacob didn't need to be told twice. From the first bite, it was as if he was breathing fire, but the food was delicious. The song she'd put on was about betrayal and revenge, as near as he could make out, the girl singing about how her brothers captured her unfaithful suitor and tied him to an oak tree for the wolves to eat.

As he ate, July appeared again, with two full pitchers in her hands, her small, square shoulders moving to the music as she poured the red liquid into his glass. 'Not too much,' he said, but she kept pouring till it was full. When she filled Alix's glass from the other pitcher, she pressed the length of her body softly against her side, and Jacob felt a voyeuristic spark of arousal, in spite of himself. He wondered if she'd snuck some rum in his punch.

With the music pouring out of the speakers and the food so delicious, he did not broach the subject but ate rather gluttonously, the heat from the sauces combining with the heat rising out of the garden, so he never noticed when the green twilight had given way to darkness, or when someone had taken time to light candles all over the kitchen. It was the same with the women, glistening in the candlelight, while music strutted ecstatically, and the drinks accumulated in their heads. At one point, he looked over at July and saw her sipping from her glass, staring darkly at him through the gap of her missing finger, as though trying to warn him about something.

'If sex had a face,' Alix said.

At least that's what it sounded like. Then again, she might have said anything, or nothing at all. The way Jacob was feeling – a curious mixture of euphoria and confusion – reminded him of times when he was younger and tried smoking pot. Even his stomach was sending him anxious messages.

He tapped at his glass with his finger, and said, 'Did you put something in this?'

Alix picked up his drink and sniffed at it, then soured her face. 'Couldn't you smell it?'

'Smell what?'

'July made you a jungle brew,' Alix told him, and another charged glance passed between the women. 'Apparently, she doesn't want you to leave.'

He turned to July, who was watching him like a cat watches a mouse, waiting for it to move. 'What kind of jungle brew?'

July's gaze bored into his brain.'*Yagé*,' she said softly. *Yah-gay*.

'What did she say?' Jacob asked.

'It's not alcohol,' Alix explained, as if that was consolation, 'but you probably shouldn't drive till it wears off.'

'Yagé?'

'Also called *ayahuasca*,' Alix said. 'It means vine of the spirits. In some parts of the world, it's a sacred ritual.'

'In July's part of the world?'

Alix shook her head at him, letting him know that he wasn't going to get any more information out of her. He was cognizant enough to know she was probably right. His head was swimming.

'How long does it last?'

'Awhile,' she said, standing. 'You might as well make yourself comfortable.'

As she passed behind July, she ran her fingers though her long hair, as if to magically draw her out of her chair, but the defiant way July flipped her hair around her shoulder, suddenly Jacob is seeing Laura, his wife, the way she snapped that black sheet up to her chin. And those eyes again, hers and Price's, dark and darting in Jacob's bed.

Green Girls

Price Ashworth, who calls himself a hypnotherapist these days, speaks first, in his assured way. 'This could be embarrassing, to say the least.' As if this were one of those episodes that might turn into a good story over time.

The movie flickers out of some lost corner of Jacob's mind, and he doesn't want to stop it. Yes, he can even see the bottle of wine on his night table – beside the clock-radio. He walks closer to the bed, an exquisite, hand-tooled piece of mahogany furniture that took him half a year to build – his engagement ring to Laura. Inset in the headboard is a backlit, stained-glass panel that Price himself had created for the couple, as a wedding gift.

Jacob can feel his heart pounding behind his eyes. He can't think of a word to say.

'Jake, please go in the other room,' Laura tells him with a shiver in her voice. Her owl-brown eyes are dilated black. She's so beautiful, Jacob thinks, even now, the way her dark hair is tossed around, the flush of her cheeks.

Price lifts one toned shoulder out of the blankets and shows Jacob his hand. It might be the start of an apology, but Price Ashworth is not accustomed to apologizing beneath his station. He's thirty-eight years old, six foot one, a fit hundred-seventy pounds, a Tae-Kwon-Do master. He owns a solar-heated house a block from the ocean. Pompous when sober, wine exalts him.

'Let's stay focused,' he says. 'Natural breathing.'

Jacob is three years younger, and lumbering by comparison. Feeling a wild trembling in his chest, he checks his breathing and finds that his lungs are filled. Once again he notices the ballgame playing quietly on Laura's clock-radio. It's a small, state-of-the-art piece of hardware that he had bought for her with the advance on his third novel, that is, before the publisher went bankrupt.

'I thought you knew it was a *make-up* double header,' Jacob says to Laura in a tightly controlled voice. Then he turns to Price. 'In a make-up double-header, people with rain-check tickets only get to see the first game, the one that got rained out last month.'

'Jake, please?' Laura says. Is she crying?

Jacob stares at the illuminated square of stained glass between their heads: the pair of fairies naked and innocent. A powerful wave comes over him, and he snaps the radio's plug out of the electrical outlet. The room becomes suddenly, contemplatively quiet. His heart is dying.

Price says, 'Jacob, is baseball really what you are wanting to discuss at this point in time?'

The movie flickers. The radio leaps. A white arm flashes into the air.

A window shade sputters up and sunlight bursts into the room. Then something shudders up from Jacob's chest, a sickening, dull horror at the sight of Laura bent over Price, holding his head in her hands . . .

'Are you okay?'

It's July talking to him.

'What?'

'Come sit down.'

Snapped from the vision, Jacob rose out of his chair as though out of a dream, to see Alix and July in the doorway, their eyes like sparks, as if they too have just watched his memory unfold. He was shaking.

'Are you okay?' July said again.

He shook his head, fished his keys out of his pocket. 'I need to leave,' he said. He needed to talk to Laura, needed to know.

'You can't drive now,' Alix told him.

He stared at July, struck with another revelation: He understood how she lost her finger. And Alix . . . He touched his fingers to his cheek. 'Her husband did that—?'

'An animal attacked me,' she said evenly, in a way that meant don't ask again. But something about the way July was watching him, that knowing, mischievous glint, made him think it was only a matter of time before all of Alix's secrets were spilled.

CHAPTER THREE

The slap of a palm on the Indian's face was loud enough to interrupt a game of dominoes from clear across the dormitory. The other prisoners paid the commotion little mind, until the sound of the guard's footsteps clocked across the room.

'Cecil, is that you disturbing the peace?' Sergeant Buford Bullens pulled his keychain out of his pocket as he approached the two men. 'What's the matter, you feelin frisky and your Injun pal's got a headache tonight?'

'He's workin root on me and I've had enough of it,' the black man said. 'Bottom line.'

Cecil was dressed in a white cutoff sweatshirt that revealed the massive biceps and sloping shoulders of a weight lifter. The prison guard, a white man who was six-one and well-proportioned, looked hard at the Colombian Indian sitting on the tile floor, wraparound sunglasses on his face and blood seeping from his nose.

'Aw, he's not doin nothin,' Bullens said with innocent pleasure.

'He's workin root on me right now.'

'Ah, you don't believe that voodoo stuff. He don't even understand English.'

'He understands everything, man,' Cecil said. 'He communicates with the damn birds.'

'Is that so, Sereno? You talk to birds?' Bullens walked over to the Indian, whose straight black hair hung down to his chest. Pulling a rubber glove onto his hand, Bullens daubed a handkerchief under the Indian's bloody nose.

'I seen him stare a flock of pelicans clean out of three coconut palms,' Cecil declared. 'And I seen him call 'em right back again. All with a look. Man's a damn root doctor, which you obviously don't seem to grasp.'

Bullens turned to Cecil. 'And you, my friend, obviously don't seem

29

to grasp the concept of "gain time."' He spoke loudly enough to inform the other sixty-eight prisoners in the dorm. 'Your cellmate here has been a model prisoner for the past four years, which means he has accumulated credit, which means he gets to leave Alligator Alley several months ahead of schedule.' Bullens leaned closer to Cecil, but continued speaking loud enough for the other prisoners to hear. 'You, on the other hand, took fifteen years just to make trusty. And now you want to throw away that privilege because this gentleman chooses to spend his time in meditation.'

'Shit,' Cecil said.

'All right, the two of you lovers, into lock-down, let's go.' The guard's keys reflected the overhead lights as he swung around to unlock a steel door.

Inside was a small table and two chairs. 'Have a seat,' Bullens said as the men filed into the room, Cecil lowering himself onto one of the chairs, Sereno on the floor. The sergeant pulled a black trash bag and a roll of Scotch Tape out of his back pocket, and he taped the trash bag over the door's portal window. Then he turned to face the men.

Biff Bullens was a handsome man, with short hair, a straight nose, and a dimpled, muscular smile. He had soft, violet-blue eyes, which women found difficult to resist, and a plastic surgeon had once given him a full chin. The US Marines had taught him to stand straight, speak straight, and stay in shape. Even in his early forties, the man was such a model of military efficiency that it was hard to disrespect him, at least until you got to know him. He lifted a corner of the trash bag and peeked out the portal window, then turned back to the men and smiled.

'You fellas know the meaning of the word "diversion?"'

'I only gave him a slap,' Cecil said, then turned to the Indian. 'You okay, man?'

Bullens chuckled. 'Looks like you flattened his damn nose.'

'You laugh, man, look at his ribs. He ain't had a morsel of solid food in a week, just that leaf and twig shit.'

Bullens studied Sereno more seriously. The Indian was shirtless, sitting cross-legged against the wall, wearing only a pair of 60s-vintage plaid Bermuda shorts – and the wraparounds. A pale, wedge-shaped scar showed just above his solar plexus; a second, similar scar winked out from between two ribs just beneath his left breast. Two more on his shoulder and neck. Twin, gnarled indentations – apparently from bullets – were located above and below his rib cage and on both arms. A longer scar ran diagonally from his collarbone across his neck and under his jawbone.

'He's right, you know,' Bullens told the Indian, checking the window again to make sure they weren't overheard. 'You've got to keep your strength up. Prison escape ain't exactly a walk on the beach.'

The way Sereno stared through the sunglasses, it was hard to tell if he was even awake.

'He coherent?' Bullens asked.

'I think.'

'Hey, Sereno,' Bullens said, pulling a rolled-up newspaper from his back pocket, 'your secret admirer sent me another package. This one came from Topeka, Kansas.'

Bullens stripped the rubber bands off the newspaper and unrolled it, and a bulky plastic bag dropped out. 'Now what's this?'

The bag contained crushed dried leaves, bits of bark and some orange specks. Someone looking through the window might have thought it marijuana, except for the thick bits of bark and orange stuff – and the stench. Cecil pushed the bag away from him, turning his head away from the smell. Bullens tossed the bag to the Indian, who barely flinched when it hit him in the chest.

'Don't rouse him, man.'

'Yeah, he's probably communing with them birds.' Bullens chuckled again.

'You laugh, man, how you suppose he made his nose stop bleedin?'

'It's called coagulation, numbnuts,' Bullens said, popping Cecil's head with the newspaper. 'Take a look at page six.'

'I don't read Spanish.'

'You ever agree to anything in your life? Page six.'

Cecil gave him a look, then picked up the paper and flipped the pages until a small piece of paper, a fragment of email, fell onto the table. Cecil picked it up, then showed it to Sereno, who seemed to study it briefly.

'Everything okay?' Cecil asked in a whisper. 'Boat coming next Saturday?'

Sereno gave a barely perceptible nod.

Cecil turned back to Bullens. 'Yeah.'

Bullens pulled a pencil from his pocket and passed it, along with the newspaper, to the black man. 'Have him write "sixteen hundred hours." That's four p.m. for you folks on Mickey Mouse time.'

Cecil set the newspaper and pencil in front of the Indian. 'Four o'clock,' he said. After a moment of apparent deliberation, Sereno picked up the pencil and scrawled something in the margin, then set the pencil down.

The black man picked up the newspaper and folded it up again, then set it on the table. Bullens snatched the pencil from him. 'Now how about you?' he said, and he crumpled the small piece of printout and pressed it in Cecil's hand. 'You're not on a hunger strike your own self, are you?' Bullens touched his finger to his own mouth.

'Aw, Bull . . .'

The smile froze on the prison guard's face. After a few seconds of scrutiny, he nodded his head and said, 'Is that how it is?'

Cecil sighed, a frustrated, apologetic sound.

How it was? The man went by Biff, not Bull. He liked to be friendly, liked to be cool, liked to walk among the prison population like this: 'How's it goin, Tommy?' 'Not bad, Biff.' 'How's the family?' 'Good, I guess.' That kind of thing. 'Sarge' was okay. Maybe Sergeant Bullens. Not Buford. Definitely not Bull. It didn't matter, guard or prisoner, if he heard you call him Bull you'd pay for it, one way or another. Which was about as stimulating as things ever got in Alligator Alley Correctional Institute. Don't call Biff Bull.

Now Bullens smiled so hard at Cecil that his dimples looked like bullet holes. 'You boys wanna call this whole thing off?' he asked softly.

'Fuck,' Cecil said, wadding up the email and sticking it in his mouth.

Bullens peeked through the window again.

'Chew it up good,' he said. 'Because if I call off this little operation, you're stuck in this place for another ten years. And Mr Sereno here, well, he'll be walking out of here a free man two weeks from Tuesday, all scheduled to go home. Right, Sereno? I mean, all the way home.'

The Indian turned slightly and, for the first time, appeared to pay attention to the prison guard.

'See, just because the boys in Administration missed your INS hold when you were admitted, they sure-as-shit won't miss it when you're released. You know what that means. Off to Krome Detention Center, and from there, deportation. Back to Colombia, where you'll get whacked the minute you step off that airplane.'

'Okay now?' Cecil said, opening his mouth to show that he'd swallowed the paper.

'I'm not sure if we're okay or not,' Bullens said quietly, patting at his cowlick, as he had done since he was fifteen, trying to make it lie down. 'Do we have a clear understanding?'

'On our end, yeah,' said Cecil, still standing, anxious to get out. 'A week from now we're gone, and we'll never have to look at your face again.'

Bullens smiled sincerely, then looked over at Sereno. 'I guess you made some people unhappy back in *Co-rum-bia*, huh?' Rolling the R in a mocking way. 'I don't blame you a bit, hey, a man finds his half-breed American wife sexin another man? In my book he's got a God-given right to waste 'em both. I mean, that's how it works in the jungle, right?'

Sereno continued staring through his shades. Bullens stared right back. 'Only, too bad you done it in the great state of Florida.'

Cecil flicked his hand in the air. 'Sarge, please, awright? You torment him, I don't sleep.'

'And too bad the wastee turned out to be connected to the Colombian drug cartel,' Bullens went on. 'I hear they found forty stab wounds in the poor bastard.' Another dimpled smile. 'Then you went and bit off your wife's finger. Is that true?'

'That's it, put me in the hole,' Cecil said, 'I don't care.'

The Indian sat stoically while Bullens gurgled in light, private laughter, as though someone were down inside his uniform tickling him. After all, no one really did like Buford Bullens – none of the prisoners, and only a couple of the guards – which was probably why he laughed like that.

'Hey, Sereno, I bet you were some surprised to find out the little woman was packin heat. These American girls, they ain't like the chicks back home. Looks like she put a half dozen slugs in you, plus half the silverware drawer.' Bullens had that private laugh of his, then looked over at Cecil. 'And he bites off her finger.'

Cecil tilted his head in a pleading way. 'I told you, Biff, everything's cool.'

'Outstanding,' Bullens said, wiping his tears away. 'That being the case, a week from now Sereno here can climb into a boat with his Injun buddies and go to South America, Central America, the Virgin Islands – anywhere he damn pleases. He can hunt down his wife, for all I care, chow down some more of that hand.'

He smiled at Sereno again. The Indian continued staring through his sunglasses, emotionless.

'Come on, I'm just trying to get a rise out of you, man. I'm worried about you. But you best understand this, Sereno. If your *caballeros* don't keep their end of the bargain' – Bull touched the side of his nose, the international drug symbol – 'we're gonna have us an Indian bloodbath that'd give John Wayne a hard-on.'

'They'll bring what they said,' Cecil interjected, then said to Sereno, 'Ain't that right?'

The Indian kept up his staring match with Bullens.

'Everything's cool, Sarge,' Cecil said. 'They're gonna bring the stuff, and you and me are gonna split fifty-fifty. Sereno gets on the boat, and

33

I'm out of this damn state before anyone knows we're missing. Awright?'

'Outstanding,' Bullens said. He ripped the trash bag off the window and opened the door to leave. Then he stopped and gave Sereno another smile.

'Hey, I bin meanin to ask,' Bullens said to the Indian. 'Your wife's finger – did you swallow?'

CHAPTER FOUR

I n the living room, Alix sat on a leather couch that was backed up to the open glass doors. July perched cross-legged on the floor, facing her. An oil lamp flickered on the coffee table between them. Jacob stood at the back wall, pretending to look through a bookcase, but the lantern light wasn't bright enough to illuminate the titles. Not that he was trying to see. He was picturing Laura again, wondering if she was with Price Ashworth now. He thought maybe the yagé had worn off enough so he could drive.

'There's room on the couch,' Alix said to him.

July said, 'He can stand if he wants.'

'Too close to the edge,' he told them. 'I don't like heights.'

From July came a soft peal of helpless laughter, a musical sound. Jacob turned to her and was struck with a most peculiar notion, that the coffee table was leaning against her, as a cat might.

Alix said to him, 'Some people believe it's dangerous to reveal your fears to anyone but your shaman.' Her face, lit by the lantern, was a mask of seriousness.

'What exactly is a shaman?' he asked. 'A priest? Medicine man?'

'Priest, physician, philosopher, psychiatrist,' Alix explained. 'In many cultures the tribal shaman is believed to possess supernatural powers.'

'My husband's a shaman,' July said abruptly.

Alix turned sharply to face her.

In a single, fluid motion, July rose to her feet and walked over to the couch, where she straddled the arm. Her eyes had the reckless glint of a child's. To Jacob, it looked like she was seated on a panther.

'Where's your husband now?' he asked, remembering that Alix had said she'd helped her leave her husband. But now she was giving July a narrow, piercing look, meant to shut her up.

July answered anyway. 'In a cage.'

'Cute,' Alix said.

'Prison?'

Alix didn't answer. Instead, she fixed July with an intensive stare, a stark expression of betrayal. Returning a delinquent look, July slid off the couch arm and landed next to her, leaving a slice of wetness like a kiss on the leather where she'd sat.

With a slap, Alix shoved off her. To Jacob, the sound echoed off the three walls of the room – *slap, slap, slap* – then sailed off, little fiery vapors, into the jungle. Alix continued glaring, while her finger marks lingered on July's thigh, a rosy palm frond. The girl's hair was disheveled. Her eyes dilated. And now she sprawled back on the couch, her feet propped on the coffee table, her scuffed knees lazily parted. And the way she stared at him . . .

He realized that the music had stopped, replaced by the loud hissing of artificial rains falling down through the leafy canopy – from water pipes attached to the greenhouse frame – as though the small, enclosed forest were alive.

'When I was young,' Alix's voice sliced the silence, 'my best friend had a dog named Patches that his parents kept chained to the back porch. They had a big sign that said, "Danger. Don't pat Patches." '

She glanced at July. The look that passed between them fairly crackled with electricity.

'Patches was so fluffy and cute,' Alix continued. 'Whenever you walked up to the porch, he'd wag his tail and whimper. He was so hard to resist, with those sad brown eyes. So you'd give in and pat him, and let him lap your hand, then he'd roll on his back and beg you to scratch his belly. So you would.

'But the minute you stopped – the instant you took your hand away – Patches would jump to his feet. His eyes would shine. Then you'd understand why you'd been warned. But then it was too late. You'd try talking to him – "Nice Patches, nice Patches" – but he'd start moving toward you, growling deep in his throat. At that point, all you could do was turn and leap off the porch. And as soon as you did, Patches would fly. Most of the time, his chain would stop him before he got a good bite. But some people weren't fast enough.'

Alix laughed a little, in a dry, cynical way, then lay back on the couch.

'The warning sign was there, big as life: "Danger. Don't pat Patches," ' she said. 'But some people . . .'

Jacob spoke up. 'What happened to Patches?'

Alix answered evenly: 'What do you think?'

He stared back at her, for the longest time. In fact, the way their eyes locked together, the way their breathing became synchronized, he felt as though they were engaged in some kind of psychic showdown.

Even when a glass shattered – by the sudden darkness in the room, Jacob realized that July's foot had knocked the oil lamp off the table – they both ignored the distraction, that is, until Alix jumped off the couch.

Jacob stepped back, staring with amazement as yellow flames spread out over the floor from where the oil had spilled, under the coffee table, under the couch. While July leaned back against the bookcase watching indifferently, Alix was trying to avoid the fire with her bare feet while attempting to lift the heavy couch over the track of the sliding door.

The crackle of a table leg igniting broke Jacob from his trance. He charged forward, grabbed the coffee table and set it spinning over the couch and out the door, its wooden legs sputtering fire into the night. When he turned to the couch, his foot slid through the flaming oil and he went down on one knee, sliding through the fire. It was all blinding motion – flames, heat, smoke – then he was standing, lifting the burning couch in his arms and heaving it down.

'Your pants!' Alix yelled, swatting at his leg, but he turned away from her and marched through the pantry door into darkness, one flaming moccasin lighting the way, his footfalls ringing off the iron treads, winding around and around, and as the glass door came around below him, he saw the couch on its back outside, smoking madly and sputtering sparks under the rainfall. When his sole hit the slate floor, he slapped out the flame on his moccasin and hurried toward the shop door, knocking into hanging pots, leaves and vines grabbing at him, then he was driving away, going to see his wife.

CHAPTER FIVE

T he house Jacob and Laura rented was at the edge of Kittery's
original suburban development, where men who worked at the
shipyard had raised their families for the past half-century. Sided in
pink vinyl, the small ranch sat at the edge of a gravel pit a half mile
from the strip malls that lined Route One. It was the fourth house they
had rented since they'd lost their ocean-view home in York Harbor
nine years earlier, and it was filled with the furniture that Jacob had
built with hand tools and wooden pegs and dovetail joints and months
of evenings planing and sanding in meditative rhythms while he
planned his following day's writing – the cherry dining-room set, the
cherry hutch, the maple cabinets, the pine bookshelves, the mahogany
armoire and bureaus . . . and bed.

Now one of the cherry chairs lay at the end of the driveway, waiting
for the trash collector, with a leg broken and a stile separated from its
rail. The leaf from the table leaned against the chair, split down the
middle, along with a cupboard door. Another flash of recollection
came to him: Trying to sit in the chair; trying to hold himself there by
holding onto the table. Then he was pacing again, up the hallway,
down the hallway, up and down, while Laura and Price huddled in the
bedroom. God, how he must have frightened her.

Now, when he walked into the kitchen – she had left the stove light
on – he saw the missing cupboard door, the missing chair. He cleared
his throat so she would know he wasn't an intruder. Maybe she'd call
the police anyway. What did he expect, coming in like a thief? Did he
think she would take him back?

'Jake, you know you can't come here,' she whispered, tying her
bathrobe closed as she came in from the hall. The way she kept her
distance, as if she were afraid of him, broke his heart.

'You know I'd never hurt you,' he said.

'You need to leave,' she told him.

'Can we go outside and talk?' he asked, not wanting to wake up Max.

She shook her head. Above the smell of his charred moccasin, he could detect the fragrance of her shampoo and added that to the things he missed about her. He could barely resist the urge to go over and take her in his arms.

They had fallen in love in Price Ashworth's waiting room when Jacob first came for treatment. Turned out Laura had read *John* – and loved it. Not only that, she was a baseball aficionado. The fact that she was a diehard Yankees fan only added fire to their flirting. The clincher, in Jacob's mind, was that Laura had transcribed all his psychological files – until they started dating, anyway – meaning she knew him intimately and still wanted him. In fact, she told him that she loved his mind. He loved everything about her.

She was intelligent and beautiful and spirited. She had her father's feistiness and her mother's drive and practicality, and she loved to cook, having mastered an eclectic cuisine that reflected her personality, a wholly agreeable marriage of Old World Italian and Downeast Maine: haddock alla florentina with fiddleheads; potatoes frittelle; maple tiramisù.

And here was Jacob, standing in the middle of her kitchen, waiting for words to come, while she stood waiting for him to go.

'Are you in love with him?' he asked finally. In the first place, Price was an incorrigible womanizer, but Laura didn't need to be told that. She'd witnessed the chaos of the man's love life for nearly fifteen years. In fact, she and Jacob used to laugh about his escapades. Now she only shook her head, refusing to listen.

'Laura, if it's money—'

'It's not money,' she said. 'Max should have gone to Belnap years ago. He should have been enrolled in that school the day we got his test scores.'

'The school costs thirty thousand dollars a year.' Jacob stopped, aware that he was no longer whispering. Besides, it was the same argument they'd been having for years – Belnap School for the Profoundly Gifted, which was Price Ashworth's *alma mater*. For some reason, maybe because it was familiar territory, they were having it again. 'Max doesn't need to be sent a thousand miles away to school. He needs his family.'

'His family is not enough.'

'He needs me.'

'Shh.'

'He needs to see that if you work hard enough, you can make it in this world – not in some private school filled with geniuses. He needs to see it every day.'

'Jake, he's seen you work all of his life,' she said. 'All you do is work. Do you know what it's like watching you? Like watching a lion in a cage, pacing and pacing. Tell me how that helps Max.'

Her words tugged at the hollow of his chest. He could see her eyes welling.

'Every day of his life is hell,' she said in a vulnerable, shaking voice. 'Come in from the playground where he's been ridiculed for being *smart*, then sit in a classroom where he's so bored out of his mind that he ends up in the principal's office or the resource room because his parents refuse to let him take Ritalin . . . meanwhile the rest of his world marches farther and farther away.'

'The solution is not to numb his brain – or take the rest of the world away from him.'

'Oh, stop. Did he tell you how he hurt his ankle?'

'He said he fell.'

'He duct-taped two kites to his arms and jumped off the school roof. Some older kids dared him.'

A heavy tear spilled onto her cheek, and she wiped it away with the back of her hand. But she did not avert her eyes.

'Jake, you'll never know how awful I feel for hurting you,' she said. 'I never meant for it to happen this way. But I can't be sorry for trying to make a better life for Max.'

'By sleeping with Price?'

'You need to go.'

'*Just tell me why!*' he whispered, then shut his eyes to stop the rising rage. He opened his eyes and tried again, keeping it down. 'At least,' he said, 'tell me when it started?'

'Why?'

'I have to understand.'

'Go.'

He shook his head, not that he was refusing to leave, he was simply lost. 'Can we call a marriage counselor?'

She stared across the dark kitchen at him, looking almost frightened. God, how he wanted to crawl into his bed beside her. 'Jake, I'm sorry,' she told him, in the saddest tones he had ever heard. 'I don't know what else to say.'

He could barely say the words . . . 'You're going to divorce me.'

She kept staring with those angelic eyes, not denying it, though how he wished to God she would. The refrigerator seemed to shimmer.

He staggered back a step, unable to take his eyes off her. She was the first girl he'd ever loved, and the only one, a woman now, and he had no idea how he'd lost her.

'You won't take Max away from me,' he vowed, anger leaping up through his skin, then he turned away dizzily, pushed the screen door open and walked down the porch steps. Crossing the lawn to his car, he could feel the roaring approach of a monstrous despair.

'Hey, Dad—'

The voice floated on the air like a ghost.

'Dad!'

Jacob turned. In the dark, he could see Max's glasses glinting behind his window screen.

Jacob took a shaky breath. 'Hey, champ, how ya doin?' The words forced from his throat.

'I was right, wasn't I?' the boy answered.

Jacob came closer in the soft grass, while he searched for something to say. But nothing came. Reaching the window, he cleared his throat, an abrupt and conspicuous sound in the suburban night.

'Go back to sleep, Maxie,' he said, and he touched the warm screen where his son's forehead lay. 'We'll figure something out.'

When he got into his car, something hard poked into his back between his shoulder blades. At first he thought a spring had popped through the upholstery. Then he reached his hand around—

—and he got out of the car again.

Staring in the open window, he stood there on the side of the road, unable to comprehend. Someone had stuck a knife in his seat.

The night was black when Jacob let himself in the musty cottage. He turned on the lamp and stripped off the clothes he was wearing, folded his shirt over the chair, dropped his charred pants on the floor. Then he climbed into bed. This was the moment he had dreaded. The sheets were stiff, the bed too short, and Laura's absence glaring.

The first thing he thought: He would never again see her come in from jogging – she ran three miles every morning before Jacob arose, rain, snow, or blistering heat – then come up to their bedroom and strip off her sweats and awaken him with a kiss, or sometimes crawl back into bed on top of him. She did that only a week ago. It was a warm, humid morning, and she was so wet with perspiration that they laughed while they made love. Last week.

Jacob turned the thought out of his mind, wanting only darkness. But he did not turn off the bedside lamp, afraid of how the darkness would compound his loneliness. Instead, he stared up at the knotty pine ceiling while he tried to replace his anguish with anger, his sadness with indignation – anything that didn't feel so infinite. Laura was divorcing him. She would take Max away from him and, with Price Ashworth's help – he was the one who had prescribed Ritalin for the boy – start him on the medication and send him away to school.

But why? How had it happened so suddenly, so completely? And Alix Callahan, what was she up to? He remembered the name of the attorney she had told him about – Willard Zabriski. He had already been paid. By whom? And why?

July was in his brain too. Her face, her shoulders, the coffee tones of her skin, the lithe muscles of her arms, her slouching dark stare . . .

Jacob rolled over, to get rid of the image. He does not desire, does not fantasize. This is how he contains his mind.

He heard a car pass slowly on the street – and his thoughts returned to the knife someone had stuck in his car seat, wondering if it was the neighborhood bullies giving Max a hard time, or just random vandalism. He thought of Max lying in his own bedroom, and remembered the stunned first days and weeks living without his own father. The ache rose in his throat; tears burned his eyes. He never imagined such confusion, such a deep and unrelenting emptiness. What scared him the most was that he had no idea how much worse it could get.

He rolled over again. And he made himself a vow. He would not let himself fall apart. For Max's sake, he would be strong. He would find out what had happened to his life.

He shut his eyes, took one more breath . . . and darkness came.

In Jacob's dream, he walks through a tropical garden, meandering along a path surrounded by lush foliage. Suddenly July is there, facing him, watching him. Hidden from the world, she pulls the delicate straps over her shoulders and willowy arms, and the dress slides down her chest, catching at her breasts. She inhales sharply as it falls the rest of the way, then stands there exposed, never taking her eyes off him.

He moves closer to her. 'What's wrong?' she asks. A long strand of hair covers one of her eyes. With his fingers, he gently brushes it behind her ear, over her shoulder, then runs his hand slowly down her breast, and her nipple carves a path along his palm.

She reaches her own hands around his neck, and then she kisses him. And the softness of her lips, the way their tongues come alive and their breathing intensifies, and now they're sinking down to the warm, moist ground . . .

'*Jacob . . .*'

★ ★ ★

'*Hey—*'

Rising to consciousness, he'd already convinced himself that Laura was here to bring him home. But when he opened his eyes, his heart bolted.

'How did you get in?' He squinted against the light. Was he still dreaming?

'Window,' July answered. The bedside lamp was still lit, the windows dark. He started to sit up, but his head hurt so much, he fell back down. His pillow was drenched. His whole body ached.

'It's the yagé,' July told him softly, placing her hand on his forehead. 'You need water.' She was wearing the same brown dress she'd had on the night before, and smelled sharply of perspiration.

He closed his eyes. 'I need to sleep,' he said tiredly. 'You can't stay here.'

For a number of seconds he lay perfectly still, letting his muscles lie down, hoping she was gone. Then he felt her finger touch his brow, lightly tracing his scowl line.

'You worry too much,' she said.

He opened his eyes and he saw her staring down at him from between the silken curtains of her hair. His heart leaped, thinking she was going to kiss him. 'Seriously,' he said, rolling onto his side away from her, 'I don't mean to be rude—'

'You were on fire when you left,' she cut him off. 'You're so strong.' She began massaging the back of his neck, and he immediately felt the pain subside. 'I started reading your book last night,' she said. 'I was afraid to fall asleep.'

'Afraid to fall asleep, why?' he asked.

'Alix,' she answered. 'Her imagination speaks to her all the time, like a gossiping old woman.'

Hearing the colloquialism, Jacob wondered again where Alix had found her.

'After she came home,' July continued, 'she started drinking again and got really weird.'

'Wait a minute.' Jacob turned back to her, remembering the knife in his car seat. 'Alix went out last night, after I left?'

July gave him an affirmative look, and his heart kicked from the adrenalin shot.

'What time?'

'Late,' she said, and started to get in bed beside him. 'Jacob, I'm so tired.'

'Hold on—' He held the blankets down.

The way her gaze turned disparaging, suddenly he saw something very American about her indeed, that disdainful look informed by shopping malls and negligent parents, by MTV, suburban schools and bad web sites. It was the look of a girl used to getting her way. She tossed the blanket at him and said, 'I just wanted to *sleep*.'

'You can't,' he told her. 'Not here.'

'Well, I can't go home,' she said. 'She'll kill me.'

'I'm sorry,' Jacob said, retrieving his jeans from beside the bed pulling them on under the blankets. 'I'd like to help you, but I really can't get involved in this.'

She gave him a narrow black look, then whipped her hair around and started for the door, when they heard a car pull off the road and roll onto the gravel dooryard outside the cottage. July stood there with one hand on the doorknob, looking back at Jacob, completely unnerved. They listened to the engine for another moment or two, then the car sped off.

July went to the window and peeked through the blinds. 'She knows I'm here,' July said. 'I told her I was going for a walk. But she knows. She is sure we're already lovers.'

'Wait a minute. How did you get here?'

'Hitched,' she said. 'A couple of drunks picked me up. The bars just closed.'

'Well, hitch home again. Please.'

'She has a gun!'

Jacob's heart caught mid-beat.

'I've been trying to tell you,' July said, 'Alix is insane, jealous. I can't go back there.' She came back to his bed and sat down as though she intended to stay.

'That's it.' Jacob got out of bed, pulled a blue work shirt from his bureau and pulled it on as he went to the door to show her out. 'Please.'

'I can't.'

'Look—' He studied her, trying to think of a way to make her leave, short of throwing her out. 'If you really believe Alix is a danger, call the police.'

'I can't call the cops, and she knows it.'

'Why not?'

'Because I can't.'

And neither could he. Involve the police in some sordid affair between a lesbian psychopath and her bisexual lover, and he'd be sure to lose custody of Max.

'Besides, it's not me I'm afraid for,' she said.

'What are you talking about?' He frowned. '*Me*?'

She looked at him with frightened, liquid eyes. 'Or your boy.'

The words sucked a cold jolt of panic from his heart. Not only the words, but the conviction with which she held his stare.

'Alix is very smart,' July told him. 'She would make it look like an accident.'

She kept her eyes on him while he tried to digest what he was being told.

Then she quietly added, 'Alix could also have an accident.'

As the next few seconds ticked by, Jacob Winter stood inside that airless cottage trying to think of something else she might have meant by those words. But any way he interpreted it, he arrived at the same conclusion: She had just suggested they kill Alix Callahan.

'Come on,' he told her, taking her hand and leading her off the bed. 'I've already forgotten you said that, but you definitely need to go.'

The telephone shrieked. Jacob wheeled. July grabbed hold of his sleeve. 'Don't answer it,' she whispered.

'Even if it's her,' he said, pulling the shirt out of her fingers, 'she's five miles away. You've got plenty of time to get out of here.'

'She has a cell phone,' July said.

The phone rang again, echoing around the cottage. Jacob picked up the receiver. A sudden thought occurred to him, that it might be Laura, lying alone in their bed, unable to sleep—

'I'm telling you this for your own good,' the voice said. 'Don't get involved with her.' It was Alix Callahan, loud and monotonic.

'I have no intention, okay?' Jacob said, glancing over at July, who stood small and frightened beside the door.

'I know what you're planning,' Alix said.

'Listen, I haven't seen July,' he lied, pacing the small path between his bed and bathroom – then he stopped. He could hear traffic in the telephone, and for a moment feared she was standing outside his window. Then he realized that the road outside his cottage was quiet.

'What did she tell you about me, that I'm insanely jealous and, what, I have a gun—?'

Jacob stopped pacing, went to the door and made sure it was locked, while she kept talking in that same hollow voice.

'. . . that I'm a threat to your life,' she raved on, 'or is it your son?'

'Listen to me.' Jacob spoke as evenly as he could. 'If you ever mention my son—'

'I know, you'll kill me.'

'Look, Alix, why don't you call someone who can help you?'

She gave an ironic laugh. 'You want to know who gave me the money?'

'No, I want you to stay out of my life.'

'Meet me on the bridge,' she said.

'I'm not going to do that,' he told her. 'If you've got something to say, say it.'

'Then you'll never know,' she said, and the line went dead.

Jacob stood there, stunned, holding the telephone to his ear. July studied him with worried eyes. He didn't need to ask which bridge, he knew damn well. She was still playing games. But what kind of game? In his mind he replayed what she had said, until he realized that there was no other way of interpreting it. She was planning to kill herself.

He grabbed his keys off the night stand and said to July, 'When I come back, would you please not be here?'

'What did she say?'

'Nothing.' He opened the door and looked nervously out at the night.

'I'm coming with you,' July said, pushing past him.

'Absolutely not,' he told her, but she walked straight to his car and got in the passenger side.

'July—' He followed her and held her door open so she could get out. 'We can't show up together.'

'It might be a trap,' July said, refusing to get out.

Jacob hesitated for only a second, wondering how her coming would avoid a trap. Not wanting to waste time arguing, he slapped the roof of his car. 'Why can't you people understand me? I cannot get mixed up in this.'

'Hurry up,' July told him.

'Was she depressed when you left?' Jacob asked, as he pounded the Mazda through its gears, squealing around the deserted rotary. 'Despondent?'

'She's crazy, I told you,' July answered.

'Did she ever talk about doing herself in?'

'Why?'

'I don't know, she sounded strange, frightened. Why else would she call from the bridge?' He cut the wheel sharply, veering onto the ramp to I-95, trying not to think about what he was doing: driving onto the monster for the first time in his life. Seeing no other choice, he pressed back in his seat and clutched the steering wheel, concentrating on his breath. 'Do you keep sleeping pills in the house?' he asked. 'Barbiturates?'

'Tylenol PM, that's all,' she answered. 'Take this.'

He tore off the ramp onto the highway, the hulking skeleton rising up steadily before them – and Jacob's heart started to pound. Trees and rooftops descending, the lights of the town spreading out below, the moonlit sky wrapping around them.

'Take it,' July said again.

He looked over. The flickering highway lights outlined a small black revolver in her hand.

'*What are you doing?*'

'I told you, she thinks we're having an affair.'

'Put it away.'

'Jacob, she told me she was going to kill us both.'

Jacob had all he could do to keep breathing, as they climbed higher and higher over the river and were swallowed by the steel work. 'July, please,' he said, with as much calm as he could muster . . . He felt increasingly faint.

'There!' July pointed.

A car parked on the side of the bridge, a small, boxy station wagon, its right directional blinking red, red, red . . . And a shadowy figure standing at the rail. Jacob caught his breath.

July slouched down in her seat.

His foot pressed the brake, and he pulled over just beyond the GREEN GIRLS wagon. Indeed, it was Alix standing there on the other side of the railing. She was facing him, unable to see July, who stayed down. Jacob leaned over her and fumbled with the window switch. 'What are you doing?' he yelled into a whistling gust.

Alix looked over her shoulder, down to the darkness below her.

Paralyzed with fear, somehow Jacob managed to open his door.

'*Don't*— ' July grabbed at him, but he was already out the door, legs turning rubbery beneath him.

Now Alix stiffened, a guileless look of terror in her face. 'You told me you were alone,' she said to him, keeping her eyes on July.

'Alix, please,' he said, his voice barely more than a whisper.

'Jacob, be careful!' July yelled.

The blast of an air horn shook him, and he grabbed the hood of his car, the bridge bouncing like a diving board as the trailer truck blew past.

'Just climb back over,' Jacob said. His voice shook, along with the rest of his body, but he could see that Alix was shaking even more. She looked down beneath her feet, then threw her face in the air, as if she couldn't believe this was happening to her.

'Alix—' He left the relative safety of his hood and grabbed onto the Volvo's roof. 'There are people who can help you,' he told her, in as

Michael Kimball

calm a voice as he could muster, as he made his way around the Volvo.

Her expression turned incredulous, almost as though she were about to laugh. Still she kept her eyes on July. 'You're so stupid,' she said, and reached one hand into the pouch of her sweatshirt—

'*Jacob!*'

An explosion sounded behind him. He fell to his knees and watched Alix's face drop between the railings.

He jerked around and saw July behind the wheel. 'Get in!' she yelled, revving the engine.

He knelt at the curb, frozen. Alix Callahan was gone.

July shouted: 'Are you going to jump down and save her? Get in!' The car started to move.

Jacob pulled himself up the side of the Volvo, in a daze. 'What did you do?' he asked.

His car was rolling away. He ran after it and jumped in the open door, she wasn't stopping, caught hold of the seat belt and pulled himself in.

'What happened?' he said, slamming the door as she raced down the bridge, the smell of gunpowder blowing through his car. He could still hear the squeak of Alix's fingers sliding off the rail. No, it was a siren rising up in the distance. He looked over at July, horrified. 'What did you get me mixed up in?'

'She had a gun, she was going to kill you,' July said evenly, aiming his car for the exit ramp.

'Where are you going?'

'Home.'

'I keep telling you, I can't be involved in this! I have a son!'

'Jacob, you need to drop me off,' she explained.

He couldn't think. 'What about the gun?'

'I'll hide it.'

He stared at her in disbelief. Reaching the bottom of the ramp, she drove through the red light without stopping. 'Don't get pulled over,' he told her, his mind beginning to return.

She turned onto her road, driving calmly between the neat brick houses.

'Oh God,' he said, dropping his head in his hands. He needed to think.

When they reached the point where the river and bridge swung into view, July pulled to the shoulder and shut off her headlights.

'What are you doing?' He wished he could stop the trembling in his voice.

48

'Shh.'

Through his open window he heard more sirens; he could see the blue lights flashing up on the bridge, the headlights of two other vehicles stopped there, and men converging like fireflies, waving their flashlights down at the river. Another siren sliced the night, moving from west to east behind them.

Divers would be coming, Jacob thought, logic slowly returning, to pick Alix's body out of the current. Would they also find a bullet?

'Are you sad?' July asked him.

He looked through the darkness at her, astonished. 'Am I *sad*?'

'That she's dead.'

'Did you shoot her?'

'She was going to kill you,' July said indignantly.

He closed his eyes, trying to replay what had happened on the bridge, but his memory had already retreated into the darkness, doors had shut. He looked up at the bridge again, the camera flashes going off like lightning. He tried to remember her phone call, how he had driven onto the bridge, what he had said to Alix – if anything – but everything had vacated his brain.

'Okay,' he said to July, 'you've been home all night. They're going to trace her license plate. Then they'll come to tell you the news.'

She stared at him.

'July, let's go.'

'I'm shaking,' she said.

He pushed the gearshift into neutral, took hold of the ignition key and started the engine. 'Please,' he said.

July shifted into first, revved up the RPMs, then popped the clutch. The car shot ahead with a chirp, then stalled. She started it again, pressed the accelerator and eased the clutch, transmission whining for a hundred feet or so, then she stopped with a jerk in front of Green Girls. Jacob turned off the key, checked the road behind them, relieved that no other houses were in sight. He got out and walked around to the driver's door, opened it for her.

'Listen now,' he said. 'It's important, it's absolutely crucial, that neither of us knows anything about this. You were home all night. You haven't seen me.'

She remained in the car, holding the wheel.

'Come on,' he said, taking her arm.

She pulled away angrily. 'I was trying to help you.'

'I know, I know,' he whispered, stepping aside so she could get out. 'Now, don't turn any lights on. Just go to bed. Do you sleep together?'

'What?'

49

'You and Alix – do you share a bed?' Realizing the tense was wrong. July realized it too, nodding up at him glassy-eyed.

'Okay, you went to bed early and never heard her go out. You'll do fine. No . . .'

'Jacob, you're making me nervous.'

He raised his fists to his head, thinking, thinking . . . 'Okay,' he told her. 'Turn all the lights on. Have your bathrobe on, whatever it is you wear to bed.'

'I don't wear anything.'

The way she said it, the look she gave him— He flinched when he saw the revolver in her hand pointing carelessly at his chest.

'Whatever,' he said, redirecting her aim as he gently led her out of the car. 'When they get here, tell them you woke up when you heard Alix leave the house, and you've been waiting up ever since. You were worried, because she's been so depressed. That way you won't have to act shocked when they tell you. Okay?'

She gave a slight, fearful nod.

'A note,' he said. 'She may have left a suicide note. You need to find it before they do.'

'Why?'

'She might have mentioned my name. I told you, I can't be implicated. Neither can you. If you find a note, flush it down the toilet. No, burn it. Is the gun registered?'

July leaned against him, her head warm on his neck. 'Jacob, I don't think I can do this.'

'You've got to,' he said. 'Is it registered?'

'I don't think so.'

'We've got to be sure.'

'I don't know,' she said. 'It belonged to Alix.'

'Okay. Just hide it.'

'Where?'

'I don't know. Someplace where . . .' Jacob drew back. 'If this is Alix's gun, whose gun did you think she had?'

July shrugged her shoulders.

'You said she had a gun.'

'I don't know! She had something!'

'Shh.' He put his hands on her arms. 'Okay. Just get rid of it.'

'I think I'm in shock,' she said, leaning her body against him.

He gently turned her toward her house. 'Just be calm,' he said. 'I've got to get out of here.'

She let out a soft gasp, then turned back to him, a fearful look in her eyes.

50

'You can do this,' he encouraged her. 'You'll do fine.'
But the way she kept staring at him.
Jacob's heart pounded. 'What's the matter?'
She shook her head, deadly earnest.
'Her cell phone.'

CHAPTER SIX

'This is supposed to be a surprise drug search, not an opportunity for you to foul the officers' latrine,' Bullens said, slapping the door open with the flat of his palm.

The only man in the room was Cecil, and he was stripped naked, sitting on one of the four toilets attached to the wall, reading a *People* magazine, not even looking up. 'Be done in a minute, Sarge. I'm enjoying the luxury.'

Bullens came and stood directly over him. 'You make sure you enjoy it, because I just wanted you to know' – the sergeant went to peek in the shower room, then he turned a couple of the showers on full, and came back – 'I have taken certain precautions.'

'What kind of *precautions*?' Cecil replied.

Bullens looked up at the ceiling, seemed to study something for a moment, then returned to the black man with a glimmer of a smile. 'Which means, if anything goes wrong with our little escapade – like if you or Sereno plan on double-crossing me – I have arranged it so that if I don't get to whack you myself, every day for the rest of your life you will wish I had.' The smile broadened on the sergeant's face. 'My friend, you will fall to your knees and *pray* for someone to put you out of your misery.'

Cecil shook his head earnestly. 'Hey, Biff, man—'

'Don't "Biff man" me,' Bullens said. 'I know you and Sereno got plans.'

'What *plans*?'

Bullens looked back at the closed door, then lowered his voice. 'I suggest you think very carefully before you say another word.'

Cecil stared at the sergeant; he didn't even blink when sweat ran into his eye.

'I happen to know that a million dollars disappeared the day Sereno whacked that drug dealer down in Plantation Key,' Bullens said. 'A million, at least.' He glanced back at the door again.

'I don't know anything about no money,' Cecil said.

Bullens fixed him with a grin. 'You know what I think? Speaking of double-crosses. I think you and Sereno and the boat people got plans for that money.'

'I just told you,' Cecil said, unwavering, 'I don't know about no money.'

'Honorable men have sold their integrity for a lot less than a million dollars. And you ain't honorable.' Bullens scrutinized the black man, and flushed the toilet under him. 'Wouldn't be hard to do,' he said. 'Put a cap in my head, then go get your million and think you're going to be free.'

Cecil spoke each word distinctly: 'I . . . don't . . . know . . . about . . . no . . . money.'

'Lower your voice.' Bull gave him another few seconds of scrutiny, then flushed the toilet again. 'I need to know if I can trust you, that's all. Yes or no.'

After the toilet stopped, Cecil said, 'Yeah,' but he didn't like saying it.

Bullens nodded thoughtfully. 'If that's the truth, then come Saturday we'll deliver Sereno to the boat people, and the boat people will hand over the product, and you can take your third and be on your merry way.'

Cecil looked up. 'What's this "third" shit?' he said, then drew back as though ready to block a punch.

Bullens regarded the black man balefully.

'I'm asking a question, not being belligerent,' Cecil said. 'Deal was, you and me split fifty-fifty.'

Bullens smiled as he drew a small tape recorder out of his pocket. 'Now I surely don't intend to stand here and quarrel with a man who just lost his bargaining position,' he said. This time when he flushed the toilet under Cecil, the vacuum made a vicious sucking sound, and seemed to draw his face into a frown.

'Oh, yes, we got you, my friend.' Bullens lightened with indifference. 'Conspiracy to traffic in a controlled substance. Bribing an officer of the law. Conspiracy to escape. You probably racked up a lifetime of felonies. And now I'm going to do you a favor.'

Tears rose thickly to Cecil's eyes. He pretended to read *People* again.

'Hey. Do you want your freedom, or not?'

The black man maintained his silence.

'As bad an individual as you think you are, you must know that the great state of Florida doesn't care if you do another day here – or the rest of your life. They're actually more concerned with that band of

Colombian Indians and the load of contraband they're bringing to trade for your buddy Sereno's freedom.'

Cecil let the magazine drop from his hands, then stared at the floor. 'What do I have to do?'

'I'll bet you're better people than I give you credit for,' Bullens said to him.

'I adhere to a particular moral code,' Cecil replied, stuck on the toilet.

Bullens' chest jiggled with silent laughter. 'Hey. Numbnuts. How long have you known me?'

'Too fuckin long.'

Bullens knocked on his head. 'Did you seriously think I was going to help you escape for a sack of cocaine?'

Cecil raised his face to the ceiling, trying to stop the pooling in his eyes. 'You want me to cross Sereno, right?'

Bullens brought his mouth close to his ear. 'This is your ticket, my friend, the only way in this lifetime you're ever gonna taste real freedom. And yes, it may require you to go against your *moral code*.'

Cecil stared hard, straight ahead.

'It ain't complicated,' Bull told him, 'Everything's the same as before – 'cept with a wrinkle.'

'Tell me the wrinkle.'

'The wrinkle?' Bullens said, and he walked over to the door. 'From now on there gonna be two of us good guys.'

Cecil watched with dark suspicion as Bullens pulled the door open, and another prison guard stepped in, a uniformed black man named Terrence Gideon.

'Not being the literary type,' Bullens said, 'you probably haven't had much occasion to make the acquaintance of O.I.C. Gideon.'

'I know him,' Cecil said, regarding the black officer with street-wary disdain.

'Then you're probably aware that Officer Gideon was once a jailbird, like yourself. For drugs, isn't that right, Officer Gideon?'

Gideon folded his arms. He wore tortoiseshell eyeglasses and had a physique that might be called portly. He was Officer in Charge of the prison library, the lowest rank in the Florida prison system, and one he'd held for twenty-one years. He was forty-six years old.

Bull came back and flushed the toilets again, as he continued speaking to Cecil. 'Officer Gideon is a reformed man nowadays,' Bullens said. 'He's been cleared for this assignment at the highest levels.'

Cecil's jaw clenched. 'What *highest levels*?'

Bullens knocked on his head again. 'The highest levels ain't about to talk to you. For obvious reasons.'

'Uh-huh,' Cecil said.

Chuckling to himself, the sergeant said, 'Do you notice the restraint I'm showing?'

'Oh, fuck, yes.'

Bullens raised a warning finger. 'Officer Gideon is a church-going man now, and he doesn't tolerate that kind of language.' Bullens started flushing again. 'Now, because I don't feel all that secure being the only white man in the company of traitors and thieves,' Bullens said, 'now there gonna be two of us good guys that you bad guys take hostage.'

'That's your wrinkle,' Cecil said – as if it were that simple.

'That,' Bullens allowed a smile. 'Plus we're gonna recapture you jailbirds. Along with Sereno's Colombian crew – and their stash.'

'And you expect to pull that off so Sereno don't know it's me who set him up – after you had me dragged outta bed in the middle of the night?' Cecil studied Bullens. Then he studied Gideon, who looked away as though unable to withstand his stare.

'No one'll know nothing,' Bullens assured him. 'You do a couple of months here, to make it look good, then we can say you got transferred upstate. We take you outta here, drop you off at the bus station in Miami, and you're gone, free at last, free at last, thank God Almighty—'

'Don't do that,' Cecil said in a low voice.

Off in a darker corner of the bathroom, Gideon gave Bullens a sober look. The gesture did not escape Cecil's notice. He kept his eye on the librarian as he said to Bullens, 'How about I get away clean, like we agreed. You can say I escaped.'

'And spend the rest of your life lookin over your shoulder?' Bullens widened his eyes.

'Word gets out I set up Sereno, I won't survive two hours in this place,' Cecil said, 'never mind your two months.'

'Lower your voice.'

Cecil gave Gideon another look, perhaps hoping for support; he got none.

Footsteps sounded outside the room, someone humming a song. The door opened and a man, prematurely gray and dressed in a robin's egg blue suit, poked his head in. It was Dale Shivers, Warden of Alligator Alley Correctional Institute, a man who seemed to take genuine interest in all of his men, both prisoners and guards, and was known for his nocturnal wanderings through the facilities, chatting with the insomniacs, sharing his philosophy. 'Everything okay in here?' he asked.

'Just fine, Warden,' Bullens replied. 'Officer Gideon and I are trying to track down a couple of overdue library books, that's all.'

Warden Shivers nodded thoughtfully. 'We wouldn't want to discourage the men from furthering themselves.'

'No, we would not,' Bullens agreed. 'Absolutely.'

Warden Shivers looked from Bullens to Cecil to Gideon, then shut the door. His footsteps went tick-tocking away.

Bullens tapped his finger on Cecil's head. 'If you apply a little thought to the matter, you'd realize that your Indian friend is living out his golden years right here in this institution. The minute he gets deported back to Colombia, he's gonna get himself executed by the drug cartel because he wasted one of their dealers on Plantation Key for screwing his wife. He ain't dumb; he knows he's marked. Even if we let him get on that boat and he goes after the million he took off that dead drug dealer then joins up with some other Indian tribe in Mexico or Argentina, you think eventually some other mud-race individual won't rat him out for a pair of polyester pants?'

'Sarge, how'd you get so enlightened?' Cecil said.

Bullens flattened his lips. 'Scenario three: Sereno sets out to find his American wife and waste her ass for not dying last time he tried. Any way you cut it, a couple days after that Injun walks outta this place, there's gonna be a bloodbath. So try to think of it this way: You're saving lives in the third world.'

'Zero weeks.' Cecil folded his arms, to show he was serious. 'You want to recapture me at the scene, to make it look good, okay. You can even bring me back here for processing. But I never set foot in the population. You can spread the word that I got sent up to Stark.'

Bullens pretended to think it over.

'And before I agree to anything else,' Cecil said, 'I want to see my new ID and bank account number.'

'The paperwork isn't ready,' Bullens said. 'That's coming from the Florida Department of Justice.'

'Where's that, next to the Florida Department of Santa Claus?'

Bullens chuckled. 'I am going to miss your sense of humor.'

But Cecil was not joking. 'You want my cooperation,' he said, 'you grant my request.'

Bullens gave him a warm, dimpled smile. 'If I want your co-operation,' he said, flushing Cecil's toilet one more time . . . 'I got your cooperation.'

CHAPTER SEVEN

When Jacob got to his cottage, and was about to pull in, at the last second he continued driving past. His front door was open. Worse, he spotted the police car was parked beside the office. What Jacob decided to do wouldn't have been a rational person's first choice. But in his state of mind, it seemed the only one.

Squeaky Frenetti's bar looked dead by the time Jacob got there – only one vehicle was parked on the road and the light above the sign – SPEEDWAY TAVERN – was turned off. Not wanting his car to be seen, Jacob pulled up the driveway in back, where Squeaky, his father-in-law, had left his Impala. The lot was dark, as was the Captain Norman House, the building it had once served. Originally built in the 1700s by a sea captain named Joshua Norman, the mansion had once been a magnificent display of gables and chimneys, with an octagonal widow's walk on top, overlooking Kittery Harbor.

Over the centuries of changing families and fortunes, the property had served as home to shipyard presidents and factory owners, then was a sanatorium and later a retirement home, until it was shut down by the town's codes enforcement office. During the same lifetime, the captain's old carriage house, which lined the roadside, had undergone similar changes, from blacksmith shop to bait and tackle shop, candy store, ice cream shop, and finally a clam shack.

When Squeaky Frenetti bought the property at a bank auction in the 70s, he dreamed of transforming the mansion into a restaurant and inn, notwithstanding the warnings from friends that he might as well throw his money to the tides. They might have been right. Structural repairs to the foundation and roof of the mansion not only drained Squeaky's savings, but when the town refused to let him turn the carriage house into a working garage, he decided to keep his little house in town, with its three-bay garage, and turn the carriage house into a bar. The Captain Norman House – which Squeaky renamed The Spite House – remained empty.

When Jacob walked through the back door of the tavern and down the stone steps, he found his father-in-law washing dishes in the tiny, stone-walled kitchen.

'You got a lot of moxie showin your mug around here,' Squeaky croaked, not even turning to look at him. Sounds of a televised car race came from the bar.

Jacob approached carefully, unsure if the old man had been drinking.

'You know I'd never hurt Laura,' he said quietly.

'So how come she kicked you out, you smart bastard? You went ape-shit with a radio, that's what I heard.' He took his hands out of the soapy water and dried them on a towel, then turned and peered up at Jacob. Squeaky Frenetti was a stocky man, five-nine in his black penny-loafers, a holdover from the 1950s side of the 1960s, with his rolled-up short-sleeves and blue jean cuffs. He was bald on top, but the white hair around his ears was greased and swept around the back of his neck into a stiff duck tail.

'Something happened tonight,' Jacob said.

The older man's face brightened. 'Oh yeah?'

Jacob lowered his voice. 'I didn't do anything wrong, but the police are probably going to be looking for me.'

'You didn't do anything wrong?'

'That's right.'

Squeaky appeared to mull over what Jacob was telling him, then he stuck his head in the doorway that led to the bar, and announced, 'He hasn't done anything wrong.'

Jacob gave his father-in-law a curious look, then stepped through the door to see Phil Fecto sitting on a barstool, watching the car race on TV. Smiling, the detective snuffed out his cigarette. 'Have a seat, I'll buy you a beer,' Fecto said, patting the stool beside him.

'Smart bastard, he seen you drive up,' Squeaky told Jacob under his breath.

Despite the fact that the tavern was across the street from the harbor, no fishing nets hung from the walls or ceiling; no lobsters or buoys, no harpoons or long oars. The walls of the Speedway Tavern were covered with pictures of cars and autographed photos of drivers: Buddy Baker, Dale Earnhardt, Richard Petty, and the local celebrity, Jeff Dakota, a twenty-four-year-old kid from town who had recently made it onto the NASCAR circuit.

Behind the bar hung a crumbled red hood from a '72 Impala, the car that Squeaky still drove. Beside the hood, framed in gilded chrome, was a poster-sized enlargement of the same Impala passing a blurred WONDER BREAD sign on a race track wall. QUAKER STATE was written on the side of the car. A brass plaque on the bottom of the frame read: 1975 WINSTON CUP. FIRST PLACE, TWO LAPS TO GO.

'The woman who telephoned you tonight – around ten twenty-five—?' Fecto gave Jacob a straight-on look. 'Alix Callahan. We found her car parked on the High-Level bridge. Keys were in it, and it started no problem, so we deduced it wasn't broke down.'

Squeaky came into the bar and set a glass of ginger ale in front of Jacob, who took a drink, trying to appear casual. He knew it would be pointless to deny Alix's phone call. He also knew he would have to lie about July's presence on the bridge, or he'd lose his son. The truth of the matter was, he had no recollection of the incident.

'Would you boys mind turning off the lights and locking up when you leave?' Squeaky said, as he turned off the television.

'No problemo,' Fecto replied, and the old man returned to the back room and was gone. Then Fecto turned back to Jacob. 'That nice couple at Breezy Acres,' he said, 'they told the police you went out around ten thirty – which would be, like, five minutes after Ms Callahan called you.'

It was E-Z Acres, but Jacob didn't bother correcting him; he figured Fecto was just having fun. The detective had pale, lifeless eyes and wore a yellow pin on his windbreaker that said, WHAT, ME FUNNY? – a reference to his sideline as a so-called Maine humorist. Meaning he told stale jokes in an exaggerated upcountry dialect. He also liked to crack jokes when he made an arrest, which was the last thing a suspect wanted to hear – which was probably why Fecto did it. When he had arrested Jacob after the radio incident, he'd said something like, 'If you don't agree with a man's taste in music, next time just ask him to change the channel.'

'I don't know why she called me,' Jacob admitted. 'I hardly know the woman.' He was careful to use the present tense.

'But she'd be the same Alix Callahan who paid your bail the other day—?' Fecto leaned back on the barstool with an assertive glint in his eye.

'I don't know why she did that, either,' he said quietly. 'We were never friends. When she called tonight, she sounded depressed, so I drove to her house.'

'Which would've been ten thirty-five, thereabouts?'

'I suppose so,' Jacob answered, and took another drink. It's impossible to have a panic attack, Price Ashworth once told him, as long as you're breathing properly. Trouble is, Price never explained how to breathe properly while you're having a panic attack. His heart was hammering at his chest.

'Because about the same time,' the detective continued, checking his notepad, 'at precisely ten forty-two, a motorist radioed dispatch and said he saw two cars parked on the bridge and two people standing outside their cars – a man and a woman. He said it looked like the woman was on the wrong side of the railing.' Fecto kept his eye on Jacob. 'You look a mite nerved up, guy.'

Jacob said nothing, wishing he'd stop the shtick.

'But you got nothin to hide, right?'

'I told you, I hardly know her.'

'But it was you she called.'

'I don't know why.' The way Fecto kept watching him, he knew the answer must have sounded ridiculous.

'And that was you up on the bridge with her.'

'No.'

'No? But you drove over the bridge.'

'I drove over. I didn't stop.'

'When you talked on the phone, did she tell you she was going to jump off the bridge?'

'Not in so many words.'

'She said what, then, she's gonna dive? Fly?'

'She didn't say she was on the bridge,' Jacob said. 'She was vague, but it sounded like she might take her life.'

'And you didn't call for help.'

'I didn't know if she was serious,' Jacob maintained. 'How often does someone actually commit suicide?'

'Usually not more'n once.'

Badda-boom. Jacob raised an eyebrow, acknowledging the detective's witticism. His stage name was The Defective Detective. Now he scrutinized Jacob while he tapped a cigarette out of his pack. 'You know, they dusted the railing and lifted prints from two people – on both sides of the railing.' He gave Jacob a smug look as he stuck the cigarette in his mouth. 'We already got your prints on file. Shouldn't be hard to tell if one set's yours.'

'I told you, I stopped,' Jacob said, fabricating now to compensate for his wayward memory. 'I looked over the rail, to see if she was in the water, but it was too dark.'

'Guess I missed that part where you got out of your car,' Fecto said.

Jacob sighed. 'Phil, you know what I'm going through with Laura and Max. The last thing I need is to be tangled up with this.' It was the first time Jacob had called Fecto by his first name, even though the detective's son had played for Jacob's baseball team for the past three years. Fecto was one of those parents Jacob wished would stay home, the variety who would stand on the sidelines offering their loud criticism to coaches, players, and umpires alike.

'Quite a coincidence,' Fecto said, ignoring Jacob's appeal. 'On that entire bridge you'd end up in the exact spot where she jumped. But you say she was gonzo by the time you got there.'

'Her car was there.'

'But the exact spot? Her prints practically touching yours. And the other thing—' Fecto paused to light his cigarette. 'That little dent in the railing?'

'I don't know what you're asking me,' said Jacob.

Fecto blew a column of smoke and said, 'The lab boys think it came from a bullet.' He examined Jacob with a tilted head, like an Irish setter watching a rock. 'Hey, you don't own a firearm of any sort, do you? Nothing came up registered under your name, but that don't mean diddley. You got a gun?'

'No. Do you really think I shot this woman? Pushed her off?'

'You do have a way with women.' Fecto snuffed the cigarette out in the ashtray and said, 'Let me see your hand.'

'What?'

He took hold of Jacob's right wrist and brought it to his nose, sniffing Jacob's fingers, then his wrist and forearm. 'When'd you wash up last?'

'I don't know, a few hours ago, I guess. Before I ate.'

'Other one,' Fecto said, picking up Jacob's left hand and sniffing. Then he took a pair of rubber gloves out of his pocket and pulled them on. Setting a blue plastic box on the bar, he flipped the lid and took out a sealed packet, opened it and produced a small moist cloth.

'Your hand again,' he said, and swabbed one, then the other, while Jacob looked away, wondering if he should call that public defender – whose name escaped him – or maybe the lawyer Alix had told him about . . . Zabriski.

'It's diluted nitric acid,' Fecto explained. 'Detects the presence of nitrates on the skin – which come from gas and powder residue released when a firearm discharges.' He stuck the swab in the bag, sealed it again, then took out a fresh one. 'Hold still,' he said, and wiped Jacob's cheek and chin. 'Lab'll analyze it. Should get the results sometime tomorrow.'

'I told you what happened,' Jacob said.

'You came upon Alix Callahan's empty car, stopped and looked over the railing, then drove away so you wouldn't get mixed up in the woman's suicide.'

'That's right.'

'You know what I think?' Fecto said. 'I think when we put you in a lineup, the driver of that trailer truck is going to put you on that bridge the same time Alix Callahan was standing there. Any chance of that?'

Jacob held the detective's dull gaze defiantly – knew Fecto was bluffing. If the police really knew the driver's identity he'd be standing in the lineup right now. Still, he wondered how July's story would jibe with his. 'Have they found a body?' he asked.

Smiling to himself, Fecto fished inside his windbreaker for another cigarette. 'I wondered when you'd get to that,' he said, as he snapped a flame from his lighter.

'Maybe she didn't jump,' Jacob suggested. 'Maybe she walked off the bridge. Or, if she did jump, maybe she swam to shore.'

Fecto shut his eyes as he inhaled a full dose of nicotine. 'Back when they were doing repairs to the bridge,' he said, easing smoke into his words, 'the workers would dump their bags of cement that got hard. I saw it. Eighty-pound bag of solid cement hits that water, you'd think it would plunge?' Fecto shook his head in a satisfied way. 'It explodes.'

Imagining Alix hitting the water, Jacob shut his eyes.

'Quite a few people have jumped off this bridge since I've been a cop. Some left notes, others left their families with big fat mysteries. One guy even jumped on a bet. Guess what? In thirty years, only two individuals have lived to tell about it. That's only because they managed to hit the water feet first, legs straight, hands by their sides. Like a human arrow.'

'Maybe Alix did the same thing,' Jacob said, trying to sound confident.

'Those winds?' The smoke laughed out Fecto's nostrils. 'Up top it blows one way, down below it blows another, off the ocean, down the river.' His hand scattered the smoke. 'A couple of years ago I helped recover the body of a jumper. When the guy hit the river, the impact tore his leg off at the crotch and snapped every bone in his body . . . flattened him. Okay? She did not swim to shore.'

While Fecto watched Jacob for a reaction, he added, 'You know, when you get the wind knocked out of you, you don't float. You sink straight to the bottom – and that river goes down about sixty feet under the bridge.'

Jacob shook his head. 'I've told you everything I know,' he said. 'May I go home now?'

'See, the thing is, I know something happened between the two of you up here,' Fecto said. 'Come on, you're a writer. Make something up. I can't go home until I file my report. How's this? She says, "I'm going to jump." And you say . . . I don't know, what?' Fecto blew smoke at Jacob. 'Something that might help me understand why you were the one she called.'

Jacob took a deep breath, then let it out slowly. 'I don't know why Alix Callahan bailed me out,' he said. 'I don't know why she called me tonight. And I don't know why she jumped.'

Fecto took a drag of his cigarette, inhaled in a meditative way, then dropped the butt in Jacob's ginger ale. 'And that's what I'll put on my report: "Witness knows nothing." ' He stood and shoved his notepad and pen in his pocket. 'You gonna lock up?'

'Yeah.'

Fecto walked to the front door. 'Tell your father-in-law thanks for the coffee.'

'If I think of anything, I'll let you know,' Jacob told him.

'I'll put that in the report too.'

In the dark, Jacob held the hood of his car open with his back while he jiggled the battery cable. Then he went back to his window, reached inside and turned the key. The motor moaned tiredly but didn't come close to starting. He opened the hood again, wondering why Squeaky had left him there with the detective. The street below was deserted, the ocean quietly churning. It wasn't like Squeaky to trust anyone, let alone his son-in-law, to close up his tavern. As Jacob jiggled the battery cable again, a pair of headlights suddenly turned up the drive. Jacob squinted into the lights, hoping it wasn't another cop.

The old Impala stopped beside him. 'Won't start?' the old man asked.

'It turns over, but won't fire,' Jacob answered.

'They don't usually do so hot without a coil wire,' Squeaky said, holding up the rubber-coated wire.

Jacob scowled at his father-in-law.

'Follow me to my house,' Squeaky said, tossing him the wire. 'I got your stuff.'

Jacob could see his boxes piled in Squeaky's back seat.

'You got evicted,' Squeaky explained. 'Imagine that.'

He took off.

★ ★ ★

Ten minutes later, Jacob pulled to a stop in front of the small brick house, with its three-bay garage. Squeaky's Impala was already there. Lights were on inside. Peepers were loud in the surrounding woods.

Jacob got his backpack out of the Impala, and walked into the kitchen. The smell of the place was familiar, a combination of transmission fluid, gasoline, hand cleaner, thirty years of cigarette smoke and canned cat food. He spotted Max's photos stuck to the refrigerator and went over for a better look. There were a dozen or so, most of which Jacob had taken. Laura always sent the doubles to her dad.

'You can sleep in here,' Squeaky said from the end of the hall, where he unlocked a door opposite Laura's old bedroom. It had been the sewing room when the family was together, but stayed locked after Laura's mother left. 'Come on, I've got a nice, soft pillow for you,' Squeaky said, and went into the room.

Jacob walked down the hall. Something wasn't right. When he stepped into the room, at first he thought the wallpaper in the dark room was patterned with big black splotches. But when the light came on, the splotches turned out to be holes. The door closed. Jacob turned.

The big fist whistled past his chest and crashed through the wallboard, gypsum dust spewing out around Squeaky's wrist. 'You mind if I blow off a little steam?' the old man asked, sucking his hand out of the wall, along with two splintered pieces of lathing.

Jacob stepped back. 'What are you doing?'

'Looking for answers,' Squeaky answered. 'Like how you give a guy a concussion and don't know how.'

Jacob shook his head, not about to sully Laura in the eyes of her father.

'You clocked 'em with a radio – Fecto told me!' From years of shouting, the old man's vocal cords had been scraped to a raspy gargle.

'We had a disagreement,' Jacob said flatly.

'Oh, yeah? We're having a disagreement now. You gonna hit me with a radio? What kinda disagreement?'

'It's personal,' Jacob told him.

'Personal, like the skirt?' Squeaky stuck his chin out. 'Okay, Casanova, who was she?'

'Who?'

'The skirt that called you tonight. The skirt that took the plunge.'

Now Jacob understood Squeaky's rage. He thought it was Jacob who'd been cheating on Laura.

'She's a lesbian,' he explained.

Squeaky's face folded into a scowl as if he'd bit into something rotten. Glaring hard at Jacob, he began nodding his head. 'You know how long it's been since I decked someone? Twenty-two years, goin on twenty-three. But I'm hearin that clock right now.' Two glistening triangles were carved out of his knuckles from punching the wall.

'Squeaky, she was helping me,' Jacob persisted.

'A lezzie helping you,' he said with a swagger in his shoulders.

'She bailed me out of jail.'

'Why?'

'I don't know.'

'You don't know. And now this other broad comes in asking all about you.'

'What are you talking about?'

'Some schoolmarm type with a hair acrost her ass – the District Attorney, that's who. Lady Evangeline. Now what's this shit about you being on drugs?'

Jacob turned and walked away from him. 'I'm not on drugs.'

Squeaky pursued him down the hall, into the kitchen. 'You're supposed to be, according to her. Which is why you clocked Dr Ponytail – that's what I hear – because he came over to tell you to take your pills. What are you, crazy in the head now?'

Jacob picked up his backpack and headed for the door.

'You must be crazy,' Squeaky persisted, 'you want to put the little man through this shit. You and your goddamned books. No wonder Dr Ponytail's gettin set to buy my business while you're holed up in heartbreak hotel.'

Jacob stopped; turned. 'Price Ashworth wants to buy the Tavern?'

'That and the Spite House,' he answered. 'You didn't know? Pony-tailed half-wit offered me five hundred large for the property.'

'Does Laura know he wants your place?'

'Does Laura know?' Squeaky blew a laugh. 'She's his frickin agent. Where have you been? Oh, yeah, Mr Sensitive's gonna turn the place into some yuppie bed and breakfast, with the frickin seashells and fishing nets, and all the beautiful people.'

Stunned, Jacob studied his father-in-law. 'Where's he getting that kind of money?'

'He works! He's made something of himself! Instead of dreamin up books no one wants to read.'

Jacob imagined Price and Laura running the inn together, and every organ in his body sank. He dropped his backpack on the floor. At least things were beginning to make sense. Price wasn't in love with Laura. He was using her, to get his hands on Squeaky's oceanfront property – just as Laura was using Price, to get Max into a good school.

The old man kept his eye on Jacob for another few seconds, then shook his head again. 'Half a mil he wants to give me, and I'm just dumb enough not to take it.'

CHAPTER EIGHT

J acob awoke when he heard the raspy voice seep through the wall. 'You tell me to mind my own business? He's my grandson!'

He was lying on the living-room couch with his head on the arm. The sun was out. Curious about Squeaky's conversation, he walked down the hallway.

'Yo,' Squeaky said when Jacob knocked. His voice was a yelp.

Jacob pushed the door open. 'Was that Laura?'

Lying in bed with his T-shirt on, Squeaky kept his eyes closed. 'Your lawyers are hard at work,' he said. 'The little man's gonna spend the weekend here.'

Despite his elation, Jacob felt a hollowness in his chest, thinking that, with Max out of the way, Price and Laura would have the weekend to themselves.

'You okay?' Squeaky said.

Jacob shrugged. 'Yeah.'

'Good. 'Cause now you're gonna tell me just what the frick you told that son of a bitch.'

'Who?'

'Your lawyer, that's who! Laura says he's been calling her friends, askin did she ever have sex affairs, does she have drug problems, drinkin problems, is she a good mother to her son.' Squeaky's hands jumped out of the blankets. 'What the hell are you tryin to pull?'

'I haven't said a word to my lawyer.'

'Zalinkski, Zaleski, Wahooski—'

Jacob stepped into Squeaky's bedroom. 'Zabriski?' Had Alix hired the attorney to defend him before she jumped?

'Frickin bloodsuckers,' Squeaky said. 'They bat around your lives like a game of ping-pong till you're both ass-high in debt. When they finally bleed you dry, *then* they settle. You get screwed for life, she goes on welfare, the kid turns to a life of crime. Great frickin country.'

Coughing deeply, Squeaky laid his head down again. 'Get outta here and let me sleep.'

'I don't understand,' Jacob said. 'Price Ashworth offered you a small fortune. You'd be set for life. Why don't you sell to him?'

'You think he's the only one who wants that place? A week don't go by without some idiot tryin to give me money. Two days ago, some shyster from Rhode Island who wants to turn it into a yacht club.' Squeaky swiped the air with both hands, like a drunken conductor. 'I gotta sleep, shut the door before you give me a heart attack.'

'Wait a minute.' Jacob stared into the room. 'Are you the one who's paying my legal fees?'

Squeaky wrinkled his face. 'Go ahead, I'll lay here. You keep firing stupid questions at me.'

Jacob remained in the doorway, waiting, while Squeaky glared up at the ceiling, his big chest heaving.

'I don't know what the frick's goin on, okay?' the old man said finally. 'With you, with Laura, Dr Ponytail, lesbians jumpin off bridges, and this whole, miserable, rotten world. But I'll tell you this. There's a little boy involved, and if you're not careful, he's gonna wind up as frigged-up as the rest of us.'

At a pay phone outside the Fishermen's Co-op, Jacob made the call.

'The cops came last night and told me about Alix,' July told him. 'I cried. I don't think they knew I was with you.'

'I'll be there in a while,' Jacob said, not wanting to discuss it on the phone. But he needed to know everything she'd told them.

'The lady at E-Z Acres said you don't live there any more.'

'You called there?'

'No, I went to see you.'

Jacob's sigh was unintentional. 'You shouldn't have,' he said, trying to hide his anxiety.

'I had to tell you.'

'Tell me what?'

'Her computer's gone.'

'What do you mean?'

'Alix's laptop – it's missing,' July said. 'I can't find it. Jacob, I'm scared.'

'Give me an hour,' he told her.

She hung up, and he looked in the phone book for his lawyer. He was shaking again.

Willard Zabriski's law office sat on the Portsmouth bank of the

Piscataqua, a block west of Market Square, with three arch-topped windows that looked out at a black and gray freighter docked in the fog. The nautical brass clock on the wall said 11:00 when Zabriski's assistant, a woman who introduced herself as 'Miss Finch,' brought Jacob into the conference room and seated him at a long table facing the river. A pitcher of ice water sat in the center, beside three drinking glasses. The overhead light was on.

After ten minutes or so, an oak-paneled door opened and a slender, well-appointed man stood there holding a folded newspaper. The first look he gave Jacob was a thinly disguised wariness, obviously wondering how to defend someone Jacob's size who was accused of bashing a man's head with a radio. The lawyer's hair was gray-specked brown, and it swept to his eyebrows from left to right. He looked to be in his early sixties, and he said, 'So.' His suit was ivory linen, his shoes calfskin. 'A mutual acquaintance has retained my services and told me that I'm to be your attorney.'

'I know that Alix Callahan paid you,' Jacob said, taking a vague dislike to the man. 'Would you mind telling me who gave her the money?'

Apparently not about to answer, the attorney dropped the newspaper on the table. It was the morning's edition of the Portsmouth Herald, with a boxed story above the fold. **Car abandoned on bridge**, the headline read. Below a photo of the Green Girls Volvo was the caption, **Woman missing, feared drowned**.

'What should you be telling me about this?' the lawyer asked.

As a light rain began painting the windows, Jacob told him the same story he'd told Fecto.

'And the reason Alix Callahan telephoned you?' Zabriski said, as he scribbled in his legal pad.

'I don't know why she called me,' Jacob said. 'I don't know why she paid my bail, why she hired you to defend me, or where she got the money.'

Zabriski kept writing. 'If someone provided Miss Callahan with the funds, I do not have that information,' he said flatly, and flipped a page in his pad. 'Now. To your assault case.'

'Can I get anyone coffee?' Zabriski's assistant broke in. Miss Finch wore a conservative tweed jacket and skirt over a white blouse. With her wire-rim glasses, she could have been Jacob's age; she could have been fifty.

'Thanks,' Jacob said, shaking his head no. She poured a cup for the lawyer, and set it in front of him. She kept her distance from Jacob.

'I've read the police report concerning the assault on Dr Ashworth and damage to your house,' Zabriski said, sifting through some photocopied documents. He glanced at Miss Finch, and she started a small tape recorder. Then he looked across the table at Jacob. 'Did your wife's lover make a motion that you might have regarded as threatening?'

'I don't think so,' Jacob replied, rising up stiffly in the straight-backed chair.

'Did he raise his arm?'

'Probably – to protect himself.'

Zabriski glanced up dispassionately. 'You must be a mind-reader.'

'What do you mean?'

'If he raised his arm, how do you discern intent? I'll ask you again: When you confronted your wife and her lover in your bed, did your wife's lover raise his arm to you?'

'Possibly,' Jacob answered, wishing he'd stop referring to Price Ashworth as Laura's lover.

'Did your son see them in the bedroom?'

Jacob said, 'I'd like to leave Max out of this.'

Zabriski stretched his legs under the table and looked out the bay window, seeming to watch a yellow kayak glide through the mist. The sky was lowering.

'Mr Winter, are you currently a patient of Dr Ashworth's?'

'I used to be,' Jacob answered. 'Laura's the receptionist and transcriptionist at the psychiatric clinic where Price Ashworth has his practice. I had a few sessions with him after my mother died, twelve years ago.'

Zabriski looked up. 'That's where you met your wife?'

'Yes,' Jacob said, trying not to read too much into the lawyer's inflection, or the way Zabriski looked him over. That's when Jacob realized what bothered him about the man. He reminded him of his father.

'Your wife,' Zabriski said distastefully, flipping a page in his legal pad. 'How often does she drink?'

Jacob felt a rumbling in his stomach. 'I'd rather not go that route, either, if you don't mind.'

The attorney leaned back and pressed his long fingers together. 'Mr Winter, in both your criminal trial as well as your divorce proceeding and custody hearing, I will be defending you from your wife, who, together with her divorce attorney, the District Attorney, and Dr Ashworth, will use every means at their disposal to destroy and demoralize you, to put you in prison and take your house and every dollar you may have saved – and every dollar you might earn in the foreseeable future. And win sole custody of your son.'

Jacob took a breath to object but could not find the words. Zabriski cut him off anyway.

'Now, does your wife drink or use drugs, pharmaceutical or otherwise?'

Jacob sighed. 'Laura doesn't have a drinking or drug problem. She's a good woman, and a good mother.'

'Fine,' the attorney said, closing his legal pad and straightening as though to stand. 'DA Evangeline has already made us an offer: You plead guilty to one count of aggravated assault, you'll receive a five-year sentence, all but two suspended.'

'Two years—?'

'In the state facility at Thomaston,' the attorney explained. 'With good-time credit, you can reduce the sentence by four months.'

Jacob leaned forward.

'On the other hand,' Zabriski continued, 'we could go to court, plead guilty and ask for mercy. With circumstances as you've described them, you could get as little as three months, with a longer suspended sentence.'

Jacob shook his head helplessly. 'I can't go to jail. My son needs me.'

Zabriski looked over at Miss Finch, then back to Jacob. 'Your alternative is to take the case to trial. But if the jury finds you guilty, you could get ten years, all but six suspended.'

Jacob stared at the attorney, reality slamming him from all sides.

'You could plead temporary insanity,' Zabriski suggested. 'But with an NGRI plea, even if it's determined that your insanity was temporary, the judge would most likely sentence you to a mental institution for an indeterminate amount of time, until you're considered no longer a danger to society. With your medical history, my best guess: five years.'

Jacob leaned his head into his folded hands, rough and calloused from years of woodworking. For the first time, the idea of going to prison became reality.

'There's always *in flagrante delicto*: crime of passion.'

Jacob looked up.

The lawyer pursed his lips doubtfully. 'Problem number one: It rarely succeeds.'

Jacob said, 'They were in my bed.'

'Problem number two.' The lawyer raised his brow. 'Dr Ashworth claims he was sitting on the living-room couch, fully clothed, when you attacked him in a psychotic rage.'

Jacob's scowl opened in disbelief. 'He said they were in the living room—?'

'So does the police report.' Zabriski stood and paced to the window, as though he were presenting the prosecution's opening argument. 'A Detective Phillip Fecto, the chief investigator, will testify for the prosecution that Dr Ashworth came to the defendant's home to persuade him to take his Haldol, a medication usually prescribed to inhibit the symptoms of psychosis. The defendant walked into the house . . . how much do you weigh?'

Jacob shook his head, not needing to answer. He understood the picture the man was painting.

'The defendant walked into the *living room*,' Zabriski said again, 'picked up the radio and viciously attacked the doctor, sending him to the ER with a concussion.'

Jacob felt his intestines start to crawl. 'It's the clock-radio my wife keeps beside her bed.'

'Which, the doctor will testify, your wife had brought into the living room so she could listen to the second game of the doubleheader, because it was not televised.'

'Laura said that?'

Zabriski shook his head. 'This is the doctor's testimony. Apparently your wife shares your memory loss. The last thing she seems to remember is hearing the knock on the front door, and letting Dr Ashworth into the house.'

Jacob sat numbly and listened.

'Mr Winter, did you ever have reason to suspect your wife was having an affair with Dr Ashworth?'

The humming behind his ears was getting louder.

'Has she ever had any previous affairs? Flirtations?'

Jacob shook his head. 'No.' It was true. Their relationship, from the start, had been ideal: Lovers, mates, best friends, parents.

'I find your reticence somewhat puzzling,' Zabriski said. 'If I caught my wife cheating on me, I don't think I'd be that keen on protecting her character. Especially if custody of my son were at stake.'

Jacob took a breath of the stifling air in the room. Indeed, the man could have passed for his father, a professor of anthropology at Brandeis University. Except Zabriski had mentioned he had a wife, and Jacob's father long ago had traded his wife for a man.

The lawyer flipped back though his legal pad. 'Before this incident, had you ever felt jealousy toward Dr Ashworth?'

'No,' Jacob answered.

'Were you drinking the day of the incident?'

'I don't drink.'

'Nor I,' Zabriski remarked without looking up from his notes, and the similarities to Jacob's father vanished. His father drank like a fish.

'Mr Winter, I'll ask you again, did your son see your wife and her lover when he came in?'

Jacob sighed, shaking his head adamantly. 'I was the one who saw them – in the bedroom. Then I closed the door and told Max to go play at the gravel pit.'

Zabriski looked up at him, his pen paused on the legal pad.

'Max doesn't have any friends in the neighborhood,' Jacob said, and left it at that, not wanting to explain that the other parents wouldn't let their kids play with him.

'Is there a chance he heard an exchange of dialogue before he left for the gravel pit?'

'I said no.'

'No, he didn't hear? Or no, you'd rather lose custody of your son than involve him in your defense?'

'It's this: I discovered that my wife was having an affair with another man, and in a moment of *in flagrante delecto*, I hit him with a radio. I don't remember.'

Zabriski gave him a wary glance. 'Mr Winter, did you know that Dr Ashworth is currently under Board review in this state?' the attorney asked abruptly. 'For allegedly engaging in improper relations with a former patient. His license to practice medicine is already under suspension in Maine, for another ill-considered dalliance. If it was known that he had relations with the wife of a former patient, he might very well be looking at the end of his career.'

And he wouldn't be able to afford to send Max away to school, Jacob realized – which must have been the reason Laura was willing to hide the truth about their being in the bedroom . . .

'Let me tell you something about the District Attorney who will be prosecuting you,' Zabriski continued.

. . . that is, if they were in the bedroom.

'Susan Evangeline has more determination than a mile of army ants. She lives in a small house and drives a ten-year-old Saab. She has no social life. She lives to prosecute violent men.'

'I'm not a violent man,' Jacob said, and felt Miss Finch's sideward glance.

'You've heard of the White Horse Inn?' Zabriski asked.

'In Rye?'

'Rye, Kennebunkport, Bar Harbor, Nantucket. They're owned by Charlie Astor, a billionaire and personal friend of three past Presidents and every New England governor, senator and congressman for the past thirty-five years. Maybe you didn't know this, but two years ago Ms

Michael Kimball

Evangeline became Mrs Astor for all of eight months – until she was elected DA. At her divorce settlement, she did not ask for a dime. She'd already got what she wanted: Power. She is the women's avenger, Mr Winter. I promise you, Susan Evangeline will learn things about your past that you've long since forgotten. Mr Winter, are you listening?'

Jacob kept his eyes on his hands. 'I'm listening.'

'Have you ever struck your wife in anger?'

'Of course not.'

'Have you ever touched her in anger?'

'No.'

Zabriski flipped through his notes again. 'In California,' he said. 'An altercation at your mother's funeral.'

Suddenly the rain was slapping at the window in waves. 'I thought someone brought a guest who shouldn't have been there,' Jacob said – not that he could remember the incident. It's what he'd been told. 'I was wrong.'

'Yes, one gentleman turned out to be the caterer,' Zabriski said, as he flipped back a page in his legal pad, then gave Jacob a searching look. 'The other man your father—?'

Jacob gave a forbearing sigh. 'I told you, I was wrong.'

'And a separate episode in the same time frame,' Zabriski said. 'A disturbance on an airplane which resulted in an emergency landing in Chicago, and your removal from the plane and subsequent arrest.'

'My mother had just died,' Jacob explained calmly. 'I was upset. I started treatment when I got back to Maine.'

He thought of his mother again, the way she had clung to him when he left for college, and wouldn't let go. It was the last time he saw her alive. Two months later he got a phone call at school telling him she'd had an accident, which turned out to be an overdose of barbiturates mixed with alcohol, which turned out to be suicide, of course, but no one ever mentioned that small fact at the funeral, only that she'd been 'getting help.'

While the attorney droned on, using words like 'pattern of behavior,' and 'conflict resolution,' Jacob's mind traveled back to his house, and once again he was walking in the back door. He hears the Red Sox game on the radio and, following the sound, walks through the kitchen . . . to the living room? Are they sitting there together, on the couch? Is there a bottle of wine on the coffee table? And where's the radio? Jacob cannot see any of it: the radio, the wine, the black silk sheet, or Laura's shoulder exposed . . .

But now, quite unexpectedly, he envisions July's brown shoulder, an image which presents itself richly hued and detailed, the seductive way

74

she had moved to the music the night before, the way she had looked at him. As the image deepens, he can even recall the smell of her, that botanical sweetness, complicated by the pungency of her natural scents wafting out of her dress – the image interrupted when he hears the lawyer's words, 'shared parental rights and responsibilities. The question remains, which of you will get "primary physical residence?" '

Jacob looked up at him, trying to appear attentive.

The attorney stood dismissively, an abrupt but graceful move that looked well-practiced. 'I won't go to court with a case I'm certain to lose. Mr Winter I suggest that you reflect on the things we've discussed. In the meantime, I'll want you back on your medication.'

Jacob closed his eyes. 'The pills were prescribed twelve years ago. I don't take the pills any more because I don't need the pills any more. They inhibit my writing.'

The lawyer looked up at Jacob with a sour face. '*John?*'

Jacob got to his feet, resisting the urge to tell the man that the book had been a bestseller.

'One more thing,' the attorney said. 'In reference to the bridge incident last night, let me say that if you even think of doing anything to embarrass this firm, I will resign as your attorney so fast it will make your head spin.'

Jacob stood there, only half hearing the words. He was staring out across the river with a sudden and powerful revelation: His next book.

'I trust we have an understanding?' Zabriski said, stepping back as Jacob passed through the door.

'Yes,' Jacob replied. 'Thank you.'

Bridge.

75

CHAPTER NINE

R ain shot out of the down spout and washed in a river across the gravel parking lot. It tore at the sheet of paper tacked to the front door, bleeding the words 'CLOSED UNTIL FURTHER NOTICE' until they were barely legible.

As soon as Jacob touched the handle, the door flew open, and a middle-aged couple stepped out, ageing hippies by the looks. In fact, they seemed startled to see him, then they continued down the fieldstone walk. The guy carried a potted plant and a green trash bag slung over his back. The woman carried a package tucked under her arm, wrapped in brown paper, sealed and addressed.

Jacob did not see where the package was headed. He assumed they were bringing something to the post office for July. What struck him as odd was the way, when he looked back at them, they were also looking back at him. And the fact that their car had New Jersey license plates. He didn't dwell on it, though, because at the same moment, July was at the door, pulling him in out of the rain.

'I didn't know where you were,' she said.

'I had to get some things from home,' he answered, not wanting to talk about his legal problems. Was she selling yagé?

'What things?'

'My tools. Who came last night?'

She closed the door, saying, 'Two guys and a woman. They looked everywhere.'

'For what?'

She shrugged. 'A suicide note, I guess.'

'Did they find anything?'

'I don't think so. They said they might come back today.'

'What about the gun?'

'I hid it.'

Jacob stepped out of his wet moccasins. The slate floor felt cold under his feet. 'What did you tell them?'

'Just what you told me: Alix went out late at night, and I waited up for her. I said she was depressed.'

'Good. They don't suspect you were on the bridge?'

She turned away from him to deadhead a black blossom. 'I don't think so.'

'But what if that truck driver spotted you in the car?'

'Then we'll tell them the truth,' she said, glancing back. 'Alix was going to kill you.'

'How?'

July's eyes narrowed for a second, then she turned and started walking down the main aisle of the humid shop toward the garden. With his fingers, Jacob combed his wet hair. Then he followed. At the door, she turned left to the circular stairs and started climbing.

'Did they ask about me?' he asked, going up behind her.

'Uh-huh,' she replied with maddening indifference.

'What did you say?'

'I told them that Alix invited you to dinner last night, and that you used to fuck her in college.'

Jacob's heart skipped. Stopping on the stairs, July looked back at him from under her hanging black hair, her eyes like black pearls.

'You're not serious.'

Without a trace of a smile, she turned and continued climbing into the pantry, a six-foot enclosure filled with groceries, and containing two facing doorways: kitchen and living room. The muffled rain hitting the roof was a comforting sound. It reminded Jacob that he was sheltered, however temporary.

July turned to face him in the tight, windowless space. 'Jacob, I want to help you write your book.'

'How could you help me?'

'You could stay here,' she said. 'I would take care of you. Feed you, wash your clothes. You wouldn't have to work. I've got some money saved. All you would have to do is write.'

Momentarily captivated by her offer, by the way she peered up at him, he abruptly turned away and went into the living room. 'Okay if I look around?'

'I wouldn't bother you,' she persisted, following him.

'I appreciate the offer,' he said. 'But, the way things are, I don't think it would be too smart. How about the bedroom?'

'I can sleep outside,' she said.

Jacob stopped. 'I mean, did they look there?'

'What do you think?' she said, brushing past him to a door. When she threw it open, he saw a queen-sized mattress on the floor, skimpy green underpants thrown beside it. As in every other room in the house, lush flowering plants hung from every window and wall. Jacob lifted a corner of the mattress, peeked underneath.

'They looked there,' she said, her arms folded tightly at her chest.

Jacob lowered the mattress, then pulled the blankets back. The sheets were discolored in two places, where they'd slept. A musky odor blew back at him when he dropped the blankets down. He realized that his mind was compromised with arousal.

'She told me herself,' July said, 'that you were lovers.'

Jacob gave her a look as he shook a pillow out of its casing. He didn't believe her, and it must have shown, the way she spun away from him and walked out of the room.

'What about the pockets of her clothes?' he called.

She didn't answer.

Ignoring the lace bra that hung from the knob, he opened the closet door and ran his hands through the pockets of every piece of clothing.

'You checked the bathroom?' he called.

Again, no answer. He went in anyway, entering through a door off the bedroom. The room was narrow and long, with a skylight set in the slanted ceiling. Rainwater ran in sheets down the glass. Against the far wall, a washer and dryer rumbled and shook the floor. Above the appliances a small, frosted window was opened an inch or two, looking down toward the road.

Aside from the noise, the room was pleasantly appointed: an antique claw-foot bathtub, pedestal sink and old-fashioned toilet. Jacob shut the door and opened the medicine cabinet. He found – no surprises here – a pair of toothbrushes in a juice glass, a pill bottle of Tylenol PM, a stick of unscented deodorant, two hairbrushes, a pack of plastic disposable razors . . . nothing, at least on the surface, that would look like a farewell message. Then, above the noise of the appliances and beating rain, he heard a man's voice. He went to the frosted window and peered out the two-inch opening, saw a blue Explorer parked in front of his car.

Behind him the door opened, and Detective Fecto looked in with a smile. 'Hope I'm not interrupting anything.' He sniffed the air, then poked a hanging pot, started it swinging. 'Looking for a note, I hear.'

'I don't think she left one,' Jacob said.

Fecto gave him a cool, imperious stare, his detective posture. He even looked the part this morning, dressed in a beige trench coat and a smart-fitting felt hat, both of them dripping rainwater. Looking out the door, he brushed water off his double-wide shoulder and muttered to Jacob, as though confiding. 'Know anything about her?'

'Like what?'

Fecto gave a shrug. 'No record. Nothing.' At the sound of footsteps approaching, he changed the subject. 'Did you know the Piscataqua is the second fastest river in the country? And the number one deepest.'

July, sliding into the room behind the detective, gave Jacob a careful look. Her wet hair stuck to her face, from having stood outside with the detective, probably trying to keep him from coming in.

Fecto reached inside his trench coat and pulled out a freezer bag. Inside was a stainless steel steak knife, with a half-inch of murky water in the corner of the bag.

Jacob tried to hide his recognition: It was the same kind of knife someone had used on his car seat.

'Divers found it about a hundred feet downriver,' Fecto explained, studying Jacob with a knowing glint. Then he turned to July. 'Look familiar?'

She gave Jacob a meaningful glance.

And he remembered. The knife was part of the dinnerware he had used here. Which meant July had been right. It was what Alix had been pulling out of her pocket on the bridge . . . And July had indeed saved his life. Her eyes lingered on him, too long.

'You recognize it?' Fecto said to her.

'I'll show you,' she said, and left the room.

Fecto eased the door closed after she went out. 'Often, when someone appears out of thin air,' he said quietly to Jacob, 'no history, no record; there's a good chance they're under Witness Protection. Not always stellar citizens.'

'What do you mean, no history?' Jacob asked, then spotted something that shot a chill through him. He tore his glance away from the skylight, where the barrel of July's revolver peeked into the room, washed onto the glass by the torrent of rainwater flowing down.

Then the door opened, July returning, steak knife in hand.

'That looks right,' Fecto said, taking it from her. 'Do you mind if I borrow it for a few days?'

July shook her head, her face full of sad innocence, then said, 'Do you think she cut her wrist?' Her red bra showed through her wet dress, and Fecto was not shy with his stare.

Jacob stepped between them, positioning himself at the door, to keep the detective facing away from the skylight. 'If you don't mind,' he said, subtly trying to get them out, 'could you give me a minute?'

'Check this out first,' Fecto said, taking a photo out of his pocket. He faced it toward Jacob, a picture of a small, misshapen slab placed

79

beside a ruler, a quarter-inch around. 'The lab boys found it this morning in the southbound lane, which is why it got away from us last night. A ricochet.'

Jacob studied the photo. 'That's a bullet?'

'When a slug collides with something hard, like a steel railing, the lead will flatten and break apart,' Fecto explained. 'Which means – see? – no lands or grooves left for Ballistics to analyze.' He showed the photo to July, who looked up at Fecto in a beautiful way.

'I don't understand. Why are you showing us these things?'

'Fortunately, they've got some pretty sophisticated equipment at the lab. Even with a piece of lead this beat up, spectrographic analysis can tell what gun it came from – or if it matches any bullets from the same gun – or even bullets still in the box.' Sticking the photo back in his pocket, Fecto turned to Jacob again. 'You don't own a firearm, do you?'

'I told you no,' Jacob said, still trying to move them out of the room.

'You, Ma'am? No guns in the house.'

July shook her head no. Then she saw it. Her eyes flashed back at Jacob.

'No access to firearms, either of you?'

She looked up at the revolver again, straight at it. Jacob felt the heat rise to his face, knew he was flushed, and he walked out of the bathroom, hoping they'd follow him. It worked. Fecto came out, July behind him.

'Do you see why we're so interested in this knife?' the detective said to July, closing his notepad and sliding it in his pocket. 'Imagine what goes through an investigator's mind. Here you've got a partial slug, a bullet mark on a railing, a steak knife that belonged to a woman who apparently jumped off a bridge, or was pushed – or shot? Sometimes I think they don't pay us enough.'

'Maybe she was going to use the knife on herself,' July suggested.

'Possibility,' Fecto said, obviously not buying it. But he did seem to be leaving. 'If either of you think of any other theories, anything at all, I hope you won't be afraid to call.'

'I won't,' Jacob said, letting them both pass him in the hall. Then he went back into the bathroom and started to close the door.

'By the way,' Fecto said. 'Did that laptop computer ever turn up?'

Jacob glanced at July, then wished he hadn't, the way Fecto looked him over. 'You knew it was missing—?'

'She just told me.'

'Weird,' Fecto said. 'They found the printer and cables, but no computer. Wasn't in her car. Figured maybe she tossed it off the bridge when she jumped.' He gave Jacob another shrug. 'Sorry to keep you from the cockpit, Captain.'

He chuckled, then finally walked away, and Jacob closed the door, then stood listening to their footsteps going away . . . then a door closing downstairs. He went to the window and, to his relief, saw Fecto get in the Explorer and start the engine. The revolver, having washed down to the middle of the skylight, was plainly visible to the road . . . if the detective decided to look up at the house. But as the vehicle started moving, he was plainly focused on July, her red underwear.

Keep going, Jacob prayed, as Fecto shifted through the first two gears, then disappeared around the corner and was gone.

Jacob unlatched the skylight and gently pushed it up. Rainwater fell in around the sides. Then the bathroom door opened.

'He's gone,' July said.

Jacob directed his attention to the skylight, trying to reach the weapon.

'So—?' she said. 'I didn't know it was going to rain.'

She climbed up on the dryer, giving him a distracting view of her buttocks, then turned and stretched up to reach around the glass. Jacob bounced the frame up and down, and the revolver slid with a gnawing squeal down the glass. Bracing herself on Jacob's shoulder, she stretched her body upward and retrieved the weapon, then climbed down and slapped it in his hand.

'You hide it,' she said, and walked out of the room.

'July, wait,' he said, not knowing whether to thank her for saving him from Alix or apologize for doubting her. Or leave.

She walked into the bedroom. He stopped outside the door.

'July, I didn't know about the knife,' he began.

With her back toward him, she pulled her wet dress over her head. Her red underwear stuck to her flesh. She stood for a moment, motionless, her wet hair clinging to her shoulders, her dripping back divided by the elegant curve of her spine.

'I just wanted to say,' he said, refusing the libidinous tug, 'I appreciate what you did for me.'

She shrugged her perfect shoulders, then turned to face him, her eyes dark and full.

'Jacob, I'm so scared,' she said in a small voice, and came toward him. She seemed to be crying. He wondered if maybe the shock of Alix's death was wearing off. Then she was in his arms.

'If we just stick to our stories, we should be all right,' he said, trying to sound comforting, despite the discomfort he felt holding her, holding the gun. 'We just need to keep our heads.'

'But I can't believe she's not coming back,' she cried, moving slightly, fitting her body against his. He felt her warm breath on his neck and wondered if she could feel his heart beating. He had to let go of her.

'No, don't,' she said, clutching him tighter. 'I'm so cold.'

'July, I can't stay.'

'Why?'

The way she looked up at him, he was about to answer, but suddenly they were kissing, her lips so incredibly soft, and then her tongue was moving warm and wet against his, their accelerated breathing overtaking the rain beating on the roof. Jacob broke it off, heart pounding, the cold revolver in his hand peeked up over her shoulder.

'I can't do this,' he said, but his breathlessness betrayed him. Why, indeed?

She gazed at him with such longing, such sadness, his heart all but melted. But he shook his head. 'I'm sorry.'

She turned away from him. 'Go then,' she said, and he did, took the gun and left before he lost the will, with no intention of ever returning.

CHAPTER TEN

'Montana, that's what I'm thinking. Ever heard of Montana?' Not that Cecil expected an answer, but he turned his head anyway, saw his comrade either studying the sky or sleeping – with Sereno's sunglasses it was hard to tell. The two men lay in the grass as far from the basketball courts as they could get, facing up at the gray dome overhead, while heavy, white-knuckled clouds sagged overhead. The temperature was up in the high 90s, and the humidity at least as high. Surrounded by the Everglades in the thick heart of summer, a day like this could suffocate a man. Just lying there, Cecil's T-shirt was soaked.

'In Montana,' he went on, 'you can buy a hundred-acre ranch for eighty grand. Horses, cattle – I mean, grow your own fruit and vegetables, raise hogs for ham and bacon. Fuck the cattle, man, I just want a horse, and wide open spaces. Imagine that? Bad-ass black man like me riding the open range—?'

Cecil laughed easily, certain that he was acting natural. One thing being inside taught a man, and that was how to cover up.

'Maybe I'll start up a dude ranch for African-Americans, Latinos, maybe a summer camp for underprivileged kids. Have us a little pond filled with catfish. Fish all day and never break a sweat as long as I live.'

He wiped his forehead with his shoulder and glanced over at the Indian, lying there dry as a bone. Christ, the way those sunglasses wrapped around his face, the man might as well have been dead.

'You never see a cop in Montana, know that? Drive your car a hundred miles an hour on the roads. Girl I used to know, Adeline. I use to look out for her kid brother, kicked his ass for her when he got outta line 'cause I knew she'd appreciate that. We talked sometimes, me and her, long talks, you know what I'm sayin, deep. When I first got here, she used to write me from time to time. Just old friends, you know. But

I saved her letters.' His chest kicked with a laugh. 'Correspondence I got from my old lady, I threw that shit away. What does that tell you?'

Laughing again, Cecil really studied Sereno now, and he realized that Bullens had been right. The man was dead if he got out of here, no matter where he ended up. So, what was the harm in letting him have his dreams? Cecil sure wasn't about to tell the man that his taste of freedom was only going to last an hour.

'Anyway, eventually the letters stopped from the both of em. Oh, but Adeline, sweet Adeline. Tell you why she stopped writing. Guy she married, tall flashy dude, showboat. It became an inner conflict to her. Yeah, but I know a day don't go by she don't think about me, wondering what her life mighta been. So. That's what I'm gonna do. Buy a ranch, two or three head of horses. Send for Adeline.'

Cecil smiled. Watching the dark sky descend, he pulled in a chestful of the steamy air, then let it out again. He turned his head. 'I bet you lay awake sometimes, dreaming what you're going to do.'

He watched the Indian for a while, but Sereno just kept facing at the lowering clouds.

'I gotta say, your silence raises some curiosity in me, you know? Like, I know you was acquitted on lack of evidence and all, but word is, the man was stabbed like *sixty times*.' Cecil kept looking at the Indian. 'My assumption is, the reason they couldn't pin it on you is 'cause you didn't do it.'

Cecil thumbed a sting of sweat from his eye.

'I know Spanish, man,' Cecil said finally. 'Enough. If you ever want to come on outta that coma and talk sometime, you know, tell me what's on your mind.'

He looked skyward again, and shifted his shoulders on the ground. 'Because, I mean, we never discussed the matter, as it's none of my business, but – being as how we're comrades – I'm wondering if you've ruminated about the safety issues involved in recovering that unaccounted-for . . . *dinero*. That is, if the rumors have validation.' He looked over at Sereno again. 'What I'm thinking here is, if anything happens, man, anything unexpected, and you got someone you'd like to have that money – a bequeathment, last will and testament, you know? – I just want you to know that you can trust me to see they get it.'

Sereno's brow furrowed suddenly, as though he had spotted something in the sky. When Cecil turned his own eyes skyward, he saw a low trio of pelicans gliding overhead—

'Ho!' he cried and tried to jump out of the way. But the fat ball of excrement slapped down on his shoulder, spattering his chin. He leapt to his feet, tore off his T-shirt.

84

'Son of a bitch ratbastard, you workin root on me?' he cried, glaring down at the Indian.

He balled up the T-shirt and furiously rubbed at his shoulder and chest, where most of the pelican shit had landed. The way Sereno kept staring at the sky gave Cecil as much answer as he needed. 'Workin root on *me?* Man, I'm the only friend you got!'

His expression unchanged, Sereno turned his face slowly toward Cecil. The yard guard, seeing the commotion, started coming over. Backing away, Cecil pitched the T-shirt at the Indian. 'But that's good. I'm glad. 'Cause now I know, man. I'll be sure to watch my back.'

CHAPTER ELEVEN

A s soon as darkness fell, Jacob drove ten miles up the coast, to a place he knew in Cape Neddick, just off King's Cove, where a dirt road cut back into the woods along the shore of a marshy duckpond. He made his way to the dead end, surprised at the number of houses that had been built over the past ten years. The night was quiet. He hoped it would stay that way.

Where the road dead-ended, a grassy old trolley bed intersected and led through the woods, straight, level and black. He took the revolver and a flashlight, and he walked fast.

The place was about three hundred feet in, a massive rock where he and Laura used to picnic when they'd first met. They called it whale rock, because of its shape. At its head was a soft patch of grass. It was the spot where Max was conceived, and now, as Jacob peeled back the turf with a garden spade he'd taken from Green Girls, he felt as though he was desecrating the place.

Of course he was, carving into the earth. When he hit bedrock he laid the revolver in and began pushing the soil back over it – when something cracked in the woods. He spun around, leaning back on the rock. Holding his breath, he tried to see through the darkness, but could make out only indistinct columns of pine trees piled one on another against the black night. He flicked on his flashlight, shone it around, turning the near trees white and darkening everything else. It had sounded like a footstep about fifty feet back – or so he imagined. Logically, he knew it must have been a curious deer or fox, perhaps a porcupine. The flashlight did not help, so he shut it off and quickly laid the turf back on his secret spot and tamped it down with his moccasin.

Then he drove to his father-in-law's house.

Surrounded by pieces of the disassembled kitchen chair – stiles, rails, legs, spindles – Jacob sat on the floor in the roomful of holes and made the furniture like new again. From years of dry winter heat and summer humidity, the glue had disintegrated.

He had done the messy work outside on the back porch, heating the joints with a propane torch, sanding down the old varnish, the old glue. When the mosquitoes got bad, he came inside. After gluing newspaper to each tenon, he poured more glue into the mortices and began clamping the chair back together, all the while immersed in his thoughts about Laura and Price, going back to comments, coincidences, odd looks, and the times he'd called her at work and she was out doing errands . . . thoughts of her infidelity alternating with notions of his own. July was inside him, and he couldn't get her out.

She had offered her house. No, she had offered much more, to take care of him so he could write his book – to be his keeper and lover. She'd already been his savior. Yet he knew if he started a relationship with July, he'd be giving up any hope for a reconciliation with Laura . . . speaking of dreams. Jacob knew now that his marriage had ended a long time ago. It had just taken him a while to realize it. For God's sake, even Maxie had been aware of it before he had.

And maybe Max was the reason for his reluctance. If Jacob went to July, he would also be deciding Max's future.

'*That was your wife,*' came the voice from above. '*Hey, Shakespeare—*'

Jacob looked up from his work to see Squeaky standing over him. The window shade flashed with lightning, followed by quiet thunder in the distance.

'The little man's ball game got rained out. She's bringin him by.'

'I'm almost done,' Jacob said.

'You gonna let her see you like that?'

'What?'

'Brush your hair, shave or somethin. You look like a bum.'

Jacob tightened a clamp on the chair. 'I can't see her anyway.'

'You can't see her, how you gonna talk to her?'

'I can't talk to her.'

'Well, I sure the hell can't do it for you!' Squeaky cried, already hoarse.

'It's a court order,' Jacob said.

'What, court order, and you lay down and die? '

'*Hey.*'

It was Max, standing in the doorway, gaping in at the room full of holes. Jacob set the chair down.

'There's the little man,' Squeaky said, lowering into a boxer's crouch. 'How'd you get here so fast?'

Max took off his cap and tossed it aside. 'Mom called on Price's car phone. What the hell happened in here?'

Squeaky stopped, dumbfounded. So did Jacob.

It wasn't his cursing. The top of his head had been shaved bald, so that the only hair left was around his ears and the back of his head. The boy's head looked 60 years old.

'What's with the trim?' Squeaky said. 'Cripes, you look like a nitwit.'

'I look like you,' Max said, and he danced forward, tossing left-hand jabs into the old man's padded hand.

'Maxie, who did that?' Jacob asked him.

'The barber,' Max said.

'Wait a minute, I'm your barber,' Jacob protested. 'I cut your hair.'

'You weren't around,' Max said. 'Price took me to his barber – his *stylist*. The guy asked me how I wanted it cut. I said, "Like yours." Cool, huh?'

'Maybe for a circus midget,' Squeaky said, moving toward Max, dodging and weaving. The boy feinted two quick lefts, then scored with a loud smack to Squeaky's arm.

Jacob stared at his son, thinking that perhaps this was his way of making him pay for the separation. 'Price let the guy cut it like that?'

'He told him to do what I wanted. He said I should follow my heart.'

'What did Mom say?'

'She said it's my head, I have to live with it.'

Jacob sighed. 'Maybe we should shave it all off. Bald's cool.'

'I like it like this,' Max told him. With his thick glasses, he could've been taken for an alien.

'Don't sweat it, the hair'll grow back,' Squeaky said, straightening.

Max looked around at the holes again. 'Gramp, you ever been in a real fight?'

Squeaky chuckled. 'Once or twice.'

The boy waited for more.

The old man gave a thoughtful frown. 'This is what you need to remember: Everyone makes mistakes in life. You, with your dumb haircut. Me. This guy.' He hitched his thumb at Jacob. 'The deal is, some mistakes are big and some are small. And some are real doozies.' He fit Max's cap back on his head. 'Know how you can tell a doozie?'

Max shook his head.

His grandfather gave Jacob a pointed look. 'That's the one you can't never take back.'

CHAPTER TWELVE

———

The July 4th weekend sailed by under sunny blue skies, while Jacob entertained Max and outlined his novel whenever he could find a minute ... and did his best to keep July out of his mind. At the movies Jacob wrote in his notepad, even during the fireworks display in Portsmouth. After Max went to bed, Jacob stayed up until three in the morning reading library books about the history of Portsmouth, New Hampshire, and Kittery, Maine, and the construction of the Piscataqua River Bridge. Even during the few hours he slept, Jacob woke up repeatedly and wrote notes to himself in the dark.

At seven in the morning they went fishing for schoolies in Spruce Creek. In the afternoon, they went body-surfing at York Beach, catching ride after ride into the sand and splashing back out again – Maxie, with his cap pulled down to hide his friar's haircut, his wet glasses strapped to his head, giving his dad a triumphant thumbs-up when he caught a good wave. When they walked to the pizza place for dinner, Max swung his arms high, the way he did when he was happy. Indeed, for Jacob the days with Max were some of the happiest of his life. Then they were gone.

'*You hate Price, don't you?*'

Jacob looked up from his notepad as Max got in the car, a towel underneath him to keep the seat dry, while he wriggled out of his bathing suit.

'Waste of energy,' Jacob replied as he started the car, hoping he wouldn't pursue this conversation, but Max was studying him through salt-stained lenses, waiting for some kind of explanation.

'Well, I hate him,' Max said, sitting naked as the car pulled out of the parking lot and onto the road.

'He's not that bad,' Jacob said.

Max tossed the bundled suit into the back seat and changed into his baseball uniform, as Jacob drove through York Village, then took the shoreline road to Kittery.

'Mom says he's a Renaissance man,' Max said with a smirk.

'Uh-huh.'

''Cause he's a *hypnotherapist* and he does that stained-glass crap and rock-climbing and all that. So what? He hates me.'

'He doesn't hate you.'

'He never talks to me.'

'Do you talk to him?'

Max took off his glasses, spat on each lens, and wiped them on his uniform. 'I listen, he talks, more like it. If Mom's around, he acts like he's one of my teachers. When she's not around, if I go in the living room, he goes in the kitchen. If I go in the kitchen, he goes in the living room. I don't care.'

And that answered Jacob's questions about whether Price had been over the house. 'Maybe he's uncomfortable around you,' he suggested.

'He thinks he's so great,' Max replied. 'He's writing this poem about Benedict Arnold, it's like three hundred pages long. Mom's all, "Oh, Price, you're such a genius." '

'That's a long poem,' Jacob said, wondering again just how long the affair had been going on.

'I think he's jealous of you,' Max said. 'He's always bragging about, you know, he's so smart, and he's this master of Tae Kwon Do, and showing off how fast he is. He drops an apple off the table and before it hits the floor he can pick four other apples off the table, one at a time.' Demonstrating, Max threw four lightning jabs at the windshield. 'I guess it's fast. Big deal.' He pulled the glove box open and reached inside. 'Hey. Where's your medal?'

'I threw it away.'

Max gave him a look. 'How come?'

Jacob slowed to pass a cyclist. His heart felt like a rock. Maxie still giving him the look.

'Dad?'

When the ballfield came in sight, Jacob pulled the car to the roadside and stopped. They could see Price's Z3 parked behind the backstop. Laura was sitting beside him. He figured they were 500 feet away, so he was obeying the law.

'The medal?' Jacob said. 'The guys at the fire house gave it to me.'

'I know.'

Jacob shifted into neutral, then confessed. 'Maxie, I wasn't an actual fireman. I was the dispatcher, the person that answers the phone.'

'I know what a dispatcher is.'

'It gave me time to write.'

Max scowled, as he absorbed this. 'What about the medal?'

Jacob said, 'I climbed a stepladder one day, to change a lightbulb. They knew I had a fear of heights. It was a joke.'

The way Max looked at him then. Kind of a smirk, the way you might look at a bug in your hand, just before you tossed it away. 'Whatever,' he said, and reached over the seat to grab his backpack. Opened the door, got halfway out—

'Maxie, wait a minute.'

Max stopped, but didn't look back.

'Adults grow up, you know – just like kids do.' Jacob turned off the engine, to make things as quiet as he could. 'We all change, Maxie. And we all need to accept the fact that Mom is changing about certain things. She still loves you – just like I do. That part never changes. But as far as the way she feels about me—'

Max leaned out of the car, trying to bail out of the conversation. 'I know what you're going to say.'

'Let me say it anyway.'

Max waited, as though on a leash.

'Just between you and me,' Jacob told him, staring out at Price Ashworth's car, 'even the Renaissance had its share of jerks.'

'That it?' Max said, clearly relieved, but humorless.

Jacob slapped the brim of his cap. 'I had a great time with you this weekend, champ.'

'Yup.' Max started walking to the field.

'Good luck tonight,' Jacob called. 'Remember: Head, not heart.'

'Later,' Max answered, without turning back.

Squeaky was at work when Jacob returned to his house. He made himself a pot of tea and, while it steeped, telephoned the agent who had negotiated his four previous novels. Maury Howard was a kind and capable man, but hard as he'd tried to sell Jacob's fourth book, after his third publisher went bankrupt, the best deal they could get was a hundred-dollar advance from a university press, and three free copies.

'It's about a bridge,' Jacob explained.

He heard the agent sigh, then light a cigarette. 'Jacob, I have to be blunt. Critics love you. Literary journals love you. I love you. But your commercial appeal? Publishers don't love you.'

'*John* sold a million copies.'

'*John* was a phenomenon – twelve years ago. And your second book set new records for returns.'

'But the reviews—'

'Reviewers don't pay the bills,' Maury said. 'Readers do. And readers want stories. I'm not saying you need a gargantuan plot and a thousand subplots. But you need some plot. Any plot. For crying out loud, in *Tree* there wasn't a woodcutter, there wasn't a thunderstorm, there wasn't even a woodpecker. Jacob, people want to read about people.'

'There's a person in this one,' Jacob said.

Maury didn't speak for a moment. 'Does he do anything?'

'He gets a flat tire and can't decide whether to change the tire or jump.'

'What, jump off the bridge, commit suicide?'

'That's right, he's depressed.'

'Is that it?'

Jacob paced the kitchen at the limit of the phone cord. 'Life doesn't have plots, Maury. Life is tedious, repetitive, senseless . . . This bridge, it's a monstrosity of a bridge. It's very high, and it connects two old New England towns – a New Hampshire shipping port with a Maine fishing village.'

He listened to Maury draw deeply on his cigarette. 'What are you asking, Jacob?'

'I want to know if you can sell it.'

'Sight unseen? No. Can I sell a great novel by a writer named Jacob Winter? I'm not sure. You know, the word is that *Fridge* singlehandedly bankrupted Antelope Press. And, frankly, I'm not that sure you can write people.'

'What do you mean?'

Maury paused, then breathed a thoughtful sigh. 'Jacob, you're a meticulous and masterful talent. If I had a checklist – the thousand rules of wonderful writing – you could check every one. Technically, there's nobody better than you.'

'But—?'

'Your writing has no heart.'

'I'm not writing romance novels, if that's what you mean.'

'What I mean is, people want to feel emotionally connected to what they're reading,' the agent said. 'What they don't want is five hundred pages about a refrigerator, I don't care how many literary reviewers say it was the most profound book ever written.'

'Emotional connection,' Jacob said.

'It's not something you get off a checklist,' Maury told him. 'It's not something you get from being *smart*. You need to put your heart in it.'

Jacob said, 'I always put everything I've got into it.'

'Heart,' Maury said.

Jacob sighed, tired of the conversation. 'Will you look at my manuscript when it's ready?'

'I'll look forward to it.'

'Thank you.'

'Jacob—' Maury paused again. 'Is everything okay?'

'Everything's fine,' he said.

They hung up, and Jacob began writing. He lost himself. Words poured from his brain to his fingers. Paragraphs fell rich and fat onto the screen, about the freighters and tugs that used the Portsmouth docks, the narrow, winding streets of the old city, the quaint blocks of red-brick buildings that overlooked the river.

Even when he began feeling hunger pangs, he never lost his concentration. When the evening turned dusky, he turned on a lamp and continued writing. Although he'd already spun out forty-five pages, so far, the man with the flat tire had not been mentioned. In fact, Jacob had not yet described the bridge. The pages he wrote described the Piscataqua River, the towns of Kittery and Portsmouth, and only hinted at the enormity of the steel structure linking them.

Finally, when the twilight turned to dark, he put on his darkest clothes and went out quietly into the night, to start finding out the darker things that Laura had kept from him – and Alix Callahan had been afraid to tell.

CHAPTER THIRTEEN

Down the rickety wooden stairs, the brown-skinned man descended to his basement bakery, weighted down by two fifty-pound bags of flour. Deftly he made his way across the boards laid on the puddled concrete floor, balancing himself with the weight until he reached the pallet, where he set the bags down. When he turned to go back and get more, the heavy door closed.

'Happy Independence Day, my immigrant amigo,' Biff Bullens said, and the baker stopped, and studied his former prison guard.

'Sorry to startle you, Pedro,' Bullens said. 'You got another email for me?' With a smile, he pulled a twenty-dollar bill out of his pocket.

The baker matched his smile. 'Ah, *gracias*, Toro.'

Bullens lost his smile. The baker added with a nod of courtesy, as he pulled a Palm Pilot out of a canvas bag, '*Sargento* Toro.'

'Just hurry it up,' Bullens said, dropping the twenty on a rack of sweet bread that was cooling.

'*Momento*,' said the baker, poking at the Pilot with a stylus.

Bullens opened a bin and helped himself to a pastry. 'Nobody knows, correct?'

'*Sí*, no one,' the baker replied.

'Good.'

'*Bien*,' said the baker, and handed the Pilot to Bullens.

'What's it say?' Bullens asked. 'Translate-o.'

The baker pointed to the small readout: 'It is raining today. The flowers are happy.'

'Flowers are happy, that's it?'

The baker nodded. '*Sí*, Toro. *Alegre*. Happy.'

'That's good, everybody's happy,' Bullens said, 'you're happy, I'm happy,' and he pulled out a suppressed semiautomatic.

The baker, stunned for a second, dropped behind the table and let out a long, loud yell. Bullens walked around the side. The baker sprang to his feet holding a ten-gallon plastic bucket of jellied apricot in front of him. Bullens fired a round into the bucket. Although the baker was barely five feet tall, he was strong and fast, and he charged at Bullens using his bucket as a shield, while the suppressor spat out fire, one round after another, and the jellied apricot spat back – until Bullens fell backward against the oven. Burning his arm, he reached around the bucket and smashed his weapon on the baker's head.

The small man stumbled back, his bucket poised for another attack. But the next two shots opened the pail like an egg, and the pile of jelly spilled glistening onto Bullens' black shoes.

The baker, looking down at himself and understanding that he was mortally wounded, dropped to his knees. As Bullens raised his weapon, the baker raised his hands, as though to catch the rest of the bullets.

Bullens was glad to oblige.

CHAPTER FOURTEEN

U ntil he unlocked the door, Jacob had never committed such a crime. Now, as he crept into the lobby, his mind buzzing with thoughts of alarm systems, guard dogs, and roving patrol cars, he reminded himself that a psychiatrist's office probably wasn't that heavily protected. What was there to steal but some used furniture and artwork that the doctors obviously didn't want in their homes?

It was a one-story brick building on a quiet Portsmouth street. Each of the four offices had two outside walls, two windows. The reception space, centered in the building, was windowless, so that once Jacob had closed the inner entry door, he was able to turn on the overhead fluorescents without fear of detection. Technically, he had already committed one crime tonight, breaking into his own house while Laura and Max were at the game, and taking her spare set of keys. Everything was relative, he told himself: crime, love, commitment. He needed to know when Laura had become more than Price Ashworth's employee.

In her desk drawer he found four different-colored appointment books, one for each of the doctors. Simple deduction: If Price Ashworth had been seeing patients every day, then he couldn't have gone somewhere else with Laura. He opened the book to the middle and found Price's patients booked solid, from nine to five.

He swiped a few pages ahead, and again, booked solid. A few more pages. There again. And again. Then Jacob stopped—

Turned back.

One patient's name stared up at him. Wednesday afternoon, 4:00–5:00.

He checked the previous week. Same day. Same time. Same name . . .

Alix Callahan.

96

Green Girls

★ ★ ★

Heartbeat accelerating, Henry Lamb swings off the approach ramp. The apple-green arch rises up against the apple-red sky, the steel web opens up and swallows all the cars and trucks. High above the river, ocean winds beat against Henry's door. Veinal fluids tap at his temples.

Jacob sat in the back of his father-in-law's house, the roomful of holes hovering silently around him as his story oozed forth out of the thousand black holes in his brain, tangling from time to time with strands of his own life.

He understood now: Price Ashworth was the one paying for Jacob's defense, by funneling money through Alix Callahan. On the surface, it seemed so implausible – unless one knew Price. Why would anyone pay the legal fees of the man who'd brained him? To take the edge off his conscience for stealing the man's wife? Or, as Price would have put it, to balance out his Karmic debt. Evidently, he could afford it. So . . . mystery solved.

Off to Henry's right, a small airplane cuts a white hook in the sky – in fact, it's the letter J, white on red. He takes in the view to his left, the wide river yawning out to the ocean, the two lift-bridges opening up, tall cranes stretching like the necks of giraffes up to the sky, while a coal freighter plows past the Portsmouth docks.

Two months ago – it was early May – Jacob and Laura had left Max with Squeaky and spent the weekend on Matinicus Island, out beyond Monhegan. They stayed in a lobsterman's shack and spent their days lying on a sunny, grassy bluff watching the migrating birds . . . and making love. Two months ago. How could she have been in love with Price?

Laura must have put Price up to paying his legal fees, Jacob thought. Despite her disenchantment with Jacob, she still wouldn't want to see him go to prison, if only for Max's sake.

A sudden, loud pop shakes Henry's car. It pulls toward the rail. He jerks the wheel, stamps the brakes. A screech of tires behind him, horn blaring, another horn, as his car pounds into the railing, then he is traveling backward, sweeping around, north, east, south, tires pummeling the roadway, green steel trusses fluttering past every window and the railing racing at him again, the open sky.

Or perhaps the reason Price had paid for Jacob's lawyer was more diabolical: to ensure that Laura would not win sole custody of Max. Of course. Why would Price want responsibility for the boy?

And why would Alix Callahan have agreed to be part of it?

The car stops with a jolt. The passenger window shears in two and flies away, fluttering like a butterfly over the rail and down. A trailer truck screams past, air horn blaring. The roadway bounces slowly in its wake, up and down.

'Hey Tippy-tap.'

Squeaky's voice intrudes out of the muted distance.

'Do you mind? There's people tryin to sleep here.'

Jacob paused, the high, windy bridge dissolving from his mind.

'Sorry, I'll get out of here,' Jacob said, saving the file then closing the lid on his laptop.

Squeaky scoffed. 'What's it, a crime now to wanna sleep?' he said. 'It's almost three.' *Tree.*

Jacob got to his feet. 'It was inconsiderate of me,' he said. 'I apologize.'

'All I said is, save the tappin shit till morning.'

Jacob slung his laptop over one shoulder, his backpack over the other, and walked out to the kitchen – having no idea where he was going, but he was going.

'Not to mention you oughta stick around where I can keep an eye on you,' Squeaky persisted, following him down the hall. 'If you expect to get Laura back, you'd better straighten up, Mr Man, get a decent job.'

Jacob opened the back door and stepped outside before he got drawn into another battle. 'I appreciate your helping me, Squeaky.'

'If you want somethin part-time till something better comes along, you can work for me.'

Jacob turned back. 'Tending bar?'

'No, swingin a radio over your head. Yeah, tendin bar. Saturday's gonna be busy, you can make a bill or two in tips.'

Taken by surprise – never would he have imagined Squeaky hiring him – Jacob gave it a moment's thought. 'I'll be there,' he said.

'Good. Now come in and get some sleep. You look like shit.'

'I can't sleep,' Jacob said. 'I need to work on this book.'

'Frig the book – face reality!' the old man cried. 'You ain't no frickin writer!'

Dogs started barking in the distance. Jacob shook his head, not intending to speak. But . . .

'Squeaky, she's divorcing me.'

For the moment, the old man stood speechless.

'I'll see you Saturday,' Jacob said, and walked to his car.

At four in the morning Rick's Restaurant in York Village was bright and lively with fishermen and wisecracking waitresses. But Jacob Winter, nursing his bottomless cup of coffee, couldn't remember ever harboring such a bottomless depression.

Green Girls

As he sat there trying to think of a compelling reason not to go to July, Alix Callahan came to mind again – she'd scarcely been out of his thoughts since he'd seen Price's appointment book. That Price Ashworth would have used Alix to pay Jacob's legal fees was understandable. But why would Alix have agreed to be the conduit? Maybe she owed him for his services. No, she had too much pride to do anything surreptitious for the likes of Price Ashworth – not in trade. She certainly wouldn't have done it as a favor.

Blackmail.

Jacob let the notion grow. If Alix had revealed something to Price under hypnosis . . .

He yawned, jittery from the coffee. It was sleep-deprivation, he told himself, the reason these crazy ideas were ricocheting around his head despite his trying to keep them down. His junior year at the university – before he was diagnosed – he'd spent seven weeks in his dormitory room, from Thanksgiving to the middle of January – writing *John* – and nobody missed him. That was after his mother died, after the episode on the airplane, the episode at the funeral home, before he started on Haldol. Not for the first time tonight, he wondered if he should start taking the medication everyone seemed so eager for him to put into his bloodstream.

Instead, he paid his check and left the restaurant, then drove to Long Sands Beach, where he parked on the road and reclined his seat, to soothe himself with the sound of the surf, hopefully to sleep . . .

. . . But sleep won't come to Jacob, no matter how hard he tries. It's his body more than his mind, as though a second body is trapped inside him, trying to push its way out. He can even hear the tone of her voice in the sound of the surf, July, too soft to distinguish. It happens when he's over-tired, over-stressed, overworked, the voices. And now July . . . beautiful, dark July . . . pushing and pulling on every part of him. He tries so hard to get rid of her, but she is imprinted on all his senses: the smell of her flesh, the taste of her lips, the heat of her breath in his ear, her soft mouth and black stare . . .

Delirium rising, Jacob pulls his seat upright. He tries talking to himself, reasoning that if he can bring at least his faithfulness to court, the custody judge will have to take that into consideration. Perhaps even Laura will realize.

Yet even as he begins this inner counsel, he pictures the shape of July's breast, ripe and swollen. He can feel her warmth under his hands, feel her mind like a ghost invading his, and once again this other creature starts pushing inside him, solid, heavy-browed, and mindless.

He lays his head back on the seat and concentrates on the surf. The ocean breathes heavily; stars burn in the sky. He closes his eyes. He counts the seconds between waves.

But he cannot dispel her. He even hears her whisper in the seawater sweeping the beach, he smells the pungency of her skin mingling with the salty air. Powerless to stop the sensations, he finally allows her ghost to move over him, cover him like a blanket, and soon falls into a fitful, sexual sleep.

A car engine wakes him with a start, a loud engine racing away.

But no car is in sight when Jacob sits up, no taillights in his mirror. The car was in his dreams.

He pictures July again, allows her fully into his mind. Then he starts his car.

And goes to her.

CHAPTER FIFTEEN

The moment the door opened, Jacob's heart came alive. The sleepiness of her gaze did nothing to diminish her beauty.

'Was Price Ashworth blackmailing Alix?' Not exactly what he meant to say, but there it was.

July narrowed her eyes. 'Who?'

'He's a psychiatrist. Alix was his patient. Did you know that?'

'Alix was crazy. So what?'

'You knew she was seeing him.'

She shrugged.

'Do you know why she jumped?'

July shook her head, holding Jacob's stare fervently, until he closed his eyes and leaned against the door jamb, so incredibly tired. He felt like crying.

Without a word, she took his hand, and then she was leading him down the aisle of her sweet green shop, and out into the cool garden. Dew-covered elephant leaves blessed him as he passed into shadows; sleeping fragrances lulled him. Then he was going through a door of her garden hut, three screened walls and a thatched ceiling from which dried herbs and fresh flowers hung, filling the air with fragrance. On the floor was a thick mattress, covered with a green, cotton quilt.

She touched his face, a blessing, and now she was kissing him, and he was kissing her, both of them breathing harder as they sank into the big mattress together, and he gently pulled down her underpants. When his fingers found her, it was like pressing on some overripe, sun-swollen fruit. At the instant of his touch, she seemed to burst, at once sucking his fingers in and spilling out over them.

Clutching at his wrist, she pressed back into the mattress, gazing up at him through half-closed eyes. In some distant part of Jacob's brain, Laura emerged . . . but, seeing July's rapturous, inward-directed scowl, the image dissolved.

Then she was on her knees, this young girl, naked, and opening his trousers just far enough to free him, and the moment she touched him a shock of ecstasy raced to the back of his brain. He reached for her, but she pushed him back down.

'I want to watch you,' she whispered, crawling over him.

He thought of Laura again.

Oh, but the sight of July.

Suddenly nothing in the world existed then but this girl, her black hair hanging over Jacob's face, her eyes gazing down.

Slowly she lowered herself.

At the instant of contact, she caught her breath. He felt the kiss of young resistance, then she sucked him inside with a soft, shuddering moan.

And there was nothing left for Jacob, nothing at all but his poor, ravaged mind spilling over.

PART TWO

CHAPTER ONE

Terrence Gideon pulled down Coconut Drive, heading out of Florida City to work. Just like any normal day, except this morning his shoulders ached, and he hadn't slept more than two hours all night. Nor had he finished the bacon and eggs Bethany had made for breakfast. And when he kissed her goodbye, the way she'd studied him, then followed him onto the porch when he left. She asked him what was wrong and he told her, nothing. Gideon's two sons came onto the landing too. His little girl looked out the window.

The couple had four children, aged six to nineteen. As a family, they attended church every Sunday and made sure they ate dinner together every night. Gideon and Bethany helped the children with homework, monitored their television watching, and saved every spare dollar for college. Bethany worked as a shift supervisor for a telemarketing company that raised money for community projects, but only during school hours and Saturdays, when Terrence was there to keep an eye on the kids. As carefully as they'd planned their lives, Gideon thought, here he was—

A horn blared in his ear, jerking him from his thoughts. His heart sank lower when he looked over and saw Biff Bullens in his pickup truck, hitching his thumb to the curb. Gideon checked behind him, then cut to the shoulder. In his mirror, he watched the pickup's door. The confident way the sergeant stepped out, Gideon felt like he was about to be busted. He rolled down his window and the morning heat charged like a bear into the Jeep.

'Stick this in your window,' Bullens said, handing him an orange sign: FOR SALE. 'And pop the back. I got something else.'

'I've been thinking about this,' Gideon said, but the sergeant was already back at his truck, hauling a spare tire out of the bed.

'We don't take no chances today,' Bullens said when he returned, opening Gideon's liftgate. He checked behind him when a delivery truck rounded the corner, then shut the liftgate and returned to Gideon's window. 'What are you listenin to in there, Lawrence Welk? Ninety point five, they're playing Beethoven's Ninth.'

He started to reach in the window for the radio, but Gideon blocked his arm. 'It's Count Basie. I'm listening to it.' A drop of sweat rolled down behind his thick glasses.

'To each his own,' Bullens said. 'You know Beethoven was stone deaf when he wrote that symphony? At the premier performance, they had to stand him up to take his bows. He wept like a baby because he knew he'd never hear a note of the greatest music ever written.'

Gideon wiped the sweat with his thumb. 'I think I need to talk to somebody.'

Bullens smiled. 'I'm your man.'

'Somebody else. I need reassurance.'

Bullens gave him a puzzled look. 'Unfortunately, we're too far along.' The implied threat was unmistakable. 'Here, stick these under your seat.' Surreptitiously, Bullens thrust four pairs of handcuffs up to the window. Gideon took them quickly and shoved them under the seat. He looked around to see if anyone was watching.

'What's the matter, you feelin kinda sickly this morning?' Bullens said.

Gideon sighed. 'So many people in that prison,' he said. 'Why me?'

Bullens shrugged. 'I guess they figure, with your reputation, the prisoners are gonna trust you.'

'Reputation,' Gideon said. 'I got caught smoking pot when I was in college.'

'You did a year inside, that's my point.'

Gideon stared out at the heat waves already rising off the pavement. 'It doesn't seem right, what we're doing.'

Bullens reached into one of his pockets and pulled out a wallet-sized card. 'Everything's perfectly Constitutional,' he said. 'Put this in your pocket. Miranda card, so when the hammer comes down, we do everything by the book. See?' He turned the card over. 'Written in Spanish on the backside. You just read it off to the Colombians, ask if they *comprenday*, then no one can say their rights were violated.'

Gideon dropped the card in his breast pocket. 'That's not what I meant anyway. Who's to say Sereno would try to escape in the first place, if we didn't set it up for him?'

'You know it's for his own good,' Bullens said, almost sounding fatherly.

Gideon showed Bullens his hands, meaning he wanted no part of it. 'You also told Cecil he'd get cut free for his cooperation.'

Bullens wagged his head. 'The boy's got a dream, at least . . . which is more than I can say for you. Cripes, man, you've been handed a chance to make the drug bust of the year. If you think that comes along every day, you better think again. Once or twice in this mundane life, my friend, every man gets an opportunity to change his fortunes. I suggest you pay attention, because while you're bellyaching, your dream may pass you by.'

He slapped the roof and walked back to his truck.

Gideon wiped his cheek on his shoulder, then sat there in the heat remembering the last words Bethany had spoken to him before he left, standing up on the porch with the boys. 'Baby, I'll see you tonight.' The way she'd looked at him, it was more like she was asking.

He'd held up his hand to them, a wave that lingered.

'Terrence, okay—?'

'Yeah, baby,' he'd told her. 'I'll see you tonight.' That's the way he'd left his family. Now, as he drove away from Biff Bullens, how he wished he'd said more.

CHAPTER TWO

J acob Winter awakens in a deep green light. He rises in silence, pulls on his shorts and walks out the door of July's garden hut, surrounded by huge, leathery leaves. All around him, the forest drips with golden, syrupy dew, as he heads toward the house. Then he realizes that he has gone the wrong way, actually deeper into the glassed-in world. He comes to an intersection of paths and turns right, but after a few steps the jungle presses in closer. Tiny yellow frogs leap from his path. Then, up ahead, he spots a mossy clearing. Yes, it's July's garden pool, the exposed underground stream, and he thinks he can get a drink of water. But as soon as he steps into the clearing, he feels a low humming in his head that tells him something is about to happen. This is the way it happens in his dreams. The humming, then—

It's Alix Callahan, standing at Jacob's right shoulder.

Taken aback, he gapes at her. 'Are you okay?'

Her chest jumps with a laugh. 'Are you *serious*? I jumped off the bridge.'

He stares. 'You jumped . . .because Price Ashworth was blackmailing you. Right?'

She laughs again. 'Jacob, go back to sleep,' she tells him. 'Figure it out in the morning.'

Back to sleep? Yes, Jacob realizes he's dreaming, so he turns away from her and rolls over in bed. It's dark again. He closes his eyes.

Then a door opens.

'I need to sleep,' he complains, but he hears the hush of footsteps coming closer, so he opens his eyes. And stares.

It's his mother standing over him. She's smiling softly and, God, the way she's looking at him.

'Honey, it's so good to see you,' she says. 'Do you want to dream together?'

Jacob stares, afraid that if he makes a sound, if he even blinks, he

108

will cause her to vanish. But he can't stop the tears from burning his
eyes, and he loses her.

'*Wait!*'

The echo of his cry hung in the garden hut, bright and hot and heavy
with silence. He tried to gauge the time of day by the garden light
coming through the window, figured it must be afternoon, by the heat.
But what a longing he felt. Seeing his mother, even in a dream, had
been wonderful.

Jacob lay back down, remembering July, in fact feeling her in his
arms, remembering her particular scent, the arousal he felt colliding
with regret. He switched off his imagination, reached for his pants on
the floor, and pulled out his watch, his notepad, his pen. As he
suspected, it was almost noon.

12:00 BREAKFAST. DISCUSS RENTAL ARRANGEMENTS
WITH J. 12:30 WRITE. 3:00 CALL Z FOR MAX ARRANGE-
MENTS. 4:30 LUMBER YARD. 5:30–6:00 DINNER.

As he wrote he realized that strange ticking sounds were coming
from a narrow wooden door adjacent to his bed. Thinking it might be
July, and the room a toilet, he stepped off the mattress and
knocked . . . listened to the ticking.

'July?'

Would she view their lovemaking as a casual thing? Or the consecra-
tion of a new love? Should he apologize and leave? Did he even want to
leave?

He opened the door and was attacked by hordes of crickets.
Furiously brushing the insects off him, he threw the door shut – but
not before registering the incredible sight inside the tiny, skylit room.
Along with a miniature forest of plant life, the entire room sprang with
crickets, a dense cloud of them.

Dreaming or awake – he could hardly tell any more. But he could
hear July's music now – some Irish jig or reel, fiddles and penny
whistles charging wildly ahead. He walked out of the hut into a humid,
green heat, where the music was louder, and he pictured the way she'd
gazed up at him when she was naked . . . and once again he thought he
should leave, so he stepped into her shop to tell her. Although there
were puddles underneath the hanging plants, as if they'd just been
watered, the place was closed. He climbed the stairs, thinking that she
might have no expectations, after all. She was younger, certainly a free
spirit unaccustomed to the conditions of marriage. Perhaps the
arrangement could be ideal: He could stay there until things were
resolved, do repairs, maybe build some furniture; their friendship

would grow, he'd learn from her, she'd learn from him, they'd keep each other company, he could fix things. But no more sex.

As he entered the living room, he found her sitting at a desk in the back of the room, working at his laptop. She was wearing one of his three-buttoned jerseys over a tan muslin skirt.

'Hey,' he said, trying to disguise his anxiety, and he saw the laptop's display change.

'I'm reading your new book,' she said. Actually, she had been typing. She raised her face toward him, as if she expected a kiss.

He looked around the room and saw that Alix's bookcase had been emptied, the books thrown in cardboard boxes and stacked in uneven piles on the floor. Three full trash bags sat in the corner, bulbous sacks poked with corners.

'It's unpolished,' he said, trying to ignore the way the baggy shirt exposed her exquisite, upturned breast.

'You're writing about the bridge?' Her searching face, her crow-black hair, the muscles of her arms . . . her nipple stood out enough to show that she knew she was showing – and was aroused by it.

'You have a grasshopper in your hair,' she said, and laughed while she stood to brush it off.

'You raise them?' he asked.

'Frog food,' she said, and sat back down.

He noticed the email icon on the task bar. 'You're writing to somebody.'

'You don't want me to?'

'I don't mind,' he said, backing away to let her know he wasn't trying to intrude on her privacy. Still he couldn't help but wonder, the way she'd tried to hide it. Now he was thinking about what Fecto had said too, that Alix's computer had disappeared. And what about that couple from New Jersey carrying the package from the shop? Was she selling her jungle brew, the yagé, over the Internet?

'Jacob, you're so suspicious,' July said, and clicked on the icon. Her email appeared. 'Come here.'

'I don't want to read your mail,' Jacob objected.

'Do you know Spanish?'

He looked over her shoulder. ' "The weather is very hot here," ' he translated. ' "I have longing – I miss – the mountain?" '

'The mountains,' July corrected.

'What mountains?'

'I'm writing to one of my cousins. My father gave some old computers to the village.' She looked up at him, searching again.

'Who's your father?' Jacob asked.

'A missionary.'

'Where?'

'You're worse than the cops,' she told him, and clicked the SEND button.

He smiled. 'I guess I was a little crazy when I showed up here this morning,' he said, seeing a chance to discuss the nature of their relationship.

'My mother worked as a cook for him and his wife,' she said, giving him a challenging look. 'After I was born, my father met with the shaman of my mother's village, and everyone agreed I should be raised American. So my mother was sent away, and I was raised in the mission, by my American father and his American wife, who never stopped hating him. And me. Okay?'

'Are they still there?'

'I wouldn't know. I left when I was twelve.'

'Left, like ran away?'

'I got married,' she said nonchalantly. He couldn't tell if she was serious. 'He was my cousin. He was thirteen. Jacob, bend down, I want to kiss you.'

'Where is he now?' he asked. 'Your cousin.'

July grabbed his belt. 'Dead,' she said impassively. 'Jacob.'

'Wait. When did he die?'

'A long time ago. A jaguar killed him. I don't want to talk about it.' The look she gave him suggested that such things were not out of the ordinary where she'd been raised.

She let go of his belt. He looked at his watch.

'I'd like to make you something, in exchange for your letting me stay here.'

'Make me what?'

'I make furniture,' he explained.

'What kind?'

'Most anything.'

'I don't want furniture,' she told him. 'I want you to write your book.'

'Carpentry relaxes me,' he said. 'I write in my head while I'm working.'

She gave him a look. 'Can you make me a bed?' He wondered if her expression had to do with what they'd done this morning – or did she know what had happened in the last bed he'd made?

'If that's what you want,' he said. 'I just need a corner somewhere. I'll hang some Poly to contain the dust.'

'You can work down in the flower shop.'

'What about your business?'

'That belonged to Alix,' she said. 'I'm closing it down.'

He thought of the couple from New Jersey again.

'Now you're scowling again,' she said. 'Why are you so serious all the time?' She leaned back in the chair and propped her heel on the arm. The way she gazed up at him, he felt his face flush.

'What kind of bed?' he asked.

'Big,' she said, and her leg fell out to the side, exposing herself to him. For a second, he felt his heart kick, as her scent rose up between them.

'July . . . queen size?'

'Yeah,' she said. 'With a big green headboard.'

'You want green?'

She nodded.

'I don't usually use stain,' he suggested diplomatically, but wanting, really, wanting nothing so much as to slide down to the floor and stare into those stoned brown eyes while he slowly sinks into her.

'Isn't there wood that's green?' she asked.

'The heartwood of poplar is green, but it's a secondary wood.'

'It's wood, isn't it?'

'Well, customarily it's used for the insides of drawers,' he explained, 'where it won't show.'

'Secondary wood is fine with me. Can you make it like the bridge?' Her eyes seemed to dilate with arousal, and Jacob felt a sudden interruption in his heart, a bright thread of warning to the back of his brain.

She gave him a coquettish look. 'You're writing a book about the bridge. I want a bed shaped like the bridge.'

'I don't bend wood,' he told her. 'The work I do is more traditional – straight lines, square corners.'

She studied him skeptically for a moment, her eyes dark and piercing. 'Jacob, the rest of the world isn't straight and square.'

'My furniture is.'

With an exasperated sigh, she spun the chair around and got to her feet. 'Don't make me anything. Write your book,' she said, and she walked out of the room with a playful gait, like some jungle cat with her tail high.

'July—'

She flipped back her hair. 'I'll make your breakfast. You write.'

Jacob took a couple of breaths, decompressing. He sat in the chair and turned to his computer. For a few seconds, he stared at his story – Henry Lamb sitting in his car high on the bridge – Jacob wondering if

112

he should continue, or if he should pack his things and leave. He could hear July in the kitchen, rummaging through the refrigerator.

'Jacob, I don't hear you typing,' she called.

He laughed to himself. Then placed two fingers on the keyboard and settled in.

Henry Lamb leans his forehead against the steering wheel. His lip is bleeding. He deduces that his right front tire is flat. The wind shakes the car so hard, Henry thinks it might float up off the roadway and blow over the railing. He opens his window, to let the wind whip through, out of the west now. He breathes in deeply. The oxygen calms him, but he is helpless to ignore the tons of interlocked steel surrounding him, groaning.

He knows he cannot drive off the bridge until he changes the tire. The bridge is nearly a mile in length, and he is stuck at the center point, over the middle of the Piscataqua River, parked under a green sign that reads:

STATE LINE
NEW HAMPSHIRE

The sign is attached to a hollow post. In fact, all the structural members that support the bridge are hollow, all of them perforated with large oval holes. Attached to the signpost are a set of steel rungs enclosed in a cage. Henry has never seen the rungs before. He imagines what it must be like to climb up there. When he looks up to see where the ladder leads – to a crow's nest, and from there all the way to the top of the arch 250 feet high – he gets dizzy and lowers his eyes.

A scissor jack is in his trunk, along with a spare tire. He takes his keys out of the ignition, opens his door and steps out onto the pavement. He does not think about jumping. He thinks about getting his scissor jack out of the trunk, and the tire iron. But, first, he steps up on the curbstone.

He holds onto the railing with his left hand. The wind makes a hard sound against his face. The sky around him is streaked with scarlet. The airplane slices it like an apple skin, inscribing the letter E. Below him, he watches a fishing boat go quietly up the tidal river, heading for the marina. He sees the smokestacks of the coal plant in the distance, all the darkening greens along the riverbank, the groves of white pine and sugar maple and white oak.

When he looks in his right hand he sees that he's cut himself on his keys, from squeezing so hard. His blood rolls across his palm and ripples with the wind.

'You like a bird's nest?'

Jacob looked up from his writing.

She had taken off his jersey and put on a pale green halter, and tied a white apron over her skirt. She carried a pewter tray.

He smiled, somewhat chagrined. 'Bird's nest?'

'Fried egg on toast,' she told him. 'Alix used to call it a bird's nest. Is that too radical?'

Resting the tray on his chair arm, she began setting things on the desk: a mug of coffee, glass of orange juice, and a platter mounded over with bacon and eggs and home-fried potatoes, red peppers and mushrooms.

Jacob sniffed at the juice, then took a sip. It tasted as if she'd just squeezed the oranges.

'Is it okay?' she asked, not joking.

He almost laughed again. 'It's fine, thank you, it's delicious. Listen . . .' She stood there as a waitress might, awaiting an order. 'Please stop that,' Jacob said.

'I'm sorry. Did you want something else?'

'Yeah,' he told her. 'I'll make you the bed.'

CHAPTER THREE

B y eleven in the morning the thermometer had reached 100, and
the forecast said it was only going to get hotter. Outside the
prison, heat waves rippled off the asphalt, making the parking lot
look vaporous. Even with binoculars, the tower guards would not be
able to see what was tucked in Biff Bullens' hand as he walked to
the Jeep. Having let it be known that he was thinking about buying
the vehicle from Gideon, he was confident that he'd raise no
suspicion by checking it out on his break. Squatting next to the
vehicle, he inspected each of the tires, then knelt on the burning
asphalt and peered underneath, at the exhaust system and drive
train. Then he got in and pulled the garage-door opener off
Gideon's visor, clipping an identical unit in its place and slipping
Gideon's in his pocket.

'What are you doing?'

Bullens jerked his head around. Gideon was there.

'Cripes alive, you gotta relax, man. You're all jittery.'

'I saw you come out here,' the black man said.

'I'm looking over your wheels,' Bullens told him. 'Remember, I'm
supposed to be buyin this piece of shit from you.'

Gideon eyed Bullens, his scowl magnified through his thick lenses.

'You keep lookin like that, we best call the whole thing off,' Bullens
said.

'Looking like what?'

'Google-eyed, that's what. You got the Miranda card?'

'I got it,' Gideon answered.

Bullens looked the Jeep up and down, shaking his head delibera-
tively, then he muckled onto the steering wheel and horsed it back and
forth. 'Go 'head back, I'll be along,' he said, pushing himself out of
the Jeep with a bright smile. 'Wouldn't appear natural, the two of us
walkin together.'

Gideon took a slow breath. Then turned and headed back to the prison.

CHAPTER FOUR

The morning fog lingered, rising off the river and dissipating just as it fingered the roadway of the bridge. Jacob stood at the top of the bank with his clipboard and pencil, close enough to smell the river, as he made his sketch. The high, graceful arch was actually comprised of two arching chords connected by thirty-two truss members of different lengths, the variation caused because the chords were differently shaped. While the bottom chord was a simple parabola, the top chord looked like a bell curve, both members seeming to run parallel along the top, but widening toward the bottom, as the top chord swept out to join the roadway and the bottom chord continued downward to join the piers – or in the case of July's bed, the posts.

'Hey,' July called. He looked up. She had walked ahead of him, in a red T-shirt and cutoff blue jeans, both turning gray. A cyclone fence appeared behind her, taking shape out of the mist. 'Come closer.'

'I can't see the bridge from there,' he told her.

When he looked up again, July was climbing the fence.

'What are you doing?'

He looked around to make sure no one was watching. 'I want to show you something,' she said, and swung her leg over the top.

'July—'

He went to the fence, the fingers of his free hand entwined through the steel, as she jumped down the other side, grabbing the asphalt simultaneously with feet and hands, like a cat. She met his eyes as she rose to her feet, and laced her fingers through the fence so her hand touched his.

'Jacob, how come you're so afraid of heights?' she asked.

His heart was beating hard. 'I don't know. Gravity.'

Her eyes held his, dark and mischievous. The pier alone was as big as a city building. Six lanes of traffic speeding overhead made a relentless, loud hum. He could feel the vibration through his feet.

'I think you're afraid of me,' she said.

Their eyes remained locked, while he sought to articulate a denial. Before he had the chance, she turned away from him and strode over to the pier, kicking off her sandals. He saw steel rungs embedded in the concrete. 'July?'

He looked up, and the underside of the bridge came into view. Overwhelmed, he lowered himself to the concrete, pressed down by the sheer enormity of the structure. And she was climbing.

Another wave of dizziness made the bridge throb above her head. Jacob shut his eyes. He tried to steady his breathing, stop his trembling. Then he heard her cry.

'Jacob!'

He looked up and saw her hanging one-handed off the top rung, framed by the green underside of the bridge. It all looked so insubstantial in the fog, he could almost pretend it was imaginary.

'Jacob, come up with me,' she called down to him.

'You're crazy!' he shouted up at her.

'So are you!' she yelled back. Pulling herself onto the top of the pier, she climbed over a railing and then stood dwarfed beside the vertical support, a hollow steel column that rose straight up to the girders that supported the roadway. On facing sides of the column, oval-shaped holes perforated the steel every three feet. While Jacob watched, astounded, July pulled her T-shirt off over her head. His heart beat harder. She tied the shirt around the railing then turned away, reached her arm inside the hole in the column, and pushed her head and shoulder in . . .

He wanted to shout at her to stop, but then the colum swallowed her. He could see her brown hand gripping the bottom of one of the holes, the small of her back in another, as she climbed, her foot in another.

Jacob stared up, amazed, the bridge humming loudly all around him as though delighted with the morsel it had just ingested. Pigeons and seagulls flew around the girders, celebrating. As he watched her climbing higher, he realized that he had never known anyone like her – so daring and impulsive, so beautiful and sexual . . . and so much his polar opposite. Yet she'd been attracted to him, and – for the first time he acknowledged this to himself – he to her. In fact, as he watched her climbing, he felt the attraction deeply, down in his chest and stomach and in some part of his brain, anxiously, almost as a kind of fear . . .

Then his mind was working at something else. Rolling onto his side, he reached behind him for his clipboard, his pencil, and started writing.

Green Girls

Henry put his hands on the steel. The paint was wet from the fog. The hole looked impossibly small, certainly too small to allow his shoulders through. But he poked one arm and his head inside, then made himself smaller to accommodate, and pulled himself all the way in, then began climbing up through the tunnel. The bridge was singing happily, actually singing. He could feel the vibration in his hands.

Then he got a strong smell – a mixture of ammonia and an acrid sweetness. 'What's that?' he called up to the girl, his voice ringing inside the tunnel.

'From the birds,' she rang back.

Henry's stomach rose. He pushed his face out of a hole and spat frothy saliva into the air, to keep from vomiting.

'Are you coming?' Her voice trailing away.

Henry raised his face, just in time to see her legs and feet squirt out a hole high above him, and white light replace her. He climbed up and up to the top of the column, then looked out and saw her standing below him, on a narrow catwalk with waist-high railings.

A twinge of fear went through him, but he was able to turn it off, filled by the mystery of this girl. He did not question her, indeed, he did not question why or how she had appeared to him, her face staring out at him while he stood at the railing. He stuck his arm through the hole, then his head. Clutching the catwalk railing, he pulled himself out. She helped ease him down to the grated steel floor. Her hands were warm.

'Thank you,' he gasped, holding tight to the railing. They were standing just beneath the loud roadway, a mosaic of concrete slabs over their heads held in place by steel girders. The concrete swayed with the traffic. He reached up and touched the underside of the slab, and felt the cars passing over his fingertips. 'Everybody going home,' he said. 'They have no idea we're here.'

The girl smiled at him. Sea smoke wafted around her legs. Then she turned and started walking along the catwalk, cutting across the bridge from the northbound to the southbound side. When she had gone perhaps twenty meters, she walked to her left. At first Henry imagined her stepping off the catwalk and walking on air. Then she looked back at him, and he followed to the place she had turned, high over the middle of the river between the north- and southbound lanes, where another catwalk intersected, this one stretching out as far as he could see, disappearing into the fog. The girl walked ahead of him. Seagulls and pigeons scattered in front of her.

'Where are we going?' he called, but he was already following her. They walked and walked until, far below him, in a gray-white haze, Henry saw

119

a phantom boat glide by. Riggings on the back dissolved and were gone in the softness. He imagined falling, and it did not frighten him, not as it had when he'd looked over the railing and she'd called to him. Nothing seemed real anyway: the bridge, the swaying, what he was doing up here.

Up ahead, she turned left again, onto another intersecting catwalk. When she reached the end, underneath the southbound lanes, she waited for him beside a huge rising column. Facing him as he approached her, she stuck her head into the oval hole of another beam, and disappeared.

Without hesitation, he followed her.

CHAPTER FIVE

J ust before three o'clock, the hottest part of the afternoon, the clean-up crew was moving like slugs. Twelve prisoners, all trusties wearing their outdoor colors – blue short-sleeved jumpsuits with white side-stripes – were picking up litter and stuffing it into trash bags. A single officer accompanied the men, Sergeant Biff Bullens, in his tan uniform. The tower guards may have wondered why Bullens was wearing long sleeves. Other than that, nothing seemed curious.

What the guards saw, if they were even paying attention this close to shift change, was OIC Terrence Gideon leaving the building a few minutes early, wearing his Marlins baseball cap and carrying a stack of books in his arms. They would have seen Bullens ask a couple of trusties to give him a hand. They'd watch Cecil and Sereno take the books from the librarian and follow him behind his Jeep. When the opened liftgate obscured their view, the guards would not have seen Cecil pull a tan officer's uniform from his trash bag and slip it on. Nor would they have seen both Gideon and Sereno climb under the brown tarp in the back of the vehicle.

They might have noticed, if they were still watching when they were replaced by new tower guards, the trusties file back into the building, while Cecil, wearing the tan officer's uniform and Marlins cap and the same kind of black-rimmed eyeglasses that Gideon wore – in fact looking remarkably like Terrence Gideon from the distance – closed the liftgate and got in the passenger side of the vehicle, while Biff Bullens climbed in behind the wheel.

Anyone knowing Biff and his racial attitudes would know that these men were not going joyriding. The logical assumption, once the Jeep pulled out of the lot and turned east on I-41, would be that Bullens was taking it for a test drive.

It was an effortless and bloodless prison break that, when eventually discovered, would be easily explainable. Bullens would say that Cecil held a shiv to his kidney and told him that his fellow officer, Terrence Gideon, in the back with Sereno, would die unless Bullens drove the Jeep where he was told.

Next inmate count wasn't until 5:00. With the second shift guard in Dorm 12, even if he saw that two of his seventy prisoners were missing, he would figure that, being trusties, they were working in the chow hall or warden's office, or somewhere else in the facility.

If by some quirk the escape was noticed, police would assume the escapees – an African-American and Colombian Indian – would head directly for Miami or take Route One down to Florida City, where they could blend into the population. Because both men were unfamiliar with the area – Cecil was from Orlando, Sereno from another continent – no one would expect the Jeep to leave the highway and take the first access road into the everglades. Then again, no one would suspect that Biff Bullens, who had poached every mosquito-infested corner of the swamp, was in on the plan.

Indeed, to make it look real in the unlikely event that they were seen, Bullens had planted a small .22 revolver under the passenger seat for Cecil, with instructions for Cecil to retrieve the gun as soon as he got in the vehicle. Cecil did exactly that.

'Oh, man, smell that freedom,' he said as he cradled the piece on his lap. 'Grass or something. Swamp.' His feet drummed the floor mat nervously. 'Almost forgot what the world smells like outside them walls.' If questioned about the gun, Bullens would be able to say he had no idea how it had gotten there. After all, it was Gideon's Jeep.

'We supposed to get rain or what?' Cecil said, and looked at Bullens for an answer.

The sergeant checked his side-view mirror and pulled onto the access road, then drew a muzzled semiautomatic from under his own seat. 'I'd just as soon we didn't talk,' he said. 'Try to remember, we ain't pals.'

Gideon tried to not breathe. In back, under the tarp with Sereno, scrunched up on either side of two spare tires, the stench of the Indian's breath was enough to make him gag. Besides, it was like an oven under there, with the sun shining through the windows onto the tarp.

'I've got to breathe,' he said finally.

'Best stay covered up,' he heard Bullens answer. 'Sereno's still dressed in his blues, in case anyone sees us.'

Just the same, Gideon pulled a corner of the tarp back, enough to let some air in. 'These tires make it awful cramped for a sizeable man,' he complained.

122

'Redundancy planning, case we get a flat or two,' Bullens replied. 'Besides, they add height, so your big heads don't show.'

Suddenly the Jeep swerved to the right, pressing Gideon against the spare tires.

'Hey, Biff, man,' he heard Cecil say, 'this one of them all-wheel drives?'

'Why, you plannin on buyin one with all that money you're gonna get?'

'Might,' Cecil said.

'All this time I figured you for a gold-plated Cadillac.'

'Man, you got outdated attitudes,' Cecil said. 'What's this thing on your visor?'

'Don't!' The vehicle jerked, and the top tire fell into Sereno, who pushed it back into place.

'What the fuck,' Cecil complained.

'Don't be touchin everything, that's all,' Bullens said.

'Yeah, you make sure you don't be touchin *me.*'

Gideon heard Bullens say, 'It's a garage-door opener, Satchmo. You ever hear the word, "garage?" '

'Yeah, I know what a garage is. Cracker. Like I said, how'd you ever get so enlightened?'

'I was born enlightened, Boyo. I didn't like your kind when I was a baby, and I never saw a reason to change. Same with Spics and faggots. In case you never noticed, my favorite word is "Hate." I hate liberals, I hate Catholics and Jews. I hate Democrats and most Republicans. I throw beer bottles out my window. I park in handicapped places. I hate the ozone layer and all endangered species. I believe women are here to fuck and make food. I hate peace. And there's nothing I hate more than the weather. Now, what is it you'd like to talk with me about?'

After a considerable pause, Cecil answered. 'What do you think of the word, "Not a damn thing?" '

'As a matter of fact, it's one of my personal favorites,' Bull replied.

Under the tarp, Gideon turned and saw Sereno's face in the dark. The Indian was not wearing his sunglasses. It was the first time Gideon had ever seen his eyes, not that he could see all that well, but it still made him nervous, the look the Indian was giving him. As if Sereno were warning *him*.

CHAPTER SIX

J acob lifted himself off the floor and shook the weariness from his right arm. He had been planing truss boards for hours, and his knees ached from the hard flower shop floor. He stepped out into the garden and took a drink from the hose.

Through the glass, he could see a bit of the green arch. The chords would be made by gluing together four twelve-foot lengths of 3/8-inch-thick poplar, then bending the lamination around a form and clamping them until the glue dried. He had spent an hour with a calculator and graph paper, until he had designed a replica.

Then he'd gone home – to Laura's house – and loaded his roof racks with plywood and the few boards of poplar heartwood he had stored neatly in his garage workshop. He went to the lumberyard for more. July went with him and paid in cash. Because he could not, with hand tools, make the individual laminate boards perfectly uniform, he brought them to a woodworker he knew in Berwick, whose shop contained a joiner and planer and a piece of machinery called a time-saver, actually a table sander. The man told Jacob he'd have the boards ready in a day.

From one o'clock on, Jacob had worked on the truss boards, sawing them to length, then sawing tenons on either end, and coding each piece in pencil according to his design, while July brought him food and drink and continued packing Alix's belongings in trash bags and boxes and carrying them down to the shop. Whenever she came down she rubbed Jacob's shoulders or sponged his neck with cool water in the heat of the afternoon, and always brought him something cold to drink. As much as he had perspired in the flower shop – it was easily a hundred degrees – he had consumed a gallon of water, lemonade, iced tea. Now he could hear July upstairs working in the kitchen, the knife knocking at the cutting board.

'Jacob, are you done?' she called. Evidently, she'd heard him stop planing.

'Just giving my arm a rest,' he answered.

'Come up, I made some iced coffee.'

From across the shop, the spine caught his eye. He went over and lifted the book out of the box. An anthropology text, written by Kennedy, Melnicove, and Winter.

J. William Winter.

His father.

'Want me to bring it down?' July called from the top of the stairs.

He paused for a moment, fact and suspicion intermingling. Then he put the book back in the box. 'I'll come up,' he replied.

When he went up to the kitchen, July had her back to him, standing at the island counter, dicing red peppers. His glass of iced coffee was waiting beside her. 'I put sugar in it, I hope you like it sweet.'

He went over and took a sip. It was indeed sweet, and creamy, and strong with caffeine. He drank some more. When he'd swallowed he said, 'Why would she get rid of her computer?'

July kept working. 'She was crazy. How should I know?'

He drank more, then asked, 'Do you know where she did her graduate work?'

Her knife stopped. 'Jacob, why are you always so concerned about her?'

'Just wondering,' he said, not sure he wanted to divulge anything. 'Don't make anything for me, okay? I'm going for a ride.'

She turned to face him. 'Where?'

'I just need to clear my head.'

'Do you want to go out to eat?'

'No, I'll get a piece of pizza somewhere,' he said, aware that she'd probably feel rejected, but he needed to go alone.

'Jacob—?' He was startled by the sharpness of her tone, but he kept walking down the stairs.

'I'll only be a couple of hours.'

CHAPTER SEVEN

A few miles southeast of Florida City, the Jeep turned off the road. The prisoners had been gone for fifteen minutes, and the police scanner had made no mention of the escape. Nevertheless, Bullens steered deeper into the cypress swamp, where anhingas sat on the low branches drying their wings, and alligators lay like half-submerged logs along the roadside, watched the vehicle slide past them as though it was potential nourishment.

'Won't be long now, boys,' Bullens said, sounding like a Boy Scout leader. At the edge of the swamp, he swung the Jeep abruptly left, taking a narrow pass into a vast prairie of tall saw grass. A squadron of brown pelicans flew over. Then, in his mirror, Bullens watched a drab green pickup truck slip out of the reeds.

'Slight delay,' he said, putting on his directional.

Cecil leaned back, checked his own side-view, fit his hand around the .22.

'This ain't the time,' Bullens told him. 'It's just a sheriff's deputy, lookin for poachers.'

He stopped the Jeep, and the pickup truck pulled up behind him. 'Everyone stay cool,' he said. He opened his window and watched the young deputy step out. The boy had a sunburned face and a tan uniform, quite like his own, so Bullens stuck his elbow out the window, let the kid see his colors.

'Makin any progress?' Bullens said.

'Hot one,' the deputy said, looking in at them. 'Guys from the prison?'

Cecil kept his eyes straight ahead. 'Just showin OIC Gideon the sights,' Bullens said. 'Hope I wun't speedin or nothin.'

The kid looked in the back seat, then in the rear. 'What do you have under the tarp back there?'

'Me? Tools, tires, whatnot.'

The deputy walked around behind the Jeep. 'Mind poppin it open?'
'Problem?' Bullens said.

'Probably not,' the deputy answered. 'We've had some poachers.'

'Yeah, we're stowin alligator hides back there.' Bullens gave a laugh.
'Pop the back, please.'

Bullens leaned forward and reached for his wallet. 'I figure we're all
on the job. Twenty take care of things?'

'Only take a second, sir.'

'You got it,' Bullens said, nonchalantly pulling a rubber glove over
his right hand as he pulled the liftgate release. Then he reached under
the seat and retrieved the suppressed .38. Seeing the piece, Cecil gave
Bullens a wide-eyed scowl. But Bullens quietly opened his door and
swung his leg out.

'Sir, remain in the vehicle, please,' the deputy said, pulling the liftgate
open.

'Just stretchin my legs.'

'I want to see your hands!' the deputy shouted suddenly, his voice
breaking. *'Everybody! Right now!'* He had jumped back five feet,
sidearm drawn.

Gideon sat up first, the tarpaulin sliding like a hood off his head.
His glasses were fogged.

'Hands in the air!' the deputy cried.

Gideon raised his hands and tried to warn the deputy by nodding his
head.

'It's a hostage situation,' Bullens called. 'I got a gun on me up here.'

'Fuck that, I surrender,' Cecil countered.

'Don't anyone move!' the deputy shouted, and he shuffled toward the
right corner of the Jeep, trying to see them all.

'I want to surrender,' Cecil repeated, and he tossed his .22 across the
dirt road. 'No trouble, just take me back.'

'Get out and lay on the ground!' the deputy shouted at him.

Cecil opened his door and stepped out. The deputy danced to the
side, shifting his aim from man to man. 'Down on the road, hands on
your head!'

Cecil sank to his knees, then lowered himself the rest of the way.

'You got another one back there, Officer,' Bullens said.

'Sir, keep your hands where I can see them,' the deputy told him.
Then he swung his revolver at the tarp. 'Who else is under there?'

Stepping forward, he caught hold of the tarp and yanked it off
Sereno, who was crouched in his prison blues beside the two spare tires.
The Indian's long black hair hung down, obscuring his face. 'Hands on
your head!'

'He doesn't understand English,' Gideon said. But Sereno did as he was ordered, kneeling up slowly with his sunglasses hiding his eyes and a hollow Bic pen stuck between his lips, like an unlit cigarette.

'Now, isn't this one sorrowful group of stowaways,' Bullens said from the front seat. 'Want me to get on the radio?'

'Sir, I need to see your hands!' the deputy ordered, stepping out from the Jeep to get a better look at Bullens.

'I wouldn't take my eye off them minorities,' Bullens said.

The deputy brought both hands to his weapon, aimed dead at the driver's door. 'I'm going to count to three,' he warned. Then he slapped at his neck, flinching as if he'd been stung. He fingered something curiously, a tiny shaft of bamboo maybe an inch long, and pulled it out of his skin. At first he looked over at Sereno, who sat stoically, the pen still in his mouth. The deputy scowled at the dart as he staggered back a step, then turned to his truck as if to run for it, but he collapsed on the road close to where Cecil lay. The deputy's legs moved, then only his shoes twitched. A few moments later he lay perfectly still, gaping out at the green haze.

Bullens stepped cautiously out his door. 'Excitement too much for him?'

Tentatively, Cecil raised his face, and he reached for the revolver in the young man's hand. A polished black shoe stepped down on his wrist. Cecil looked up and saw the .38 aimed down at his neck.

'You were just gonna feel his pulse, that it?' Bullens said.

'Tryin to disarm the man, that's all,' Cecil answered.

Bullens placed his shoe on the deputy's arm. The young man continued staring into the swamp haze. 'We must be living right, boys,' Bullens said, bending and prying the gun from the deputy's hand, then tossing it in the swamp.

'Nothin to do with right or wrong,' Gideon said from the back of the Jeep, as he took the pen from Sereno's lips. Examining the plastic tube, he said, 'It's a blow-gun.'

Behind his sunglasses, the Indian showed no expression.

Bullens looked him over and said, 'Officer Gideon, please make sure our Indian friend is relieved of his weaponry.'

Carefully, Gideon reached into the breast pocket of Sereno's blue jumpsuit and took out another pen. 'Unless you're planning on writing someone a postcard,' he said, clipping it securely in his own pocket.

'This boy's barely breathin,' Cecil called, pressing his ear to the deputy's chest.

'Put him in his truck,' Bullens said. 'People'll think he's sleepin one off.'

'I'd feel better if we got him some medical help,' Gideon said.

Ignoring him, Bullens picked up Cecil's .22, then walked around to the back of his Jeep. "'Kay, boys, scootch down.' Reluctantly, Gideon resumed his position, doubling up beside the spare tires while Sereno got down on the other side. Bullens picked the tarp off the road and threw it over them, then shut the liftgate, while Cecil lifted the deputy under the arms and started dragging him back to the pickup truck.

'Stupid, you're makin heel tracks,' Bullens said.

Cecil stopped. 'What now?'

'Pick him up.'

Cecil bent and hoisted the young man over his shoulder. 'Too hot for this shit,' he grumbled.

Bullens went over and walked beside him. 'Watch my back,' he said quietly.

Cecil jerked around and almost fell under the weight of the deputy.

'I'm talking about your soul brother,' Bullens muttered. 'Officer Gideon.'

'What's this now?'

'Keep walkin. I happen to know that Brother Gideon's been talking to Sereno, and they got the both of us fitted for body bags. I'm just sayin, you're gonna have a gun. Be prepared to use it.'

Cecil turned to look at the Jeep, his eyes darkened. 'I never wasted nobody,' he whispered solidly, 'never had a hand in wastin nobody, and I ain't about to start now.'

'Did I say waste someone? All I said is, you might be called upon to act swiftly and decisively.'

Reaching the deputy's truck, Cecil dumped the man over the side rail. Bullens was right beside him.

'This ain't summer camp,' he murmured. 'I offered you freedom and a rich way of life, you actually thought it was a handout? This is a serious and bleak side of life we're in, dog. Tell me something. You believe in self-defense?'

Cecil studied the officer for a full five seconds. 'Yeah, I believe in *self-defense*.'

'Then tell me what you'd do if another man was about to take *your* life? *Your* freedom? Because that's what Brother Gideon aims to do.'

They both stared hard at the Jeep.

'I'm just saying,' Bull croaked. 'When we get to the boat, be prepared to improvise.'

129

CHAPTER EIGHT

Jacob's father was unlisted in the Waltham telephone directory. Even a statewide search of Massachusetts came up empty. Jacob could not convince the University switchboard operator, nor even the Dean's assistant, when he showed up in her office, to release his father's phone number or address. The assistant told him to wait in an outer office while she tried to reach Professor Winter. Fifteen minutes later, he was there. In the dozen years since Jacob had last seen him, his father's hair had turned from bronze to white, though it was still thick and wavy.

'Jake, how are you?' his father said, offering his hand. Jacob took it and said he was fine, thank you, relieved that the old man hadn't wanted to hug him. J. William Winter III was as tall as his son, but slender to the point of being bony. His face was an unhealthy shade of pink, except for the crescent-moon scar at the corner of his lip. Jacob had never seen the scar till now. In the ensuing awkward moments, Jacob realized that his father was going to wait him out.

'I don't mean to bother you,' he began.

'No bother at all.'

'Did you ever have a student named Alix Callahan?'

At the sound of her name, a look of pleasant bewilderment came to his father. 'You knew Alix?'

'Barely,' Jacob replied, realizing that his father had heard of her death. 'We were at UNH together.'

His father gave him a lingering look – watery eyes peering over half glasses. His nose was enlarged, either from sunburn or wine, his cheeks marked with spider veins. 'Let's walk,' he said.

They took a worn path that cut the corner of the campus while Jacob's father talked. 'Alix did her graduate work here at Brandeis.'

'Anthropology?'

'Ethnobotany. Fantastic dedication. Fantastic mind. Fantastic

130

scholar. I always thought she'd be one of the ones who really made a mark.' They joined the sidewalk. 'Rumor had it she got her heart broken.'

'Do you know anything about it?'

His father furrowed his brow in a wistful way and shook his head. 'She went off to Colombia, to work on her doctorate, but she never sent a thing back, never wrote. I contacted her parents in Vermont, but they hadn't heard from her, either; not that they seemed to care.' He said this with a lightness that might have been directed at Jacob. 'Then, a couple of years ago, someone said she was running an exotic flower shop up in New Hampshire.'

'Portsmouth,' Jacob said.

'I guess she was drinking pretty heavily.'

Jacob tried to detect something in his father's tone – remorse, maybe self-consciousness – but failed. 'Funny she never mentioned you,' he said, and a thought hit him. 'Did you give her money recently?'

'Did I give Alix money? No. As I said, I lost touch with her. When I heard she was in Portsmouth I telephoned and left a couple of messages, but she never called back.'

At the intersection, they turned onto the main street.

'What about Colombia?' Jacob asked.

'All I know is, she went to live with the Kogis.'

'Indians?'

'The Kogi Indians.' He smiled reverently, as if there were something that set them apart from the rest.

'Kogis,' Jacob repeated, thinking about July now, as much as Alix. 'They live in the mountains, don't they?'

His father gave him an approving look. 'To be precise, in the northern and western slopes of the Sierra Nevada de Santa Marta. Do you know about them?'

'I know they take a drug called yagé.'

'Yes,' exclaimed his father, as though relishing the delight of sharing his knowledge with his son. 'Jake, have you eaten?'

'I'm all set,' Jacob answered, preempting an invitation. 'Actually, I should be getting back.'

They stopped walking. 'Jake, what would you like to know?'

'I'm not sure,' he replied. 'What are they like, the Kogis?'

'Fascinating, fascinating people,' his father said. 'For one thing, they populate one of the most diverse eco-systems in the world: rain forest, woodlands, mountains, valleys. They're semi-nomadic, meaning they plant crops in several different environmental zones, depending on the time of year. Yet they wear no shoes, in the belief that shoes would break their contact with the earth.'

They started walking across a campus lawn. The grass was freshly mown and fragrant.

'What distinguishes the Kogis from other indigenous peoples of South and Central America,' his father continued, 'is the prominence of spirituality in their society. In fact, the Kogi shaman is so revered for his metaphysical knowledge that priests from other, far more affluent tribes will travel hundreds of miles to consult with him about spiritual matters.'

'Including American missionaries?' Jacob asked, thinking of what July had told him about her own father.

The professor chuckled. 'Western culture is woefully unequipped to understand Kogi traditions. For example, when a Kogi girl first menstruates, she is considered a woman and encouraged to marry. As part of the marriage ritual, the village shaman must deflower the bride.'

Jacob looked askance at his father. 'The priest has sex with twelve- and thirteen-year-old girls?' Once again he was thinking of July, who had told him that she'd first gotten married when she was twelve. Not only that, but hadn't she also revealed – if Jacob could trust his memory – that she was now married to the shaman himself, a man who was in prison?

'Don't get hung up on sex,' his father said – and Jacob detected in his tone more than simple instruction. 'To the Kogis, everything that exists, both physically and metaphysically, has to do with procreation. The sun's journey divides the sky into masculine and feminine halves. Huts are built with masculine and feminine logs. Even the earth around them – mountains, valleys, forest, lakes and ocean – these are erotic things, erotic ideas, erotic visions. In the Kogi language, the word for dawn is also the word for vagina: *Munse*.'

'Sounds like a strange place to go if you just had your heart broken,' Jacob said, although he was really wondering how Alix ever expected to fit in such a society, indeed, how his father felt about a world where everything centered on male-female union. Or perhaps that's the reason Alix went, hoping to understand herself . . . or punish herself.

'Unfortunately, what makes it strange has nothing to do with the Kogis. They live in a very structured, hierarchical system the same way they've lived for centuries. The Kogis were the only people in South America who survived the Spanish invasion of the sixteenth century – by moving into the mountains. But nowadays they're being invaded from all sides. On the lower slopes are the *colonos*, poor Colombian farmers who are rapidly moving into Kogi territory, slashing and burning the land as they come. And what do they grow?

Marijuana and coca, because those are the only crops that pay them a subsistence living . . . but they also bring in the drug barons, who in turn attract soldiers and mercenaries and thieves. Then you have the revolutionaries and professional kidnappers who use the mountains as hideouts, and that brings the counter-revolutionaries and the army. And, of course, there have always been the gringos looking to exploit their natural resources.' Jacob stopped outside the parking lot where he'd left his car, and his father said, 'Do you know the biggest threat to Kogi culture?'

Pop quiz. Rather than risk failure, Jacob waited to be told.

'Money,' the old man said, giving him a meaningful look. 'Money,' he repeated. 'Always and forever. The almighty dollar.'

As a young man, J. William Winter had been disinherited from the family lumber exporting fortune when he turned his back on the 300-year-old business – to study anthropology. Fearing a lecture, Jacob looked at his watch again.

'I guess you need to go,' the old man said.

Jacob nodded. His father put his hands behind his back in a professorial way, poised for a collegial goodbye. 'How's everything else, Jake?'

'Fine.'

'Wife? Son?' The man could've been some kindly television dad, bestowing on his son some parting wisdom.

'Fine,' Jacob answered again, grateful that his father didn't ask about his writing. 'Yourself?'

His father smiled. 'Okay,' he said, and Jacob knew they were both lying. 'Sure I can't buy you a beer?'

Jacob shook his head. 'I need to get back,' he said, and headed for his car.

'I always look for you in the bookstores,' his father called after him.

Jacob kept walking through the hot parking lot, wanting to say something in reply. But he couldn't think of anything good enough, so he just waved as he went.

CHAPTER NINE

T he eighteen miles of Route One from Florida City to Key Largo is called, by locals, 'The Stretch' – shortened from the Death Stretch, the nickname assigned to the highway because of the volume of fatalities racked up year after year. Despite the fact that Route One is the major access route into the Florida Keys, the Stretch is a road better fit for the 1950s, when the Keys weren't so popular, and people weren't in such a rush.

There's another way to Key Largo, called Card Sound Road, much less-traveled and two-lane all the way. On the west side of the road, a makeshift canal cuts through the mangroves, wide enough for a small motorboat. Except for the occasional sunbathing alligator, the scenery doesn't change until the road becomes a causeway, with Card Sound on one side and Barnes Sound on the other, where houseboats share rickety docks with working boats, crab pens, clotheslines, radio and television antennae. Hand-painted signs say BLUE CRABS and NO TRESPASSING. These are the homes of crabbers and fishermen, maybe a dozen such places along the mile-long stretch before the road ramps up to Card Sound Bridge.

Halfway along the causeway, on its south side, is a thumb-print of land covered in mangroves and scrawny Australian pines. On the opposite side of the road, another peninsula extends into Little Card Sound like a long, bent leg.

At four o'clock Terrence Gideon's Jeep pulled off the causeway onto the thumb-print, carefully navigating the vehicle over the bed of coral and crushed shells until they were hidden from the road.

At the same time, a small fishing boat wended its way between Old Elliot Key and North Key Largo into Card Sound, looking no different than any of the old boats coming into the row on this blazing afternoon, loaded with crabs, mullet or bait. The three Indians aboard, two men and a woman, could easily have passed for residents or

134

associates of Houseboat Row as they chugged lazily past the string of docks, then moved around the point of land. The boat was only eighteen feet long and open, except for the canvas canopy slung over the cockpit.

Thirty feet from shore, the Jeep pulled to the edge of the coral drive, stopping on a ridge that had once been a reef. When the driver's door opened, Bullens stepped out with his hands raised, and Cecil slid out the passenger door, aiming his revolver at his back. The masquerade was for the benefit of anyone who might have followed the boat or Jeep to this slice of secret shore, so they would see what Bullens wanted them to see: an escaped con holding a prison guard hostage.

Above the idle of the vehicle and the gurgle of the boat coming in, they could hear only the oomp-pah bass from Alabama Jack's, the bar up at the bridge, and the drifting conglomeration of music from the houseboats on their right and left.

With Cecil's revolver trained on him, Bullens looked hard at the boat coming in, looked all around, seeming to sniff the air. Satisfied that they hadn't been tailed, he reached in his pocket, pulled out the rubber glove and snugged it on his right hand. Then he drew his silenced .38 from inside his pants.

'Remember what I said,' Bullens muttered, and Cecil shoved the revolver down the front of his pants as he circled around behind the Jeep and popped the latch. When the liftback came up, Gideon sat up and threw off the tarp. His face shone with perspiration, his glasses dripped. He took them off and wiped them on the tail of his uniform. He wiped his brow with his sleeve and, with a grunt, lowered himself to the ground.

'So this is Sereno's crew,' Bullens said, eyeing the boat puttering in. 'Those men or women?'

As the bow scraped into shore, the woman pushed the anchor, a rusted two-stroke engine, over the bow rail and it dropped into the weeds.

'Squaw's got muscles,' Bullens remarked. Then he slapped his .38 in Gideon's hand. 'Here, I want you to stay by the Jeep and keep an eye on Sereno. He puts another ballpoint pen in his mouth, shoot him in the head.'

Gideon returned a tentative look.

'Lord almighty, Officer Gideon,' Bullens said. 'I don't know how you see through them Coke bottles.'

'I'd just as soon you didn't use my name any more,' Gideon told him.

'My mistake,' Bullens said. 'Go on. And you,' he said to Cecil, 'go check those boat Indians for weapons. If they get funny, shoot 'em all.'

Holding his .22 over his shoulder, Cecil approached the boat cautiously. Out in the water, the stern bounced gently, its motor bubbling up blue smoke. When his shoe hit the water, Cecil took hold of the gunwale and motioned all three Indians to the bow, holding the pistol on each of them as they raised their arms and turned a circle, as though familiar with the routine. They all had long black hair, and they were dressed all in white. Finished, Cecil looked back to Bullens.

'So far, so good,' Bullens said. 'Let's have the stuff.'

The Indian who had skippered the boat shook his head, then pointed toward Sereno, who was still crouched in the back of the Jeep.

Bullens snapped toward Gideon. 'Sereno stays put.' Back to Cecil: 'I want the product first. Have the girl bring it down.'

Once again the skipper shook his head.

'Kneecap that cocksucker,' Bullens said.

Cecil looked back at him, then up at the Indian, whose eyes moved down to the engine block.

'Inside the anchor?' Cecil asked.

The skipper gave an affirmative stare.

'No shit.' Cecil laughed as he moved toward the rusted engine.

'Have Pocahontas get it,' Bullens told him.

The two men on the boat exchanged a wary glance.

'Only two ways this is gonna go,' Bullens said to them, coming down to the boat, 'my way or the highway.' He stepped into the water and raised his gloved hand to help the woman down.

She leaned on the gunwale and, disdaining the sergeant's hand, swung out of the boat and dropped five feet, landing feet-first in the weeds. She flipped her hair behind her shoulder.

'Watch the skipper,' Bullens said to Cecil, as the Indian opened a door below the cockpit and pulled out a blue plastic box. Cecil's revolver followed the Indian as he reached into the box and took out a socket wrench, then came to the bow and dropped the ratchet down into the woman's hand.

With Bullens standing over her, she squatted beside the engine block, fit the socket over a bolt and, with a jerk of her arm, broke the seal. When she had removed the last bolt, she rapped the block with the wrench, then pried open the valve cover with her fingers. The engine had been completely hollowed out, and the package she withdrew was wrapped in waxy white paper which itself was sealed in a thick plastic bag.

Bullens poked her brown arm with the back of his hand. He lifted the package from her, gauged its weight, then gave it back to her. 'Have her put it on my front seat,' Bullens told the skipper.

The woman, seeming to understand, rose to her feet and started toward the Jeep. As Bullens watched her, he called to Sereno, 'If that isn't twelve pounds pure, Sereno, I'll know in due time. One phone call, my amigo, and you munchkins'll go down so fast you'll think you were in a shark attack. You'll *wish* it was a shark attack.' He widened his eyes to accentuate the threat.

When the woman had placed the package on the front seat, Bullens said to Gideon, 'Okay, now Sereno.' He shot Cecil a furtive glance.

Keeping his .38 aimed at the ground, Gideon gestured to Sereno, who climbed out of the Jeep and followed the woman down to the water.

Readying his .22, Cecil kept his eyes on Gideon's weapon, wanting to avoid Sereno's eyes anyway, as the Indian passed him.

'Hold your horses,' Bullens said, coming alongside and poking Cecil's arm, taking the revolver from him.

'*Alto*,' Gideon said, setting his hand on Sereno's shoulder.

The Indian stared darkly at him.

Bullens raised his weapon up at the boat. 'You other two, come down here, pronto.'

'Wait a minute, Sarge, what are you doing?' Cecil said. Whether it was his timing, delivery, or the way he screwed up his face, it wasn't difficult to see that he was a lousy actor.

'That's right, you're all busted,' Bullens said, turning his weapon on Cecil. 'Officer Gideon, go get the cuffs, under my seat. Hurry up.'

While Gideon hustled to the Jeep, he heard Bullens say, 'You two nitwits best get down off that boat, or I'll shoot this woman. Uno, doze, trays . . .'

Gideon opened the driver's door and fished under the seat. He was shaking, and hoping Bullens didn't mean it, but he had no idea what the man was capable of. He only knew that he did not trust him, and wished to God he had never agreed to this. By the time he had grabbed the four sets of handcuffs and headed back toward the boat, all four Indians and Cecil were standing onshore with their hands clasped on their heads, while Bullens held his weapon on them.

All the while, Cecil continued his tirade. 'I trusted you, man. You gave us your word—'

Bullens swung the revolver toward him, and Cecil shut up. 'You have the right to remain silent, remember? Do it, 'cause you sure as shit ain't gonna win no Oscar.'

'The fuck you talkin about?'

Bullens straightened his arm. Cecil closed his mouth, not sure if the man was acting or not. Then Gideon arrived with the cuffs.

'Good work, Officer,' Bullens said, reaching with his free hand. Gideon handed him the cuffs.

'Not them, your weapon,' Bullens told him, taking the .38 from him. 'You can read these drug-runnin sonovabitches their rights in Spanish while you give them their bracelets. Shackle 'em in a line, with the skipper at the end. I'll take care of this one separately.'

Cecil gaped at the sergeant.

Gideon walked behind the Indians, saying, *'Usted tiene el derecho de guardar silencio,'* as he shackled the first two men together, then the woman to the second man. His command of Spanish was rudimentary, at best, but he'd managed to memorize the Miranda card Bullens had given him.

'I don't know what you just said,' Bullens told him, 'but it sounded like a damn welfare office, so it must be right.'

Before Gideon cuffed Sereno to the woman, he came around in front of them and said, *'Comprende usted estos derechos?'*

The woman nodded her head fearfully. Sereno, with his shades on, gave no indication that he understood.

'Put your hands down so I can handcuff you,' Gideon told him, taking the loose cuff that hung from the woman's wrist and clamping it around Sereno's. Then he withdrew the Miranda card from his pocket and slipped it into Sereno's shirt pocket, saying in a voice that sounded as if he were chastising him, *'No me confianzan estos hombres.'*

'Hombres, you got that right,' Bullens said.

'I do not trust these men,' Gideon had told the Indian in Spanish. When he closed the handcuff around Sereno's wrist, he furtively slipped his own thumb inside the manacle to prevent it from locking tight.

Suddenly the other Indians ducked and covered their faces. The crack from the muzzle was surprisingly sharp, despite the suppressor.

Gideon spun around to see Bullens bent at the knees.

'Yeow-zah!' he said, with a clenched grin. For a couple of seconds, he watched the underside of his sleeve darken with blood. Then he looked up at Gideon and said, 'How y'all doin?'

Since he still held both weapons, it appeared that he must have shot himself – which made no sense to Gideon. Until he tossed the .22 to Cecil. It was more the look of urgency he gave the black man.

'Do it,' Bullens growled.

'I don't see a threat, to speak of,' Cecil replied, holding the revolver by his side.

'I just been shot, Dumbbell. By the same black-assed traitor who's all set to take your sorry life.'

That's when Gideon broke for the shore, charging into the water beside the boat, running, swimming, stumbling, and splashing half of Card Sound up into the mangroves trying to escape.

Bullens wheeled with his weapon, but he didn't fire. 'Put him down!' he shouted at Cecil, while Gideon beat his way around the point of land. 'Get in there after him!'

'You!' Cecil yelled back.

Both men ran along the shore until the thickening mangroves held them back.

'Wade in there, you prick!' Bullens snarled, his .38 aimed at Cecil's forehead.

'You wade!' Cecil snarled back, bringing his .22 to the sergeant's chest.

Bullens glared with a livid grin at the black man. The standoff lasted no more than five seconds, by which time Gideon was gone.

Then Bullens snorted a laugh and lowered his gun. 'Officer Gideon's treachery will not succeed,' he said in a loud voice. 'He's screwed six ways to Sunday, and he knows it.'

'Sarge,' Cecil said, nodding toward the boat.

Bullens spun around and fired a shot. A chip of the gunwale flew off into the air. The Indians, who had climbed aboard during the commotion, ducked inside the boat.

Bullens marched over, his .38 held high. 'Hands up, everyone,'

Two by two, the shackled hands rose into sight.

Bullens laughed. 'They may not understand English, but they sure as shit know American.'

As Cecil trudged back through the weeds, Bullens said to him, 'Slight change of plans. I decided to let everyone go.'

Cecil gave the sergeant a skeptical look.

'We got the stuff, what do we care? Screw 'em,' Bullens said. 'In the back of the Jeep, go get that spare tire, the one on top, and put it in the boat.'

'What for?'

'Don't be argumentative, I'm getting nervous,' he replied, keeping his weapon trained on the Indians.

Cecil walked off to the Jeep, but he didn't hurry. In fact, he kept his eye on Bullens all the way. While he reached into the back and hauled out the spare tire, he kept his .22 ready. 'What's this for?' he said when he lugged the tire back to the boat.

'Life preserver,' Bullens said, eyeing Sereno. 'In case the ship goes down, the boat people can have something to hang onto till they're rescued. Go put it in.'

Cecil carried the tire into the shallows and, with a grunt, hoisted it up to his shoulder, balanced it on the gunwale, then tipped it over the side. When it fell onto the deck, the boat rocked.

With his wounded arm, Bullens gingerly reached into his pocket and pulled out another pair of handcuffs. 'Come get this,' he told Cecil. 'Climb up there and latch the tire to the captain's wrist.'

'Shouldn't be wastin time, not with a man on the loose,' Cecil argued. 'Gideon gets to a phone, this is Florida. Firearms while smuggling drugs. Maybe for you, that's a big fat promotion. For me, it's mandatory life.'

'You're the one wasting time.' Bullens held out his hand. 'Give me your piece and bring them nippers up. I'll watch your back.'

'You climb up. I'll watch your back.'

'I been shot, stupid. I don't climb so good,' Bullens said, keeping his hand extended. 'Anyway, my people didn't live in trees.'

'Keep that shit up,' Cecil said.

Bullens pressed lightly on his bloody arm, as if checking for sensation, then looked back to Cecil. 'Take your time, I'll just bleed to death here. Don't forget, we still gotta split up the stash and get you to your car.'

Cecil spat on the ground, a show of resolution. 'I'll go up there,' he allowed, 'but not without this.' Showing Bullens his .22, he stuck the handcuffs in his pocket and turned to the boat.

'Knucklehead, you got your back to me now,' Bullens said.

Cecil stopped, looked off at the horizon, as though waiting to be shot. He turned to Bullens, who stepped back and held his .38 out to the side, inviting Cecil to shoot him.

'Boyo, you take your weapon up there,' he said with a kindhearted smile, 'they'll snatch it away and shove it up your ass in a heartbeat. You know they will.'

Cecil stared at him for another few seconds . . . then gave Bullens a warning of his own. 'I got folks expectin me. Just like you do. They know exactly what's up. I told 'em everything. So . . .' He pitched the .22 into the weeds at the sergeant's feet, then sloshed angrily to the boat and grabbed hold of the gunwale.

Bullens stepped on the gun. 'Nice to be trusted,' he said, as he aimed his .38 into the Indians sitting on the deck. 'Okay, boys and girls, keep those hands up, we're gonna give you a nice American life preserver. When you get back to the jungle you can put it on the tribal bus.'

While Cecil climbed aboard, Bullens issued a warning to surrounding pines, meant for Gideon. 'Word to the wise, anyone thinking anything stupid better think again.'

Once on deck, Cecil picked up the tire and rolled it over to the Indians, then balanced it between his legs while he passed the open cuff through the lug hole and hub.

'Outstanding,' Bullens said as Cecil clamped the cuff onto the skipper's free hand.

Cecil said, 'Okay? Now throw me my gun.'

'Go start the engine,' Bullens told him.

Cecil wiped his hands on his uniform. 'I want my gun first.'

Bullens looked down at the pistol in his hand, then gave Cecil a long, calm smile. 'You're too argumentative.'

'I'm doing it!' Cecil snapped, stepping around the cockpit, muttering, 'Like I know how to start a boat.'

'Same as an automobile, turn the key,' Bullens told him. Cecil did as instructed, and the Evinrude sputtered smoke. 'Now put it in reverse,' Bullens said. 'Shift down.'

Cecil looked at the console. 'Yeah, then how am I supposed to get off the boat?'

'Jump in the water, how you think?'

'Biff, man, I told you I don't swim.'

'Then you better be quick.'

'Okay, but I want my gun,' Cecil told him.

'I want my gun, I want my gun. Do you do anything without bellyachin?' His pistol suddenly aimed at the black man's stomach.

Cecil jerked down behind the cockpit, shouting wildly, 'Sarge, I been completely trustworthy to you!'

'You've been paranoid and distrustful,' Bullens replied. 'Now shove that bastard in reverse. Push that gearshift down till you hear it pop.'

Cecil grabbed the shift lever and pulled it down. The motor clattered and the boat began crawling backwards, dragging the makeshift anchor under water. 'Sarge, you *know* I'm solid!' Cecil cried.

'Ease up,' Bullens said, and Cecil cut the throttle to a chugging idle.

''Kay, hop on down,' Bullens said, 'unless you got plans to turn Injun.'

'Fuck, you're gonna shoot me!'

'I might just do that, if you intend to keep pissing me off,' Bullens said. 'Look, I put the gun away. See?'

Cecil stayed down behind the cockpit. 'I got folks expectin me,' he said again. 'I don't show up, they're instructed to call the governor and tell him everything that transpired here.'

141

He didn't see Bullens until it was too late, the big beaming face rising up beside the boat, the long muzzle aimed – and then Cecil didn't have time to do anything but twist away, before the bullet tore through his side. He dropped to his knee, then sprang up again, to jump over the side. But the sergeant's second slug shattered the back of his skull, and Cecil collapsed in a pile.

'Mind another passenger?' Bullens said to the Indians as he caught hold of the bow and gave the boat a slight sidewards realignment, enough so it headed straight back toward open water. Then he pressed the muzzle of his gun against the anchor rope and fired. The rope snapped and the boat moved out, Sereno staring back at him all the while.

'That's right, you give me the evil eye,' Bullens said. He picked Cecil's revolver out of the weeds and stuck it in his trouser pocket, then walked back to Gideon's Jeep. Opening the door, holding the .38 down by his leg, he called out, 'Officer Gideon, come on out, dog, you're a hero now. We got the drug dealers tied up in their boat, we confiscated the stash, and you took down the escapee that wounded me. Let's go back home and get our 'attaboys.'

Off to the left, Gideon lay in the shallows motionless as a crocodile, face in the weeds, mosquitoes whining like fiddles all around him, feeding off his forehead and ears.

'I know you can hear me. You intend screwing me, boy, you may's well step barefoot into hell.'

Bullens reached into the Jeep and pulled the garage-door opener off the visor, then walked away from the Jeep, listening for footsteps in the mangroves, but all he could hear was the chugging of the Indians' boat making distance in the sound.

As they rocked and puttered away from shore, Sereno pulled the woman's hand to his mouth. Taking the cuff into his teeth, he squeezed his fingers together and started pulling his hand through. When the heel of his hand caught, he pulled harder, until his mouth began to bleed. From under the cuff, a slice of flesh lifted off the back of his hand like a carrot peel – and the steel, greased with his blood, suddenly let him go.

Sereno walked back to the cockpit. As the shore continued backing away, he took the gearshift and pushed up into neutral. He cut the wheel, and the boat made a lazy, rocking turn. Now the starboard came around, and he watched Bullens climb to the top of the knoll. He could see that the sergeant had a pistol in one hand. In the other hand, he held something smaller.

★ ★ ★

At the top of the knoll, Bullens called out to the mangroves that surrounded him. 'Last chance, Officer Gideon. If I go back alone, this'll go down as an inside job, perpetrated by the only person who could possibly perpetrate it: OIC Terrence Gideon, Officer in Charge of the library for twenty-one years. Never promoted, disgruntled, past police record to boot. Don't forget, I got the gun that shot me. Your prints are all over it. Same gun that killed your partner in crime.'

Bullens listened again. Then he turned back to the water so he could see the boat. And there was Sereno behind the cockpit. Bullens chuckled, and pointed the garage-door opener at him.

'You don't know how long I've been waitin for this,' he said. 'You prick.'

Gideon crawled up between two Australian pines, his eyes level with the top of the grass, shivering with indecision. He knew that Bullens would kill him if he showed his face. On the other hand, if he allowed the sergeant to return to the prison with a bullet in his arm, the man could tell whatever lies he wanted. Who would the authorities believe, the wounded sergeant or some disgruntled OIC, a black man with a criminal record?

His entire life, Gideon realized with pounding terror, had come down to seconds. His only option was to attack the Jeep. But that meant an uphill charge, unarmed. Never mind the noise, he was 100 pounds overweight. And what if he died here? Despite how Bethany might defend her husband's name, Gideon knew that his children would grow up never really knowing the truth. He poked his head up a little more, just in time to see Bullens aim that garage-door opener at the boat.

'Hey, Gideon,' the sergeant yelled, 'want to see what happens to people who cross me?'

Bullens aimed the little gray device at the boat and pushed the button with his thumb.

The explosion was so massive that the shock waves nearly capsized the fishing boat a hundred feet from shore, as parts of the Jeep whickered through the air and rained down in the water. Along the shore, three small Australian pines crackled in flames.

When the boat stopped rocking, Sereno lifted Cecil's body off the deck and dropped it into the water. Then he stepped behind the cockpit and threw the shift into forward, maneuvering the boat around floating logs and slabs of rubber and foam, heading to shore. His

143

tribespeople, still cuffed together, moved behind the cockpit with him. The woman, who had a free hand, took the wheel from Sereno. The captain told Sereno to take his mochila, a leather pouch filled with toasted coca leaves, from around his neck. Sereno did so, and the other man offered his poporo, a small gourd filled with seashell dust used to activate the coca. Sereno hung both gifts around his neck. The woman told him to make himself invisible and fly.

As they reached shore, Sereno swung over the rail and landed feet-first in the shallow water. The motor revved, then the boat backed away from land and swung around. The stern dropped as the boat sped away. Sereno did not wave goodbye.

Up on the land, a grisly black hole had been carved in the coral ground. The Jeep's axles and drive train hung up in a blown-down tree. There was no other sound, nor any sight of the two prison guards. Parts of the vehicle – doors, seats, and scraps of upholstery – were strewn about the mangroves, crackling in flames and sending up mustard-gray smoke.

Then a groan rose up.

CHAPTER TEN

Jacob heard the Irish music from the street. But it was so much louder inside the shop – the hanging plants actually vibrated – that he almost didn't hear the telephone ringing on the checkout counter. When he answered, he heard Laura's voice.

'You're not coming?' she said.

'I'm sorry?' He looked at the clock – almost eight – and could smell wood smoke from the garden.

'Coming where?'

'I'm at the ballfield.'

Seeing a tail of yellowish smoke working up through the foliage, he wondered if July was there.

'At Maxie's playoff game,' Laura said.

'What playoff game?'

'I called you this afternoon,' she said. 'I left a message with the girl you're with, to say I was going too.'

'Laura, I'm not *with* anyone—'

'Max called yesterday and left a message with her. He said you never called him back.'

'I never got the message.'

'They won,' Laura said. 'Max pitched a no-hitter. He wanted to tell you.'

'I never got the message,' Jacob repeated, wondering how much Laura knew about July – and why July hadn't let him know. 'Tell Maxie I'm on my way. And, just so you know, this is only a roof over my head—'

Laura hung up.

Jacob tossed the phone on the counter and went out to the garden, but didn't see any sign of her. He heard a quiet crackling from the direction of the hut, and smelled the wood smoke stronger. It was a sour smell, probably poplar burning. He started on the garden path, carefully watching the foliage for any flicker of yellow.

'July?'

He spotted movement behind the garden hut. Then he saw her standing with her back to him, holding a pitchfork over a flaming charcoal grill, as though toasting marshmallows.

'Maxie's playing ball tonight,' he said as he made his way over to her. 'I've got to go out again.'

She ignored him, eyes dark and downcast, while the yellow smoke went snaking around her. She was wearing a butterfly-print dress, and she'd tied back her hair.

'That was Laura who just called,' Jacob said. 'She said that Maxie called for me?'

'I forgot to tell you,' she said.

'July, he's been calling all day.'

'She must want to see you bad.'

'Laura?'

She turned and gave him a look. Her face shone with perspiration, strands of hair stuck to her cheek. Then he saw her pitchfork . . . Not marshmallows. Stuck on the end of each of the four tines was a tiny yellow frog, the steel inserted deep in its gaping mouth, where thick white foam bubbled out.

'Why should I tell you anything?' July said. 'You just walk out the door, don't tell me where you're going.'

'I'm sorry, I just needed to be by myself.' He took a closer look at the frogs. 'They're not alive—?'

She turned back to the grill and lowered the pitchfork nearer to the flame, and he heard a high-pitched squeal as more froth oozed out the wide yellow mouths and gathered on the tines. On the ground beside her was a glass jar filled with the foam, along with poplar shavings that she was burning.

'That's the poison?' he asked, thinking about what Alix had said – that one frog could kill 20,000 mice . . . or ten humans.

She gave him a derisive scowl. 'I make insecticide with it,' she said. Her gaze lingered on him, her beauty stunned him, yet her expression was absolutely unreadable. Was it wry humor? Or anger, that he was leaving again? Sadness? Bewilderment? She'd had sex with the village shaman when she was twelve, Jacob told himself. Later she married him. At some point she'd taken up with Alix Callahan, and the shaman ended up going to prison. Now she was living here, possibly under witness protection. He couldn't help but feel sorry for her.

'Do you want to come with me?' he asked, hoping she would refuse. The last thing he needed was for Laura to see him with July.

146

Her look turned sarcastic. 'Should I wear a cheerleader's outfit?'

He smiled. 'I'd like to see that.'

'You'd better hurry, Jacob,' she told him, humorless. 'You'll miss the big game.'

He stood there for a second or two, trying to think of something to say that would resolve the situation. Nothing came to him.

'I'll be back as soon as it's over,' he said, then hesitated before he turned his back on her, while another part of his mind flickered with sudden, chilling clarity, that perhaps moving in with July had been a mistake. In fact, it might've been a doozie.

CHAPTER ELEVEN

Terrence Gideon heard the whistles, piercing and high-pitched – and he dreamed he was running. The prison walls had been blown. Yes, running as fast as he could, but not fast enough. Looking back, he was blinded by searchlights. Up in the guard towers, he could see silhouettes of men with rifles trained, their muzzle flashes going off like strobes. Gideon cried out—

—then opened his eyes. His body was cramped with pain: arms, legs, back – everything hurt. Groggily, he felt around the branches for his glasses, which were no longer on his face. He smelled burning rubber mixed with sweet burning pine. Without his glasses, the sun was enormous in the low sky, wavering through the yellow smoke. Then something fell out of a tree and splashed in the water. He jumped, imagining it was an alligator, but when he saw the flash, he realized with amazement that it was the mangled bumper of his jeep. He closed his eyes, wanting to sleep again.

But a shadow moved over him, and he felt someone's hands on him. Opening his eyes, he saw Sereno bending close to his face, trying to lift his overweight body out of the mangroves. Gideon rolled his head to the side – and his heart thumped. He could see a body hanging in the branches beside him. By the tan color of the uniform, it had to be Biff Bullens. He could make out red spatters, like flower petals, on the leaves. When Sereno pulled Gideon free of the vegetation, something else fell, bouncing down through the branches and landing on Gideon's chest. Sereno frowned at the thing before he touched it. Then it was in his hand. Gideon knew what it was, but it made no sense. A garage-door opener. He watched Sereno clip it in his shirt pocket. Then he was gone.

As Gideon struggled to his knees, he let out a sharp groan, the sound of which he barely heard, as though his voice had been soaked up in his porous bones.

Again he felt around him for his glasses. He could see the mangrove stalk clutched in his hand, and that was as far as he could see. Summoning all his strength, he pulled himself to his knees, then brought the hand close to his face. A shard of glass was stuck in his palm. He pulled it out with his teeth.

Then, through his gauze of deafness, he heard a faint siren. He dropped down and quickly crawled to his left, toward the foliated thicket. He was running away again, he thought, as if this might still be his dream. All around him trees and saplings leaned toward the water, as though after a hurricane, except their limbs were all blackened on one side. Twisted metal hung from naked branches . . . and Gideon realized: The spare tire had been a bomb. Bullens had stashed it in the Jeep, then used the garage-door opener to detonate it.

Gideon climbed over the hot steel springs that had been his car seat, and pushed on, keeping an arm in front of his face to ward off the branches. A police car appeared and he ducked down. Through the thicket, he saw the cruiser turn slowly off the road, with another one following close behind. Then the muffled bang of a car door closing. Dark movement between branches. Low sounds of men's voices.

No.

Bullens had not meant to blow up the Jeep. He had meant to kill Sereno and the Indians. Gideon turned and looked toward the light of open water.

But how would he have explained the boat blowing up? With Gideon and Cecil both dead, he could have blamed either of them – or both of them, saying they must have been in cahoots. He could have implicated the Colombian drug cartel.

More cars pulled in, flashing blue lights.

Yes, the crime scene would tell the story. Cecil shot dead. Bullens hanging in the trees, shot in the arm, Gideon's fingerprints baked on the pistol stock. Cocaine residue spattered everywhere. And Gideon on the run.

While the voices grew louder, Gideon moved further to the left, until trees began standing straighter and leaves began reappearing.

In his slowly clearing confusion, he thought of Sereno dragging him out of the mangroves. Or was that a dream? He felt in his shirt pocket. The Bic pen was gone.

Sereno.

Yes. Sereno had switched the tires when he was alone in the back of the Jeep.

Another vehicle drove onto the scene, this one with red lights flashing. Gideon lowered himself, and his options became clear: Come forward and tell the police everything. Or run.

Are you telling us you believed the warden was in on this escapade?

Out on the road a siren blared and another patrol car screeched to a stop. He needed to decide. But what could he say? Would his eyes shift when he told his story? Would his throat go dry?

Bethany entered his mind. He could even hear her voice. *'Goodness always prevails,'* she'd say. That's what she'd always told the children. *'Be true. Have faith. Goodness always prevails.'*

Gideon heard a muffled shout, and suddenly men were running to the place where Bullens' body hung in the mangroves.

Be true.

Would they drag him into an interrogation room? Would they shout and pace and belittle him until he began to doubt himself?

Yes, he could hear Bethany as if she were right beside him. *Terrence, have faith.* He could see her soft brown faithful eyes. She was sanctified, and she lived a gracious life. No anger, no bitterness. *Have faith,* she'd tell the children, and she'd mean it in a thousand different ways.

Trouble is, Bethany had never been through the system, never had to dwell with men who lived like snakes.

More sirens cried out, two fire trucks coming in, white men shouting over the noise.

Goodness always prevails. Yes, that's what Bethany always said. And maybe she was right.

But sometimes goodness takes so long.

Staying close to the ground, Gideon slithered backward, between bushes and grasses and trees, sliding down into the wet green shadows. He had made his decision.

CHAPTER TWELVE

Jacob reached the baseball field in the gathering dusk, fully expecting everyone to be gone, but the kids were still playing under lights, six blazing floods distributed around the perimeter of the diamond.

Stepping out of his car, Jacob saw by the scoreboard that it was the bottom of the tenth inning. Speedway Tavern – Max's team – was losing, 10–9, and they were at bat – with two outs and a runner on first. He spotted Max swinging a pair of bats in the on-deck circle, and he gave the boy an apologetic brow gesture. Max looked away.

As Jacob walked down the right side of the field, looking for a spot where he could be by himself, he noticed Laura and Price sitting in the little green convertible. Price was reading a book in the dying light and wearing a safari hat.

A voice came up behind him. 'So, how's the coach tonight? I mean, *former* coach?'

Jacob turned. 'Not supposed to be talking to you,' he said, and found a place to stand. So much for being alone.

Fecto was sporting a golf shirt and doubleknit trousers, uncommonly upscale. Jacob understood the reason when he saw the woman accompanying the detective. It was immediately apparent – maybe not to Fecto, but certainly to Jacob – that she was out of Fecto's class. Evidently she hadn't known him long.

'Hey, just a couple of dads watching their sons play ball,' the detective said, actually putting his hand on Jacob's back. 'This is Mr Winter, our local celebrity,' Fecto said to the woman. 'He's a famous author.'

Looking up at Jacob as though intrigued, she took her place on his other side, close enough to make him self-conscious. She was obviously not Fecto's date, he thought, taking in the black rectangle of her eyeglasses, the short brown hair, the well-made jersey and khaki slacks, an aura of fit conservatism.

'What is it you write?' she asked in a way that let him know she hadn't the slightest interest. Not that it mattered to Jacob how she asked. The question always felt like a minefield.

'*John*, right?' Fecto, popping a cigarette out of his pack. 'About a toilet.'

Now the woman seemed to scrutinize Jacob. 'I remember,' she said. 'I thought the premise was fascinating.'

'Thank you,' Jacob said, weathering the assault. He turned back to the game in time to see the opposing pitcher blow a three–two count and walk the batter, putting runners on first and second, and bringing Max to the plate.

'This pitcher's good, probably the best in the league,' Fecto explained to the woman – which was an obvious dig at Max. 'But he's tired, should be easy to hit.'

The pitcher – who was easily six inches taller than Max, outweighed him by thirty pounds, and had already started shaving – was in his last year of Little League. A year younger, Max had better stats, both pitching and hitting.

Fecto took hold of the fence. 'A walk ties the game and loads the bases for Luke. That's my son,' he told the woman. 'Luke – on deck there.'

They hardly know each other, Jacob confirmed. 'Looking for a hit, Maxie!' he yelled, putting his fists together and snapping his wrists. Then he touched his chest, his hand, his head.

Fecto chuckled. 'See that?' he said to the woman, touching his own head. 'He just told his kid to take the pitch – not to swing. Smart. Load 'em up for Luke.'

Fecto was right about one thing. Jacob had indeed signaled a take, but not so Fecto's son could come to the plate swinging. The pitcher was clearly exhausted and would keep walking batters – and Jacob knew the opposing coach had no one to relieve him.

The pitcher took his stretch. Checked the runners . . . and fired. Max swung from the ground. The force of his missing propelled his body out of the batter's box and his glasses off his face. Boys from both teams let loose with lusty laughter.

'Guess he didn't see your signal,' Fecto said with a smirk.

Picking up his glasses and fitting them on his face, Max shot a look back at Jacob, who held a hand up to his eyebrows, showing him how high the ball had been.

The right fielder, scrawny and beak-nosed, yodeled, 'Batter's a geek! Batter's a geek!'

Max glared off in the kid's direction. Jacob whistled, got his attention. 'Base hit ties it, Maxie.' He touched his head again.

'I understand you used to coach the team,' the woman asked.

The pitcher went into his stretch.

'Mr Winter is on, what do you call it, Little League probation?' Fecto volunteered.

The ball came in shoulder-high, a hanging curve. As Jacob gripped the fence helplessly, Max whipped the bat around and missed again, by half a foot. His helmet swung around sideways on his head. A spontaneous jeer exploded from the opposition.

Fecto let out a snort. 'Classic sucker pitch.'

'Geekballs! Geekballs!' cried the right fielder.

Straightening his helmet and glasses, Max looked over. Jacob clapped his hands. 'Ignore them, Maxie,' he called, but wondered why his son was ignoring him.

The pitcher, standing taller on the mound, shook off a sign from the catcher, then went into his stretch.

'July,' Fecto said abruptly. 'Now that's a strange name for a girl.'

The ball sailed in head-high, fat and slow, exactly like the previous pitch. Max wanted to swing, looked like he was going to swing – his hips turned, his shoulders jerked – but at the last instant he laid off. Ball one.

'Way to watch 'em!' Jacob yelled.

'This doesn't have anything to do with the assault case,' Fecto said assuringly. 'I've been looking into that bridge incident. It's kind of a funny coincidence that you'd move into the woman's house, with her what-do-you-call-it – *partner* – if that's what they call it these days.'

'Make him come to you, Maxie!' Jacob yelled. He was trying to ignore Fecto, but it was increasingly difficult, with July's name in the air.

Max dug in his back foot. The pitcher tossed down his resin bag, then looked to the catcher for a sign.

'Low and away,' Fecto said. 'He'll get him reaching.'

'Whose side are you on?' Jacob said, unable to resist.

'I'm just saying, this pitcher's smart. He doesn't make many mistakes.'

The smart kid went into his stretch. And Max stepped out of the batter's box.

'Time!' The ump stepped around the catcher, arms raised.

'What do you think would make someone do something so drastic?' Fecto continued. 'Jumping off the bridge, I mean . . . that is, if she did jump.'

Jacob turned to the detective – who suddenly gazed off toward home plate, distracted.

'What the hell is that supposed to be?'

Jacob looked back at Max. The boy had leaned his bat against his legs and taken off his helmet, as if to examine it. For a moment or two, the entire baseball field turned silent, as everyone – players and parents alike – stared at his friar's tonsure. Then the murmur started in the stands, a pocket of laughter here and there, and cries of ridicule from the opposing team. Even the coach was shaking his head, as Max's teammates howled in the dugout. Jacob heard the coach yell at them to shut up.

But Maxie never cracked a smile. He scratched the hair above his ear, like an old man might, then replaced his helmet, picked up his bat and stepped back in the box, never for a second taking his eyes off the pitcher.

'You condone that?' Fecto said. He was the kind of guy who could be genuinely tormented by a haircut.

Jacob yelled: 'Go get him, Maxie!'

'Cut the shit,' Fecto said. 'He looks like one of the Seven Dwarfs.'

With supreme confidence, Max raised his bat.

The pitcher glowered at him as he went into his stretch.

'Low and away,' Fecto said softly.

And it was. Much too low, too far way. The ball hit the dirt and the catcher lunged – then threw off his mask and scrambled to the backstop. The runners raced ahead to second and third.

'Good eye, Maxie!' Jacob yelled.

'Good eye,' Fecto muttered sarcastically. 'Christ, how can he see with those glasses?'

The pitcher, who had run to the plate, took the catcher's toss with a disgusted swipe of his glove, then said something to Max as he stalked back to the mound. Max responded by removing his helmet again, and he kept it off his head until the pitcher had a chance to turn around and have another look.

'You think maybe Alix had something to hide from?' Fecto said.

The noise rose suddenly on the field, in the stands, and in both dugouts, as Max took his place in the batter's box, giving the pitcher a kind of smile. The pitcher did not smile back.

'Maybe July has some idea.'

'Talk to her,' Jacob said.

'I tried. She won't.'

Even though the pitcher took a full windup, the runners only danced off the bases. It might have been the older boy's fierce grimace that unnerved them, the shadow of his adolescent mustache, or the savage way he flung his body off the mound when he fired. The catcher leaped

154

in the air, snagged the ball way over his head, then feigned a pick-off throw, driving the runners back.

'Three and two, two men out, pressure's on,' Fecto said. 'First time you met July, from what I gather, was the night you had dinner over there. What was it, just you and the two girls?' Fecto chuckled. 'Hey, no potential for trouble there.'

Jacob kept his focus on the game. By now the players from both teams had come off their benches to clutch at their dugout screens. Parents were standing in the bleachers. Even Price Ashworth had lowered his book.

'Geekballs!' cried the right fielder. 'Geekballs!'

The pitcher walked a circle around the mound, bent for the resin bag, squeezed it a couple of times, dropped it back on the ground. At the plate, Max stepped out of the box and removed his helmet again.

'Inner vision, Maxie,' Price Ashworth called. 'Follow your heart!'

Max looked back at the Roadster, where Price was conferring with Laura, who appeared to be agreeing with him. 'Maxie, home run!' she called.

'Max!' Jacob started clapping his hands, trying to get his son's attention. 'Max!'

But Max wouldn't look his way.

'Hey, Squeaky!' he yelled.

Now Max glanced over, trying to contain a smile. He leaned over his bat as if it were a cane, then bent at the waist and started shaking his legs, his impression of an old man, squinting out at Jacob, as if nearsighted.

'What's he doing?' the woman asked.

Jacob touched his head.

The boy stopped clowning . . . and held his father's stare.

'You just told the kid to take, with three and two?' Fecto said, loud enough for the players to hear.

Max kept squinting.

The umpire came out and said something to him.

Jacob touched his head again.

Max finally looked away. Pulling his helmet back on, he stepped back in the box.

'You're dreaming,' Fecto said. 'He's got a chance to be the big hero. I mean, cripes, even a normal kid . . .'

Jacob leaned on the cyclone fence, trying not to listen.

'You know what I mean – too much pressure,' Fecto said. 'Cripes, he gets called out, and that's the game. That's the season.'

The pitcher started his windup. The runners took off.

'Watch this. Big, fat curve,' Fecto said. 'A fin says he bites for it.'

Then came the pitch, high and slow, just as the detective had predicted. Max reared back, as though to pulverize it. Jacob squeezed the fence. Max stopped. Jacob caught his breath. Then, suddenly, the boy's shoulders jerked, and the silver bat whipped around, shoulder-high. As the ball arced down to the catcher's mitt, a vicious ping shot it skyward, high above the bright, upturned face of the beak-nosed right-fielder, and way over the floodlights.

'That's foul,' Fecto said knowingly, but he was wrong. The baseball, lost in the night sky, cleared the outfield fence, actually cleared the playground beyond, and eventually bounced high off the well-lit school parking lot. While Max's teammates went on howling and drumming the dugout walls and running to the plate, and the parents cheered with elation, Maxie threw off his helmet and rounded first, showing his big shiny head to the pitcher.

'You know, the team ain't done half bad since you clocked that hypnotist,' Fecto said, nudging Jacob, as if they were best friends.

Jacob ignored the needling, as he watched his son stomp chalk dust off second base with both feet. 'Way to tag 'em, Squeak!' he hollered, in spite of himself, waiting for Max to look up so he could wave, at least. But Max kept rounding the bases without looking back; then he was swarmed by his teammates and new coach. Laura was there too, giving Max a hug. Even Price was high-fiving him. Then Max was walking off with both of them.

'I'd say the kid kinda dissed you there, dad.' Fecto's voice registered slowly, as Jacob watched his son squeeze into the Roadster with Laura and Price.

Jacob turned, gave the detective a long look. He knew the badgering was simply Fecto's MO. Rattle a suspect, rattle him and rattle him until he wore him down, until the guy couldn't think straight, couldn't sleep, couldn't stop brooding about all the ways he had screwed up his life . . . until he wanted nothing in the world so much as to confess his sins to the detective, clear his conscience and get some peace, even if it meant a clear conscience in a prison cell.

The detective's hand landed on Jacob's shoulder again, his tone abruptly amenable. 'It's good the boy's got a positive outlet,' he said, then gave him a cocky smile, the kind of smile that suggested he had a little secret, and Jacob was in for a big surprise.

'Mr Winter, could we talk for a minute?' The woman tried to keep pace with Jacob's stride, but he wasn't about to stop. Although he wasn't a drinker, he thought that he'd like to buy a bottle of Jack Daniels, go home to July, and drink himself into oblivion.

'I know Alix Callahan talked to you before she jumped off that bridge,' the woman said.

Suddenly realizing who she was, Jacob shook his head, refusing to even look at her.

'My name is Susan Evangeline.'

'I'm not supposed to be talking to you, either,' he told her.

'All I want to know is what she said to you,' Evangeline said, keeping up.

'I told your partner everything I remember,' he said as he reached his car and opened the door.

'Detective Fecto is not my partner,' she persisted, grabbing his door, preventing him from shutting it.

'Please, Mr Winter, this is not business. I'm asking you for a personal favor.'

He stared off at the darkened sky, skeptically.

'Alix Callahan was a family friend,' she explained in a quiet voice.

He turned to her, peered through her no-nonsense glasses – and found no glimmer of compassion in her gray eyes. In fact, she looked like a woman who had no potential for anything *but* business. But if he ever needed an ally, this was the time.

'I will not discuss your assault case with you,' Evangeline told him, 'nor will I take part in any discussion regarding that case that you might initiate.'

Jacob held tightly to his steering wheel. 'What do you want to know?'

Even while he gave his tacit consent, a part of his mind skittered back over the field of lies he'd already sown, wondering what new deception he'd have to concoct – and whether he could muster the composure to do so.

'Ms Callahan's family would like to make sense of this,' Evangeline explained. 'They're desperate to know why she did what she did. Absent a body, all they can do is speculate. Did she say anything to you?' The words, spoken by someone else, might have had a ring of despair. But exasperation was as much emotion as Evangeline conveyed, as though she just wanted to get this unpleasantness behind her. A district attorney who married to further her career . . . Why not? These days it seemed that people fell in love for less.

'I told the detective everything she said to me on the phone. Didn't he show you the report?'

'Yes, he did,' Evangeline answered. 'But I think there's something he didn't show you.'

157

CHAPTER THIRTEEN

The five-year-old black Saab fit the woman to a tee. There was no point in asking where Evangeline was taking him. Jacob knew precisely. As she veered onto I-95, taking the ramp twice as fast as she should have, the car leaned hard to the left, and Jacob grabbed the shoulder strap.

'We lost the light,' she complained, as if it were Jacob's fault. The vista widened suddenly, the skeletal arch rising into view against the sky, the beacon at its top blinking like a single, all-knowing eye. Treetops and roofs dropped away on their left and right, while across the river window lights spread across the town like the evening's first stars. In all respects, it was the onset of a pleasant summer evening. But as they ascended toward the steel arch, Jacob felt himself swimming against waves of panic. Then he saw the emergency flashers in the distance, the square back of Fecto's blue Explorer parked on the bridge.

'Not business,' he said, pressed back in the seat.

'In your statement to Detective Fecto, you claimed that you saw Alix Callahan's car parked here,' she said. 'You stopped your car, got out, and put your hand on the railing. You looked down to the river, but you couldn't see any sign of her because it was too dark.'

He closed his eyes. 'When I came home from Boston last Friday,' he said, 'Price Ashworth was in my bed, not in the living room.'

'Mr Winter,' Evangeline persisted, 'did you see her body in the river?'

'No.'

Evangeline snapped her right directional on, checked her rearview mirror, then jerked the wheel, pulling abruptly around Fecto's Explorer into the breakdown lane. She hit the brakes hard, and Jacob grabbed the dashboard. Turning off the engine, she switched on her emergency flashers. Trying to keep breathing, Jacob turned his head enough to see Fecto sitting on the hood of his vehicle, smoking a cigarette.

'The Coast Guard called off the search this afternoon,' Evangeline said, as a trailer truck roared past. The roadway went up and down.

Jacob stared out ahead of them, at the stationary green sign:

STATE LINE
NEW HAMPSHIRE

'Which means we have a steak knife and part of a bullet. And that's all. Unless a fishing boat finds her in their nets or she washes up on shore, most likely her body will never be found . . . If there is a body.'

Jacob looked over at her. This new theory – of Alix hiding – was what Fecto had intimated earlier. He glanced in the sideview mirror, at the detective.

'Detective Fecto is here in case you want to revise your statement,' Evangeline told him.

'What do you mean, "If there is a body?" '

'The truck driver who saw Alix Callahan told police that a man was standing with her.' Evangeline looked over at him. 'A little over six feet, two hundred twenty pounds.'

Jacob shook his head.

'If you were with Ms Callahan when she jumped, if you *saw* her jump and you don't want to admit it because you're embarrassed that you didn't stop her—?' She gave him a look. 'Or maybe you're afraid this might complicate your assault case or custody hearing. Mr Winter, I understand your reluctance.'

Jacob met those determined eyes again. For a moment, he considered telling her this much: Yes, he had been here with Alix, he tried to talk her out of it, but she jumped before he could stop her. As for July's presence and the bullet . . .

No, he could not risk telling even a half-truth. He could not trust this woman.

'Do you know any reason Ms Callahan might have wanted to disappear?'

'I keep telling you people, I didn't *know* her,' Jacob said. 'I don't know anything *about* her. I never talked to her until the day she bailed me out of jail.'

Evangeline sat quietly for a moment; then abruptly leaned over him to open her glove compartment and pull out a flashlight. 'I need you to get out of the car,' she said, and opened her door.

Jacob sighed. 'There's nothing I can tell you out there that I haven't told you here.'

'You need to see something,' she said, shutting her door. The change in her voice told Jacob it was pointless to refuse. Then she opened his door, making it more pointless. 'Please,' she told him, not a request.

'Hey, guy,' Fecto called, snapping his cigarette over the railing.

Jacob swung his leg out the door and tested his moccasin on the pavement, then pushed himself out. A couple of cars flew past, flashing their bright lights. The hot gust in their wake gave Jacob the sensation of being blown over the rail, and he leaned back against Evangeline's car, trying not to let them see his trousers shaking.

'This is where your prints were found,' said Evangeline, already at the railing.

Fecto leaned back against his windshield, clamping his fingers behind his head. 'Hell of a game, coach. You know, the one thing you can't force a kid to do? Respect you – once he's lost it.'

Not that Jacob planned to respond, but Evangeline interceded before he had the chance.

'In your statement, you said when you looked down it was too dark to see anything in the river—?'

'That's right.'

She held the rail with one hand, waiting for Jacob to join her, but his leaden legs refused to carry him away from her car.

'Go ahead, take a look-see,' Fecto said, as he tried to light another a cigarette in the wind. 'By the way, that's where the knife was found,' he said, pointing upriver, 'out there a hundred feet or so. Which is pretty weird, considering.'

Ignoring him, Jacob took a deep breath, trying to counteract the vertigo.

'I mean, considering,' Fecto flicked his cigarette, and sparks flew crazily off the bright tip, 'the night Alix Callahan disappeared, the tide was going out.'

Jacob looked at the detective. Then looked back at Evangeline, when a sudden screech of tires alerted them all.

Jacob spun around as blinding headlights burst against the back of the Explorer with an explosion of steel, and he caught the Explorer's grill in his hands, thinking very clearly, *Who is trying to kill me?* the impact throwing him into Susan Evangeline as the corner of the vehicle rammed the railing and miraculously rebounded around them, but only after launching Detective Fecto from its hood.

The way time stretched out, Jacob saw the detective leap into the air, executing what looked like a handspring off the railing as he vaulted over it, even twisting back in a last-ditch reach for Jacob's hand, which was at the precise moment occupied in the seeming act of shoving the Explorer away. In the detective's startled eyes, Jacob saw the split-second recognition that his last slim chance at survival had passed, as he slapped three ringing beats on the railing and fell from sight, his hoarse cry immediately lost beneath the steady blare of a car horn.

Jacob felt the railing sliding up his back as he fell to the pavement beside the damaged Explorer, watching curiously as a white Dodge Caravan with a folded front quarter rolled slowly across two unoccupied lanes, horn sounding, its driver sprawled across the steering wheel. Beside Jacob, Susan Evangeline straightened her eyeglasses as she pulled herself up. Throwing her hand out at an oncoming car, she climbed over Fecto's bumper. 'Get on my phone and call 911!' she shouted back at Jacob.

Jacob got to his feet, legs trembling.

'Hurry up!' Evangeline yelled at him, limping across the lanes, waving her arms at an oncoming trailer truck. Jacob heard the fierce hissing of air brakes as it tried to stop.

'Radio for help!' she yelled to the trucker, then he revved his diesel and went ahead. Thankfully, the Caravan's horn stopped . . . and a sobbing groan rose up on the wind.

Jacob turned back to the railing.

'What are you doing?' Evangeline cried. She was helping the Caravan's driver out of his vehicle.

Hearing the groan again, Jacob stepped up onto the curbstone, clutched the railing securely in his arms . . . and looked over.

There, about ten feet below the roadway, he saw Phil Fecto sprawled on a ledge, actually a steel maintenance platform that extended four feet out from the girder that supported the roadway. The detective appeared semiconscious, lying on his side facing in toward the bridge. His baseball cap lay between his head and elbow. He let out another painful groan, and his knee started to bend.

'Don't move!' he called down, then turned back to Evangeline, who was leading the injured driver across the roadway.

'I never saw 'em, they had their headlights off,' the man was saying in wavering tones.

'Over here!' Jacob called Evangeline over.

Responding to his urgency, Evangeline helped the driver into her car. 'Wait here,' she told him, then came over to Jacob and looked down.

'Detective!' she snapped. '*Fecto!*'

At the sound of her voice, Fecto's head lolled. His arm straightened, knocking his cap off the platform. Watching it tumble through the air, Jacob's legs weakened. He clutched the railing.

'*Detective Fecto!*' Evangeline shouted, shining her light on his face.

Jacob warned, 'I wouldn't—'

161

Fecto moaned angrily, sounding like a boy being summoned from a good sleep. He threw his arm defiantly.

'Detective Fecto, don't you move!'

Fecto's eyes opened. He looked up into the flashlight dazedly, his leg dangling out over the beam, exploring the open air.

'I said, "Don't move!"'

'Yeah, fuck you,' he slurred, and turned his head to look out at the sky. With a startled jerk, he kicked himself off the beam.

To the detective's credit, he showed admirable alertness in putting into practice the advice he'd given Jacob. Almost immediately upon his descent his body snapped to attention and he plummeted feet-first, like a javelin. Unfortunately, as he had also explained, the wind under the bridge could be notoriously uncooperative. While Jacob and Evangeline watched helplessly, the detective's stiffened legs began drifting upward in the wind. When he hit the water, his body sent out a terrible spray halfway across the river, and in the two or three seconds before he sank out of sight, Jacob could see the head dangling from his shoulders like some unnecessary appendage.

Jacob's legs gave out. As he felt the concrete collect his body, a wave of darkness swept over his head, like the river below, and sucked him down.

'Look. The moon isn't even out.'

Jacob tried to breathe, but he felt like he was going to vomit. He was sitting. The woman was holding him up.

'Look down, Mr Winter.' Evangeline directed his face between two railings. He could see the lights of a boat twisting in each ripple. And something was bobbing as it moved slowly downriver, a piece of wood, or was it Fecto's head?

'Can you see that?'

Jacob turned away. Sirens wailed in the distance. Cars raced past. Shadows moved back and forth along the green railing. The roadway went up and down, up and down.

'You were here when Alix Callahan jumped,' Evangeline told him. 'You were here. But you never looked over that railing, did you?'

'I told you what happened,' Jacob said, pulling himself to his feet.

'You lied.'

He started walking away from her, into the flashing headlights.

'You lied, Mr Winter,' Evangeline said. 'You lied, and I will crucify you.'

He kept walking.

'You let her jump,' she said, pursuing him.

He walked faster. Emergency vehicles were converging. The bridge swaying and bouncing.

'You think you're in trouble now?'

'There was nothing I could do!' he shouted, and pounded the railing with the flat of his hand. He turned to face Evangeline and was struck by the animosity in her eyes. No one had ever looked at him with such loathing. 'I couldn't stop her,' he said.

'How hard did you try?'

He just stared. How hard, really?

'Did you see her fall?'

'I saw her jump.'

'Did you see her fall? Did you even look over the railing afterwards?'

'No,' he said quietly. 'May I go now?'

Evangeline looked back at the spot where Fecto had gone over. She took a couple of breaths, evidently to regain her composure, then said in a disgusted tone, 'I'll have someone drive you to your car.'

'I'll walk,' he said, and started off into the glare of headlights.

'Mr Winter, you need to wait,' Evangeline warned him. 'It's against the law to walk on this bridge.'

'Then you can charge me with that too,' Jacob said, and he went on his way.

CHAPTER FOURTEEN

The Florida boy would search the trailer for his orange T-shirt, the one that said HIALEAH SAND AND GRAVEL on the front. He would blame his mother for losing it, and she would tell him she didn't remember taking it off the clothesline. His stepfather would blame the boy, might even ground him, depending on the kind of week he'd had at the bottling plant. None of the three was likely to call the Hialeah Police, not for a missing baseball jersey.

Neither would the police be notified when, in the same neighborhood, a family cat failed to report for breakfast; or when a bird-feeder that had been filled with sunflower seeds in the evening was found emptied in the morning.

As for the Florida State Police, they were still running their dogs through the glades that surrounded Card Sound Road, fighting off clouds of mosquitoes. They'd canvassed all the residents of houseboat row, the patrons of Alabama Jack's, as well as certain sections of Florida City, where the fugitives might have been hiding. They'd set up roadblocks on the bridge and below, searching all boats leaving Card Sound. But, outside of the small mangrove hideaway where the Jeep had exploded, they had not found a trace of either of the two missing men. With good reason.

The missing prison guard had stowed away on a flatbed of cinder blocks bound for Orlando before anyone realized he was missing, while the Indian had made his way deep into the fuming heart of the swamp. Who in his right mind would imagine a man surviving – on foot, at night, in places where even bloodhounds were afraid to venture? The glades were filled with saw grass that would tear human flesh to jerky strips, if the alligators and crocodiles didn't get him. The mosquitoes alone were enough to bleed a man dry, if they didn't drive him to drowning himself first, for the pure relief of it.

Sereno did not stay in the swamp, however. By ten o'clock he was also northbound, courtesy of a sugar cane truck that slowed to avoid a dead alligator in the road, then he hopped the sugar train out of Miami. It was well past midnight when two state cops finally stopped to drag the reptile out of the road . . . and discovered it was missing its heart.

CHAPTER FIFTEEN

B y the time Jacob had walked the three miles back to the baseball field and retrieved his car, he hadn't a single doubt that Alix Callahan was alive and stalking him, certain that she was the one who had forced the Caravan into Fecto's Explorer. Driving back to Portsmouth over the Route One lift-bridge, he looked upriver and saw traffic flowing normally over the High-Level bridge, as though nothing out of the ordinary had taken place.

When he got to Green Girls, July's car was there, but the house and shop were dark. Now he wished he hadn't left July alone. He walked cautiously up the fieldstone walk, eyes moving from one corner of the building to the other. Just as he stuck his key into the lock, the door fell open. Jacob froze . . . but it was July in the doorway, wearing his Red Sox T-shirt as a nightie, peering sleepily out from her black curtain of hair.

'I didn't know where you were,' she said.

He came inside and shut the door behind him, making sure to lock it. When he turned to face her, she slipped her arms under his. 'Jacob, what's the matter?'

'I think someone tried to kill me on the bridge tonight,' he said.

She leaned back, far enough to see him.

'Fecto fell. Remember the detective who was here yesterday?'

'Fell – like died?'

'The District Attorney brought me up there,' Jacob explained. 'Susan Evangeline, you said she came here the other night.'

July's eyes narrowed.

'Someone ditched a car into us. It wasn't an accident.'

She scowled. 'What are you saying?'

'Whoever ran the car into us had their lights off,' Jacob told her, then stopped, not knowing whether to tell her . . .

'Jacob, what?'

He said, 'It might have been Alix.'

She pulled away from him as if he'd given her an electric shock.

'There's a beam below the roadway she might've landed on,' he explained, and she turned from him and started toward the stairs. He followed and climbed the iron treads behind her. 'July, you've been up there. All those ladders and catwalks—'

'You want her to be alive,' July said – an accusation.

'I want to know who tried to kill me,' he shot back, louder than he'd intended.

Reaching the top, she stopped and looked down at him.

He held the iron railing, felt the humid air rising up around him. 'That night, on the bridge, how many shots did you fire?'

'I wasn't there,' she answered sullenly.

He was glad it was dark downstairs, so he couldn't see the floor. 'July, more than one?'

She gave him a fierce look, then spun away. In a few seconds he heard a door slam, and he knew it was stupid to try and reason with her until she'd had time to absorb what he'd said. But stupid seemed to be what he did best these days, so he went to the bedroom and knocked.

'July?'

He opened the door and peeked in. The room was dark, but he could see her lying on her mattress, turned away from him.

'Even if that wasn't Alix,' he said, 'if her body turns up and they find she was shot, then I'm their number one suspect. I'm their *only* suspect.'

'How? You weren't there when she jumped.'

He sighed. 'I told Evangeline.'

'Told her what?'

'That I was with Alix on the bridge,' he said.

He saw July's head move.

'She doesn't know you were with me,' he said. 'But they're interested in you. Nobody knows anything about you.'

As he waited for her to say something, his eyes became acclimated to the dark and he realized he wasn't looking at the back of her head. She had been facing him all along, staring wistfully out of the darkness. He went to her, sat on the edge of the mattress.

She took his hand. 'Are you okay?'

He sighed. 'Yeah. A little sore. But Phil Fecto had a son Maxie's age.'

She kissed his thumb, then ran the back of his hand across her cheek. 'Do you really think it was Alix?'

'I don't know.' He ran his hand down the side of her head, the length of her hair. Then he asked. 'You met her when she went to Colombia, didn't you?'

July turned away from him, pulling the quilt over her shoulder.

'She went to live with Kogi Indians,' he said.

'I already told you, Jacob, why are you asking? I told you, my mother was a Kogi. My father was an American missionary.'

No, you didn't tell me . . . Jacob almost objected. But he thought better of it. 'Alix said she helped you get away from your husband. Was that a Kogi shaman?'

July turned her head toward him. 'Jacob, are you a fucking detective?'

'I'm asking.'

'Well, stop asking.'

'If Alix is hiding from something, or someone, I want to know what's going on.'

July said, 'My husband is in prison. When he gets out, he'll be sent back to Colombia, where he'll be killed.'

'Why?'

'Because it's Colombia. Okay?'

'Maybe that's what she's hiding from.'

'Jacob, they don't know her. Nobody knows her. She's not hiding. She was crazy and depressed, and she wanted to hurt me by killing herself and taking you with her. Now stop talking about her.'

He watched her eyes in the near darkness, blinking up at the ceiling.

'I'm sorry,' he said, though he didn't know why he was apologizing. 'I'm just so afraid of losing Max.'

July turned and looked at him again. Then she lowered the blanket and invited him in. He lay down beside her, but left his feet on the floor, half committed. She took his hand and brought it to her mouth, and meditatively kissed the places between his fingers. He sighed.

'You know the kind of kid who'll do anything on a dare?'

She lowered his hand to her chest. Between the softness of her breasts he could feel the quiet beating of her heart.

'He scares me,' Jacob said. 'He's got a hundred-eighty-one IQ . . . and learning disabilities. So he's classified "twice special," which simply means, he doesn't fit. He has no social skills. And he thinks he's indestructible. The kids egg him on. Want someone to rig the fire alarm? Build a rocket? Fly? Talk to Maxie Winter.'

'He sounds like a lot of trouble,' she said, reaching down and pulling off her T-shirt.

Jacob smiled. 'He's had his share of problems – and broken bones.

He can't sit still in school, can't pay attention to his teachers for more than five seconds – his mind moves at light speed, constantly juggling twenty things at a time – he can't have any sugar, no caffeine. But put him in front of a computer? Total concentration . . .' All of a sudden, Jacob's throat closed up.

July threw the blanket over him, then pulled his legs onto the mattress.

'I couldn't take it if I lost him,' he whispered.

Then she brought his arm under her cheek, as though it were a pillow, and wrapped her legs around his. They remained still for a few moments.

'You'll never lose me,' she said, her voice soft as a bee's wing, and she pulled him into her arms.

CHAPTER SIXTEEN

Thick as the mosquitoes were in the north Florida woods – they were louder than the sugar train going away – most of them kept their distance from the Indian. Those that landed on his skin immediately flew away again. Even in Sereno's native forests, mosquitoes never bothered him half as much as did the sun. With his shades protecting his eyes from the morning light, he crept down to the river bank, where the water ran slow and shallow. Cupping his hand in the current, already he knew this was wrong. The water was too warm. He took a taste. No salt.

He climbed back up the bank, worked his way to the right, away from the railroad bed, then crawled into a sweet bed of juniper. A balled-up armadillo awoke, gazed at the Indian, then got to its feet, took a couple of hops and waddled out of the patch. The Indian laughed, and found a place where the juniper was softest. As the train grew quieter, he made himself a pillow.

There would come another train in the night.

Terrence Gideon stumbled through the maze of eighteen-wheelers, his body an itching, stinging, sweating, swollen mass. During the night mosquitoes had stung every centimeter of his skin, drawing his blood even through the blue Nike sweatsuit he had taken off a clothesline somewhere outside of Orlando. The shirt was ridiculously tight. His ears burned, and his entire world was a blur.

Carrying his uniform in a plastic trash bag, he found his way through the door of the truck stop, then followed the smell of bacon and coffee until he collided with a rack of sunglasses beside a cash register. Luckily, he was able to keep the thing from crashing to the floor.

'Go ahead and seat yourself,' the cashier said pleasantly. She was a black woman, dressed in light blue, and she smelled of coconut. She must have thought he was drunk.

Now he could hear the ring of teaspoons against coffee mugs and waitresses calling to cooks. As he walked past the line of men's backs at the counter, smelling their hash-browns and gravy, his big stomach rumbled like an empty barrel. But he kept walking, pursuing a different smell, the cloying odor of pink urinal cakes, through a wooden swinging door.

As near as he could make out, two men were standing at the urinals; another was bent over at a sink brushing his teeth. Gideon walked over beside the man and furtively dragged his hand along the counter top until he snagged the prize, which turned out to be – not eyeglasses, but a disposable razor. The man reared back, staring, and Gideon dropped the razor and mumbled an apology, then crossed to the toilet stalls. Closing himself inside, he pulled down his sweatpants and boxers, and sat. Leaned his elbows on his knees, his head in his hands. He wanted to cry. He wanted to sleep. But he could not allow either.

He knew that his glasses would have been found in the shallow water where the Jeep had exploded. Any detective worth his salt, realizing how nearsighted Gideon was, would alert local opticians to watch out for any fat, stumbling black man looking for glasses.

Momentarily, Gideon heard the bathroom door open and close. He listened to the footsteps, listened to the water come on. He pulled up his pants and stepped out of the stall. He could tell that the man was washing his face, so he went to the sink beside him and turned on both faucets.

'Early start, beat the heat,' he said, in a friendly way.

He could make out some objects on the counter between them. Knowing he had to make his move, he quickly ran his hand over the counter until he felt a plastic soap dish, wet toothbrush, and . . . nestled in a small terrycloth towel, a pair of glasses. He closed his hand around them, turned and slipped them on his face as he headed for the door.

The restaurant flipped up and down with each step. Realizing he had lifted a pair of bifocals, Gideon lowered his head and looked out the upper lenses. Seeing the sunglass rack coming at him, he could smell that coconut again. And there was the woman in blue, the cashier, smiling as he came. He misjudged the distance and kicked the base of her counter with a hollow bang, then mumbled an apology and walked out into the low, morning sunlight, heading directly for the line of trucks as if he owned one of them, all the while looking for an open box in which to hide . . .

And he spotted one.

Black cab, yellow box, hydraulic lift. The back was open, with a chain strung across to keep the cargo from falling out. Not much chance of that. The truck was loaded with used, industrial-type stoves and refrigerators. He looked around to make sure he wasn't seen, then climbed inside. Squeezed around a refrigerator, crawled over a stove, and found himself a piece of the wheel well, where he lay down and fell instantly asleep.

CHAPTER SEVENTEEN

'*Tighter.*'

Jacob pulled on the wood with every bit of his strength, his biceps burning with the strain, while July screwed the clamp lever with both hands. Their arms trembled. They sat in the shop, on a sheet of polyurethane laid on half-inch plywood, onto which Jacob had nailed the form, three-quarter plywood that he had bow-sawn in a simple arch. Jacob pressed his feet against the door jamb and pulled back on the long strips of green poplar. Because he had slathered wood glue between the four sheets, they were battling time. July's halter was drenched with sweat. Jacob worked without a shirt, something he had never done – but neither had he ever bent a piece of wood. Her shoulder slid hard against his arm while she turned the lever.

'Set?'

'Yes,' she answered in a gasp, letting go. She reached behind her and picked up the water bottle they kept close by.

He slid back on the poly six inches, realigned his grip . . . and pulled. 'Go.'

She fit the clamp in place and turned the screw, and the glue oozed out of the seams.

'Is this different from Alix?' Jacob asked her.

'She wasn't a carpenter,' July said, as she turned the lever. 'If that's what you mean.'

'It just seems strange,' Jacob said, 'how you could be with a woman for so long, then switch to a man.'

July pushed on the lever. Sweat dripped off her nose, fell on his arm and mixed with his own perspiration.

'It must be different,' Jacob said. To make sure the unclamped boards ahead of them remained aligned, he grabbed the four-foot board and mallet and pounded it along the side of the chord.

'Alix was crazy.'

'Jealous crazy?'

'Crazy crazy,' July said. 'Always accusing me of things.'

'Accusing you of what?'

'Jacob, pull!' She applied such force to the lever that the caul cracked. 'Shit.'

'Back off,' he said. 'We'll get another piece.' The caul was a short length of pine that they fit on the outside of the laminate, to spread the pressure and keep the clamp from gouging the poplar. While he kept pulling back on the wood, she loosened the clamp, grabbed another piece of pine and slipped it between the clamp jaw and the poplar, and started turning the lever.

'Accusing you of what?' Jacob persisted.

'Crazy things, I told you. I lie to her, I did this, I did that.'

'She must have been depressed,' Jacob offered.

'She was the liar,' July said. 'Always sneaking around, as if I didn't know.'

'She cheated on you?'

'She was insane,' July said again, straining. 'I'm glad she's gone.'

'Tight enough,' Jacob said, relieved that he could let go. 'One more.' He slid back. His arms were exhausted, his hands and wrists. With his mallet and level board, he tapped at the top. There was only about a foot remaining, from which he would saw a few inches, and it adhered to the form without coercion. Nevertheless, he got a grip with his fingers and squeezed. July inserted the caul, fit the clamp into place, and started to turn.

The telephone rang. They ignored it, until the message machine picked up and the voice started. A woman's voice.

'This message is for Jacob Winter.'

July looked at him.

'This is Attorney Zabriski's office. We need to speak with you as soon as possible.'

Detective killed in fall; witness changes story of bridge jumper.

As soon as Jacob walked into the lawyer's office, he spotted the newspaper on the reception desk.

'Mr Winter?'

Jacob glanced up, to see Miss Finch coming in from Zabriski's office.

'I meant for you to call,' she said, giving him a disapproving look. Although he had put on a clean shirt, his khaki work pants were stained and stuck with glue. 'Attorney Zabriski cannot see you now. He'll be tied up for the rest of the day.'

'Susan Evangeline told me that my conversation with her was personal,' he tried to explain.

Miss Finch folded her arms, not about to discuss the case. 'If you'd like,' she said, 'I'll see if he'll telephone you when he's free.'

'I need to see him,' Jacob said, refusing to leave. 'I need to explain.'

Miss Finch stood waiting for him to go. He wondered if her next move was to quietly leave the room and call the police. He bet she was the kind of woman who wouldn't warn him first.

'Look,' he said, 'if I'm charged with failure to report a suicide, or lying to the police, or anything to do with Alix Callahan jumping off that bridge—'

'Mr Winter, you lied to *him*,' she said in a sacrosanct tone. 'You jeopardized our credibility.'

The woman's use of the word 'our' did not escape him. Jacob took a deep breath, trying to stop the jittering that had started inside him, but it did little good.

'How can you expect us to defend you?' she asked. 'First you say you weren't on the bridge, then you tell the DA that you were. You claim that Dr Ashworth's version of the assault in your home is a fabrication, yet you won't allow Attorney Zabriski to speak with the one person who might be able to shed some light on the incident.'

Her words hung in the room, and every impulse pushed him toward the door.

'Mr Winter?'

Jacob turned his head.

'Let us talk to your son,' she said, her tone softened. 'Whatever happened that day, one thing is certain. If you end up in prison, custody will no longer be an issue.'

He turned away from her and looked out to the river, thinking, once again, about the way Max had climbed into Price's car the night before. Nothing in his life had prepared him for the pain he felt thinking that he might lose Max, not the separation from his own father, not Laura's unfaithfulness, not even his mother's death.

'When would you like him here?' he said, though he could hardly believe the words were coming from his mouth.

Willard Zabriski's door opened.

Jacob turned.

Standing stiffly at the threshold, the attorney gave him a long, sober look. 'Bear this in mind,' he said. 'I will not hesitate to drag your wife and her lover through an open cesspool, if that's what it takes to defend you. Are you prepared for that?'

Jacob looked back to the wide river, despising himself for giving in.

He looked back at the attorney. 'When you talk to Max,' he said, 'if he verifies Price's version, that they were in the living room, then I want you to stop. If I did what he says I did, I don't want to be defended.'

Zabriski stepped over to the office chair and hooked two thumbs over its back. 'If it gives you any comfort,' he said, 'I happen to believe your version.'

Jacob shook his head, not sure what to believe. 'Just don't put Max in the position where he has to decide between me and his mother.'

'I'll do everything in my power,' the attorney said.

'I mean it,' Jacob said. 'If it comes down to Max having to choose, or my losing him . . .'

'I understand,' Zabriski said, and for the first time, Jacob felt that perhaps he could trust this man. The attorney walked around the front of the desk. He shoved the telephone back and sat on the corner. Miss Finch looked like someone trying not to look annoyed.

'DA Evangeline did not lie to you about one thing,' the attorney said. 'This case has indeed become personal. Even given her notoriety for prosecuting domestic assault cases, we thought she was taking a more-than-professional interest in you, so Miss Finch did some investigation of her own.'

The woman folded her arms, striking a neutral pose.

'It seems that when your late benefactor, Alix Callahan, did her graduate work at Brandeis University, she was commuting from the town of Newburyport, where she held a three-year lease on a small beach house. Do you know who her roommate was?' The attorney raised his eyebrows, and the cauldron of facts bubbled up in Jacob's mind. He looked at Miss Finch, who nodded with satisfaction.

'Susan Evangeline?' he said, amazed. 'Alix and Evangeline?'

The Alix Callahan he'd known in college – and lately – had preferred the company of girls who were young, hip, exquisite and wild, but hardly erudite. In Susan Evangeline, he realized, Alix had found her intellectual equal. A perfectly suited pair, one earning her doctorate, the other her law degree.

'That was before Lady Evangeline married Lord Astor to get herself elected,' said Miss Finch, unable to disguise her delight. 'Which might explain why DA Evangeline is so keen to investigate Alix Callahan's disappearance herself and then close the case. Because maybe Evangeline never came out of the closet, and she intends to keep it that way.'

In Jacob's mind the cauldron bubbled over. Alix Callahan had not only found her high-achieving soul mate, she had fallen in love. And Evangeline had left her for the sake of her career. Alix responded by going to Colombia . . . where she met up with July.

'You'll also be interested to know that we've found added incentive for Dr Ashworth to falsify the chain of events that led to his injury.' He gave a hint of a smile.

'Alimony,' Miss Finch spoke up. 'He's paying off two former wives, to the tune of twelve hundred dollars a month, and a thousand-dollar mortgage on his house and another five hundred a month for his share of the office building. Unless he's hiding money in an offshore bank, he can't afford to lose his license to practice medicine.'

'But he offered Laura's father a half million dollars for his property.'

'Maybe he hypnotized a loan officer,' Zabriski suggested, with uncharacteristic humor, and once again Jacob puzzled over his theory – that Price had retained the attorney's legal services for Jacob to ensure that Price and Laura would not win sole custody of Max.

'Prepare your son,' Zabriski said. 'We'll expect him here on Monday morning.' He gave Miss Finch a glance. 'Nine o'clock?'

She glanced in her appointment book. 'Nine,' she confirmed.

The attorney straightened. 'If the boy's memory corroborates yours, hopefully we can get this settled out of court.'

Jacob got to his feet. 'Then what?'

'Best case?' Zabriski shrugged his slight shoulders. 'No time, no probation. In your divorce settlement, shared support, shared custody.'

'What are my chances?'

Zabriski went through his office door. 'I'll tell you Monday, after I talk to your son.'

CHAPTER EIGHTEEN

A squeal jerked Terrence Gideon upright. Heart pounding, he found his leg wedged between a refrigerator and stove, and realized he'd been sleeping – and the truck had just stopped. Hearing the cab door shut, he stayed down, expecting the driver to come around the back. But after a minute or so, when no one appeared, he took a chance and raised himself up behind the appliances to peek out.

The truck was parked in a small lot on the side of the highway. Traffic roared past. A wooden sign propped in the corner of the lot read EAT HERE. Then Gideon could smell the food, a rich amalgam of greasy chicken, ribs, and fried onions. His stomach made a sound like a pump, and he crawled over the top of two gas stoves and climbed down, staying close to the truck to make sure that no one saw him. When he peeked around the side, he saw the small stucco building, with people waiting at the windows, maybe twenty, in three lines. Once again, Gideon's stomach groaned. He had enough money on him – eighty dollars or more – but then he saw something more urgent than food: a public telephone right beside him, in fact, hidden from the snack bar by the truck.

He fished in his pockets for change, then called Florida Directory Assistance for the number of the Monroe County District Court. Dropping more money in the telephone, he navigated through the automated menu until he was connected to the Probation Office. Finally a woman answered.

'Thank you, I need to speak with Probation Officer B.J. Landry,' Gideon said.

'Officer Landry is off for the weekend and won't be in his office again until Monday,' the woman replied curtly.

'Would you please contact him for me?' Gideon said, doing his best to sound official. 'This is quite urgent.'

'May I tell him what it concerns?'

'Well . . . It's in reference to an escaped convict from Alligator Alley Correctional Institute.'

'The man needs to revise his strategy,' a voice said. Gideon spun around to see a black man standing at the back of the truck, holding a paper bag. The man wore a white jumpsuit with some kind of logo emblazoned on the breast. Gideon guessed he was the driver of the truck. At least, he hoped so.

'Just tell Officer Landry an innocent woman is going to be murdered unless he calls me back in the next two minutes.'

The driver scowled deeply.

'How can he reach you?' the woman asked, suddenly paying attention.

Gideon turned his back on the driver and told her the number printed on the pay phone, then hung up. He turned to the driver, who said, 'I got you a couple of cheeseburgers and a coffee, in case you're hungry.'

'Me?'

'I just gave you a ride a hundred miles,' the driver said, reaching into the bag and handing him a sandwich. 'Might as well buy you lunch.'

Gideon studied the guy.

'You snore like a grizzly bear, in case no one ever told you.'

Gideon reached for his wallet. 'What do I owe you?'

'Five,' said the man. 'You want, I'm headed up to Lake City, north of Gainesville. I'll bring you that far.'

Gideon handed him the money.

'But I don't have all day,' the driver said.

'I have to wait for this call,' Gideon told him again. 'I appreciate your kindness. But you don't owe me. Go ahead on your way.'

'I can wait a couple of minutes,' the driver said, and the telephone rang.

Gideon picked up instantly, but hesitated before he spoke.

'How you want to go about this?' B.J. Landry said.

Gideon felt a warm wave of relief at the sound of a familiar voice. 'I trusted the wrong man,' he began.

'You want me to come get you?'

'What for?'

'You want to come in, right?'

'Not yet. I need to talk to my wife.'

'Why don't you call her on the phone?'

Neither man spoke for a few seconds, both of them knowing that Gideon's home phone would be tapped. B.J. Landry had been Gideon's probation officer twenty years earlier. Even though Landry was a white man, and kind of a redneck to boot, he had taken an interest in

Gideon, had even cut him a break once when he spotted the parolee carrying a six-pack of beer out of a Piggly Wiggly – which was breaking the rules and could've landed Gideon back in prison for another few months. But Landry had looked the other way. In fact, he was the one who got Gideon his job at the prison library.

'Officer Landry, I called you because I had faith you'd believe me.'

The driver let out a sputtering laugh. Gideon turned away from him.

'Let me put it this way,' Landry said. 'I wasn't there. But you're damn sure gonna make the situation worse by running.'

'I can't turn myself in yet,' Gideon told him. 'The prisoner who escaped, a Colombian Indian by the name of Sereno? I think he's looking to have revenge on his wife. If she doesn't know he's on the loose, somebody'd better warn her.'

'I can pass the word to the police,' Landry said. 'But from what I gather, they pretty much figure he's right there with you.'

'He's not. I'm tracking him.'

'Whereabouts?'

'I have no idea,' Gideon said. 'But I need you to keep the police from killing this man. He's the only one alive who knows I'm innocent.'

'Hoss, you know as well as I do, if this escaped Colombian was involved with the drug trade, and he's looking to harm his wife, plus he blew up an officer of the law, there ain't a whole lot anyone can do to guarantee his safety. Not to mention, ain't a whole lot of jurors likely to believe his testimony about your innocence.'

Gideon looked around. Then he said, 'Mr Landry, I'd like to ask you a favor.'

'You did already.'

'I've got to get word to my family, but I'm afraid my phone is tapped.'

'Good chance.'

'You can say no if you want, but I'd appreciate it very much if you'd go see my wife Bethany. She'd be at home today, being the weekend.'

'I was about to go fishing, as a matter of fact.'

'I'd like you to pick her up and bring her to your house,' Gideon said. 'If you'd give me your number, I'll call there tonight, between nine and ten.'

'Sure that's all you need?' Landry had a way of talking that you couldn't tell, even if you were looking in his eye, if he was serious. After a second or two, he added, 'You know, if you really are innocent and you get yourself a good lawyer, you'll probably make out all right.'

'You don't believe that,' Gideon told him. 'In Florida?'

Landry cleared his throat, as if he might have been thinking up a reply.

'The man who set the whole thing up, Sergeant Biff Bullens, he told me it was a sting operation, sanctioned by Warden Shivers and the DEA,' Gideon said. 'Then he went and murdered the other prisoner in cold blood. He tried to kill me, but I ran.'

'He got blown up himself, this Bullens,' Landry came back. 'Right now you and the Colombian look pretty doggone good. You see where I'm comin from?'

'Bullens killed that prisoner,' Gideon said. 'And neither Sereno nor myself was responsible for killing Biff Bullens.'

'I know that,' Landry said.

'Excuse me?'

'I said I know you didn't kill Bullens,' Landry repeated. 'Because Bullens ain't dead.'

Gideon scowled, stunned. 'Not dead—?'

'Alive and laid up in a hospital bed, talkin up a storm, all about you and the Colombian.'

Gideon looked back, saw the truck driver pretending to tighten a noose around his neck. 'Saying what, exactly?'

'Oh, this and that, how the two prisoners took you and him hostage, and you and the Colombian murdered the other prisoner and tried to blow him up. Which was when he figured out that it was you who masterminded the whole thing.'

'Mr Landry, you know me better than that,' Gideon said.

'Twenty years ago I mighta known you,' Landry said, 'some.'

'I haven't changed.'

A few seconds passed. As Gideon tried to interpret the silence, Landry suddenly recited a phone number. 'Got that?'

Gideon repeated it. The truck driver wrote it in his receipt book.

Landry said, 'I'll have her there at nine.'

'I appreciate it,' Gideon said, but the man had already hung up.

Sitting on the edge of his hospital bed, Biff Bullens patted down his cowlick with his good hand, while an attractive, red-headed nurse pulled his shirt over his shoulder. His broken arm hung by his chest in a dark blue sling. She was telling him he needed to rest for another couple of days, as far as he could make out, while the warden, Dale Shivers, stood at the foot of the bed, probably agreeing with her. Mostly Bullens heard the whistling in his ears. The nurse said something else, which came across as a murmur.

'Lean down closer, sweetheart,' Bullens said. 'I need to read your lips.' Christ, he could barely hear himself.

The warden came closer, standing over him. In fact, Shivers never sat down, which he considered his management style. He had brought in a cellophane-wrapped basket of fruit – big spender – then stood there yammering about god-knows-what, him and his blue alligator cowboy boots. He was ten years younger than Bullens and insisted his officers call him Dale outside the company of prisoners. While Bullens turned the tiny dial on his hearing aid, Shivers' voice suddenly cut through the whistling like a bullhorn.

'Medical leave, full benefits, two weeks,' that's what Bullens heard. Then, 'Agent Connolly something something something . . . talk to you.'

'Talk talk,' Bullens returned. 'They got their pictures, they got their prints, they got their DNA.' He slid off the bed painfully and stepped into his black suede loafers. 'What I'd like to know is, when the fuck are they gonna get results?' He turned to the nurse and patted his cowlick again. 'Pardon my language, I've been through considerable trauma.' Then back to Shivers. 'Man gets blown up, wants to take a little R and R, FBI don't like it, they can kiss my charcoal-broiled ass, sorry again, Ma'am.'

He walked stiffly to the closet and got his overnight bag. When he turned around, the warden was right there, looking worried.

'Biff, they'll want to know where you're gonna be. At all times.'

'Last I knew, I was the victim.'

Shivers turned to the nurse and smiled. 'Could we have a little privacy, please?'

'Of course,' she said, and gave him a pointed look, meaning she hoped he would talk the patient into staying in bed. Then she went out into the corridor.

Shivers closed the door behind her, then came close to Bullens and pointed to his hearing aid, aiming a thumb to the ceiling. Bullens turned the volume up. Shivers put his hand on his shoulder and leaned in close. Also part of his style. Touchy-feely.

'I don't have to tell you, this is bad, Biff.'

Bullens jerked back. 'Goddamn fuckin whistle.' When he stopped poking at his hearing aid, the warden was still there, just as close.

'Very, very bad,' he mouthed.

'No, Dale, you don't have to tell me,' Bullens said, 'but you did.' He picked up his bag and hobbled to the door.

'Help yourself to the fruit,' he said, leaving it behind.

CHAPTER NINETEEN

W hen Jacob let himself in the flower shop, the first thing he heard was his father's voice. He stopped with a chill . . . then realized that the message machine was on. He picked up the phone, said hello.

'Yes, Jake, regarding the earlier message I left for you. Afraid it's rather urgent you give them an answer.'

'I'm sorry. What's urgent?'

'I know it's short notice,' his father said, 'but the headmaster needs a decision by tomorrow morning.'

'About?'

'You didn't get my message?'

'I've been busy,' Jacob said. Actually, July hadn't told him.

'Glad I tried back, then. I called in a favor for you, Jake. Dunston Academy needs a writing teacher for their summer program. The woman who was scheduled to teach went off to Rome.'

'Dunston?'

'New Hampshire,' his father said. 'A forty minutes' commute for you. It's not a great deal of money, somewhere around four thousand for eight weeks. But they'll give you breakfast and lunch, and you can be home by four. You'd be responsible for a couple of remedial English classes and three creative writing groups. The position is yours if you want it, Jake. Who knows? They may decide to keep you on for the school year.'

Jacob tried to shuffle the information through his overloaded mind: his father, offering to help him . . . Maybe this wasn't the first time either. Maybe, despite his father's earlier denial, Jacob's mysterious benefactor wasn't Price Ashworth after all, paying Jacob's legal bills to ensure that he didn't get custody of Max. Maybe . . . 'When would it start?'

'Immediately,' his father said. 'Of course, there's a recreation program that's open to children of resident faculty, nothing extravagant, tennis, baseball, basketball, and such. And your son could enroll in the classes. I'm sure he'd make friends.'

Of course, if it was his father who had paid his legal bills, he would have done so anonymously, knowing that Jacob would have refused his help. Yes, and who would Professor Winter have called upon to make the payments for him, but his former prize student, Alix Callahan?

'I've got to leave for work in a few minutes,' Jacob said. 'How late can I get back to you?'

'Whenever suits you, Jake. If you want to call at four in the morning, that's perfectly fine.'

'I'll call you,' Jacob said, intending to hang up. But . . . 'I wanted to ask you something – about Alix Callahan.'

'Uh-huh?'

Because if it was indeed his father, and not Price Ashworth, who had enlisted Alix to pay Jacob's legal bills . . . then what was Alix's real connection to Price? He knew their relationship had been more than simple doctor-patient – or why, in all their conversations, hadn't she mentioned at least that she knew the man he had clubbed with his radio? Because he'd been blackmailing her, Jacob was still convinced – but blackmailing her how? What had he learned from her? And what had he wanted from her?

'You wanted to ask—?' his father said.

'Just . . . How well you knew her,' Jacob asked. Hearing a car out front, he looked out to the street and saw July pulling into the driveway.

'In an academic sense, quite well, in fact. Are you talking about her personal life?'

'That's right.' Jacob lowered his voice as he kept an eye on July, walking around to the back of the Volvo.

'Alix was rather secretive, I'm afraid.'

He watched July pull a grocery bag out of the wagon, then close the liftgate.

'Do you have any idea what she might've been afraid of?' Jacob asked.

'Alix afraid?' His father made a deliberative sound. 'She always struck me as particularly fearless.'

As July came up the fieldstone walk, Jacob retreated toward the garden door. 'What about the Kogi Indians?'

'I'm sorry, Jake, what are you asking?'

'Would she have reason to fear the Kogis?'

'I can't imagine why.'

He heard the key in the lock, and he walked around his temporary

184

wood shop and out to the garden. 'Are they violent people?'

'Not in the least. Good God, why?'

Jacob heard the door open. 'What about the shamans?' he said quietly, walking quickly for the cover of green.

'Violent?' The old man hesitated . . . and Jacob peeked between a fan of succulent leaves and saw July walking through the shop toward the stairs.

'I'm sorry, something came up, I'll get back to you,' Jacob said. He hung up, then listened to her footsteps on the iron stairs. Before she reached the top, and the glassed-in walls, he hurried back into the shop and replaced the phone on its cradle, then walked up the stairs trying to assemble his thoughts. He found July in the kitchen, putting groceries in the refrigerator.

'I didn't hear you come in,' he said. 'I was out in the garden.' He went into the bedroom, where he found a clean white shirt in the bureau. 'I start work today at the Tavern,' he called, pulling the shirt over his head. 'Don't wait up for me, I'm going to be late.'

He could hear July turning the faucet on and off, on and off, then he heard a skillet fall into the sink. He stepped into a fresh pair of khakis, then went into the bathroom and brushed his teeth. 'Squeaky doesn't usually leave till two or three,' he said, returning to the kitchen . . . but she wasn't there. He went to the open glass doors, where he looked down and saw her pushing a wheelbarrow into her rainforest.

'July?'

She kept walking.

Buttoning his shirt, he went down the stairs and out to the garden. He had planned to ask her what she knew about Alix's relationship with Evangeline, but he knew that would have to wait for a quieter time. Likewise, he decided not to mention the teaching job until he made a decision. As he started along the main path, watching around his moccasins for yellow frogs, he heard a quick rustle of leaves, and she came pushing the wheelbarrow through the greenery. Wearing a sleeveless T-shirt, her arms shone with perspiration. 'I wasn't sure if you heard me.' He reached for her but she tensed at his touch, muscling past him with the load, a single small plant, a shovel and pitchfork.

'July, is something wrong?'

She went a few more steps, then stopped at a small clearing, where she'd left the garden hose. 'Nothing's wrong,' she answered, taking the pitchfork in her hands. 'You're going to the bar, and you don't want me to wait up.' She stuck the pitchfork into the ground, stepped on it with her bare foot, and turned over a hunk of dark, moist soil. 'If I wanted to see someone, that's what I would do.'

'Laura's not going to be there – she hates the place,' he said, while July filled the hole with water. 'I told you, I took the job because I need the money.'

July set the seedling in. 'And I told you, I have money,' she said patiently, as she shoved dirt back in the hole with her hands, covering the roots.

'But I need my money,' he said, then felt foolish saying it, especially with the look she was giving him, perplexity turning to a smile. 'You need *your* money?' She stood up. Her knees were muddy, as were her hands and feet. 'Oh, Jacob, such an American,' she said, as she threaded her dirty hands under his arms, her eyes pooling with seduction. 'He needs *his* money.'

Laughing, he took hold of her arms. 'Come on, this is a clean shirt, and I'm already late,' he said, but she wouldn't release him. 'He wanted me in early so he could show me what to do.'

'I'm not letting you go,' she teased. 'You need to stay here and write your book.'

Still trying to pull away without getting mud on him, he joked, 'I don't think I'd get much writing done.'

'Jacob, I want you to *stay*.' She lost her smile. 'I'm very horny.'

He shook his head, refusing the tease. 'July . . . It's only a couple of nights a week.' As gently as he could, he pulled her arms out from his.

'Fine, go to your job,' she said, turning away from him. 'Anyway, I think she's been here.'

'Laura?'

'Not her,' she said, then took hold of the wheelbarrow and started walking away from him.

'Alix?' He stiffened, tempted to pursue her. But he didn't.

'I could smell her,' she said, as she was swallowed by the greenery.

Jacob left. Walked back through the shop and out the entrance door, then turned back to make sure it was locked. He wondered if July had been like this with Alix – or if it was Alix who had made her this way. Now recalling Alix's story about Patches, the porch dog, as he headed down the fieldstone walk toward his car – he kept it parked on the street, to give the impression of transience – he was struck with a sudden and most unwelcome thought: the mystery vehicle that had caused the accident on the bridge . . .

He walked around the GREEN GIRLS Volvo and ran his hand over its front quarter. Seeing no damage to the fender or bumper – not even a scratch – he chided himself for his wayward imagination. But he also couldn't help feeling a lift of relief, however short-lived.

When he glanced back to the house, there was July, standing behind the shop door, watching out the window.

Jacob got to the tavern a half hour before it opened, which meant he was a half hour late on his first day at work. He came in through the back door and said to Squeaky, 'Sorry, something came up.'

'They want you at the hospital,' Squeaky told him.

'What?'

'The little man—'

Jacob's heart stopped. 'What about him?'

Squeaky held up his hands. 'He's okay. He got into somethin, had his stomach pumped. He's fine.'

Max was asleep when Jacob walked into his room. He had his baseball cap on his head and an IV in his arm. The television was on. His glasses were on the bedside table. When Jacob turned the volume down, the brown eyes opened.

'Maxie, what happened?'

'Price saved my life,' the boy said.

Jacob picked up his glasses and gently slid them on Maxie's face.

'That's what Mom says, anyway. Then Price tells her I took drugs, which I didn't.' His eyes were glassy and a little bloodshot, but his speech seemed normal. 'Anyway, Mom grounded me for two weeks.'

Feeling a surge of weakness, which was probably relief, Jacob sat on the bed. 'What happened?'

'I got home from school. Did the usual.'

Jacob said, 'Computer games.'

'Next thing I know, I woke up here. They pumped out my stomach. Which is pretty cool.'

Jacob touched his face and felt more comforted by the warmth in his cheek. 'So, why do they think you took drugs?'

Another voice pitched in, 'Because it was a drug overdose.'

Jacob turned to see a nurse in the room with them, heavy-set, with blue-framed glasses and a satisfied sort of smile. 'Was it Ritalin?' he asked, certain that Price had finally persuaded Laura to start medicating Max.

'We're not sure what kind, but the contents of his stomach went to the lab for analysis.'

Jacob studied his son. He couldn't help thinking of his own mother, wondering if Max had tried to take his life.

'He's going to be fine,' the nurse said, then added, 'for now. The doctor wants to keep him overnight, just to make sure.' By the look she gave Max, she seemed to derive some pleasure in saying it.

'Thanks for taking care of him,' Jacob said. 'Could we have a few minutes?'

'He *is* supposed to be resting . . . but I'll give you a few minutes,' she allowed. 'Unfortunately, the time to talk about drugs is *before* they get the temptation.' Then she went out.

'I didn't,' Max said, as soon as the door shut.

Jacob leaned in closer to his son. 'I know this is upsetting, what's going on between Mom and me,' he said. 'But you wouldn't try to hurt yourself, would you?'

Max wrinkled his face. 'I'm not stupid, you know.'

'I know. Price didn't give you any pills to take, did he?'

Max shook his head no.

Jacob breathed a sigh. But he couldn't get it out of his head that some kids had given Max the pills to swallow – the same assholes who'd dared him to fly – maybe they told him it was candy, and Max was embarrassed to admit he fell for it.

'They said if it wasn't for Price, I might be dead,' Max said.

'Price found you?'

'Yeah. He called an ambulance.'

Jacob nodded. Well, good for Price. He reached for Max's cap and squeezed the visor, rounding it the way Max liked. 'Hey, that was some home run you hit.'

'I did what you told me,' Max said.

'How's that?' Jacob asked good-naturedly. 'I was telling you to take the pitch.'

'Head, not heart,' Max said. 'Remember?'

Jacob laughed. 'You used your head, all right.'

'Also, Price hypnotized me.'

'What?'

'Yeah, while I was hypnotized, I told him I wanted to hit one out of the park. So he told me to describe how it would be, and I did. Then he told me to visualize the same thing before I got up to bat. Cool, huh? I shellacked it.'

'Yeah,' Jacob said, but he was thinking about Alix Callahan again, and what she might have told Price under hypnosis—

Then he remembered: Zabriski was expecting to see Max on Monday. Wonderful timing.

'Maxie, something came up,' he said. 'Good news and bad news. Well, maybe not that bad.' How good could it be, asking your son to testify against his mother?

'I've got the same thing, basically,' Max said. 'Good news – bad news. You first.'

188

Jacob hesitated too, but started with the easy one. 'I had a job offer,' he said, 'teaching in New Hampshire for the rest of the summer. Which means you could go with me, you know, get away from the jerks. They've got baseball . . .'

Max didn't say anything.

'That was the good news,' Jacob told him, buying time.

'Huh.'

'Okay, what's your good news?'

'Not sure it's that good, really,' Max said. 'Just, Price got me into Belnap. I go the end of August.'

The casual way Maxie said the words, it felt to Jacob as though a vacuum had sucked up his heart. Two things bothered him, although he wouldn't be able to articulate either until later. One, Max sounded like he didn't mind leaving him. Two, he had called Price by name again, as if they'd become buddies.

Jacob felt the chill continue washing through him. 'Was someone planning to tell me?'

'We tried,' Max said. 'Mom called you. Then I called a buncha times. The lady that answered said you'd call me back. I figured you were busy writing.'

'She's not great with messages,' Jacob said, and he thought of Zabriski again. 'Maxie, I had something else to talk to you about.'

'Yeah?'

Hey, champ, you remember that day we came back from the Red Sox game . . . Without Max's testimony, Jacob knew he didn't stand a chance of winning his assault case – which meant he'd probably end up losing custody of Max. He felt his thoughts sinking under the weight of confusion. He rubbed Max's shoulder. 'Actually, I'm not sure I'm going to be taking that teaching job,' he told him, struggling to think of anything else to say, while he watched his last chance fade. 'Did you say you had *bad* news?'

'Well,' Max said, 'actually, I think it was the grape soda.'

Jacob scowled.

'Ah,' Max said, as though disgusted with himself. 'It was in the refrigerator. I snuck some.'

Jacob said, 'Why was there grape soda in the refrigerator?' They never kept anything sugary in the house – no soda, cookies, candy . . . unless Price had left it. But Price was the one who'd told them to keep sugar away from Max.

'I drank it,' Max said. 'Half of it, actually. It sucked big-time. Then I filled the bottle with water and put some food coloring in, so Mom wouldn't know.'

189

'Yeah, but sugar wouldn't . . .' Jacob's heart walloped. 'Maxie,' he said, his brain screaming. 'Did you tell Mom about the soda?'

Max shrugged. 'Price already got her thinking I took drugs. Why make it worse?'

Jacob picked up the telephone on the bedside table and dialed. When Laura answered, he said, 'Look in the refrigerator.'

'Are you at the hospital?' she asked.

'Laura, is there a bottle of grape soda in the refrigerator?'

'Why would there be?' She stopped for a second, then added, 'Wait a minute. Yes.'

Because someone tried to poison him. Jacob did not say that aloud.

'Don't dump it,' he told her. 'Wait there.'

'You're right about your old friend,' he said, when Evangeline came to the phone.

'Excuse me?'

'Alix Callahan isn't dead,' he said. 'She just tried to poison my son.'

Evangeline didn't respond.

'My boy is in the hospital,' Jacob told her. 'Alix Callahan broke into his mother's house and put a bottle of grape soda in the refrigerator. It was spiked with something.'

'Are you at the house now?' Evangeline asked.

'I'm at the hospital, in the lobby,' he said. 'Max is okay. But I don't want him to know what happened. I don't want him frightened.'

'What makes you think Alix Callahan had anything to do with this?'

'I know she did,' he said. Furthermore, he suspected that the reason wasn't because he was sleeping with July – but because he'd been trying to find out the reason Alix was hiding.

'Have you called the police?' Evangeline asked.

'I'm calling you,' he said, and hung up. Then he called July. He was almost surprised to hear her answer.

'She poisoned Max,' he said.

July didn't speak at first, and he regretted the way he must have frightened her. 'Is he okay?'

'He's fine.'

'What happened?'

'I'll tell you about it later. Do you have a way of padlocking the door?' Even as he said it, he realized how easy it would be for anyone to smash their way in through the greenhouse.

'No, but I have a knife,' July said. 'And I'm a light sleeper.'

'Do you want me to come home?' *Home.* The word came out of his mouth unplanned. But there it was. And she'd heard it too.

190

'Oh, Jacob,' she said, sounding apologetic. 'I don't mind if you work at the bar. I just wanted to be with you.'

'I know.'

'I'm not afraid of Alix,' she said. 'I can lock the bedroom door, if it makes you feel better. Promise you'll be home right after work?'

'I promise,' he said, but he suddenly had a different plan.

She said, 'I'll be waiting for you.'

CHAPTER TWENTY

———

'How is he?' Squeaky said, when Jacob returned to the Speedway. 'He'll be fine,' Jacob said.

'What the hell was he thinking?'

There were a dozen people in the place, mostly men, standing at the right side of the bar drinking beer.

'He'll be all right.' Jacob did not want to tell him anything more – the grape soda, his phone call to Evangeline, or the fact that Max would be going to school in California.

'Take care of the setups,' Squeaky replied, tossing him an apron.

'Okay, I don't know what setups are.'

'Knives, forks, and spoons rolled up in napkins. Jeff Dakota's racing in Loudon this weekend. This place'll be packed if he stops in.'

Jacob tied his apron in back. 'I need to use the phone first.'

Jacob didn't wait for permission, but walked into the office, aware that Squeaky's eyes followed him all the way. He shut the door when he was inside, then sat at Squeaky's desk and started to dial the number his father had given him, before he knew what he was going to say. The door opened.

'So the kid screwed up, what the hell you expect, with all this bullshit?' Squeaky said, standing there.

'Give me a minute, would you?' Jacob asked.

'You, yourself, I bet, when you were his age, with the wacky tobaccy. Don't tell me different.'

'One minute. I need to make the call.'

Squeaky pulled the door shut. Jacob finished dialing, while he stared at the photo of Squeaky's Impala on the wall. It was from the same race that was depicted on the poster behind the bar, both shots taken from newspapers. In this one, the Impala was lying on its roof, its front end mangled. BRISTOL, the dateline read. It had been Squeaky's last race. The article, if there had been one, did not accompany the photo.

The ringing stopped abruptly. Then a pause. 'Please leave your message with the correct date and time,' said his father's machine, ever so distinctly.

'I'll be here till two,' Jacob said, checking the Penzoil clock on Squeaky's desk. He recited the Tavern's phone number, then hung up.

As it turned out, Jeff Dakota did come into the Speedway Tavern after his race, along with his entourage of fans, his pit crew, and old friends from town. By eleven o'clock, Jacob had poured a reservoir of beer, a pint at a time, and mixed countless whiskey-gingers and rum-cokes. He recognized some of the local guys, by face if not name. Many of them worked at local garages or auto parts stores, most were old gearheads, like Squeaky. Everyone showed up whenever Jeff Dakota was in town, especially if he did well – and tonight, apparently, he'd come in second.

At one point Squeaky took Jacob aside. 'Look at this kid,' he said, with a fire in his eye. 'They're all talking to him, kissin his butt, and all he's thinking about is those last two laps.'

And all Jacob was thinking about was where he was going when he left the bar: to find out exactly what it was that Alix Callahan told Price Ashworth.

CHAPTER TWENTY ONE

As the '65 Stingray swung through the pillars of River View Estates, the insurance salesman turned off his CD player and smiled. He was young and single, and tonight he was celebrating his third promotion of the year – and a bonus check for fifty thou, along with an equal amount in company shares. He'd decided on his way home that he'd pay off the mortgage.

He had borrowed a little under three hundred thousand for the house six months ago, a 3,000 square-foot ranch in the most expensive part of Deltaville, with a spectacular view of the river and bridge, and out beyond, the wide Georgia coast. The way his portfolio was climbing, he could pay off the mortgage and still be a millionaire before his thirtieth birthday.

At the cul de sac, he hit his garage door opener, then turned into his driveway. The garage door rose up. He drove inside and hit the button. As the door slid down again he did not see the shadow that followed behind the car. A neighbor might have gotten a glimpse, if they were watching at that precise second – but they would've only thought a dog had gotten in.

The insurance salesman stepped out of the car, briefcase in one hand, a bottle of Dom Perignon in the other, a twenty-dollar Cohiba stuck in his teeth. His only question was who to share the champagne with. Between Angela, Roxie and Katie-Lou, it was a tossup. Angela was the girl he'd marry someday, when he was ready, well-mannered and practical – and he'd told her that – but he was not ready yet, definitely not ready. Roxie, he liked to party with; she was a wild sex partner as long as she didn't get too drunk. Katie-Lou wasn't as attractive or smart, but she was the most politically compatible, which meant she stood up for the white race – and she sported a swastika tattoo on her butt, which never failed to stir the insurance man's kinky side.

194

He stepped out of the Stingray, a little unbalanced from the drinks he'd had with the company president, but he remembered to disarm the alarm system before he opened the door into the house. Setting his briefcase on the floor he turned on the foyer lights. Looked at his Rolex. Nine thirty. Hundred-sixty-thousand-dollar day.

He decided on Katie-Lou.

Stripping off his necktie, he unbuttoned his shirt as he brought the bottle of champagne to the refrigerator, slid it in on the bottom shelf, then brought out a block of Muenster cheese. He set his cigar on the granite-topped island, then turned and grabbed a steak knife from the dishwasher. As he sliced into the cheese, he felt a sharp sting on the back of his neck, and swiped at it, expecting to find a squashed mosquito in his fingers. But what he pulled out of his skin was some kind of long, slender splinter. When he turned around, he swallowed his cigar smoke.

On the other side of the island from him stood a very short man with long black hair and sunglasses, wearing an orange T-shirt that said HIALEAH SAND AND GRAVEL, and holding a Bic pen to his mouth.

The insurance salesman dropped the cheese and raised the knife, then moved to his right.

The Indian went the opposite way, keeping the island between them.

The insurance salesman changed direction. So did Sereno.

They did this two more times, until the insurance salesman went down.

Then Sereno came around the island and pulled the man away from the refrigerator, dropping him flat on the floor. Taking the knife out of his hand, he unbuttoned the man's shirt, then located his heart with his free hand, felt the faint beat. The insurance man stared up helplessly as the Indian leaned over him with the knife. Then he retrieved the Muenster from the floor and sliced off a sizeable chunk.

His coca had enabled Sereno to go for days without food or sleep, but he could no longer deny his hollow stomach. Sitting in front of the open refrigerator, Sereno ate leftover pizza and barbecued chicken legs and all the cheese he could find. He sucked ketchup from a squeeze bottle, drank orange juice from the carton, and when the orange juice was gone, he took the bottle of champagne into the bathroom, where he ran hot water into a deep Jacuzzi tub and had a long soak.

When the flame burned his finger, Gideon dropped the match. Between his bifocals and the complications of the pay phone, he was surprised when he heard the connection finally made, even more surprised when he heard B.J. Landry answer. Gideon started to talk but was cut off by a recorded voice asking if Landry would accept a collect call from a Mr Goodman.

Landry said, 'You bet.'

'Thank you very much,' Gideon said. 'May I speak with Mrs Goodman, please?'

'Before I put her on, I wanted to let you know, I checked on the woman you were concerned about – this Colombian's wife. The court has no record of her. Neither does Criminal Justice or the Florida State Police. Which might mean she's a figment of someone's imagination. Or it might mean that she's part of a state or federal witness security program. Either way, she's safe.'

'How safe?'

'Safe enough so you don't need to worry about her. Ain't nobody in the world knows where she's at.'

'I see.'

'Also, I checked your story,' Landry went on. 'Warden Shivers never heard about a sting operation. DEA has no knowledge, either.'

'I figured that,' Gideon said. 'May I speak to my wife now?'

'Hold on.'

Gideon turned and squinted out across the water behind him, the Suwannee River. The telephone was attached to the side of a gas station that had closed at six. Gideon turned back to the road, watching for police. Then he heard Bethany say his name. Overcome at first, Gideon's voice caught in his throat.

'Terrence?'

'It's me.'

'Oh Lord, are you okay?'

'Yeah, baby, I'm okay,' he said. Truth? He was starving, mosquito-massacred, exhausted, footsore, knee-sore, back-sore, and wallowing in discouragement. 'Now, you know I didn't do the things I'm accused of.'

'I know that,' she said, and the tears flooded down Gideon's cheeks. He pulled off his bifocals and the night disappeared in a blur.

'You tell me where you are, and I'll come get you,' Bethany told him.

'Baby, I love you so much,' he said, 'but I don't think I can come in, not just yet.'

'Sugar, why?'

'I've got to find a man.'

'Who?'

'This man is my only witness,' he explained. 'If the police find him before I do, they're sure to kill him. Then there's nothing to stop them from killing me.'

'Terrence Gideon, where is your faith?'

'Baby, please don't use my name over the wire,' he implored. 'You know my faith is strong. Now I've thought hard about this, and I've got to trust my own instincts. I just need you to bring me some provisions.'

'Mr Landry has given me a list of good lawyers who can defend you.'

'I trusted the wrong man,' he told her. 'I thought I was making an arrest, a drug arrest, but it was a setup. The sergeant tried to kill me, tried to kill us all. I'm innocent.'

'Of course you are.'

He stopped for a second, to replay the tone of her voice. 'Baby, don't you know,' he said, 'if I thought you believed one word of what they're saying about me, I'd lay down and die, don't you know that?'

A moment of silence followed, then Bethany said, 'What kind of provisions?'

'Deodorant,' he said. 'Soap and a towel. Toothbrush. Some good shirts and pants. Long sleeves, long pants. My old prescription sunglasses and bathing trunks.'

'Terrence, you sound like you're going on vacation.'

'And all the money you can get.'

Bethany got quiet again.

'You can't use your credit union, they'll know it's for me. Go borrow from your sister.'

'Ida May?'

'Listen to me,' he told her. 'A white prison guard lies in the hospital, almost blown to bits. The chief suspects are a Colombian Indian and a black man with priors.'

'Now, you know this is not a black and white issue,' she told him.

'All right, attempted murder of an officer of the law,' he said, getting short with her. 'Drugs were involved. The way it looks, the perpetrators are a junior officer who was once incarcerated for drugs, and an escaped prisoner who was doing time for murder, drug trafficking, and mutilating his wife. Baby, in their eyes we're both guilty five times over – and they can't wait to bury us.'

Bethany sighed again.

'The man I'm after, the Colombian?' Gideon said. 'I gave him a Miranda card when I arrested him – that's proof that I was acting properly. I also did him a favor. If I can find him before the police do, I think he'll stand up for me.'

'These lawyers,' she said. 'Mr Landry said that they'd probably defend you pro bono.'

'Baby, I'd never get to court. Don't you understand, they're gonna kill me unless I find my witness.'

Neither of them spoke as a loud delivery truck rumbled past. Then Bethany's voice, barely audible, came back to him. 'Where are you?'

Gideon looked out at the river again. 'Can you get up to Jacksonville tomorrow?'

'That's a long drive for my tired old car. If I had the Jeep—'

'I don't want you using your car anyway. Borrow your sister's car.'

'Oh, baby.'

'Tell Miss Ida you need her car because you're cooperating with the police,' Gideon said. 'Tell her you're going to help get me apprehended.'

Bethany laughed softly. 'I guess then I'd get her car – and her money.'

'Listen, now, there's two Holiday Inns in Jacksonville—'

'Is that where you are?'

'No, baby, I'm somewhere else. Don't let on to Mr Landry. Just listen. There's two Holiday Inns, one on the beach and one by the airport. You come to the one on the beach. Be there at twelve noon, and make sure no one follows you. Tell your sister it might take a day or two. If the coast is clear, we'll maybe rent us a room. Okay?'

He listened to her breathing.

'Would you wear your red dress, please?'

'I will,' she promised, and he could almost feel her warm, solid body in his arms.

'Baby, I love you,' he said, and he hung up before she could talk him out of it.

CHAPTER TWENTY TWO

Jacob's father did not return his phone call until almost midnight, sometime after Jeff Dakota left, taking most of the racing fans with him. Squeaky answered the phone behind the bar. Jacob knew by the roll of his eyes who was calling.

'I'll take it in your office,' he said, walking out from behind the bar.

'Hello, Jacob!' his father said when Jacob picked up. Not hard to tell he had spent the night drinking. 'You've come to a decision then.'

'You know, I'm working on this novel,' Jacob began.

'Wonderful!'

'Which means, I can either take the job and give up my writing,' Jacob said, 'or finish the novel.'

His father grew quieter. 'And you're leaning toward the latter.'

'That's right.'

'I see.' In the spell of silence that followed, Jacob realized that the television had gone off in the bar. 'Jacob, earlier you asked about the Kogi shamans, whether they are violent.'

'Uh-huh?' Jacob faced away from the door, not wanting to be overheard.

'I've given some thought to the matter. In a physical sense, I would have to say no, because I don't believe violence, as we know it, even exists as a concept among Kogis. In the metaphysical, however – and here I still wouldn't use the word "violence" – but you must realize that the shaman's duty is to protect his people and their world from evil, in all its forms.'

'I don't have much time,' Jacob said, fearing a lecture.

'The condensed version, then.' His father paused again. 'A Kogi shaman is chosen at birth by the reigning village shaman. He is taken away from his parents as an infant, then raised by the shaman and his wife for the next eighteen years, in total darkness.'

'In darkness – how?'

199

'He's kept in a cave or a hut with no windows,' his father explained. 'They take him outside at night, but only when there is no moon.'

'For eighteen years?'

'Give or take. You see, he must learn to use his vision.'

'Vision. Does he take yagé?'

'From the earliest age,' his father replied. 'It's his mother's milk. Before he can assume the position of shaman, he must learn to leave his body and fly over the forest and mountains among the spirits.'

'Fly, you mean, like in hallucinations—?'

'Hey' – the office door opened. Turning to see Squeaky looking in, Jacob covered the phone.

'Just tell him you'll take the job.'

'I'll be out in a minute,' Jacob said, then got back on with his father. 'I need to go.'

His father paused. 'You're sure I can't talk you into the teaching position, then.'

'No, but I appreciate the referral,' Jacob told him. 'Also, I want you to know that I'll pay you back for your help with my legal affairs.'

He heard his father say something else, perhaps another denial, but the phone was already on its way to the cradle. The door opened again.

'If ignorance is bliss, you oughta be happy as a pig in shit,' Squeaky said. 'Now call him back and take that job.'

Jacob lowered his head. Took a breath. Then turned the chair to face Squeaky. 'How come you quit racing?'

'Don't start with me, I'm too frickin tired. Just pick up the phone.'

'Laura said you were good,' Jacob persisted. 'You were leading the pack at Winston, with two laps to go. What happened, did somebody die?'

Squeaky's brow folded into a mask of sarcasm. 'Yeah, somebody died.'

'Who died?'

'Nobody died, I had a kid to support – like you. And no job – like you. Call the old man.' The way Squeaky stared, his eyes seemed to shine. 'Anyway, what the hell you got to tell the world that's so frickin important you wanna throw away your family?'

'Writing is what I'm good at,' Jacob replied. 'It's what I do.'

'What you *do* is clean up my bar. That's what you *do*.' Squeaky swiped his hand across the top of his head. 'Let me put it another way: You get back on the phone and take that teaching job – or you ain't got this job.'

'You're firing me?'

'That's right, smart guy.'

Jacob pushed himself out of the chair, ready to walk out. But before he did, he tried again. 'She said you loved racing,' he said. 'You were one of the best—'

'Get it through your head. You . . . ain't . . . no . . . writer!'

Jacob met the old man's eyes, waiting him out.

Squeaky slammed the side of his fist into the door jamb. The calendar fell off the door.

'Because I lost my ring toe, okay?'

'What?'

'You heard me.' Squeaky snatched the calendar off the floor and tossed it on his desk.

'What's a ring toe?'

A dangerous look of sobriety darkening him, Squeaky sat on the desk. 'Friggin half-wit,' he muttered, kicked off his penny loafer. 'And they want you teachin school?' He stripped off his white sock and said, 'Happy now?'

Jacob looked at the pink foot. It took a second to realize that Squeaky's third toe was gone at the knuckle.

'That?'

'Go fry your ass,' Squeaky told him, pulling his sock back on.

'That's the reason you quit . . . because you lost a toe?'

'A toe off my body, smartass. I had a wife and daughter to support.'

'And this is how I support my son,' Jacob said. 'By *not* quitting.'

Squeaky looked up, his blue eyes burning as he buried the foot back in the loafer on his way to the door. 'Here you go, smart guy,' he said, turning back to the door with a grandiose sweep of his arm. 'Here's the rest of your life.'

'Fine.' Jacob shone right back at him. 'Just don't tell me you quit racing over a toe.'

Squeaky's smile brightened. The two of them matched glares for another second or two, until Squeaky backed away from the door, and Jacob left, to find the woman who had tried to murder his son.

CHAPTER TWENTY THREE

The black Stingray slices through the night like a phantom, Sereno keeping the car on the old roads, his headlights off. Driving past sleeping farms and settlements of asphalt-sided houses, stalwart trailers, gas pumps and school buses, maybe some poor farmer's son is lying awake, coveting any other future but his own, when he hears the dark sound come out of the south and roar on past like a hot gust of wind.

Sitting on the briefcase he had taken, gleaming out over the steering wheel, a fat cigar glowing in his mouth, Sereno flew like an eagle, wide-winged and delirious. A white-tailed buck looks up from a magnolia blossom, amazed at the black thing going by. Skunk stops on the roadside, twisting back for a look. But fox is too startled to do anything but crouch and squint, water-eyed. It's not the car, or the speed, or the fact that the black thing has roared into their world with no warning. They're used to surprises. It's the eyes of the man soaring past. His eyes, and that cold, adrenalin-socked prayer that stops each one: They know he has seen them.

When a pair of headlights comes out of the distance toward him, riding in the center of the road, Sereno steers the Vette to the right, and his right wheels beat through the sand. The headlights blind him, then the pickup swerves past, with a screech of tires and an explosion of music. Sereno laughs when he sees the car's brake lights flashing in the mirror, knowing that the driver believes he has just passed a ghost.

A ways farther, the Indian stops in the road and walks around to the back of the car. With a rock he smashes his own brake lights. Then he takes the cigarette lighter out of his pocket and relights his cigar. He takes the smoke into his lungs. He looks to the north.

In his vision he has seen the girl many times, crouching in a garden beside moving water, salty, deep and brown, a wide strong river of ocean water and cargo ships. He has seen the tall arched bridge made of green steel. And a gumbo-limbo tree crowned with crimson bougainvillaea. Such a garden is warm and wet. Yet the river is cold. He cannot understand the combination. But this is where he is headed.

CHAPTER TWENTY FOUR

Though he was still asleep, the psychiatrist grabbed his phone before the second ring and was already reaching for his pen, expecting his answering service with an emergency. In fact it was an emergency, but not his answering service.

'I'm at your office,' Jacob said.

In a low-toned voice Price replied, 'Then I suggest you get the hell out of there, because I'm about to hang up and call the police.'

'Alix Callahan left a suicide note,' Jacob told him. It was a fabrication, but one he hoped would shake some information free.

'Alix Callahan was a pathological liar,' Price replied.

Jacob felt a glow of satisfaction, knowing not only that he was nicking at a nerve – but that Laura wasn't in bed with him. Otherwise, he never would have been talking like that. 'She was a patient for a couple of months, every Wednesday, her last session June twenty-two.'

'And?' Price's confidence returning, like he was fishing to see what Jacob had put together.

'She revealed something to you in therapy. You used it against her.'

'Doesn't her suicide note explain it?' Price, back on the offensive.

Jacob's brain stumbled for a second, then he returned. 'So far, I haven't mentioned any of this to the police,' he said, 'but someone tried to poison my son today, and I think you know who, and why. So go ahead and call 911. I'll wait for them.' He hung up.

Twenty minutes later he was sitting at Laura's desk when Price unlocked the front door. Behind him, two of the oak file drawers had been pried open.

'If you want to call the police,' Jacob said, sliding the phone to the front of the desk, 'I had to do some damage in here.'

Price walked across the room and opened his office door. Looking in, he sighed. 'Nice.'

204

Shards of colored glass covered the carpet beneath the hole where one of his stained-glass windows had been: Jacob's entry this time. The room was decorated with his diplomas and framed photos – Price Ashworth rappelling down a cliff face; Price Ashworth in his Taekwondo robe; Price Ashworth drumming at a men's Pow-Wow – probably to demonstrate to his confidence-shaken patients the range of his many skills.

'In the first place,' Price began, 'Maxie's drug episode – which your mind interprets as attempted murder – was nothing more than a confused and angry boy vying for the attention of his parents. Jacob, believe me, it's a commonplace occurrence among adolescents in the presence of divorce.'

'I see by your session notes,' Jacob said, ignoring him, 'that Alix Callahan started coming to you because she had a drinking problem.' He walked in and opened a manila folder on Price's desk, started flipping through the sheets of paper inside. ' "Excessive drinking," ' he read. ' "Problems with relationship." "Promiscuousness of partner." "Jealousy issues." Not a lot of detail, just enough to satisfy the insurance companies or a judge, in case you ever get subpoenaed. The details you keep somewhere else, right? Along with the tapes that Laura transcribes.'

Price turned to face Jacob, his face a study of stifled aggression. 'I don't doubt that's what you think—'

'Tell me what you had on Alix Callahan,' Jacob said, cutting him short. 'You know why she jumped off that bridge.'

'Jake, you have an extremely active imagination. Do you understand that? This business about someone poisoning Max, and now . . . I blackmailed Alix?' Price gave him an incredulous and sympathetic smile. 'I know you don't want to hear this,' he said, 'but until you start taking your medication again, your imagination is going to continue running your life. And ruining it.'

Jacob turned toward the window, the star-spattered sky outlining all the old gabled roofs. The night seemed to brighten with his mounting anger. He turned back to Price, who folded his arms in a professional way and said, 'You know, Maxie told us about your job offer, and how you turned it down in order to pursue your writing. Perhaps you should start giving some thought about how your imagination is impacting Maxie's life—'

Jacob turned, not that he intended violence, but with blinding speed Price's arm shot up, and he kicked a leg back, snapping into defensive posture.

Jacob gave him a studied look. 'Max told me how fast you were.'

'I have an overactive metabolic rate,' Price explained. Covering his embarrassment, he pulled his leather chair around for himself and motioned Jacob to the couch. They sat down.

'Jacob, Jacob, Jacob,' Price began. Then he breathed a sigh. 'Okay.' He leaned forward on his elbows, as if ready to confide a secret. 'The only thing I know that might be pertinent' – the chair came closer – 'one day when Alix came in to see me – technically, this happened before her session began, which is the reason I can divulge it to you – well, on this particular day Alix was pretty charged up, and she told me that her partner wanted her to find a man for a threesome. Which was an obvious invitation.'

Jacob studied him. 'You, with Alix and July?'

'In case you're unaware, Jake, sex with a patient is one of those little ethical details the profession frowns upon.'

'It wouldn't have been the first time.'

Price absorbed the dig, then fixed him with a wizened look. 'One does not need a degree in psychiatry to understand that pleasure was not Alix's primary motivation.'

Jacob said, 'I don't follow.'

'Genetic material, my friend.' Price was writing something in a pad – another prescription, Jacob assumed. 'She saw in me a potential seed donor.'

'Are you saying that's why Alix contacted me?'

Price looked up. 'You? No.' Rising smoothly from his chair, he went to the door, to usher Jacob out. 'I believe that she saw in you a kindred soul.'

Jacob got off the couch and went through to the reception area, where the men walked side by side to the door. 'Alix Callahan suffered from profound depression,' Price said, pushing open the entrance door with his back. 'You have demons of your own.' He offered Jacob the prescription. 'Please,' he said. 'Take your Haldol. Take the job. And see if you can't get your life back on track. For everyone's sake.'

Standing in the foyer, Jacob nodded agreeably, pretending to think it over. He was sure now: When hypnosis broke down Alix's inhibitions, she ended up telling Price Ashworth something she'd never intended him, nor anyone, to know. And Price had used it against her.

Jacob took the prescription from him. 'You know that look Laura gives you,' he said, 'makes you think she can see right through you?'

'Never noticed,' Price said – as if he didn't care, either.

Jacob smiled, then went outside and took three or four steps down the sidewalk before he turned back, caught Price watching.

'It's only a matter of time,' he said.

CHAPTER TWENTY FIVE

The night stirs up color in the east as the Stingray pushes through the marsh, Sereno looking out at the last fading stars hanging up above the mango-toned horizon. He turns onto a dirt road that leads him into cypress woods. Mosquitoes thicken as the trees press in, and the road all but disappears in the undergrowth. He burrows the Corvette into a rough-cut clearing, perhaps the place where the workers who built the road finally had surrendered to the insects and quit. When he gets out of the car, mosquitoes sing loudly around his head, but they don't land. He hears ocean waves breaking in the distance. He smells salt in the air. But he cannot detect even her slightest scent, and the dawn light filters down through the trees. Taking his briefcase out of the car, he looks for a soft place to sleep.

PART THREE

CHAPTER ONE

'*You're so stupid.*'
Alix Callahan again, her hands around her neck, strangling him—

No . . . Jacob snapped to consciousness.

'Shhhh,' July breathed heavily in his ear. She was on top of him, her body in feverish motion, trying to get him inside her.

Jacob's heart came to life. The sun sliced through the windows. July gasped . . . she stiffened . . . fingernails firing into the back of his arms, while he gripped her hard buttocks. She quivered in orgasm. Then she collapsed on him.

He listened to her breathing for a while, then he turned his head to look at her.

'Did I wake you up?' she said, and laughed in that musical way. Taking care not to hurt her, he tried to extricate himself, but she let out a moan and clung to him with her arms and legs.

'I'd love to stay in bed with you,' Jacob said, reaching off the mattress for his boxers.

July opened her eyes.

'My book,' he explained. 'I've got to start writing.'

She gazed at him, wounded, and he remembered the tension between them when he had left for work the day before.

'How was work last night?' she asked.

'I quit.'

July studied him. When he came back after leaving Price's office, he'd found the bedroom door unlocked and July lying under the blankets perfectly still. Alarmed, he'd dropped to his knees and placed his ear close to her face, to make sure she was breathing.

'Things didn't work out,' he explained.

She lay her face on his chest, her eyes softened sympathetically. He ran his fingers through her hair.

'What time?' she asked.

'Mm?'

'Did you quit.'

'I don't know. Late.' Was she fishing for his whereabouts after he left Squeaky's place? 'I went for a ride,' he explained.

'Jacob, get on top,' she said, and tried to pull him onto her. 'Where?'

'Are you checking up on me?' he teased, not wanting to tell her about breaking into Price Ashworth's office. Not wanting to have sex with her, either.

'I was very horny, you know,' she said, and she opened her legs around him.

'You told me,' he said. 'Really, I've got to write.'

She slapped his butt, a surprisingly hard shot. 'Hey—'

'You're not done here,' she told him. He could see the arousal the slap had brought her. His buttock stung. He resisted the urge to retaliate, knowing she'd consider it foreplay.

'Is it true,' he teased, 'that in the Kogi language, the word for "vagina" is also the word for "dawn?" '

'Why?' She gazed up at him as he opened the door to leave, her mouth opened in slack ecstasy, her fingers already engaged . . . 'Don't you want to feel the sun rise?'

The humming grew quieter as Henry Lamb climbed, high above the traffic now, safe inside the tunnel. Each oval hole he passed looked out left, upriver, and right, toward the ocean. He felt as though he were a virus invading the bones of some great steel god. When he looked up he saw the girl pushing herself out of a hole, the white skylight pouring in over her leg.

He pulled himself up to the same hole and saw her standing just below him inside a square crow's nest. The crow's nest was about five foot square, with a three-rail cage all around. Single-mindedly, Henry started to pull himself out, then looked down – and stopped.

They were near the top of the entire bridge structure, just beneath the highest point of the arch, high over the roadway. The fog was blowing away, and he could see plainly the tops of cars and trucks rushing north and south, oblivious to his presence, as though in another world.

But the girl. It was the first time he had seen her, all of her, and she was a more beautiful creature that he'd ever seen, indeed, ever imagined. Draped in a simple white dress that was smudged with rust and dirt and carbon black.

'What are you doing here?' he whispered.

'Same thing you are,' the girl said. She was smiling at him, and as she

spoke, a breeze came into the tunnel behind him, cooling the back of his neck. He took a deep, freeing breath, then reached out of the hole and grabbed the top of the crow's nest railing. Still smiling at him – when was the last time anyone had smiled at him? – amazingly, she began pulling her dress over her head. Pulling himself out into the open, naked air, he swung a foot down to a lower railing, then climbed into the crow's nest, where she gently took him in her arms.

'I just wrote a sex scene,' Jacob said, when his agent came to the phone.

'You mean the guy on the bridge?'

'That's right.'

Maury paused. 'He's alone, isn't he?'

'No, there's a girl.'

'*Two* characters?' Maury exclaimed. 'Jacob, you're teasing me.'

'She lives inside the bridge.'

Maury paused. 'Inside.'

'The beams are hollow,' Jacob told him.

'Why is a girl living inside the bridge?'

'Why?' Jacob paced away from the counter. 'Does she need a reason?'

'A girl living inside the beams of a bridge? Of course she needs a reason. Unless this is a fairy tale, we need to know who she is, where she came from . . .'

He paced back again. 'See, this is why I don't write plots.'

'Now, wait a minute,' Maury said. 'I'm intrigued. Do they fall in love?'

'Yes, they fall in love.'

'And she ends up saving him, talking him out of jumping.'

'I don't know,' Jacob said. 'Maybe he saves her.'

'Saves her. From what?'

'The bridge. I don't know, I haven't figured it out.'

'Jacob.'

'What?'

'I need to ask you again. Is everything okay?'

Jacob sighed.

'Because I've got to be honest with you,' the agent said. 'A guy with a flat tire, a woman living inside a bridge. Who the hell do you expect is going to publish this?'

CHAPTER TWO

To Gideon, it was like he'd stuck his feet in twin ovens, his prison shoes broiling in the hot sand. He had stripped down to his T-shirt and rolled up his borrowed pants to his knees, but he was still sweating like a hog. He had walked up the beach three miles or more, carrying his guard's uniform and borrowed sweatshirt in the trash bag, until he finally spotted the Holiday Inn. In five minutes Bethany would be there, and he was afraid.

Something was wrong, he could feel it all through his body. Like maybe his phone call with Bethany had been overheard; for that matter, B.J. Landry could have called the FBI himself. What if the local cops, who patrolled the beach in their three-wheelers and Expeditions, had been watching him? Well, he'd given them plenty of chances to grab him up, walking the beach for the past hour and a half. He had watched a pickup football game for a while, watched women of all ages strolling in their bathing suits, wading in the cool dying waves, lying on blankets reading books. He wasn't the only black man on the beach, but he sure was the only one dressed in long pants and carrying a trash bag. Feeling just a little conspicuous.

He checked his watch for the hundredth time. 11:57.

With a shudder, he rolled his pants back down, wiped his face with his shoulder, then started making his way toward the hotel. Away from the football game, things were quiet, mostly people sitting in canvas chairs, reading magazines and newspapers.

The beach was separated from the line of hotels by about fifty feet of dunes and beach grass. Wooden boardwalks cut over the dunes, protected by a wind fence strung about four feet high. Reaching the Holiday Inn, Gideon stepped cautiously onto the boardwalk and started walking. The hotel's pool came into view, then the parking lot.

Twelve o'clock.

A few people were visible scattered around the pool, another couple

214

of men taking suitcases out of their vehicles. Gideon's heart started making noise. He scanned the lot for Bethany's car. Or her sister's car. Seeing neither, he took a few more steps down the boardwalk, and more of the parking lot opened up to him. That's when he spotted the gold SUV. Two heads inside. They appeared to be watching him. Reflections on the glass obscured his view, but the passenger looked like a woman. She took off her sunglasses. Indeed, the way her head was cocked . . .

Yes, it was Bethany. But – the driver.

The man got out – tall, cowboy hat, handlebar mustache. B.J. Landry.

Wanting to retreat, Gideon looked behind him, back toward the beach, and a panic shot through him. Six or seven of the sunbathers had been men, he realized, sitting alone. FBI agents, to be sure. And the people gathered around the pool. Two were eyeing him that very moment, one talking on a cell phone – or radio. Gideon looked back to the gold SUV just as the passenger door opened and Bethany started to get out. Thirty feet away, a man was pulling a canvas bag out of his station wagon.

Gideon looked up and down the strip of sand dunes. No escape there, with all the fences. He turned back to the hotel. Landry was leaning on the SUV roof now, his chin in his hands, watching Gideon through sunglasses. Bethany, standing beside the vehicle, was staring at him in a beseeching way, a kind of shrug, as if she was wondering why he wouldn't come to her. Then she opened the back door and lifted out his brown leather suitcase. She turned to Gideon and held the suitcase in front of her legs. Oh, baby, what did you do? Didn't she know it was a trap?

Bethany looked back at Landry, then she started walking toward Gideon . . .

And he began backing away, shaking his head at her. She stopped again, at the beginning of the boardwalk. Wearing her red dress, her white sandals, red lipstick. For several seconds they stared at one another. How he wanted to go to her, ambush or not, just for the chance to hold her for ten precious seconds, to feel her strong arms squeezing him, to swear his innocence to her once again, to hear her say she loved him. But these men who were so anxious to bring him down, would they hesitate if a black woman got caught in the crossfire? Would anyone care if four more African-American children became orphans?

Bethany set the suitcase down on the boardwalk and backed away a couple of steps, then stopped to wait for him to come to her. He felt like a starving bear about to be captured . . . and Bethany was the bait. But he stood his ground. And, oh, the look she gave him before she turned away, an expression of utter sadness and confusion – as though it was *he* who had betrayed her.

Then she was walking back toward the hotel, and Gideon's heart was pounding. It was all he could do to keep from calling out her name, or running after her. Then she disappeared around the wind fence, and as he stood there staring at that suitcase, he heard the SUV doors close. He saw the vehicle pull slowly past the boardwalk. He felt such an ache in his chest. Then she was gone.

And he was left with the boardwalk, the suitcase, and more terror than he had ever known.

He stood there for a minute, maybe ten minutes, while his poor mind labored, until he finally came to the conclusion that if it was an ambush, he would be grabbed whether he picked up the suitcase or not.

So he went ahead and picked it up, and he walked into the lobby of the hotel with his head high, and he asked the concierge to have a taxi there in fifteen minutes. Then he went into the bathroom.

At the top of his suitcase, Bethany had folded his good linen blazer, mint green, along with his matching slacks. Black and blue striped necktie, to go with his beige shirt. Tucked in the blazer's inside pocket was a white envelope containing a bunch of tens and twenties. He reached down and found four pairs of underpants, some handkerchiefs and socks. Wrapped carefully in one of his socks were his old prescription sunglasses. Inside another sock was a small, brown cell phone, cracked around the earpiece – obviously used. A short piece of masking tape affixed to it had the word 'OK' written in pen.

Perhaps Bethany had gotten it from her hoodlum brother Marlin, thought Gideon – at least he hoped so. Then 'OK' might mean 'untraceable.' In any case, he was tempted to call his house right then and there, just to talk to his children and let them know he was thinking of them. Maybe one of them would know why their mother had brought Landry with her. Then again, what if it was Landry who had supplied the cell phone? In that case, a call home could mean not only Gideon's death sentence, but murder for an innocent woman, when Sereno found her.

Gideon smacked the phone against his temple, cursing his dull mind, wishing he could figure out what to do. Having no idea where Sereno was heading, he could think of only two options: turn himself in – or keep running. He smacked his head again and cursed his cowardice.

'Mister, you okay in there?' Someone standing outside his stall wearing Air Jordans, white man's voice.

'Fine, thank you,' Gideon answered, and the Jordans went away.

He took the hat out of the suitcase, put it on, then reached under some T-shirts – and found a book: *The Chaneysville Incident*, by an African-American writer named David Bradley. Gideon had first read it in prison, as an inmate, and it had affected him deeply. Changed his life, really. He smiled to think of Bethany packing it for him. There were also six tins of sardines held together with a rubber band; his plaid bathing suit, blue Bermuda shorts; and tucked inside the shorts a big plastic bag of toll house cookies, his favorites. Which was a kiss from his children.

Gideon's tears came back.

Then he found something else, inside the cloth pocket of the suitcase: a long, flat, piece of plastic with a hooked end . . . By God, it was a slim jim. He fished his hand inside the pocket and found two four-inch lengths of insulated wire, with tiny alligator clips at the ends . . . and he knew for sure that Bethany had been to see her brother, a seasoned car thief. With a shudder, he slipped the tools back in the suitcase pocket.

'Oh, baby,' he whispered.

CHAPTER THREE

By noontime, Jacob had sweated a gallon already, sitting in the garden doorway with a mallet and chisel, chipping out the last notch in the upper chord of July's bed. Arm-weary, he had cut sixty-four such notches, all precisely measured and spaced. It was delicate work when what he really felt like doing was pounding something.

After all, Maury was right. His story was preposterous. Not only the book, but this other story he had concocted – of Price Ashworth blackmailing Alix Callahan over something she supposedly confessed under hypnosis . . .

It was his imagination run amok. Just as Price had told him, as Laura had told him and, yes, both attorneys and Squeaky. Even Max seemed to know what Jacob refused to face. He could not trust his own mind. Speaking of Max . . .To celebrate his release from the hospital – and as an apology for accusing him of taking drugs – Price and Laura had taken him to see the Red Sox, courtesy of a pharmaceutical sales rep who'd given Price three front row box seats on first base.

Jacob had called the hospital once and the state police twice, to find out what they'd discovered in the grape soda Max had drunk – or in the contents of his stomach. Each time, he was told that the results weren't finalized, and assured him that he'd be notified as soon as they were.

'Jacob, you're so lazy.'

July's voice, a teasing lilt, came from behind him. Jacob turned as she squeezed past him, pressing her leg against his shoulder on her way out to the garden. She had on a short yellow shift, which her high buttocks tossed back and forth as she sauntered past.

'Federal law says I'm entitled to a coffee break,' he replied.

She turned a graceful half circle and continued walking backwards. 'I've got something a lot stronger than coffee,' she told him, running her hand up her thigh. 'Sweeter too.'

As she spun away and headed deeper into the rainforest, he stood there in the wake of her musky fragrance, his determination to resist her retreating behind his rising libido, until he could think of nothing more than the delicate pressure of her body receiving his. Arousal mounting, he set the chord on the shop floor and started after her, wiping poplar chips off his chest with his T-shirt while he came through the garden like a boar, trampling the underbrush, heedless of whatever alien frogs might have wandered in his path.

He found her standing on the grassy bank of her pool, waiting for him. Of course, she had known he would follow her, so not a word was exchanged. They met and grappled and pulled one another down to the hot grass. An onlooker might have thought it a rape, the sex was so ferocious, though it would have been impossible to tell which was the aggressor.

A thousand miles away, in South Carolina, Sereno sat on a long sandy dune, with the sea smoke out ahead of him, moistening the high grass in its breath. Fog wrapped around the pines behind him. He could hear ocean waves. He could not see them.

He set his briefcase on his lap and manipulated the latches until they snapped open, then he took out the can of Sprite and popped the lid; took a drink. Opening the plastic freezer bag, he filled his fingers with the dried vegetation, stuck some in his mouth and chewed. Washed it down with another mouthful of the sweet drink. He found a piece of yagé bark in the bag, and stuck it in his mouth, between his cheek and gum. Then he reached inside the briefcase again and took the snapshot out of the leather pocket. He lay back and stared at the image, stared and stared, while he fell under the spell of the drug, and the milkwhite fog caressed his face.

Enclosed in the greenhouse, Jacob lay in pleasant exhaustion. July, lying on her back beside him, watched him tenderly, as he watched her. Here on the flat, grassy bank of the pool, they had made love for hours, it seemed. With his fingertips, he traced the smooth curve of July's breast, not sure if he had ever seen anything so perfect. Below them, the water moved quietly inside the clear pool. Outside the glass, the arched bridge reached way up in the summer sky, while down on the river an oil tanker the size of four city blocks moved past them in magnificent silence.

'Don't you wish we could stay here forever?' she said. 'Just you and me.'

Jacob studied the goosebumps on her breast. He touched the tip of his finger to the tip of her nipple and watched it stand stiff and tender. She took hold of his hand, kissed his finger. Then she lowered her own hand down his chest and stomach, his abdomen. He stopped her before she went any lower.

'Never leave?' he asked.

'Never,' she breathed, then captured him in her hand, soft and useless.

He took hold of her wrist. 'Really, I'm dead.'

She released him and collapsed on the grass. 'No wonder your wife wanted somebody else.'

He chuckled. 'July, you'd wear out Superman.'

'Superman's a pussy,' she murmured. 'All Americans are pussies.'

He kissed her shoulder. 'And Kogi men can go all day and night.'

'Kogi men are pussies too,' she said.

'Your husband?'

'My husband's a shaman.'

'Right,' Jacob said, hearing the pride in her voice. Remembering the things his father had told him, he said, 'This is the same man who had sex with you when you were twelve . . .?'

She turned her back on him.

They both lay still for a spell. Ridiculous, he thought. He shouldn't even have been here, living with her, sleeping with her. Now they were having a lover's spat. He touched her arm. 'I didn't mean that. Sorry.'

She sighed after a moment and rolled onto her back again.

Jacob raised her hand to his mouth and tenderly kissed the stub of her index finger. 'He's the one who did this to you, isn't he?'

Her eyes narrowed a bit, then she took her hand back.

'July, I'm only trying to understand.'

'Understand what?'

'Why you'd mail him things in prison.' He was thinking of the packages he had seen leave the shop. It was a bluff – but it worked. Her face clouded over. She gave him a studied look, then stared up at the green canopy.

'I torment him,' she said.

'How?'

She turned to Jacob, and a lewd, mischievous smile came over her. 'By staying alive.'

The edges of the snapshot were worn and dirt-stained. The photo itself was creased with wrinkles. It was a picture of July, from the waist down, naked, sitting on the bank of the pool with her legs spread. The image was off center, so that only one knee showed. Beside the knee was an elephant ear leaf, behind that the trunk of a sapling palm. Greenhouse glass showed behind the leaves.

Looking closely at the picture, one could make out, beyond the glass, a massive arched bridge, with a dark river below. A concrete pier showed a water line that was higher than the level of the river, an indication that the water was tidal. But it was the white bird flying over the bridge, with its black wingtips and yellow head, that spoke to Sereno.

Limón-cabeza.

When he was a fisherman working off the Florida Keys, in the winter when the water was cold he would sometimes encounter the seabird, a Northern Gannet, far from land, diving from great heights and plunging like an arrow into the water. When it burst from the sea again, shedding sundrops off its yellow head, all the fishermen would whistle, and the bird would swoop a great circle for them before flying off to its home in the north.

Limón-cabeza, they called it. Lemon-head.

They all considered it a sign of luck if they spotted *Limón-cabeza.*

Sereno moved to the edge of the dune and stared northward into the fog. With the surf murmuring off to his right, he let out a loud whistle. Even as far north as he had already journeyed, he knew that the water was too warm for such a bird. Still, he whistled again.

Then he stared into the fog.

And he stared.

And the ocean began to shine like silver.

He stared.

And golden sand ran up to his feet like honey.

He stared.

And out of a cool, sighing breeze that rose off the ocean, the great yellow-headed bird suddenly appeared, slicing the whiteness with its wings, sweeping off toward the north.

Sereno stared.

And the fog gathered at its wingtips and chased after the bird. *Limón-cabeza.*

Sereno stared.

And a soft line appeared out ahead, dividing ocean from sky.

Sereno stared.

And out of the fog, there appeared before him the great steel bridge, its arched top graceful as a woman's hip, spanning a wide salt river.

Sereno closed his eyes. In his mind, he rose upward on the air currents and hovered like a raven in the wind above the bridge. From here he could see the glassed-in garden on the green bank, lush and warm and sweet with color.

Yes, she was there.

He could see her, but not see her; hear her voice, but not hear her. Like the knowledge of music when there were no musicians; the knowledge of heat when there was no fire.

She was there.

'His name is Sereno,' July said, as she ran the back of her hand over Jacob's chest. 'When Alix lived with my people in Colombia, she wanted to try yagé, but only Kogi men are allowed to take it, no women. She kept hearing stories about Sereno, all the scandal, and how we were sent away. She came looking for us.'

'What scandal?'

July looked back at him coyly, and in one fluid move, swung her leg over him and was sitting astride his hard stomach gazing down at him hungrily.

'Me.'

Her word coincided with the crash of breaking glass, and she sprang off him. Then the shards came raining out of the foliage, like ice crystals.

'July?'

He was on his feet. She stared off into the garden.

'Stay here,' Jacob mouthed, while he quietly stepped into his trousers. Then he reached into the pool and pried a small rock out of the bed. Not much of a weapon, the size of a tennis ball, but the best he could do. He crept onto the path that led toward the middle of the garden, where the crash had come from.

Now he was alert to everything – the tap of a water droplet somewhere ahead of him, the flick of a leaf under a sprung grass-hopper . . . His eyes darted. Then he heard a rustle of brush . . .

'*Jacob!*'

The cry came from his left. He shouldered through the jungle brush, heedless of frogs, and found her staring up, terrified. At the top of the glass wall, a seagull was caught in the shattered pane, hanging dead by a leg and wing, its thin blood dripping down the glass.

Jacob put his arms around her, flooding with relief. 'Are you okay?'

She stood there trembling, her eyes downcast, dark with fear.

'July, what's the matter?'

Pushing away from him, she gazed at him as though it was the stupidest question she'd ever heard.

CHAPTER FOUR

The man who emerged from the Holiday Inn bathroom looked like he had won the Kentucky Derby. Beige Stetson hat with a mint-green band. Matching slacks and jacket, with over five hundred dollars tucked in his pockets. Sharp Ray-Bans. And a fine leather suitcase in his hand.

Gideon spotted the bank of telephones in the lobby, chose the one with a telephone book still attached. Looked up GOVERNMENT NUMBERS, then dialed his cell phone as he walked out the front door. By the time a human voice came on, saying, 'Department of Justice, Criminal Division,' Gideon had located his taxi.

'I'd like to speak with someone in the Witness Protection Program, please,' he said.

'You mean WITSEC, the Witness Security Program?'

'That's what I said.' Gideon held up his finger to the cabbie, to hold him there. Funny how clothes could change a man.

Then a cordial voice came on the phone and Gideon said, 'I'm calling with information concerning one of the people in your program. This person is in grave danger.'

'To whom am I speaking?' the official asked.

'There's an escaped convict on the loose,' Gideon said. 'He is a Colombian Indian who goes by the name Sereno. He escaped from Alligator Alley Correctional Institution a few days ago.'

'Your name, please?' the man repeated.

'To the best of my knowledge, Mr Sereno is looking for his ex-wife, who I believe is part of your program. I don't know her name or where she lives, but you need to get her relocated right away.'

After a moment of silence, the Justice Department official said, 'Sir, I appreciate your concern, but our policy is to neither confirm nor deny—'

'*My* policy,' Gideon began, then looked around to make sure his volume hadn't attracted attention. 'My policy is: Don't you people use that woman as a decoy. I've had experience with this individual. He may not be much bigger than a child, but he is extremely resourceful and extremely dangerous. He is determined, and he will find her.'

'I understand you, sir.' Everything the man said sounded rehearsed, as though he was reading from a script. 'You should be aware that, if the woman in question is part of our program, she is quite safe. However, if she has violated the rules and is no longer part of WITSEC, then we have no information on her.'

'What rules?'

'Any number of conditions, the violation of which would have triggered immediate forfeiture of protection. For example, if she ever tried to make contact with family or friends – or even the convict – from that point forward, she is on her own.'

'You're not listening to me. This man, Sereno—'

'If she is in our program, she is protected,' the man interrupted. 'If she is not in the program, then she is a citizen of some community, no different than any other citizen. If there's a problem, she'll need to contact her local police department. Now, is there a telephone number there, in case we need to get in touch with you?'

Gideon cut him off, slipped the cell phone in his pocket, and walked briskly to the cab, got in the back seat and said, 'Tallahassee, please.'

The cabbie turned and gave him an incredulous look. 'You need to go to the bus station, man,' he said in a Latino lilt. 'I don't go to Tallahassee.'

'I don't care for buses. How far do you go?' Gideon said pleasantly, acting like money was no concern. In fact, he was planning to head west until he found an African-American community that felt safe, then check into a motel and buy a newspaper, to see if Sereno had been sighted.

'Lake City,' the driver said.

'Fine, take me.'

The driver shrugged, hit his meter and pulled away from the curb. Before he had driven a quarter mile, three times Gideon caught him peeking in the rear-view. 'How's it going?' he said.

The cabbie's eyes darted back to the road.

'Some reason I shouldn't go to Lake City?' Gideon asked.

'We've been instructed by the police that two dangerous criminals are in the vicinity.'

'What vicinity?'

'You don't look like them,' the driver said.

Gideon stroked the stubble on his cheek, the scruffy start of a beard that was coming in much grayer than his hair. 'What did they do, these two criminals?'

'Blew up a prison,' the cabbie said. 'A Black and a Brown – they turn men to stone.'

'To stone?'

'And cut their hearts out,' said the cabbie, his dark eyes in the mirror again.

Gideon laughed easily. At least he tried to. 'Sound like bad men.'

'This is true,' said the cabbie, somewhat defensively. 'The other day, a sheriff's deputy down in the Everglades – turned to stone. Last night another one.'

'Another what?'

'A man in Deltaville, Georgia,' the cabbie said. 'Turned to stone.'

'Last night?'

The cabbie swung onto Route 10 heading west. 'Where in Lake City are you going?'

'Actually,' Gideon said, 'I want you to turn around and take me to Deltaville, Georgia. And please stay off the radio.'

The cabbie's eyes rose into the mirror.

'You're aware of the X-Files?' Gideon said.

The eyes sparkled.

'I work undercover, for the FBI, and this is top-secret,' he continued, weaving the lie.

The head nodded.

'It's true, what you say,' Gideon told him. 'This man turns people to stone.'

The driver's hand left the steering wheel, to bless himself. Gideon looked at the ID taped to the glass partition.

'Mr Ortega?'

The eyes again.

'It is imperative that you tell no one about this conversation, or where you drove me. Is that clear?'

'Yes, sir. Tell no one.'

'If anyone asks, you took me to Lake City and dropped me off at the bus station. *Comprendez?*'

'Sí, *yes,*' stammered the driver. 'I understand.'

CHAPTER FIVE

T he Mazda's air conditioner blew full blast, but on days like this it
    hardly mattered. By three o'clock, the temperature in southern
Maine had reached 96 Fahrenheit, in a dead, bluish haze.

When Jacob pulled into Squeaky's dooryard he didn't see the
Impala, and figured the old man was holed up at the bar, where he had
air conditioning. But as he was about to drive away, he noticed the
steel-blue smoke coming from the exhaust hole in the garage door.
Curious, he turned off his key, stepped out into a blast-furnace of heat
and went around to the side door.

What he saw through the window startled him – Squeaky sitting
inside a BMW, engine running, windows up. Wondering if he was
gassing himself, Jacob hurried into the garage, pulled open the
passenger door.

'Jesus H. Christ—'

Squeaky jumped, and a slug of beer leaped from the can in his hand.
'You tryin to give me a frickin heart attack?'

Jacob looked in at him, still uncertain. A small color TV was sitting
on a towel draped across the car's hood – a car race was on. The sound
came from the car radio. A bowl of mixed nuts sat atop a small
Styrofoam cooler on the passenger seat.

'You're lettin the heat in, close the door,' Squeaky told him.

Jacob set the cooler in the back and sat in the passenger seat.
Squeaky let out a suffering sound as he set the bowl of peanuts on the
dash, then took a long drink of beer, never taking his attention from
the TV. The interior was tan leather and pleasantly chilled, with a sweet
balsam fragrance from the air freshener that hung from the mirror.

'I quit writing,' Jacob said. 'I came to ask you for my job back.'

Squeaky finished his beer, rolled his window down, and tossed out
the empty. It clattered on the cement floor. 'Gimme another one,' he
said. 'Get one for yourself, you want. I don't have any ginger ale.'

Jacob turned, reached into the back seat, and pushed back the lid, grabbed two cans out of the ice. 'Don't shake 'em up, this ain't my car,' Squeaky told him.

Jacob handed him the can. 'Whose is it?'

Squeaky popped the top, then nodded at the TV. 'His – Jeff Dakota's. I'm the only one he trusts to do his body work.'

Jacob opened his beer, first one he'd had since he was twenty. 'I quit writing,' he repeated.

Squeaky slapped the steering wheel. 'See, I told him!' He slapped it again. 'I told him, stay high on the fourth turn. See that? I told him, and he did it. He just moved up, from fourth to second, that hot shit.'

Jacob took a sip of beer – his first in over ten years. His eyes watered and he burped. 'If you could give me a few hours,' he said, 'just to hold me over till I find something permanent . . . I'll do what you said, call my father and see if he knows of any other teaching jobs.'

Squeaky drank a good amount of beer, then doubled his chin and doubled Jacob's burp. 'I might only have a few hours myself. Your buddy Doctor A upped the ante, you know. Eight hundred large for the Spite House. That's nothin to sneeze at.' He looked at the TV for a while, but from the expression on his face, Jacob could tell he wasn't really watching it. In fact, a scowl had dug itself into his brow, and was deepening there. Finally he turned the radio down and gave Jacob a disgusted look.

'All right, smart guy, you wanna know why I quit racing?'

Jacob waited.

'My wife left me,' Squeaky said. 'Okay?'

Although he did not meet Jacob's gaze, there was no sarcasm in his tone, no anger. He had said his piece and was asking if Jacob understood.

Jacob nodded, took another drink of beer. In fact, Laura had already told him that much: the family version. Then Squeaky told him more.

'Day I cracked up the car at Winston,' he said, laying his head back, 'afterwards I went after the sonovabitch that ran me into the wall. We all got into it, pit crew, everyone. Couple of broken noses, couple of teeth. I got a suspension and fine. Not to mention, my leg got screwed up in the crash, some broken ribs, and that ring-toe I lost.'

A glance at Jacob, daring him to make some smart-ass remark. Another drink of beer.

'Next day, when I got home from the hospital, she had my bags packed.' Squeaky finished his beer and rolled down the window, dropped the empty out, then hitched his thumb at the cooler.

Jacob got him another beer. 'She didn't like you racing?'

Squeaky snapped the top. 'Didn't like the smell of gas on my hands, my greasy clothes, my friends, their wives.' He took his first sip, closed his eyes as it went down. 'That car.' He gestured to his Impala that was parked beside them. 'Ever seen a woman jealous of an inanimate object?'

'So you quit racing,' Jacob said.

'Oh yes, I quit.' A bitter glee crept into Squeaky's voice. 'I got myself a steady job selling spark plugs up and down the east coast.'

'And she didn't take you back.'

'Did I say that?' Squeaky gave him an impatient look. 'Yeah, I moved back. It lasted a month. Then *she* took off with Laura. Said she never liked salesmen. So I quit the salesman job and bought the bar. And that's my sad tale. So.' He took another drink. 'You want a nine-to-five job, hey, be my guest.'

Squeaky turned up the radio volume and returned his attention to the race. Then he turned it down again. 'Wanna know the bitch of it all?'

Jacob gave him a look.

'She ended up marrying the prick that won that race.'

'She married another driver?' Jacob realized he was smiling. He shrugged to show that he meant no disrespect.

The older man waved it off. 'Go write your book.'

CHAPTER SIX

*R*ung over rung Henry climbed, up from the crow's nest, keeping his eyes on the green steel in front of his face, not out at the distance, nor down into the fog, nor up at the girl who led him higher and higher over the exposed skeleton of this monster. The ladder was enclosed in a cylindrical cage, welded to the center column of the bridge and leading all the way to the top of the arch. Up here, Henry could no longer hear the traffic below him. All he could hear was wind.

A chime rang above the hum of the table fan. Jacob heard the shop door close. July had been gone when he'd returned from Squeaky's. He assumed she was out buying glass to replace the pane the seagull had smashed. But after a minute, when she didn't come up, he became curious and went down to find her. As he reached the floor of the shop, he heard the slap of the door in the garden hut.

He went out into the steamy shade, directly on the garden path. With the heat inside the house, he had taken off his shirt, wearing only his work pants and moccasins, imagining now that he'd find her inside the hut and pull her down on the mattress. But as he rounded the corner of the hut, the door flew open, and Susan Evangeline fell out, swiping frantically at grasshoppers, stumbling over a fat striped plant.

'They won't hurt you,' he said, and tried to steady her but she shoved him off, and instantly regained her composure, despite the grasshoppers that clung to her gray summer suit.

'What are they doing in there?' she demanded. A grasshopper snapped past her chin.

Jacob stepped into the hut and closed the inner door on the grasshoppers, embarrassed about his shirtlessness. 'Breeding, by the looks of it,' he said, not wanting to tell her about July's frogs. But he lingered a moment, to round up his wits. What was she doing here? He looked through the screen to see her briskly brushing the remaining insects off herself.

'You should probably stay on the path,' he told her as he came out. 'Poison ivy.'

She stepped out of the foliage, the slit in her skirt revealing more of her leg than she would ever intentionally show him, he guessed. And her hair had an orange tint that he didn't remember, or maybe it just appeared that way, set against all the greens.

'The lab results came in,' she said.

'I've been waiting for the call,' he said, looking down at a bag in her hand, a plastic shopping bag.

'The substance analyzed in both the soda bottle and the contents of your son's stomach was a combination,' she said. 'Acetaminophen – a common pain reliever – and Diphenhydramine, commercially known as Benadryl.'

'Benadryl?' Jacob said.

'For allergies. Some doctors prescribe it as a sleep aid.'

'Laura takes Benadryl for her hay fever,' Jacob said. Now he wondered about Price's theory, that Max swallowed the pills deliberately, as a way of pulling his parents together. Would he have bought the grape soda himself and dissolved the pills in it? Why?

'But the combination of the two,' Evangeline said, interrupting his thoughts. 'Acetaminophen and Benadryl – and in this particular ratio – those are the active ingredients in Tylenol PM.'

Jacob gave her a look. Tylenol PM.

'In a child your son's age, an overdose can be serious, even fatal. Fortunately Dr Ashworth got him to the hospital before his body had a chance to absorb it all.'

'It was dissolved in the soda—?'

'That's right. Your wife said she doesn't have Tylenol PM at home.'

'No, we never did,' Jacob said . . .then tightened with fear. Now he knew where he had seen the bottle. Here, upstairs, in the medicine cabinet.

Evangeline gave him a puzzled look.

'She's been here too,' Jacob said. 'Alix.'

'You saw her—?'

He shook his head. 'July told me today, she had a feeling. . .' He gave Evangeline a look, not sure if she believed him – or if he should even trust her. But he pushed aside a branch and started back through the garden toward the house, and she followed, saying, 'Are you alone here now?'

'I don't know where July is,' he said, and stole another peek at her bag. Not exactly hiding it from him, he could see something red inside, maybe a shirt. 'Is that something to do with Alix?'

'I can't discuss it with you,' Evangeline answered, 'not without your counsel present. Do you expect her home shortly?'

'I have no idea,' he told her, as the house came into view.

'Oh, yes, the nonexistent girl,' Evangeline said. Her contempt for July was not hard to detect. Knowing about Evangeline's past with Alix, Jacob wasn't surprised – even though it had been Evangeline who had made the break.

'Did you know that the mortgage here, the business, and all the insurances – were in Alix Callahan's name? "July" is the only name on her driver's license. "July" *was* the name registered as beneficiary on Alix's life insurance.'

'Alix changed it?' he asked, trying not to sound concerned, though he stole a look at her as he stepped into the shop.

'Alix dropped the policy last year,' she said, the plastic bag gently swinging from her hand, baiting him.

'The medicine cabinet's upstairs,' he said, not biting.

'I'll follow you,' Evangeline said.

Why argue? He led her around the cordoned-off area where his green headboard lay in pieces behind a translucent plastic wall, and they climbed the stairs without talking. Emerging in the pantry, he led her through the living room, past the bedroom, and into the bathroom, where he went directly to the medicine cabinet and pulled it open.

Gone.

A pair of toothbrushes in a juice glass – his had replaced Alix's – a stick of unscented deodorant, July's hairbrush, a pack of plastic disposable razors, Jacob's razor and shaving cream. But no Tylenol PM. Goosebumps blossomed on his skin.

Then a door slammed in the next room.

Jacob stuck his head out the door and looked down the short hallway, saw that the bedroom door was shut.

'Wind?' Evangeline suggested.

Jacob went and knocked.

'July?'

He knocked again. Listened. Then opened the door.

There she was, with her back to him, pulling a sleeveless white T-shirt over her head.

'The District Attorney is here,' he said, as Evangeline appeared beside him in the doorway, mystery bag in hand.

July turned to face them, snugging the T-shirt over her breasts.

Jacob walked into the room, grabbed a blue work shirt off a hook and put it on. 'She wanted to talk with you,' he said, then added casually, 'Wasn't there a bottle of Tylenol PM in the medicine cabinet?'

'Why, is someone having trouble sleeping?' She ignored Evangeline.

'They found out how Max was poisoned,' Jacob said, and July's head snapped around to him.

'Maybe now you believe me,' she replied. 'That bitch.'

Evangeline said, 'I understand you think Alix Callahan was in your house recently—?'

'I know she was,' July answered sullenly. The slouched way she stood there in her tattered jeans and mustard-brown work boots – arms folded, head cocked, pelvis stuck forward – she looked like some street tough.

Evangeline seemed more interested in the open closet. 'How do you know?'

'Because I do.'

She walked to the closet, ran her hand along the clothes hanging there. Jacob saw her thumb run ponderously over a flannel shirt. 'Do you mind if I ask you some questions?' she said, presumably to July. 'Mr Winter, you may leave the room if you want, or you can stay, as long as you're aware that anything you might say to me, you do so voluntarily. Do you understand?'

'I'll stay.'

Evangeline turned to face July, who continued leaning brazenly against the oak dresser, chewing her thumbnail.

'Have you seen her?'

'I don't have to see her.' July turned to Jacob again. It was that look of hers, bewilderment, hurt, or whatever, impossible to decipher. 'Stop looking at me,' she told him. He averted his eyes.

'Is July the name your parents gave you?' Evangeline asked her.

'Someone tried to kill me once, and I had my name changed.'

'Was it a state or federal agency that facilitated the identity change?'

July stuck her hands in her back pockets and shrugged, her dark nipples showing through the thin T-shirt.

'The other night when I was here,' Evangeline pressed on, 'you told me that you were Alix Callahan's business partner for three years before she disappeared, is that correct?'

She nodded.

Evangeline took a step closer. 'And that you were here, in the house, on the night that she jumped off the bridge—?'

July stared straight at her. 'I was in bed, waiting for her to come home.'

Evangeline held her stare. 'Can you remember what she was wearing when she left the house?'

The bag. Something washed up on the rocks, Jacob realized. A jersey? Jacket? Sweater? He tried to picture Alix that night. Was it chilly? Windy?

'A sweatshirt,' July said.

'Describe it.'

She shrugged again, maintaining her defiance. 'Red. With a hood. Black corduroy pants. Leather sandals.'

A scowl deepened in Evangeline's brow. She turned to Jacob. 'Is that the way you remember her dressed?'

He said nothing. The more he tried to picture Alix on the bridge, the more his memory escaped him, as though a huge magnet had been turned toward him, pulling his mind away. Then it hit him: a bullet hole—

'Do you recall any printing on the shirt, a logo or insignia?'

Evangeline had directed the question at him, but July answered. 'Plant seeds,' she said.

Jacob tried to picture her. Red hooded sweatshirt emblazoned with PLANT SEEDS. He formed the image in his mind, but it was not from memory.

In front of his eyes, the bag opened and the sweatshirt came out, red, hooded, ripped and green-stained. With some surprise, Jacob noticed it was dry. Why wouldn't it be? Evangeline held it up and showed him. PLANT SEEDS. And there, in the middle of the letter S . . .

Jacob's heart stopped.

Evangeline caught him staring at the hole, small and neat, then she turned the sweatshirt around and showed him the other side, same kind of hole. She scrutinized him for another moment, but he only shook his head, a dull nausea going through him.

'It turned up in a fisherman's net, not even a mile out,' Evangeline explained. 'Do you recognize it now?'

July nodded soberly. But Evangeline was still watching Jacob, as though waiting for some word or gesture.

'Memory fail you, Mr Winter?'

'Is that a bullet hole?' he asked, foregoing the cat and mouse.

'Why would there be a bullet hole, if you didn't shoot her? You told me that you two were the only ones on the bridge, and that you stood there and watched her jump.'

'I *saw* her jump. I tried to stop her—'

'Jacob, don't say any more,' July said, moving toward him, no longer the slouching punk but the concerned girlfriend. The change did not escape Evangeline, who stuffed the shirt back in the bag.

'Can I see that?' Jacob asked.

'Of course not, it's evidence.'

'Why would I shoot Alix Callahan?' he asked. 'She bailed me out of jail, paid for my lawyer.'

'Jacob, shut up,' July told him.

He looked at her in astonishment, then turned back to Evangeline, who surprised him even more when she walked out the door. 'Make sure you notify my office if you're planning on traveling out of state,' she said.

Then she was leaving – just like that – with more than enough evidence to read him his rights. Unless something about the sweatshirt wasn't right.

'Alix called *me*,' he said. 'She waited for me on the bridge.' He followed Evangeline to the stairs and went down behind her, bristling with fear. 'You know I didn't kill Alix Callahan.'

All the way down the stairs and through the shop, Evangeline didn't respond. But, reaching the door, Jacob couldn't stop himself.

'Any more than you did,' he said.

Now she turned, and the look she gave him reflected a certain exhilaration, like the glint of a hangman watching the condemned mount the gallows. 'Mr Winter, you should pay attention to your friend,' she said. 'Shut up.'

She opened the door and the bell rang. Then she walked across the lawn to her car.

Jacob became aware that July was beside him. With her hands tucked into her back pockets, that cocky, delinquent pose, she watched Susan Evangeline get in her car and drive away.

'Were you flirting with her?' Jacob asked.

'No more than you were,' she said with breezy innocence.

He studied her. Was she serious? 'July, it sounded like you were trying to make me look guilty up there.'

She smirked. 'Oh, like you weren't trying to make me look guilty, bringing her up to see the medicine cabinet.'

He studied her, wracked with confusion. 'You told me Alix had been here,' he said. 'I thought this was proof that you were right.'

He searched for some sign of understanding in her eyes – when he thought of that story again. *Don't pat Patches.* Yes, the warning signs were there, Alix had told him, big as life. But some people . . .

'Fuck you, Jacob,' July said, spinning away from him and marching off to the stairs. He started after her, then stopped himself. As the iron treads rang beneath her heels, he was suddenly certain of one thing: He would leave her.

For some reason, that prospect frightened him even more than Evangeline did.

★ ★ ★

'I think I'm being set up,' he said, when Miss Finch answered the telephone.

'Mr Winter, I don't know how you expect us to defend you,' she replied.

'Please, may I come in?' He stretched the pay phone to the window of the Commerce Building, while he watched the street for the Green Girls Volvo.

'I'm sorry, Attorney Zabriski will be unavailable for the rest of the day,' she told him. 'I left three messages for you.'

Suddenly he remembered. Monday. He was supposed to have brought Maxie in.

'I'll be right there,' Jacob said, and hung up before Miss Finch could tell him no.

CHAPTER SEVEN

G ideon rang the doorbell, then turned away, wanting to appear
nonchalant when the door opened. From the front porch, he
could see the river parting the flat green land below, the highway
cutting across the marsh, climbing up to the tall arched bridge,
climbing back down again. It amazed him sometimes, how engineers
came up with such things.

The door opened.

Gideon turned. 'Good afternoon,' he said to the woman. She wore a
white nurse's uniform. 'Have any of the other therapists been here
today?'

'The physical therapist was here earlier.'

'No one else?'

'The doctor came twice. Cops and FBI most of the day, taking
fingerprints and pictures and all. Now who the hell are you?' The
woman had blonde hair piled up on her head – or else it was a wig –
thick red lips and a half-pound of eye makeup.

Gideon smiled. 'I'm Mr Sweeney, Mr Dunn's speech therapist. Sorry
I'm late. My supervisor gave me bad directions.' Gideon felt himself
blushing from the lie.

'Come in,' said the nurse. 'He's watching TV.'

'Isn't this a beautiful house,' Gideon said, stepping into the foyer.
'Are you staying here tonight?'

'Round the clock,' she said. 'As long as he needs me, I'm here. The
doctor thinks another couple of days, judging by that park ranger in
Florida. They say he's up and around already.'

'Walking? Talking?' Gideon asked.

'Wheelchair. But they got high hopes.' She stuck her head in the
doorway. 'Speech therapist?'

Gideon heard a murmur, sounding like someone talking through a
mouthful of glue.

236

'I don't know what the hell he's babblin about,' she complained. 'He didn't even know his car was gone until the cops told him there was only one in the garage.'

'Know what kind of car he had stolen?'

'Must've been special,' she said. 'The one they left behind's a brand new Cadillac SUV.'

'I should say,' Gideon answered, not knowing how to take the woman.

'How long are you going to be?' she asked. 'I might as well grab a nap while you're here.'

'Hour or so, I imagine,' he said. 'Go ahead and get some sleep. I'll wake you up when I'm done.'

The insurance man sat in a leather recliner in front of the TV. He was dressed in a blue sweat suit, with a filthy terrycloth bib tied around his neck. He'd been eating baby food, by the looks of the spatters. A plastic shower curtain protected the carpet.

'Mr Dunn,' Gideon said. 'How are you today?'

When he entered the salesman's field of vision, the man garbled something that sounded like a curse. Gideon turned to the woman, who shrugged.

'I have no idea what you just said,' Gideon told the man, then noticed the Confederate flag hanging above the fireplace. He turned back to the nurse. 'We'll be fine.'

She shrugged and said, 'You'd make me very happy if you could get him to stop drooling.'

'I'll do what I can,' Gideon said. 'Go ahead and take your rest.'

He listened for her footsteps going down the hallway. Then a door closed. Gideon turned to the television. A show was on in which three white cops were wrestling a young African-American to the asphalt. Gideon found the remote and turned down the volume.

'Mr Dunn, the man who did this to you, was he smallish?' Gideon held his hand down at his chest.

The paralyzed man looked like he wanted to nod. He made a humming sound in his throat.

'Like an Indian? Long black hair?'

All of a sudden, the man's eyes shone fearfully.

Gideon lowered his voice. 'Mr Dunn, I'm a police detective and I'd appreciate it if you wouldn't say anything about my coming here. I'm trying to track down the man who did this to you, and bring him to justice.'

The blue eyes glared out at him.

'I understand he made off with your car,' he said. 'What kind?'

Staring emphatically, the young man blurted out a long, loud murmur, his fat tongue twitching like a giant slug in his mouth.

'Don't strain yourself, that's gibberish to me,' Gideon said, not unkindly. 'Was it a Ford?'

The man groaned.

'Chevy?'

A grunt.

'Tell you what. Don't make any sound unless you mean yes. Okay?'

The man let out a series of excited grunts, sounding almost apelike.

'You're saying it was a Chevy?'

'Uh! Uh!'

'Very good,' Gideon said. 'Now, was that a Chevy . . . Malibu?'

The man lay silently.

'Cavalier? . . . Blazer? . . . truck, van, SUV?'

The man stared. Gideon imagined his eyes rolling.

'Sports car?'

'Uh! Uh!'

'Camaro.'

Nothing.

'Oh.' Gideon smiled. 'You had yourself a Corvette?'

The man let out a long noise that sounded like he was trying to sing.

'No kidding,' Gideon said. 'New one?'

The man's breathing accelerated, but he kept quiet.

'Old one.'

A sharp sound now, almost a cry.

In this way, Gideon came up with the date and color of the car and the fact that it was a convertible.

'Mr Dunn, just a few more minutes. Do you own a weapon of any kind?'

'Uh.'

'Gun?'

'Uh.'

'Do you know if he took it?'

The man said nothing. Then Gideon had run out of ideas. All he knew was that Sereno was driving a black 1965 Corvette Stingray convertible. Somewhere. And he had to call another taxi and get out of here before anyone else came.

'Sorry to bother you,' he said, and he patted the man's knee.

'Uhhh!' the man said, trying to tell him something. 'Uhhh!'

'Oh boy,' Gideon said.

The man's face brightened. Gideon thought he might be having a heart attack. 'Wait there, I'll get the nurse.'

The man practically shouted. 'Uh! Uh! Uh!' His head rolled to his shoulder, and he stared.

'You okay, Mr Dunn? I'll take your silence as a yes. Okay. You're looking at . . . the table? . . . the newspaper? . . . the telephone?'

'Nnn! Nnn!'

'Telephone.' Gideon sat down again. 'You want me to call someone for you?'

The man stared like a well-trained hound . . . at the phone. And Gideon got it.

'You've got a car phone in your 'Vette—?'

The insurance salesman answered with a long, satisfied moan.

'Now that might be a help.' And it became a simple matter for Gideon to extract the phone number. That accomplished, he stood again and helped the man turn his head back toward the television. 'You've been very helpful, Mr Dunn,' he said. 'I'll go wake up your nurse and be on my way.'

He walked out of the living room and down the hallway, where a door was closed. He could hear the nurse snoring inside, and he knocked lightly. 'Excuse me, Ma'am?' he said, but the snoring continued. 'Ma'am?'

He needed to ask her if there was a taxi service in town and, if not, where the nearest bus station was. But when he opened the door—

'Ma'am?'

There, above the bed, hung a large, framed portrait of the assassin, James Earl Ray. The woman lay fast asleep, mouth open, snoring like an engine. From atop an oak bureau, another picture stared out at Gideon: a group photo of around twenty men dressed in sheets and hoods, standing in a field. Gideon wandered closer, feeling like he had wandered inside the dark, stinking entrails of a monster.

A brass plaque attached to the bottom of the frame read: 'David D. Dunn, American Patriot. Brother in Arms. Defender of the Way. Secret Order of the Righteous White Warriors.'

Gideon felt the heat rise up the back of his neck and converge at the top of his head. That's when he saw the key ring lying on the bureau.

'Not so secret any more,' he muttered as he shut the door quietly behind him, leaving the nurse snoring.

Instead of calling for a taxi, he went back in the living room and held the keys in front of the insurance man's face. 'See this man?' he said, showing him the decal. 'His name is Chief Cadillac, an American native. Your people took his country, you dumb, pasty-faced motherfucker. So now I'm taking your Cadillac.'

The man glared fiercely, but didn't make a sound. In fact, if it weren't for his quick, shallow breathing, Gideon would have thought him dead.

He picked up the remote control off the coffee table and flipped through the channels until he came to a show – public television, by the looks – closeup of a beetle climbing over a leaf.

'Have a good, long recuperation,' he told the man. 'See if you can't educate yourself.'

Gideon entered the phone number as he drove, the SUV breezing down the highway so smooth and quiet that, even at eighty, Gideon felt like he was sitting in his own living room. He knew he shouldn't have taken the car – and it was big mistake to tell the guy he was doing so – but if he could save the life of the woman Sereno was hunting, then perhaps the authorities would take that into consideration. He figured the nurse would sleep for the rest of the night, judging by the way she'd been snoring. So he had an hour or two, to be safe, before he'd have to ditch the car.

When he dialed the telephone number the man had given him, he slowed down so he could hear. He hoped it was ringing in Sereno's car. After four rings, he heard the telephone picked up. Gideon pressed the cell phone to his ear, while he waited for a voice. When no one spoke, he felt his heart start beating. He knew he'd found his man. He pulled into the breakdown lane and came to a stop.

'You know who this is,' he said, not asking. 'Man, if you can hear me . . .'

Gideon listened closely, and was sure he could hear someone breathing on the other end.

'You've got to stop and let me take you back. They think you and I conspired together. Do you understand? They think we're murderers.'

He listened again, and now, besides the breathing on the other end, he could hear something else, a steady rising and falling, a shooshing sound. It wasn't road noise or even a car engine.

'Man, I'm your only witness. The only one who can vouch for your innocence. But we've got to go in together. That's our only chance. If we don't, they're going to kill you the minute you're spotted. And they'll do the same to me—'

Gideon heard a click on the line. And he was disconnected.

He blew a deep sigh, then dropped the phone on the seat. From some distance behind him, headlights came toward him in the mirror. He shifted gears and floored it, leaving a five-second screech behind him as he took to the highway again. Then it hit him . . . the sound on Sereno's car phone.

The ocean.

CHAPTER EIGHT

W hen Jacob walked into the attorney's office, Miss Finch took off her glasses and studied him for a second, then pushed a button on her phone. 'He's here.'

While she awaited an answer, the door behind her opened and Zabriski appeared in his white shirt and tie, hands loosely in his trouser pockets, an unspoken gesture of indifference.

'Max wouldn't be a credible witness,' Jacob said.

'Oh?'

Jacob sighed, not sure he wanted to explain. 'He has disabilities.'

Zabriski frowned. 'I see.'

'Hyperactivity, attention deficit disorder, behavioral disorder, nobody knows. But Evangeline could parade a dozen social workers and teachers and school psychologists to the bench and convince the jury that he's no more credible than I am. They'll humiliate him. I won't allow it.'

'Your decision,' Zabriski replied, and he reached behind him for his doorknob.

'Mr Zabriski, they found Alix Callahan's sweatshirt, the one she was wearing when she jumped off the bridge. With a bullet hole in it.'

Zabriski paused in the doorway, but did not respond.

'Something's not right,' Jacob told him. 'I just spoke to Evangeline. I've already admitted I was the only one on the bridge that night, with Alix. Why didn't she arrest me?'

The attorney smiled. 'Perhaps she feels as I do, Mr Winter, that given enough time you'll eventually arrest yourself.' Zabriski raised his brow hopelessly. 'Guilty or not.'

With that, he backed into his office and closed the door.

Jacob looked to Miss Finch for help. But she only shrugged. 'Is that it?' he said.

'I'm afraid so.'

Green Girls

★ ★ ★

As Jacob waited for traffic to pass so he could cross the street to his car, he felt the throbbing start behind his ears. Even his attorney had deserted him. But he was more worried about how to leave July – whether to tell her, or just steal away when she was asleep, pack his single bag and his computer and go.

Yes, and how would she retaliate?

Once again he wondered how Alix had stayed with July so long. Maybe the booze made it possible, keeping her in a constant stupor. And the yagé. The sex.

Or maybe Alix was also afraid to leave . . .

Until Jacob came along.

He turned around and looked out at the High-Level bridge spanning the river. Against his will, once again he imagined Alix falling, and he almost fell himself, had to lean against a van parked on the curb. No, not falling.

Jumping.

He was sure of it now. Jumping ten feet down to the narrow ledge that might have caught her, if she landed just right. Risking everything . . . to get free of July.

But wait. She'd already done that, gotten free of July.

He thought of Alix's dinner invitation, recalling the tension between her and July that night, and everything started making sense . . . the way Alix praised his writing in front of July. Yes, even the words she chose: 'I've never seen violence treated so sexually.'

And what did she tell him about July? 'If sex had a face.'

Playing both of them at the same time. Showing enough interest in Jacob to make July retaliate. Showing enough cruelty toward July to make Jacob want to rescue her.

You're so stupid, Alix had told him. How right she had been. He recalled Price's story, about Alix's offer of a threesome. But now Jacob understood her real motivation: Not to harvest his genes, as Price's vanity had led him to believe. She had intended to palm July off on him.

He stepped up onto the sidewalk and looked back at the high bridge again, imagining Alix crawling along the ledge, climbing down the rungs to the catwalk, disappearing inside the hollow beams, the tunnels, erasing herself from this life, abandoning all she'd ever accomplished . . .

To get away.

He stepped off the curb and crossed the street, cutting around the traffic—

'He's right, you know.'

Jacob looked back, to see Miss Finch standing outside the building. He didn't recognize her at first, in her sunglasses.

'Whether you think so or not, Attorney Zabriski is on your side,' she said. Traffic began moving again, left and right as he stood in the middle of Market Street.

'You know what I think?' Jacob replied. 'I think he doesn't want to spoil his batting record against Susan Evangeline. He doesn't care about me. Or my son.'

'He definitely does not want to lose to Evangeline,' she agreed, with an almost traitorous glance at the office building behind her. She took off her sunglasses when she turned back to Jacob, and he wondered if he detected sympathy in her plain face. 'He was paid good money to defend you, and he would have fought for you tooth and nail,' she said. 'But if you think you're entitled to a piece of his heart, you're even more naive than you act.'

Jacob walked away from her, directly into the path of a pickup truck, which skidded to a screeching stop. The horn was still blowing when he stepped onto the sidewalk and headed for his car.

'Do you know why you won't fight?' she called after him.

He opened his car door and was about to get in.

'I think you've convinced yourself that your son would be better off without you.'

He turned back, ready to tell her that she didn't know the first thing about him. But the way she was looking at him, he was struck silent. Her eyes were big with tears.

'You're wrong, Jacob,' she said. Then she put her sunglasses back on and went back to her office.

And he went to visit his old friend, Price Ashworth, to make him an offer.

CHAPTER NINE

———————

'Good evening, Ma'am, I take it you're the lady of the house?'
The nurse, wrestled from sleep by the incessant doorbell,
squinted at the man on the other side of the screen door. He was
dressed in a tie and jacket – which seemed odd in this heat, at this hour.
One arm, not inside his sleeve, hung across his chest in a dark blue
sling.

'Do you think I'd be wearing a uniform if I was the lady of the
house? I'm Mr Dunn's private-duty nurse.' From behind her came an
angry, guttural shout. 'I'm coming, hold your horses!' she yelled, then
turned back to the stranger. 'What time is it?'

The man gave her a boyish, dimpled grin. 'Late, I do heartily
apologize,' he said. Oh, yeah. Mr Charm. Then he showed her his
shield. 'I'm a detective with the Florida State Police.'

'The Georgia police were here all day,' she complained, not exactly
turning him away.

'Well, now I'd like to ask you some Florida questions,' he said. 'May
I come in?'

She puffed up her hair. 'If you must.'

Biff Bullens took the door from her and stepped into the foyer, then
turned to close the door with his good hand.

The woman led him into the living room, where the paralyzed man
lay sprawled on the floor in front of a leather recliner. He was barking
hoarsely out of his throat, while an orchestra on television performed
Dvorak's *New World Symphony*.

'I see you can move when you want to,' said the nurse, bending to lift
the insurance man. 'Don't just stand there,' she said to Bullens, who
was focused on the music.

'You like that highbrow stuff?' she said. With his good arm, the
ruddy-faced stranger helped her lift the patient back onto his chair,
while the man issued another series of gruff complaints.

'Sounds like he's trying to tell us something,' Bullens said to the woman. 'Lassie, what's wrong?' He flashed that smile again. 'No offense.'

'You do have an odd bedside manner,' she said, pushing out her abundant chest while she smoothed the front of her uniform.

Mr Dunn's tirade grew louder, more insistent, in fact sounding quite like a race car shifting through its gears.

'I can't understand you!' the nurse yelled at him. 'Jesus.' As she wiped his mouth with his bib, she asked Bullens, 'What did you say your name was again?'

'Detective Smith,' he told her. 'Just a few questions.'

'All right, but you're wasting your time,' she said, sitting on the edge of the couch. 'Like I told you, we've had police here most of the day, along with the FBI, doctors, reporters, speech therapists. Imagine, sending over a speech therapist with the likes of him.'

'Looks like he did some good,' Bullens said. 'The man does an admirable imitation of an automobile.'

The salesman's foot jerked, and he began making a wailing noise, like a siren.

'Here come the cops,' Bullens said.

'Hold on a sec,' said the nurse, getting up and walking out of the room. In a few moments she returned.

'I hate to tell you,' she said, 'but I think that speech therapist stole his Caddie.'

Terrence Gideon had never been in Savannah, Georgia. In fact, he'd never been out of Florida until now. But even in this unfamiliar place it wasn't difficult to find the right part of town, where trees refused to grow, where cars and appliances sat abandoned in the city shadows, along with another generation of discarded black men.

Gideon drove the slick new SUV slowly down the street, watching the heads turn, all the dispassionate eyes, until he saw the HOTEL sign. Ramshackle place a block from the river. Pulling the vehicle to the curb, he stuffed the cell phone back into his suitcase, then got out of the car. Left the keys in the ignition.

He asked for a front room on the third floor, which was the top, and he paid the desk clerk $25. There was a fan in the window, but no air conditioning. The room was sweltering. There was a sink, a bed, a lamp, and a small television. The wallpaper was old and dirty, Scotch-taped down the seams. The clerk told him the bathroom was down the hall.

As soon as he checked in, Gideon turned the fan on high and the room light off. Then he returned to the window and looked down at the vehicle he had stolen, while he listened to people in the next room having sex. Not that he was trying to. The walls were so thin, they could have been in his own room, with the springs wheezing and the bed legs rocking on the floor – and the way they carried on, especially the woman: 'Oh, baby, baby, baby, baby, you're so good, baby, no one do it like you . . .' On and on. Fortunately, Gideon didn't have to wait long, only fifteen minutes or so, before the boys came upon the SUV, looking around like this must be some kind of trick, way too good to be true, probably some kinda sting. So what? The very next minute, the vehicle was gone, probably on its way to some garage somewhere, to be painted or stripped. Gideon was sure it would never be seen again, at least not in Georgia.

'I went to the rock to hide my face, the rock cried out, "No hiding place!"
There's no hiding place down here.'
While Gideon waited on the phone, the gospel chorus filled the phone. Then the organ stopped. 'Oh, my Lord,' the woman said, breathless, her footsteps echoing over the receiver. 'Hello!'
'Miss Ida, please don't hang up.'
A moment of silence followed. Then the terrible voice: 'Is this who I think it is?'
'Ida May, I'm in sore need of your Christian charity.'
The big woman bellowed a single laugh. 'If you think Miss Ida's going to lift one little finger to get *your* sorry butt out of trouble, I think you've probably lost the last bit of mind you didn't dee-stroy on drugs.'
'I'm begging you, sister—'
'Y'all go on with your practicing!' he heard her holler. 'Don't you be eavesdroppin me!' When the voices started up again, she returned. 'Terrence Gideon, you must be delirious calling me here.'
'Miss Ida, I need to speak to my wife.' Suddenly, the couple in the next room started again, bumping and squeaking, and the woman going on again, 'Oh, baby, slow down. Uhh . . . uhhh . . . oh, baby, slow . . .'
'Far as I'm concerned, the best thing that's ever happened to her was the day she got rid of you. What's that noise?'
'Ida May, I did not do the things they're accusing me of,' Gideon said, moving to the far side of the room, 'I swear to God. A dishonest white man put me in these circumstances.'
That got her going, but he knew it would. And when Miss Ida got going, she could talk the ribs off a rubber. 'Terrence Gideon, you're

always so sure the white man's got his foot on you, you tell me this: If he got his foot on you all the time, how's he going to get anyplace himself?'

'Ida May—'

'Head full of self-righteousness and a heart full of blame. And no room left for personal responsibility!'

'Yes, Ma'am,' he said. 'You're a hundred percent right, Miss Ida, the good Lord knows you are, but, please, I need you to do something for me. I'm on my knees now.'

She said nothing for a moment. First time in all their years that Gideon had been able to shut her up – if only for that moment. When she started up again, she was oddly composed. 'Boy, are you in the middle of your midlife crisis?'

'Yes, Ma'am, I believe I am. Miss Ida, I need you to bring Bethany to your house tonight.'

'What?' She blew the word at him, which meant her composure was wearing thin. Any moment she'd slam the phone down.

'I need to beg her forgiveness.'

Once again Ida May let him hear her breathing – sounded like a winded workhorse. Then, from the next room, a man let out an ecstatic howl. Either that or he was being murdered.

'Lord knows I've done some bad things in my youth,' Gideon blurted into the phone. 'But I've always tried to be a good husband and father. Now, Ida May, I'm pleading with you to grant me this one kindness. I need to trust you not to betray me. For the sake of Bethany's children, your nieces and nephews. Please.'

He waited. And waited. Luckily, the couple had quieted down in the next room. Then, as he was about to plead again, Miss Ida blew a heavy sigh. 'I will pray on it,' she allowed.

'Oh, God bless you—'

'You best believe,' she cut him off. 'I've got a lot of praying to do.'

All but in flight, the Indian feels the cool night wind lift his hair and wash the back of his neck. A hazy half moon has risen hours ago, bright enough to turn the ocean green. He wets his lime stick in his mouth, then dips it in the *poporo*, coating it well, then takes the stick back into his mouth, excites the wad of coca in his cheek.

He sees yellow-gray light in the north, a buzzing kind of light, and he steers toward it. As the settlement rises up ahead, signs and streetlights fly at him. He slides his shades over his eyes. When he sees the big yellow M, he steers into the parking lot, almost clipping the EXIT sign. Driving around the back of the building, he parks behind

248

Green Girls

the fenced-in dumpster. On the other side of the rail fence, a convenience store sits up on an asphalt plateau, with two gas pumps in front. Sereno thinks about fueling the Corvette, but then he smells the fried food blowing out the exhaust fans, and he feels a hollow pang in his stomach. Still, it's not food he's stopped for. Or gasoline.

It's the silver-blue Porsche he spotted from the road, a 1957 Speedster, with the top down and a short-haired woman sitting in the passenger seat. The Speedster, this silver-blue shark, has New York license plates, but Sereno does not understand the significance of the colors or numbers or even the state name. Nor does he care about the music coming from the car's speakers, which sounds to him like thunder being released in increments.

He is more focused on the woman sitting in the passenger seat, the way she is trying not to look at him as he walks toward her, briefcase in hand, yet how all her other senses perk at his approach. In fact, her jaw is clenched, and she has stopped breathing.

The instant his hand touches the door handle, the woman scrambles out of the car and walks quickly around the building. Sereno nestles into the driver's seat. He steps on the clutch and turns the key. The gas gauge needle jumps to nearly full. The engine catches and rumbles, sending a warm vibration through the Indian's chest. He pulls the stick into reverse and backs out of the parking place, then watches a different girl walking toward the car, carrying a paper bag. She is a McDonald's girl, with yellow Ms on her shirt and on the bag she's carrying. And the way her head tilts when she sees him, the way she shows her teeth, she appears to be smiling. Sereno steps on the brake.

'I have your specialty order,' she says. 'Fish sandwich without cheese?'

He studies her melon breasts.

'Large fries and chocolate shake?'

Sereno stares, and she hands him the bag.

'Extra ketchup?' she asks.

Sereno stares, and she reaches into her uniform pocket and comes out with three, which she drops into his hand. He studies her head. Her red hair appears to be streaked with blue dye, and she is wearing a cardboard hat with the yellow M but no top.

'More?' she asks, reaching into her pocket again. 'You must love ketchup.' The packets spill out over Sereno's hand. He looks up at her with delight.

'This is all I have,' she tells him, just as the short-haired woman comes around the corner and stops, pointing, while a man wearing a

249

ball cap and another man wearing a topless M hat come running, tentatively.

Sereno watches them while he shifts into first and drives out on the road, keeping his headlights off. By the time he shifts into second, the Speedster has blended with the night.

PART FOUR

CHAPTER ONE

Price Ashworth's decorous, solar-powered home was situated near enough to Kittery Point that, in winter when the trees were bare, from an upstairs window he could boast of an ocean view, and he did. The house had three bedrooms, three Jacuzzi baths inside, a hot tub on the deck, and a glass-enclosed great room, where Price and Laura were presently seated at a cherry table Jacob had once built for him in exchange for Price's early work with Max.

Laura hadn't said much during the meal – spaghetti and sauce – except to tell him she was depressed at the thought of Max leaving in six weeks. Now, while he massaged her hand, and meditative Tibetan flutes wafted from built-in speakers, the motion-detector on the front porch lit up the pines that bordered the property. Price didn't pay any mind. The neighbor's cat triggered the light twenty times a night. In fifteen seconds the light went out again.

. . . And Jacob sliced through the basement window screen.

He had worked out the possibilities on the drive over. Because Price would have accumulated several years' worth of files that Laura transcribed from his tape-recorded sessions – and neither the files nor tapes had been in his office – he must have kept them somewhere in his house. But not in his bedroom, or living room, or great room, or any room where guests might see them. Probably not even in his home office. The basement seemed the logical place.

Jacob was right. Price's wine cellar, a windowless, atmosphere-controlled chamber, was located in an alcove off the carpeted basement. Jacob found the light switch and turned it on, moving quickly. The wine, maybe 200 bottles, was stacked along an entire wall. On the end wall was a mahogany desk, beside which stood three file cabinets with cheap, wood-grain finish, the furniture probably scavenged from Price's early offices.

253

It was almost too easy. While he listened to the murmur of conversation above him, Jacob quietly pulled out the C drawer, and there they were: three Alix Callahan folders, three months' worth – April, May, and June. He shuffled through them, found that each contained a few sheets of typed, single-spaced notes and two sixty-minute cassettes, their labels dated, one session per side. He was most interested in June 22, the date of Alix's final appointment, and went through the papers until he found the documentation. 'Discussed excessive drinking, problems with relationships,' the transcription read – and that was it. Unlike the other session notes in all other files, the record from June 22 provided no more information than did Price's office notes – with one exception. The added, penciled-in word: 'Florida.'

'I didn't *say* "lie." ' Price's voice suddenly rang clear, as a door opened above. 'I'm merely suggesting that you represent an alternative reality.'

Jacob hurried to the alcove doorway, flicked off the lights and waited in the dark.

Footsteps came down the stairs. 'Are you sure you want Pinot noir?'

Stuffing the tape in his pocket, Jacob felt his way back to the file cabinets and quietly slid the drawer closed. Outside the room, a light came on, seeping under the door. 'Pinot noir is hardly a *digestif.*' Price's voice, louder. 'I'll pick out a nice bottle of Port, if you'd rather.'

Jacob ducked behind the file cabinets. Then the room lights came on. While Jacob held his breath, he heard Price mutter the words, '*Pinot noir,*' as if he were cursing. A bottle slid against the wooden rack, then the light went off again.

Jacob felt his heart stir. The honeymoon was over. And he was about to make sure it stayed that way.

'I let myself in, I'm sorry,' Jacob said, appearing in the dining room by way of the swinging kitchen door. Price and Laura were seated at the table, partway through a late dinner. 'I won't stay,' Jacob said, brushing a string of cobwebs off his sleeve.

Laura gave him a searing look. Price reached for her hand, but she moved it. In fact, they weren't getting along tonight, evidenced by the dinner Laura had prepared: spaghetti from a box and sauce from a jar.

Jacob said, 'Is Maxie here?'

'You can't see him now, it's after ten,' Laura told him. 'He's asleep, up in the guest room.'

'How is he?'

'Fine, if appetite is any indication,' Price said. 'He must have cleaned out three concession stands at Fenway.'

Jacob said to Laura, 'Did I hear he's been accepted to Belnap?'

'Jake, not now—'

'As an alumnus, I have privileges,' Price said, 'not to mention friends on the Board of Regents and discounted tuition.'

'Sounds like a good deal for everyone,' Jacob said.

Price agreed. 'For once he'll be in an environment that challenges his intellectual curiosity.'

'Good for you too,' Jacob said. 'Why would you want a kid around the house all the time? He's not yours.'

Laura sighed.

'Baiting,' Price cautioned her, and she leveled her eyes at him.

'You're not going to put him on Ritalin,' Jacob said to Price. He wasn't asking.

'No, we're not. Of course, I feel differently about the matter. However, I'll respect your wishes.'

'Okay?' Laura said. 'Now you've made your point.'

'I'm not finished,' Jacob told her.

'I think you are,' Price said.

The house became suddenly quiet, except for the Tibetan flutes.

Price took his hands off the table and set them on his knees. 'We've asked you nicely,' he said. 'Please. Don't make me stand up.'

'Oh, Price, give it a rest,' Laura said in a longsuffering way. Yes, the wine was working on her.

'I don't mean to start trouble,' Jacob said.

'You're not starting trouble,' Price was quick to say.

'The reason I came was to see if we could get together and talk things over sometime.'

'We're not *supposed* to be talking,' Laura shot back. 'You're not supposed to be here.'

'Laura?' Price said, and he motioned to her wine glass.

She picked up the glass and drained it, while she eyed him over the rim.

Price turned to Jacob and said lightly, 'Are you enjoying this?'

Jacob showed them his hands, an apology, then pulled a chair and sat down. 'Look, we all want to save Max the pain of a drawn-out custody hearing, with lawyers parceling out every little piece of our lives. I'm proposing we meet somewhere, in a quiet restaurant—'

'What are you doing?' Laura peered at him, narrow-eyed.

'No lawyers,' he said. 'To act as mediators, you could bring Price, I'd bring July. We'll have a nice dinner, a bottle of wine or champagne . . . on second thought, champagne goes to July's head.'

He resisted the urge to look over at Price.

'And then what,' Laura said, 'when it all blows up in our faces?'

She gave him a long, resonant look. He couldn't tell if it was suspicion he was seeing, or regret. Whatever, it was breaking his heart. Still he persisted.

'We probably won't agree on everything,' he said. 'But shouldn't we try – for Maxie's sake?'

Laura lowered her eyes. Jacob looked over at Price, who offered a conciliatory shrug.

'It might be a step in the right direction,' he said to Laura.

Oh, yes. Jacob knew he could count on his old friend.

CHAPTER TWO

———

The silver Speedster glides through the Carolina night like a soaring bat, Sereno making his way northward along narrow black roads, past buildings and houses and trailers. He can *feel* the river, can *feel* the bridge, even though they're still miles away. Eventually, as the Porsche follows a long bend in the road, he watches the horizon fall away and the river take its place, widening, drifting through marshlands and dunes, down to the sea. And far off to the north, the steel arch rises up in the sky, growing nearer.

But Sereno is troubled, and a half mile before the structure, he stops the car. He doesn't need to taste the water or feel its warmth to know. She is not here. The night is quiet, except for the water washing along the grassy banks. The low clouds glow across the river, where there's a shopping mall.

He starts the engine again and drives on, staying on the dark side of the river. He drives slowly past the bridge. The Speedster is low on gas. Soon he sees a light on the roadside. A small square building with a illuminated sign and three vehicles parked out front. Sereno pulls to the edge of the riverbank and shuts off the engine. He can hear the steady thud of music inside the place. He takes his briefcase out of the car, turns the steering wheel hard to the right, then pushes the Speedster down the bank. The river swallows the car with hardly a splash. The music rises up in the night.

LITTLE BOB'S BAR AND GRILL, the place was called. It squatted in a clearing carved out of the North Carolina pines. Sometime after midnight, only three vehicles were parked there: a '98 GMC pickup, belonging to Little Bob himself. A few feet away was a brand new Thunderbird hardtop, bright red. In front of the building, actually parked sideways underneath the sign, kind of showcased there, was a two-tone 1965 F-100 pickup, turquoise and cream, with fat white-walls.

Inside Little Bob's, the insect-encrusted window fan was going hard, competing with the jukebox, the combination sending a steady WUH-WUH-WUH vibration out the windows. A piece of cardboard tacked above the Fryolator said 'CRAB CAKES SPECIAL $4.99.' Other than that, the only food served were onion rings and french fries, not to mention the two big jars of jerky and pickled eggs.

On some nights the place felt cramped, especially with a lot of eye contact going on, the way it was tonight, with the three local boys in the corner booth, smoking their Camels, drinking their Buds, and watching two muscleboys from Deepwater playing bumper pool, while their Deepwater girlfriends sat at the lunch counter, smoking Marlboros and eating three pounds of french fries with malt vinegar and lots of salt, and drinking Corona from bottles.

They'd started a thing with the jukebox, these two groups. The Deepwater girls favored Dwight Yoakam, Alan Jackson, the Dixie Chicks. The local boys preferred Led Zeppelin, Pantera. So they had this sort of teasing, flirting thing going, that is, until one of the local boys decided to shovel half a week's pay into the machine. So now they were into 'Stairway to Heaven' for the seventh time, and the Deepwater girls were getting worked up, a lot of squinting through smoke rings.

Probably no one would have noticed the roof light come on inside the F-100, except one of the Deepwater girls decided to show one of the locals her middle finger, which caused him to smirk and turn his head toward the window.

The locals came out first, one of them the owner of the pickup. When he saw Sereno trying to hot-wire the truck he almost laughed. Long-haired and wearing wraparound shades, the Indian could barely see over the wheel.

'Fuckin Mexicans,' he said.

The Deepwater muscle boys came to the door to watch the action. Their girls pushed past them for a look, one saying, 'Aw, a little Mexican midget.'

Now they all came out and surrounded the pickup. The owner was complaining, 'I don't give a fuck, okay? He's a fuckin illegal, and they steal our jobs.'

'What job is that?' said one of his buddies, and the Deepwater guys cut loose with a laugh, at which point the owner puffed himself up, spread his legs, and said to Sereno, 'You want to steal my fuckin truck, too, Pedro?'

The brown-skinned man gazed at him through his shades.

'I don't think he understands English,' said one of the girls.

Green Girls

'Maybe we should teach him,' said the other. 'He looks like he wants a lesson, with that pen in his mouth.'

One of the Deepwater boys – the biggest one – opened the passenger door, grinned in at the Indian and said, 'Welcome to our country, *señor*,' then ducked inside and punched Sereno's ear, knocking the sunglasses askew. 'This word means "ass-kick." '

'Kurt, don't hurt him,' one of the girls said. 'Let's call the cops.'

'Here, you want the keys?' said the owner, dangling his jack-knife key ring in front of Sereno.

'I think he wants a haircut,' Kurt said, reaching in the other door to haul the Indian out of the truck, which is when something curious happened. Kurt said, 'Shit,' and grabbed at his neck. Then he stumbled backwards, trying to keep from falling. But he sat hard on the ground.

One of the girls laughed, thought he was clowning.

'Kurt, what?' said the other, as the musclebound boy let out a pitiful groan and curled up on the ground, shaking.

'Kurt?' one of the girls said, coming over, *'Kurt!'*

In the moment of distraction, the Indian slid out of the truck and ran.

'Get him!' yelled one of the locals, and they gave chase around the back of the building, into the pine woods. The other Deepwater boy took off around the front of the place.

'Marcus, no!' a girl cried, but she was drowned out by the other cries in the darkness. 'Go around, go around!' 'He went up the hill!' 'Circle around!'

'Somebody help him!' the other girl screamed, kneeling beside the fallen boy. 'We've gotta get Kurt to the hospital!'

'Get behind him!' someone shouted from the pines. The night crackled with footsteps and breaking twigs.

'Marcus, it's not your problem!' cried the boy's girlfriend, from the corner of the building,

'I got him!' a voice shouted – then the same voice broke in a guttural exclamation.

'Marcus?' the girl called, leaning toward the night. 'Marcus!'

All at once she spun away from the building, as a shadow broke out of the trees, footsteps pounding, branches snapping, two boys charging hard for the T-bird, joined by the girls, all of them pulling at the door handles, jumping inside. The new car roared to life, sprayed gravel at the building, and fishtailed out of the lot . . .

. . . while a slight, solitary figure walked around LITTLE BOB'S BAR AND GRILL, climbed into the Ford pickup, and started the engine. Then he was gone, joining the night.

259

CHAPTER THREE

———

A fine drizzle covered Jacob's windshield. Under a chilly, moonless midnight, the beach was quiet except for the waves pounding close to the road. Not a good night for tourists or teens to be out cruising. Jacob's dashboard clock showed 12:25, and he wondered if July would be waiting up for him when he got home.

He slid the cassette into the tape player and Price's voice came on: '... I want you to imagine the most peaceful, most relaxing, most wonderful place ...' Jacob hit FAST-FORWARD, then tried again. '...You take another step closer. Your breathing is slower, more relaxed ... easy, deep breathing. You're so comfortable ...' Fast-forward again. This time when Jacob hit PLAY, he heard Alix's voice.

'... Plantation Key.'

Price: 'That's in Florida—?'

'Yes. When I was in Colombia, I'd heard stories about her sexual escapades. And I knew they were raising a number of plants I was interested in.'

'They being?'

'July. And her husband, Sereno.'

'The Indian shaman.'

'Yes. Only her name wasn't July then. It was Juliette.'

A car came down the road, headlights flaring inside Jacob's car. He slunk low in the seat. Juliette, he repeated to himself.

'... how you found them?'

'I met July first. I never actually talked to Sereno.' Alix's speech, Jacob noted, was flat and slow, no doubt due to hypnosis.

Price: 'Were you attracted to her when you first met?'

Pause. 'At the time, I don't think I was capable of being attracted to anyone,' Alix replied ponderously. 'I did know that she was quite young and beautiful.'

'Did you think she was attracted to you?'

'I don't know. She was working in the garden, transplanting into clay pots. I told her who I was and that I wanted to spend a few days studying her plants. While we talked, her husband came home.'

'Sereno.'

'He was a fisherman. Their property backed up to a canal where he docked his boat. When he saw me, he walked into the house. The way she watched him, I could tell she was agitated about something. She told me if I wanted, I could come back in the morning, after he went out fishing. Then she went in the house, and I left.'

'Did you perceive any sort of suggestive undertone in her invitation?'

'No.'

'But you did return.'

'She came to my motel room about five the next morning and told me that she was afraid for her life.'

'Afraid of her husband?'

A pause. Jacob nudged up the volume. 'She said she hadn't slept all night because he was so jealous. She was afraid he was going to murder her.'

'She told you her husband was jealous,' Price said. 'Interesting transference.'

'She asked if she could sleep in my room for a couple of hours.'

Hearing Alix's words, Jacob tensed as he recalled his own experience, July's predawn visit to E-Z Acres. Another car went by. The mist, he noticed, had turned to a light rain on his windshield.

'Was that when your attraction turned physical?' Price said.

'It's not important.'

'It would help me understand how your relationship evolved,' Price replied. 'When July asked to sleep in your room, did you take that as a sexual proposition?'

'I don't think so.'

'Did you get into bed together?'

Alix, breathing, not answering.

'Take your time,' Price couched.

'Asshole,' Jacob muttered.

'Can you see what July was wearing?' Price said.

'She took off her top,' Alix said.

'She was naked?'

'She had on a pair of white bikinis. Other than that, yes.'

'And you were aroused at that point?'

Again, the car became quiet, except for the fingertips tapping at the roof.

'And yourself,' Price continued. 'What you were wearing.'

Alix said slowly, distinctly, 'I'd put my robe on when I answered the door. I kept it on. Is this turning you on, *Doctor?*'

Jacob chuckled. Even hypnotized, she hadn't lost her spark.

'Shall we stop?' Price said.

'No.'

'Then. You got into bed together . . .'

Pause. 'July got in first. When I got in beside her, she held onto me.'

'Does it occur to you that she might have sexual feelings toward you?'

Jacob noticed Price's continued attempt to shift into present tense. He turned up the volume.

'I wanted to kiss her,' Alix replied, staying in the past, maintaining some degree of control.

'Do you kiss her?'

'I put my arm around her.'

'And . . .'

'Her back was very warm. Her hair was cool. I remember that.'

'You can feel this now.'

Alix's slow breathing was suddenly drowned out by the rainfall's louder pattering. 'She curls up, like a little girl. I can feel her breathing on me. Then she's brushing her lips against my neck.'

'And you're aroused—?'

'We started kissing.' Alix coming out of the present, yet still speaking without emotion.

Price coaching her: 'Breathing. That's it. Nice, deep breaths. So relaxed. So safe here.'

'We made love most of the morning,' Alix said, her voice slow again. 'I'd never imagined sex could be so intense. Then she asked me to give her a bath. I did. And we made love again in the afternoon.'

'I see.'

'For the rest of the week—'

'Yes.'

Pause.

Price again: 'I'm sorry. Continue, please.'

'For the rest of the week she came to my motel room every morning, after her husband went out fishing. We took yagé, we made love, we slept in each other's arms, and later we worked in her garden . . .'

'You were falling in love with her.'

Silence.

'Alix, tell me what you're thinking now.'

'Huh?'

'What do you remember? You're safe here. You're safe with me.'

'Friday morning.'

'Friday morning,' Price said. 'Four days later. Take your time.'

'On Friday morning July told me that she'd had an affair with a man.'

'After she had started with you?'

'No. Before. His name was Kiefer. He lived in Key Largo, and he had connections with a couple of fishermen who were running cocaine from Santa Marta.'

Alix stopped again, and took a contemplative breath.

'You're completely safe,' Price assured her. 'Deep breathing.'

'July let Kiefer use her dock when Sereno was out fishing,' she continued. 'And they would have sex.'

'Why did she tell you about this man?'

'Because he was dead.'

Silence.

'The police found him stabbed to death, and July told me she was afraid Sereno had murdered him because he'd found out about them. And now . . .'

'Breathing.'

More silence.

'Alix, do you want to stop?'

' . . and now she was afraid Sereno was going to kill her.'

'Do you want to stop?'

'No, I want to keep going,' Alix answered clearly. 'I told July she should call the police, but she was afraid they would connect her with the drugs and deport her—'

'Steady, slow. Remember, Alix, you're completely safe.'

'We were in the garden that afternoon, Friday afternoon, when Sereno came home.'

'You were afraid of him.'

'Of course.'

'Did he seem agitated? Was he acting different?'

'He didn't say anything, but he never did.

'So he went in the house. What did July do?'

'She went in with him. I was afraid for her. I was afraid for myself. I stayed close to the house and listened. Then I heard—'

Rain pounding the car roof, ocean waves battering the beach. A car came toward Jacob, headlights flashing bright to dim. He leaned closer to the dash, lowering his head.

Price: 'What do you hear?'

'A gunshot,' Alix said. 'Two gunshots. And I went in the house.'

'Do you run, or do you walk?'

263

Hesitation. 'Ran,' Alix said. 'When I got inside, I could hear July screaming. I ran upstairs, and they were in the bedroom—'

'Slow, slow—'

'He's lying across her on the floor. They're both covered in blood, and neither of them moving . . . Her mouth is open like she should have been screaming . . . but they both look dead, and then I see he has her finger in his mouth, and he's . . .'

'Okay, Alix. Shh. That's enough—'

'. . . He's chewing. She's letting him. So I look for the gun, but the gun isn't there, and now I'm stabbing him—'

'Slow down, Alix. Breathing. Breathing.'

'—in the back, in the side, and he's not moving, not even trying to stop me, but he won't let go of her finger—'

'Alix, I think we need to stop—'

'When I pull him off her, he rolls over, his face is all blood, and he's staring up at me and not moving, not breathing any more, like he's dead . . . and that's when I see inside his mouth . . . her finger—'

'Alix—'

'I just want to get her finger—'

'I'm going to count—'

'I'm trying to get it!'

'Yes, I know, he bit her finger off. Okay. *Shhh.* You're safe now. I'm going to count.'

'He should be dead. I'm trying to get her finger. He jumps up, and he won't let go! I can hear his teeth going into my cheek. July's stabbing him over and over. He won't die!'

'Alix,' Price said sharply. 'I'm going to start counting backwards now.'

'Listen to me!'

'From five to one—'

'We ran out,' Alix said, not stopping. 'I dropped July at the police station, then I went back to my motel and picked up my things and I drove all night, with toilet paper to stop the blood. When I got to North Carolina I went to a hospital and said a dog had attacked me while I was jogging.'

'Alix, we're out of time now. When you hear me say the number one, you are going to be fully awake and rested. You are going to feel comfortable and at peace—'

'I dream about him,' she said.

'He is dead now, and you're safe.'

'No, he didn't die,' she said. 'He went to prison.'

'And you had to testify at his trial.'

'No. Nobody knows I was there.'

'Does he know your name, where you live?'

'He doesn't know a thing. When he's released, he'll be deported back to Colombia. It's not important. I'm not afraid of him.'

'Very good,' Price said. 'Five . . . You're already beginning to feel a change—'

'I am trying to tell you something.'

'You're too agitated, Alix.'

'Of course I'm agitated. I just told you I tried to kill someone.'

'You have nothing to be ashamed of.'

'You're not listening.'

'Alix, you were protecting yourself. You were protecting someone you loved—'

'*Listen to me! I'm telling you—!*'

Her voice cut off. Jacob turned up the volume, until he heard nothing but tape hiss. He fast-forwarded for a second or two, then tried again. Nothing, but the rain whacking at his roof, the ocean waves crashing in.

Then he realized why the tape had been left in Price's files. Whatever Alix had continued to say – Jacob shuddered to think it could be more incriminating than what he'd just heard – Price had erased it. Either that, or it was transferred to digital and encrypted, stored on a hard drive or floppy disk. Whatever the case, Jacob knew he was never going to find it.

Another car came down the street behind him, headlights brightening the interior of his car, then flashing past, tires slapping at the wet pavement. He glanced in his rearview mirror . . . then looked again. Suddenly alert, he turned and looked over the seat, at the car parked behind him. About fifty feet back, dark, seemingly unoccupied . . . July's Volvo? Through the rain-streaked back window, he couldn't tell. What troubled him most: the car hadn't been there when he'd arrived. Neither had he seen it pull up – at least he hadn't seen its headlights.

He turned back to start the car – and jumped in his seat.

July was at his window. Standing in the rain.

'Jesus,' he said, rolling the window down, 'what are you doing there?'

'Aren't you coming home?' She sounded so sad. Thinking about what he'd just heard, he suddenly felt nothing but pity for her. He opened his door and gathered her wet body in his arms. She crawled in on top of him, shivering, and he closed the door.

'You're soaking wet. How long have you been out there?'

Her cheek was cold. He turned on the engine, pushed the heater to full. She kissed his neck, and it made him shiver.

'July, what's the matter?'

She kept silent. Had she heard what he'd been listening to?

'Tell me.'

'You went to see her?' she said in a small voice.

'Laura?' Yes, he thought, back to the plan – though his enthusiasm for it had all but vanished. 'She was at Price's,' he admitted. 'I went there to make a deal.'

He felt her arm stiffen.

'I was planning to tell you about it,' he said, and tried to turn her into his arms, but she pulled rigidly away from him and glared out at the rain.

'July,' he said tenderly. Although he couldn't help but feel sympathy for her, his determination to break free was quickly returning. He touched her again, but it was like touching stone.

'I don't want her back,' he whispered. 'The only reason I went over there is because I think I know how to beat the lawyers.'

She looked up at him, paying attention now.

'I've made a good deal of furniture over the years,' he explained. 'Our dining room set, armoire, bookcases, bureaus, a vanity. Besides custody of Max, that's all I want – my furniture. Now, Price, on the other hand, owns a big new house with ocean views, you know what I mean, the hot tub, the huge sound system, the home theater. He's got all kinds of money, belongs to the Yacht Club, eats at the best restaurants every day of the week. What I'm getting at is, he's incredibly materialistic. But he's got this other side: giving and caring, the attentive, sensitive lover. How would it look to Laura if he takes all my furniture?'

She eyed him suspiciously.

'That's why I arranged for us to meet with both of them for dinner tomorrow night,' Jacob said. 'Just the four of us.'

July didn't even look at him. She flung open the door and walked out in the rain.

'July?'

She kept walking.

Jacob closed the door and took a deep, uncertain breath. The plan was in play, past the point of no return. As a web of lightning shattered the sky, he wondered if he should ever have started.

CHAPTER FOUR

G ideon heated two packages of freeze-dried chicken noodle soup in
the coffee pot, ate a can of sardines, and finished it off with a
couple of cookies that the kids had made him, washed it all down with a
cup of chicken-flavored coffee. Then he got into bed and started reread-
ing his book, *The Chaneysville Incident*, all about John Washington, an
African-American scholar who returns to his hometown and begins
unearthing the dark secrets of his family's past. Yes, Bethany had put the
book in his suitcase for a reason, because John Washington uncovers a
thing or two about his own dark self in the process. No matter. Gideon
only managed to read a page before he fell asleep.

He had set the alarm clock for eleven. Good thing, too. Because
when his cell phone rang, the radio had been playing for a half hour.
He had fallen asleep with the book on his chest. He shut off the radio,
picked up his cell phone and answered. 'Yeah?'

'Baby, is that you?' It was Bethany.

'It's me,' he said, softly, wanting to apologize for his actions in
Jacksonville, but not wanting to admit that he'd mistrusted her. 'Babe,
are you okay? How are the children?'

'Everyone's well,' she answered. 'But we miss you so.'

He laid his head against the headboard, awash with grief. 'I'm so
sorry to get you mixed up in my troubles. But I told you, I can't trust
that honky Landry.'

Honky, because she'd brought Landry to Jacksonville, and because
she'd given him that book, as if he needed a lesson. He waited for her
to come back at him. But she didn't. B.J. Landry did.

'You listening to the news, Jasper? Where are you?'

Jasper, the nickname Landry used to call him.

Gideon jumped off the bed and went to the door, to make sure it
was locked. 'Where are *you?*'

'Well,' Landry drawled, 'let's just say I believe your story. Let's also say that I'm currently under suspension because there were some FBI agents waiting at your house when I drove your wife home last night, and I refused to say where we'd been.'

'I see,' Gideon said, unconvinced.

'That's right. Because I believe you're just hard-headed enough to think you're gonna be a hero and cancel out that half-assed possession rap that any sensible man woulda forgot a long time ago.'

'Sensible *white* man.'

'Yeah, well, screw that shit. Have you heard the radio in the last few minutes? Seen the TV?'

'Not recently.'

'Well, you're both on the news, you and the Indian.'

'I'm not surprised.'

'Are you driving a Cadillac Escalade by any chance, that you got in Delta City?'

Gideon was quiet for a moment. 'I do what I need to,' he said.

'Including murder?'

Gideon fell silent.

'Did you go to that man's house?' Landry asked.

'What are you saying, *murder?*'

Landry raised his voice. 'Were you in that house?'

'I asked the man some questions, but he couldn't speak,' Gideon said. 'Then, yes, I commandeered his vehicle, and I'd do it again. What murder?'

'You probably left fingerprints,' Landry said in a sober voice. 'And they're dead.'

'Who?'

'Both of 'em,' Landry said. 'The man and his nurse, executed, shot in the head.'

Gideon sat hard on the bed.

'The nurse's boyfriend found them a short while ago.'

Gideon turned on the TV and started searching for a news channel. 'How do you know all this?'

'I got a friend,' Landry said.

'It was Bullens,' Gideon said. 'Had to be. But why would he kill them?'

'Because he didn't want cops to know about that Cadillac you took.'

'Why?'

'Because wherever you are, he's right behind you.' An unmistakable urgency had overtaken Landry's voice. 'You've got to move – now. That Cadillac comes with GPS, which means it can be traced – where it's at presently, and anyplace it's stopped along the way. A respectable car thief would know enough to smash the thing and throw it in the river. But I have a feeling you didn't think to do that.'

'I never stole a thing in my life, before this,' Gideon told him, tracking through the TV channels, looking for news. 'Bubble gum, maybe.'

'Hey—'

'But I've sure never killed anyone.'

'Get to a phone in a public place – a good restaurant – and call the cops. Turn yourself in.'

'I turn myself in, and I'm guilty a hundred times over.'

'Think about this,' Landry persisted. 'Dead, you can't defend yourself.'

'If I spend one hour in prison, any prison, with Bullens wanting me dead?' Gideon shot back. 'I never get to trial. You know it.'

Gideon stopped on a channel. Yellow police tape fluttering in a breeze. A road house just behind, with the sign – LITTLE BOB'S BAR AND GRILLE.

'Listen to me—'

'Wait a minute.'

CLOSE ON: Sereno. The mug shot filling the screen. Goosebumps raced up Gideon's sides.

'It's him,' Gideon said.

'Who?'

CUT TO: State Troopers and detectives walking inside the crime scene.

PAN BACK: a road sign: DEEPWATER 3.

'Deepwater . . . Where's Deepwater?'

'Don't you go after that Colombian,' Landry said. 'If you find him, he'll have to kill you. I don't care if you once did him a favor. I don't care about no Miranda card.'

PAN: The road house, the sign, the river . . . Rising in the background, a tall, skeletal, arched bridge comes into view above the treetops, its flashing beacon on top . . .

Landry was still talking when Gideon hung up the phone. He stared hard at the television . . . and a single, clear thought came to him. The bridge looked exactly like the one he had seen in Georgia, the last place Sereno had struck.

Gideon pushed up the volume, heard the newscaster say, 'As our elected leaders attempt to deal with the myriad problems of immigration, underfunded prisons, and violence in our society, tonight the quiet town of Deepwater, North Carolina, finds itself at the center of our national multicultural experiment. And asks why.'

★ ★ ★

269

Gideon threw on his trousers and shirt, stuffed his jacket and book and bathroom stuff into his suitcase, then walked out into the dingy hall and headed for the stairs – while a slender black woman came creeping warily up. She was in her thirties, but dressed like a kid, in a tight-fitting skirt and Minnie Mouse T-shirt. She hurried past Gideon and murmured, 'If you ain't s'posed to be here, I'd hold up.'

Gideon stopped . . . heard the squeak of stairs being climbed. When he turned back, he saw the woman unlocking the door next to his.

'Ma'am,' he whispered, summoning her. She frowned and shook her head at him. He hurried toward her as she tried to get inside, but he got there first.

'You can't—'

He covered her mouth and shut the door. 'I've been unjustly accused,' he whispered in her ear, as he set his suitcase on the floor.

By the apathetic look in her eyes, he could tell that she not only didn't care, but she wasn't even frightened – at least, not of him. But the way she reached a hand out of his clutches and turned the lock on the door, he knew she wanted nothing to do with whoever was coming up those stairs.

'Thank you,' he mouthed, then he let her go. She crept to the bed and turned off her lamp, and the room went dark, except for the street light filtering through the tattered shades, a cold and bluish haze. They could hear a television in the next room, sounded like porno. Whoever had it on was snoring loudly.

Then they heard voices in the hall. 'I don't mind doing my part to help the police, but I can't have no affiliation, you know what I mean, Boss, if I want to stay in business—'

'Be quiet and unlock the door.'

'I'm doin that right now.'

It was Bullens and the desk clerk. Gideon recognized both their voices. Hearing the door open, he pressed his ear to the wall and listened to the two men walk into his room. He could see the woman's eyes in the darkness. Now she was plenty scared.

Gideon heard Bullens say to the desk clerk: 'I thought you said he was still here.'

'What I said is, I never seen him leave.'

The conversation was as present as if they were standing beside Gideon. He listened to their footsteps, then the shushing of the closet curtain being torn aside, metal clothes-hangers clinking together.

Bullens said: 'When you see him last?'

The desk clerk said: 'I guess, I don't know, four, five hours ago. Back when he checked in. Boss, he looked way too big to fit under there.'

Gideon imagined Bullens getting down on his knees to look under the bed.

Bullens said: 'Okay, then. I need to know I can count on your confidentiality.'

The desk clerk said: 'Absolutely.'

'Outstanding. Other officers are gonna be coming around, asking questions. This is important. I was never here.'

'Boss, no one was ever here.'

Gideon listened to footsteps.

Bullens said: 'Well now.'

The desk clerk said: 'Huh?'

Bullens said: 'The TV's still warm.'

In the darkness, Gideon saw the woman's eyes intensify.

Bullens said: 'You been at that desk this whole time?'

The clerk said: 'Never left once.'

'Not even to use the bathroom?'

'Maybe once.'

Bullens made a sound, a laugh or a grunt. Footsteps moved from right to left. Then a door closed.

The clerk said: 'What are we doing, Boss?'

Bullens said: 'I think I just found a clue.' They were still inside Gideon's room. 'Yes, I did find a clue. Outstanding. Tell me, do you see something funny?'

The clerk said: 'I see you holding two pillows.'

Bullens said: 'Not that. Look closer.'

The clerk said: 'Boss, I don't see—'

It sounded like someone slammed a car door – and a tiny beam of light suddenly shot across the room. An answering beam came in from a hole in the wall of the snorer's room. Then the snoring stopped. The television went off.

The woman held her hand to her mouth. Her eyes were wide. They both knew: Bullens had shot the clerk. Gideon gave her a look, inquiring if she was okay. She nodded that she was.

Then, from Gideon's room, the shaft of light was cut off . . . probably Bullens trying to peek through the bullet hole. When the beam reappeared, Gideon heard the floor boards squeak, Bullens leaving the room.

Gideon kept his eye on the woman. She was trembling, her eyes fixed on something beyond him. He turned and saw the shadow appear under the door. Then the sound of the doorknob being turned.

The woman looked as though she was about to start screaming. Gideon shook his head at her.

The door rattled.

Gideon looked around for a weapon but saw nothing except the bedside lamp, so he reached out his hand. The woman understood. She lifted the lamp off the table and handed it to him – but didn't think to unplug it from the wall.

The sudden knock at the door almost made him drop it.

The woman shrank back, terrified.

'Room service,' Bullens said softly. 'Somebody sent up a bottle of good red wine and a big bucket of chicken wings.'

Gideon pulled on the lamp until the power cord stretched taut against the woman's leg. She looked down helplessly. The outlet was behind the bed.

Now the door creaked, straining against the lock, Bullens leaning in against it. 'All paid for,' he said. 'I just need a little signature.' The knocking started, louder.

Gideon gave the lamp a hard tug, and the power cord snapped free, whipped past the woman's hip and slapped the door.

The knocking stopped.

Gideon didn't move, didn't even twitch. Neither did the woman. In fact they stood so silently that they could hear Bullens breathing on the other side of the door.

Then a succession of sounds from down on the street. Car engines, car doors closing. Police radios. Bullens must have heard it too, because all at once the shadow moved away from under the door.

Gideon met the woman's eyes.

'Shh,' he said, and tiptoed around the bed, to the window, where he pulled the shade aside. Down on the street, where he'd left the SUV, the vehicles were gathering – unmarked vans and wagons. Men in dark windbreakers huddled on the sidewalk. One of them was talking into a radio, pointing his finger this way and that. Gideon ducked away from the window and whispered to the woman. 'Is there a back way?'

Her eyes widened. 'Better.'

Gideon unlocked the door and peeked out. The hallway ran front to back, cutting the building in two. It was empty . . . unless Bullens was waiting inside one of the doors.

'Come on,' mouthed the woman, handing him his suitcase. She pushed past him and tiptoed out to the hall, but away from the stairs. He followed. At the end of the hall, there was a door. But when she opened it, Gideon saw it was only a closet, where the vacuum cleaner and chambermaid's cart were stored.

He shook his head. 'They're sure to look in here.'

272

The woman pulled out the cart, pulled out the vacuum cleaner, then stepped inside and shoved her shoulder against the right-hand wall, which suddenly rotated at its center, revealing a narrow, dark stairway down.

'Hurry up,' she said, backing out again.

Gideon squeezed through, holding his suitcase in front of his chest. 'Where's it go?'

'Shush,' she said, and pulled the vacuum cleaner back inside, then the chambermaid's cart. They could already hear men's voices inside the building when she quietly closed the closet door behind them. Then she joined him on the stairway and pushed the wall closed again.

'Ever hear of the Underground Railroad?' she whispered as they began creeping down.

'Where's it go?' he asked again.

'Underground,' she said. 'All the way to the river.'

'Then what?' he said.

'Honey, then you're on your own.'

CHAPTER FIVE

W hen Jacob smelled coffee, he awoke and wandered out into the kitchen. Seeing July down in the garden, uprooting plants with her pitchfork, he remembered his dinner plans with Laura and Price – and how July had gone out to her garden hut when he got home, and stayed there all night. He went to the open glass door and called down to her.

'Thanks for letting me sleep late.'

She kept digging. In fact, it looked like she'd already torn out a fair amount of vegetation and left it on the ground to die. He poured himself a mug of coffee, then went down to the shop to assemble July's headboard. As he laid two sheets of plywood on the floor, one on top of the other, then spread a sheet of poly on top, he wondered if she'd forgotten to replace the broken pane of glass and the plants had died of a night chill – or if she was thinning out some weak plants as a normal part of gardening. Then again, perhaps his dinner plans had unhinged her.

Soon he forgot about dinner, as he began assembling the truss pieces according to code, and gathered his glue and various clamps, and got down on his knees with his tape measure, nailing blocks in the plywood to position the chords. He forgot about July and Laura and Price, and all that he might have set in motion the night before, as, hour upon hour, the headboard came together with glue and clamp. When the thirty-two truss members were in place, sixteen Vs, eight Ws, reinforcing the two chords around their gracefully curving arch, he glued the caps over the faces of the chords – hiding the laminate and the notches – then clamped his work and began preparing the heavy bedposts, chiseling two angled mortices into each, to accept the tenon ends of the chords.

All the while he worked he would glimpse July in the garden, toiling over her plants, and deep inside he would have vague but growing feelings of regret, that he had schemed to be rid of her. Later, when he saw her wearing only her underpants as she knelt on the ground working the black soil around with her hands, his regret turned to arousal and a conscious willingness to overlook his misgivings, one after another, until he felt nothing but desire—

Then he stopped.

He backed away from his carpentry . . . gazing deeply at the green trussed arch . . . and all his misgivings returned.

He went upstairs, turned on his laptop, then went to the phone. His agent's message machine answered.

'It's Jacob Winter,' he said to the machine, keeping an eye on July, out in the garden. 'The girl inside the bridge,' he said. 'I just figured out who she is.'

A great time to figure things out. The young man and his heart plummeting from the top of the bridge, his mind scattering in the ocean wind. A girl falls beside him, reaching for the sky, the two of them silent, weightless, floating like fairies, balanced in the air, wings spread blissfully against the crescent moon.

The way time slows down, as the trussed steel of the bridge whispers past, Henry Lamb not only can smell the river that rises to meet him, he has time to consider how a particular mustiness tinges the odour.

It's metabolism, the reason time slows down. Hummingbirds, for example, have such a high metabolic rate, they perceive human movement in slow motion. To a fruit fly, we are statues; their day on earth lasts a lifetime.

In humans, fear increases metabolism . . . which is why the victim of a car wreck will describe the accident as though it happened in slow-motion. Extreme fear causes extreme time stall. What is the limit? It's long been acknowledged that some people who fall to their deaths actually die of heart failure before they land. Perhaps they die of old age.

In the 4.03 seconds it takes to fall 250 feet, from the top of the Piscataqua River Bridge to the water, a man with an active mind can do a lot of thinking.

'You're going to be late.'

Jacob jumped, and spun in his chair.

July gave him a brief, disdainful stare. 'What's the matter with you?'

'I didn't hear you come up,' he told her.

She walked away from him.

He blinked, then realized that his eyes were welled with tears.

From the kitchen, he heard a cupboard door slam. He pulled his handkerchief from his pocket and blew his nose. Funny, he couldn't remember ever getting choked up while he wrote. Seeing that it was after six, he shut off the computer, then went into the bathroom and took a shower. When he was through, July was still in the kitchen, pouring rum into the blender. He went behind her and gently laid his hands on her shoulders.

'Are you sure you won't come to dinner?'

'So you can all laugh at me?' Her voice had a soft and hollow sound.

'July,' he began, and she started the blender. 'I told you what this dinner was about,' he said loud enough so she could hear him over the shrieking of the machine.

'Because you can't stand to be away from your wife.'

'If all she's interested in is a big dick and a pile of money . . .' Jacob tried to keep the conversation light, despite the volume he needed to compete with the blender. '. . . then good riddance. Right?'

July turned around. Her eyes narrowed, as if she was going to say something, then she went back to her work, tossing in ice cubes, one at a time. To Jacob, it was the gesture of someone who had just made a decision. Or so he hoped.

CHAPTER SIX

Good luck, bad luck, Gideon thought. Damned ridiculous, all this luck. He'd spent the night huddled under a sink in some fisherman's building, listening to the Savannah River bubbling in and out of the crab tanks, listening for footsteps or voices all night long, while hundreds of tiny claws scraped at the stainless steel and the crabs wrestled clumsily around.

Now he was freezing half to death in the back of a crab truck, bound for God-knows-where, probably inland – why would anyone drive for hours to deliver crabs to the coast? His suitcase lay on the cold, wet floor. Gideon sat bouncing on it in the crab-wet darkness, punching in the number with his thumb.

While he waited for the phone to pick up, he leaned back against the crates, heard the crabs scratching against the flimsy wood . . . and he remembered something his uncle once told him about the crabs that fishermen use for bait. They're kept in open pails, his uncle said, and any one of them crabs could climb out any old time he wanted to. In fact, they all could climb out if they had the will. Trouble is, whenever one tries to, the others reach up and pull him down again. 'Ain't a single crab ever climbed out of one of them pails,' his uncle said to him, 'and that's a historical fact.'

The phone clicked. 'I hope this isn't who I think it is.'

'Miss Ida,' he whispered. 'Please put my wife on the line.' His voice quivered like a boy calling for a first date.

'I'm sorry, I can't speak now,' she said, 'because I'm too busy trying to teach someone's children their table manners.'

'Miss Ida, please.' He spoke louder. 'I need to speak to Bethany.'

'Then you best get yourself a pen and paper, because she can't be reached here, and I have no intention of jibber-jabbering with the likes of you.'

'I haven't got a pen and paper,' Gideon said, but she was already rattling off the phone number. Then she hung up.

While her voice still rang in his head, he dialed. The answer came immediately. 'We've been trying to call you,' said B.J. Landry.

'I was told I could reach my wife at this number,' Gideon replied testily, as a crab started tapping his shoulder in the dark. He leaned forward.

'She's right here.'

'With you? Where?' Gideon tried to see his watch, but it was too dark.

'Same place you are, Jasper. Just outside Deepwater, North Carolina. We figured you'd come tracking your prisoner, so we came to bring you home.'

Sereno was not in Deepwater, Gideon knew that much. Or why would he have been trying to steal a pickup truck to leave Deepwater? Anyway, as far as Gideon could tell, the crab truck he was in was probably somewhere in Virginia by now.

'If you really want to help me,' Gideon said, 'you could tell me more about Sereno's wife. Do you know her name?'

'What difference does it make? It was changed, and changed again. Juliette, back when she lived in Florida. Juliette Whitestone. Okay?'

'Okay,' Gideon said. 'Now I'd like to talk to my wife.'

'You know, they found a hotel clerk in Savannah,' Landry said. 'Same MO as Delta City. Same weapon, nine millimeter. And your prints everywhere.'

'I was there,' said Gideon. 'So was Bullens.'

Landry blew a frustrated sigh. 'He's gonna keep making you look guiltier and guiltier until you come in. You know that, don't you?'

Gideon took a deep breath of the fish-stinking air.

'You're also aware that they found a shitload of cocaine residue all over the interior of your Jeep,' Landry said. 'And they know that the explosives were packed in a spare tire, in the back.'

'Right. Bullens detonated it himself – with a garage-door opener.'

'Why would the man blow himself up?'

'He didn't *mean* to.' Gideon sighed. 'Sereno switched tires on him. Bullens meant to blow up the boat, with Sereno and the other Colombians.'

'Well, okay then,' Landry said with put-on confidence.

'You don't believe that,' Gideon told him. 'Who's to say I didn't rig the explosives to double-cross him, then make off with half the cocaine?'

'If you was gonna blow him up, why take only half the cocaine?'

Gideon was struck by a notion. 'Wait a minute.' He almost stood up, but the truck's rocking kept him down. 'Sereno took that garage-door opener with him.'

'I thought you said Bullens had it.'

'After the explosion Sereno picked it up off the ground,' Gideon said, the idea still blossoming in his head. 'What if it still has Bullens' fingerprints?'

'Not likely, if Sereno's had it all this time.'

'I mean *inside*,' Gideon said. 'If Bullens' fingerprints were on the batteries, wouldn't that prove that he was the one who rigged it?'

'It wouldn't hurt your case,' Landry allowed. 'But now we've got a dead baker on our hands.'

'What?'

'A Cuban baker down in Florida City by the name of González, a former resident of Alligator Alley – which means you probably knew him. Shot to death the day before the break. They're pretty sure it was the same .38 that Bull Bullens and Cecil were shot with.'

'Bullens shot himself,' Gideon said.

'Anyway, they think this baker might've been involved somehow. There was loose money in his pocket, and he still had his wallet on him. Only thing missing, according to his wife, was his Palm Pilot. He took it with him everywhere, she said. There's some speculation that González was the go-between, the one who made arrangements with the fishing boat. Or at least his Palm Pilot was the go-between and González didn't know what he was doing. His wife swears he was doing well in his bakery, and would never have jeopardized it.'

'Put my wife on, please,' Gideon said, with a tone of finality.

'I'm telling you again,' Landry said, 'you do not want to meet up with this Colombian. Do you have any idea what he was in prison for?'

'Yes, I know.'

'Stabbed a man forty times over his wife. Forty times. Cold-blooded, cold-hearted murder. You think about that.'

'He was acquitted of those charges.'

'He was not acquitted. The judge threw out the conviction, probably because of some technicality. But that don't mean he didn't do it, you know that! Here's somethin I bet you don't know: The dead guy's blood was laced with something called – hold on – *batracho-toxin*. I don't know how to pronounce it, but it comes from poison frogs in the rain forest. Which means the man was paralyzed when Sereno killed him – most likely had to lie there and watch himself get perforated.' Landry paused, for effect, while crabs scratched noisily at their crates. 'That's some very sadistic behavior, my friend.'

'I don't know how much battery I've got left,' Gideon told him, trying to keep the shiver out of his voice.

'They also got him for trying to waste his wife Juliette, and that's a charge he didn't beat.'

'And he's going after her again,' Gideon said.

'That may be. But you don't want to get between 'em. His wife was *armed*, do you know that? She had a gun and she emptied the clip into him, she even cut him with his own knife. And he still managed to bite off her finger. This man is half monster.'

'And I'm going to stop him,' Gideon said. 'Find him and stop him.'

Landry sighed again. 'Your picture's on TV, Jasper,' he said in a different tone, one of resignation. The shiver it gave Gideon was worse than the chill of the refrigerator truck. 'You been on TV a hundred times in the past week. Do you know how many people in this country own guns?'

'Yeah, everyone,' Gideon said, 'but me.'

CHAPTER SEVEN

E ven though the sky was aglow with the sunset, the harbor-front restaurant managed to be pleasantly gloomy. Jacob had called ahead and reserved a table at the window, and he asked the waitress to bring a bottle of $40 champagne on ice. Ten minutes after he sat down, they came in. Jacob stood and pulled out the chair to his left for Laura, but she took the seat opposite him. Price sat on his right.

'Are you alone?' Price asked. Laura was already perusing her menu.

'July wasn't feeling well,' Jacob answered. 'Champagne?'

'Probably best not to drink if we're discussing business,' Price suggested.

'I'll have a glass,' Laura said, not bothering to look at either of them.

Jacob could tell that they'd probably had words on the ride.

'I guess we could all use a little relaxing,' Price said, sliding both their glasses closer.

Laura took a steno pad out of her purse and set it on the table, opened and ready for business. 'Can we order?'

'I thought perhaps we might discuss preliminaries,' Price suggested.

'I don't want to be up late again tonight,' she said, perhaps as a way of asking him to shove his preliminaries.

'I'm kind of worn out myself,' Jacob said.

Laura gave him a look. Price placed his hand gently on hers. 'What do you say we establish the ground rules?'

'Where's Maxie?'

'My father's watching him.'

'At the Tavern?'

'He's got him sitting up at the bar, eating microwave pizza, and watching a car race on TV,' Price said. 'All-American dinner. Max promised to wash dishes.'

Laura started to take a sip of champagne, then stopped. Her eyes narrowed. 'Oh, it must be prom night.'

Jacob didn't have to turn to know that July was on her way to the table. But he did turn. And she did not disappoint.

Lightly across the floor she came, wearing a very short, practically sheer summer dress. The fabric fell off her shoulders, touched her nipples and abdomen, and brushed her thighs with each step she took. Every other man in the dining room, and most of the women, were watching too. What caught Jacob's attention was the glazed glare she focused on him as she came.

Price pressed his long fingers on the table and rose to his full height, then pulled out July's chair. Jacob stood when she arrived, but she pretended not to see, nestling in the chair without speaking.

Knowing it was his place to make introductions, Jacob nonetheless took his time pouring July's champagne, waiting to see how the cards would fall.

Price played first. 'I take it you're July,' he said. 'I'm Price Ashworth. This, of course, is Laura.'

'His assistant,' Laura said with a smile.

'Not outside the office,' Price explained, as though confiding. 'I'm a hypnotherapist. Laura is my transcriptionist and office manager.'

Jacob topped off their glasses, emptying the bottle, then hailed the waitress, who came directly. She looked like a college student, young, fresh-faced, and quite lovely. 'You need to be faster to keep up with us,' he said, and she gave him a smile. 'Could you bring another bottle?'

'As fast as I can,' she joked. He could feel July bristle beside him.

'And perhaps an order of oysters on the half-shell,' Price added, then said to July, 'If you have a weakness for oysters – I crave them – they're positively delectable here.'

'Do they raise their own?' Laura said, as the waitress went away.

Price gave her a quizzical look, then turned back to July. As she reached for a dinner roll, her dress fell away from her breast. 'Let me help,' Price offered, passing her the basket while pretending not to look, but Jacob could tell he was already examining the mental snapshot he had taken.

'So, I understand you specialize in esoteric plants indigenous to the rain forest,' Price said. 'That must be a comforting pastime, staying in touch with your roots, so to speak.' He smiled at his witticism.

July sipped her champagne.

Jacob sipped his water.

'And such a cute sun dress,' Laura said. 'I remember when I could wear things like that.'

'Don't be silly, you can wear anything you like,' Price said. 'I only questioned your choice of denim, because I know the restaurant, and was afraid you might feel conspicuous.'

Laura ignored him.

'I always thought you looked amazing in jeans and a plain white shirt,' Jacob said to her.

The comment was as much for July's benefit, and she responded more or less as he'd hoped, angling a glance at Price, who said, 'If I were to guess, I'd wager your particular heritage was from the mountains of South America – perhaps the north coast?'

'Does that make you a genius?' she said, sinking her thumbs into her dinner roll and slowly tearing it apart.

Price gave her a glinting look, then buttered his roll with a surgeon's precision. 'Tell me, July, did your family live in a *selva*?'

'What's a *selva*?' Jacob asked.

'I'm sorry,' Price said. 'Rainforest.'

'Why didn't you say "rainforest?" ' Laura asked.

'The word *selva* has cultural connotations,' he explained.

'Something else you'll have to teach me.'

'Laura, when does Max leave for Belnap?' Jacob asked. He was being sincere, but she didn't answer. Price did.

'As you might expect with such an exclusive school, there's an extended orientation session for incoming students,' he said. 'For Max, school would effectively begin the third week in August.'

'Will they let him come home for weekends,' Jacob asked Price, somewhat less sincere, 'or would that be your decision?'

Laura let out an audible sigh.

The waitress returned with a plate of oysters and another bottle of champagne. Setting the oysters down, she covered the champagne bottle with a towel and proceeded to uncork it, wincing as she did so.

Jacob smiled while he watched her. He knew July was watching him. When the cork popped, the waitress waited for a second or two, then peeked under the towel.

'I'm always afraid I'm gonna spray someone,' she said, catching his smile. Ready to pour, she offered first to July, who turned her head away. Jacob nodded, and the waitress topped off her glass, then moved to Laura, who covered hers. Jacob did the same. 'I'll stick with water.'

'A smidgeon for me,' Price said.

She poured, then turned to Jacob again. 'Ready to order?'

'Maybe you should give us another few minutes,' he said.

As soon as she went away, Price picked up the conversation. 'I've actually sailed along the Colombian-Venezuelan coast,' he said to July.

'Spent a long weekend in Cartagena. Have you ever been there?'

July lifted an oyster to her mouth. 'Mmm,' she said, which may have meant yes, may have meant no, or she might have been simply enjoying the oyster – except, with July, nothing was simple. The way she pressed the opened shell to her lips, the way her gaze turned inward when she sucked up the meat, it looked like an obscene kiss. As if on cue, both Price and Laura lifted their glasses and drank.

July reached her hand under the table. 'I need to use your napkin,' she said, swiping her hand roughly across Jacob's lap.

'Don't you have one?' he asked.

'I don't want to get it dirty,' she replied.

'Who said chivalry's dead?' the doctor piped in brightly.

Jacob knew that July's seduction of Price was nothing but revenge – for his smiling at the waitress, his arranging this meeting with Laura. He could also tell, the way Price was looking at her, that it was working.

'So,' Jacob said to Laura, 'how are negotiations going on your father's property?'

She held her menu stiffly in her lap and looked to Price. 'Are we ready to order?'

Price gave Jacob the look of a confidant. 'We're closing in,' he said.

'Maybe your dad mentioned to you' – Jacob still focused on Laura – 'we've been spending a lot of time together.'

She tossed her menu on the table. 'Excuse me,' she said, getting up and heading for the bathrooms.

Jacob watched her make a path between the tables. 'I upset her,' he said, taking his napkin off his lap and placing it on his plate. 'Would either of you object if I went and apologized?'

'I think that might be appropriate,' Price replied.

'July?'

She responded by sucking another oyster indulgently from its shell, with her eye on Price. So Jacob got up, excused himself, and walked to the lobby. Momentarily, Laura came out of the women's room.

'I'm sorry,' he told her. 'Laura, can we talk?'

Shaking her head, she walked briskly past. He started following.

'I was wondering if your parents ever told you why they got divorced,' he said quietly.

She stopped. Then turned to face him, folding her arms as if pleasantly unaffected. 'Could you be any more obvious?' She moved a step closer, if only to make sure they weren't overheard. 'Trying to dump your little girlfriend on Price,' she whispered. 'Do you think we're that stupid?'

'No, you're both very smart, I've never doubted that. I mean, look at the arrangement you've worked out. Price gets your dad's property, you get Max into private school. That's a very intelligent relationship.'

She stared at him, her eyes so familiar, so deeply a part of him. Suddenly he felt that if he wanted to take her in his arms – and he did, more than ever – she would have let him. But he didn't have time. She turned away from him and headed back to the table.

'Because he lost his ring toe,' Jacob said, keeping pace.

Laura kept walking. 'I know he lost his ring toe.'

Jacob pursued her through the dining room, weaving between tables. 'He told me that after he lost the toe, your mom wanted him to quit racing. So he quit and got himself a steady job.'

Laura stopped; spun around to face him. A man and woman beside them continued eating, pretending not to listen.

'Laura, she left him for another driver,' Jacob said.

'No, she left him for a winner,' Laura said, then closed her eyes as though wishing she hadn't said it. Nevertheless, inside Jacob's chest, he felt the awful emptiness return, and he moved back, to let her return to their table. Then she touched him. 'I meant the guy had money,' she explained, 'enough to get us out of Lowell.'

'Laura, she left your dad for a guy who screwed married women.'

'You think she didn't know that?' Laura raised her voice.

Beside them, the woman put down her fork and stared unabashedly. Across the room, July watched them too, while Price talked on and on.

'Jake, I was fourteen years old. I was drinking, doing drugs. My mother took me away from all that.'

'For money,' he said. 'She left your dad for money.'

'She did what she had to,' Laura replied.

The woman touched Jake's hand, said, 'Listen to her.'

'Maybe she made a mistake,' Laura added. 'Then again, maybe my father was incapable of loving anything but his car.'

With that, she turned and walked to their table, where Price was speaking in Spanish, and July was giving Jacob the squinting examination of an animal ready to pounce.

Laura did not sit down. 'I'm leaving,' she announced.

'Not hungry?' Price asked, gesturing with a concerned but clandestine smile, wanting to keep things under control.

'Don't put yourself out, I'll call a cab,' Laura told him. She was already walking away.

Price stood quickly, although still trying to retain his grace. 'Her electrolytes are low,' he explained, pulling three twenties out of his pocket and dropping them on the table. 'July, it's been a pure delight.'

Jacob watched him leave, then sat down beside July, who stared at the champagne bottle like she was trying to shatter it with her eyes.

'I guess that could've gone better,' he said.

Then July left too.

Jacob took another drink of water. In fact, he thought it went just perfectly . . . until the waitress came with the check and an envelope addressed to: 'Man with white shirt and moccasins.'

Jacob gave her a curious look, and she shrugged. 'Some guy found it in the men's room,' the waitress said. 'Maybe you've got a secret admirer.'

'The men's room?' he replied. He looked around the dining room, to see if anyone was paying particular attention. But no takers. 'Where's the guy?'

'Left.'

He added a twenty to the cash Price had left. 'I don't need change,' he said, and she went away.

As he walked out of the dining room, he stuck his thumb under the flap and ripped the envelope open. A restaurant receipt was inside, with writing on the back:

IT WON'T WORK. STOP TRYING.

CHAPTER EIGHT

J acob was not surprised to find Green Girls dark and empty when he got back from the restaurant. Up in the kitchen he made a full pot of coffee, then went straight to his computer in hopes of finishing his novel. In a matter of seconds he lost himself in his story, his fingers massaging the keys as if he were creating music. Indeed, he might have been Beethoven on some insomniac night, improvising while waiting for dawn and stumbling upon the Eroica.

Metabolism rises. Time slows down. Henry falls slowly.

So slowly, in fact, that the police cars on the roadway appear stationary, perched on a cloud. A white and orange ambulance pulls out to pass, floating. Policemen themselves cling to the misty bridge like spiders . . . poised on top of the arch, in the crow's nest, on catwalks and on rungs.

But wait—

Under the NEW HAMPSHIRE sign, Henry spots a car, its trunk left open. It's his own car . . . still parked there. His tire . . . still flat.

The roadway rises.

Henry looks up, but the girl is no longer falling with him. The airplane is stationary, a cross hung in the sky, caught in the process of finishing the V in the statement JESUS SAV . . . which, obviously, is JESUS SAVES. But why is the pilot skywriting when no one on the ground could possibly see his message through the fog?

Time slows down.

As he enters the cloud, the mist moistens his face. When the clouds swirl away from his feet, he begins to see people crowding the banks, and boats on the river like tractors stopped in a field, having plowed furrows behind them.

Henry knows something.

He looks down, sees the red sky reflected in the river, tiny insects flitting across the surface, the backs of two hungry stripers.

*The girl, he realizes, was in his imagination. But the airplane was real.
The pilot was writing to him.*
The stripers dart.
Yeah, a great time to figure things out.

Jacob leapt from his chair, he was so excited. Or had he heard a noise
from the kitchen? He walked through the pantry and turned on the
kitchen light.

'July?'

His voice was dry. Outside, in the garden, the overhead sprinklers
had come on, and a sweet, warm mist rolled in through the open glass
doors. He went to the sink for a glass of water, and saw by the clock
that it was past three. As far as he could tell, July was not home. He
gave the matter no more thought, but returned to the living room, and
his novel.

After reading what he had written, his eyes stung; his throat
constricted and ached.

He pushed away from the desk and lay his head back in the chair.
Tears broke quietly and ran down his cheeks, wetting his ears. He
couldn't remember ever crying before, not from writing – certainly not
from reaching the end of a novel. Maybe this wasn't from writing.
Regardless, he slumped over his knees and let the tears flow – not that
he could have stopped if he wanted to.

Then he did stop . . .

Another noise stopped him.

He turned in his chair and faced the pantry. The room was dark
and quiet, except for the rain in the garden. The noise he had heard
was a soft, low ring, the sound the iron stairs might have made under
a heel.

'Hello?'

He went to the pantry; looked down the stairs. There was no light
coming up from the shop. He stepped into the kitchen and looked out
into the garden, but that was dark too. In fact, aside from the wet rattle
of leaves and toxic trilling of frogs, Jacob's world felt lifeless. He went
to the bedroom, then to the bathroom, wondering if July had slipped
in while he was finishing his book. But her bed was empty and her car
wasn't in the driveway.

Which meant his plan had worked, and better than he'd hoped. July
was with Price somewhere.

And he was alone.

He returned to the kitchen, to the phone, and he dialed. After two
rings, Laura answered, quietly.

'I wanted to tell you,' he began, then stopped, to keep the rush of emotion down. He cleared his throat. 'The book I'm writing' – although he didn't know why he was telling her this – 'I just finished. It's printing right now.'

'Jake, it's four in the morning,' she replied sleepily, but he could tell that she hadn't been sleeping either.

'I'm sorry,' he told her.

The telephone hummed quietly in his ear.

'I mean . . . I'm sorry. The way things turned out.'

The silence that answered him did nothing to dispel the emptiness he felt.

'Price never made it home,' she said finally.

'I wasn't looking for Price.' Tempted as he was to let her know that July wasn't home either, he was not finding this small victory as pleasing as he'd once anticipated.

'Jake, what I told you earlier, about what my mother did – the reason she left my dad—?'

'Uh-huh.'

'I'm just not sure—' Laura's voice caught on the word. She stopped, and Jacob heard her sigh.

'Not sure?'

'I really missed my dad,' she whispered, then hung up the phone.

When Jacob awoke in the morning, the room was hot and filled with sunlight, but the house was still quiet. He didn't think July had come home while he'd slept, because the bedroom door was closed as he'd left it, and her side of the bed had not been slept in.

In fact, a lightness came over him, remembering that he had finished his novel. Without hesitation, he went downstairs and began removing the clamps from July's headboard, and that's when he thought he smelled smoke, and he assumed that July was here, after all.

'Hello?'

He stepped through the open doors.

'July?'

She didn't answer. He went back into the shop, went to the front and looked out the door. Her car wasn't there. So . . . perhaps she'd stopped home early in the morning, while he was asleep. Paying no further mind to the smoke, he set about the task at hand, and sanded the entire piece of furniture, top to bottom, until the seams disappeared and the green took on a pleasant sheen. Then he carried the finished parts out to the hut, where he slid the rails into the headboard and footboard posts so they would lock in place. Because July had no box spring, Jacob cut plywood to fit the rails, then lifted her mattress onto the plywood. The bed took up nearly the entire hut, but, surrounded by hanging vines and flowers, it was a handsome piece of furniture – indeed, a good enough replication to set Jacob on edge. He was glad he'd never see it again. Later, she could apply a coat of polyurethane, to preserve the wood. Right now – Jacob checked his watch and saw that it was almost two – he was going to take a quick shower, gather his manuscript pages and computer, pack his clothes into his backpack, then drive to UPS and ship the novel off to Maury Howard in New York. Then go to work at the Tavern. The bed would be his thank-you to her for taking him in, and inspiring him.

Pulling himself up the circular stairs, caked with fine, sour sawdust, he was looking forward to the shower. But as soon as he passed through the living room—

The missing computer hadn't registered this morning. But now, peering at the bare desk, his heart hammered home the alert. He dropped to his knees and looked under the desk. Even his early draft pages were gone. He stood there, trying to remember. In his tiredness the night before, had he already put everything in his backpack?

Then he was in the bedroom, searching through the backpack, then walking all through the house, then stalking mindlessly into her garden, smelling the stale smoke and bristling with fear—

'July?'

Mindless of poison frogs, mindless of everything, he bypassed the hut, heading toward the pool . . . then heard a snap. He stopped, lifted his foot and saw – the plastic letter G. And there in the blade of a bromeliad, a B and a T. Jacob fell to his knees, heart pumping, and found the rest of his computer ground into the chewed-up earth, scattered amongst the torn branches and leaves. She had beaten the thing with an axe, by the looks of it.

He wanted to scream, but couldn't take a breath—

Then a spark of hope.

Marching back to the house, he tore through the shop and ran out the front door and down the fieldstone walk to his car, threw open the door, dived across his seat and pulled open the glove box. His backup disks. Gone.

He turned to the house, but he did not run back. He walked in disbelief, flagstones passing slowly beneath his feet, though his mind was a blur, and then he was in her garden again.

'You'd better not be here,' he managed to say in a low voice, as he walked straight to the hut, and around back.

With his first glimpse of the charcoal grill, he leaned heavily against the back of the building. Even though he'd prepared himself for the worst, here it was, stark and real. A red gasoline can lay on the ground beside the grill, near a rough circle of blackened soil. Flecks of ash lay scattered like snowflakes on the green leaves all around him – his manuscript pages. Inside the barbecue grill, his floppy disks lay curled and ruffled on the coals, blackened, smoldering.

CHAPTER NINE

In the middle of Richmond, Virginia, Terrence Gideon sat at an orange table in the college library, his face hidden behind a computer. Dressed in his mint green suit and striped tie, his suitcase under his table, he could have been a student, a professor, even a journalist – who stank badly of fish. Beside him stood a stack of books, *Bridge Design and Structural Specifications* on top. He could hear two students tapping at computer keyboards all around him, and he could hear whispered conversations that he imagined were all about him.

In less than a minute he had identified the type of bridge he had seen in both Georgia and North Carolina, then began trying to locate others. Luckily, the college library subscribed to WorldCat, a database of all library catalogues in the country. He was hoping to find an atlas of American cantilever through-trussed-arch bridges – but apparently no such book existed. And apparently that particular style of bridge was not too common, at least not along the eastern seaboard. So he switched to Compendex, an engineering database that indexed journal articles, and he started with the narrowest range possible, using the words *steel, arch, cantilever, through-truss,* and *tidal river*, but eliminating other words: *suspension, railroad, mountain*. That's when he scored. 'Your search has produced three results,' the monitor read.

He clicked on the first, a bridge in Baltimore, then he printed it out. The second was located in Massachusetts, and he printed that one.

'Can I help you find anything?'

Startled, Gideon sat forward, returning to the menu in the same motion, while he tore his paper out of the printer. Then turned to look up at the woman, who was young and white and quite attractive.

'Compendex,' she said. 'You certainly seem like a man who knows his way around a library. And a boolean search, at that.'

Gideon felt humidity rising up from his chest, his glasses starting to fog. 'Yes, Ma'am,' he said, doing his best to appear confident despite the fact that he smelled like crabs. 'I write for a magazine called *Libraries Illustrated*, which is out of New York City.'

'Libraries, as they pertain to bridges,' the woman said.

'Yes, Ma'am.'

'Because the young man at the circulation desk – don't turn around' – she was still smiling pleasantly – 'now, he's got this queer notion that you're a librarian yourself, actually a particular librarian who's been in the news recently, I mean, like, twenty-four hours a day? He's waiting for me to go back there and tell him I agree with his suspicions.'

Gideon started to laugh, but the woman leaned over and pretended to type something on his keyboard. Actually, she was exiting Compendex, while she laid her newspaper in front of him, so he could see the police drawing of himself. Looked older than the ID photo that he'd seen on the news, this likeness of him dead-on, down to the scruffy white beard.

'I see,' Gideon said, and he reached his hand into his jacket pocket, as if he had a gun. 'We're just having a friendly conversation,' he said, the way Robert Redford took Faye Dunaway hostage in *Three Days of the Condor*, 'but I'm going to need you to walk out of here with me.'

'Don't be silly,' the woman said quietly, folding the paper back up. She wore lilac perfume and had fine, manicured nails. In fact, she could have been a Miss Virginia contestant, the way she smiled. 'I'm an excellent judge of character,' she told him. 'I also happen to be one of those people who believe the librarian was framed.'

'I guess I haven't been watching enough TV,' Gideon said, and he did his best with another laugh, even though he felt sick to his stomach. He removed his hand from his pocket. 'I'm sorry.'

She placed her hand on his back with some urgency, enough to make him stop talking, and she turned the top book face-down.

'Chardonnay, were you able to help the gentleman?' The male voice, sounding pinched in the throat, came from a considerable distance behind them. Gideon didn't turn. He knew it was the young man she had mentioned.

'We're working on it,' the woman said, friendly enough. But Gideon could tell that the guy was suspicious, by the way he seemed to lose his power of speech.

'You, then,' he continued, 'wouldn't mind watching the desk for a minute, while I step out the door and go out . . . to get a fresh breath of air?'

'Go on,' she said. 'I'll watch the desk.'

As soon as the young man went away, the woman said to Gideon,

'He's got a thing for me, can you tell? I just let him know that you definitely were not the man in question. And I think he's going to look for the nearest toilet and relieve himself. Then he'll find a campus cop. So you'd better scoot.'

'Ma'am—'

'No. Scoot.' She leaned close and spoke quietly and fast. 'And unless you *want* people to think you're this man, I suggest you stay out of public places. And definitely do something about your appearance. Hon, from here on, the Uncle Remus look is out.'

Then she picked up his books and spun around – if she'd been wearing petticoats, they would have fanned the entire building – and sashayed off to the stacks.

Gideon grabbed his suitcase and went the opposite way, head down, breezing through the double doors. As soon as he hit the sidewalk, he veered across the lawn, practically running – but not wanting to call attention to himself. In Richmond, in July, nobody runs, least of all a 260-pound black man carrying a suitcase.

He passed two big buildings, then an old rowhouse. Don't look around, he told himself, just keep walking like you know where you're going. Cutting around the rowhouse, he spotted a brick church on the next lawn. Hearing no sirens, no whistles, no feet running up behind him, he quickened his pace, and in a matter of seconds was hustling up the concrete steps. To his relief, the front doors were unlocked and he walked inside, then stood behind the heavy door for a few seconds, his chest aching. The building seemed empty.

He looked out the window, saw a few cars going by, but still no sign yet of police. He did not allow himself to hope that the young man had been dissuaded from his suspicions – more likely that the campus police were waiting for the state police to mobilize. In any case, Gideon knew he wasn't out of danger.

He walked to the back of the church hoping to find a hiding place, some secret room or closet in which to wait for nightfall, then tried a door to the right of the altar and found a small office that had a closet full of white shirts and black trousers and robes in three colors, black, white and burgundy. The closet smelled sweetly of frankincense.

As he reached for a shirt, a whistle went off. He spun toward the office door. Not a whistle, but his cell phone. He dug the telephone out of his pocket and clicked it on. 'Okay,' he said.

'I've been working on a theory,' Landry said.

'This isn't a good time,' Gideon said.

'Just listen. The DEA knows that a shitload of cocaine used to funnel through Alligator Alley and then on to the entire Florida prison system – that is, until the day Sereno wasted this dealer named Kiefer, at which point the supply dried up. I'm talking the entire Florida correctional system, Jasper, and that's not chump change. Now, even though Mrs Sereno gave up a few names in exchange for immunity and witness protection – mostly Colombian mules and small-timers – the feds never learned who Kiefer's prison contact was. But they do know it had to be someone at Alligator Alley . . . cook, dental assistant, truck driver . . . or maybe one of the prison guards.'

'If it was Bullens—'

'Then his vendetta against Sereno makes sense.'

Gideon sidled to a window and peeked through the blinds. Cars moved inconspicuously along the streets. People walked and talked and smiled. If police were running, or pointing, or even gathering – no one was paying the slightest bit of attention. Neither did Gideon hear sirens in the air.

'Why wouldn't he just have Sereno whacked in prison?' Gideon asked. 'It's not hard to do.'

'No profit in it,' Landry said. 'Listen now. If Bullens was the man funneling cocaine through the system, then he lost a very lucrative sideline business the day Kiefer was murdered. From everything I know that happened in Card Sound the other day, your friend Bullens was not only gonna have his vendetta against Sereno, but about six-hundred grand in product, besides.'

'And that's why I got brought in,' Gideon said. Anger tightened his stomach. 'To die there, then take the blame.'

'But things got screwed up. You didn't die, and Sereno got away.'

Gideon thought for a moment. 'That's a theory,' he said, ready to hang up. 'Maybe you could convince someone who matters.'

'Wait a minute, your wife wants to talk—'

'Can't, I'm sorry,' Gideon said, not because he'd just shut off his phone, but because he was suddenly considering a horrendous offense, and then he was actually watching himself do it, stealing from a church of God. Taking off his smelly shirt and tossing it on the closet floor, he slipped a white shirt off a hanger and held it up to himself, grateful that the minister seemed to be as portly as he. Then he selected a pair of black trousers, a little narrow in the waist, but wearable. Taking the black robe with billowing sleeves, it was almost as if he were watching someone else doing this.

Next he went into the bathroom, where he stripped off his under-shirt and washed himself, then opened the medicine cabinet and found an electric razor. He plugged it in and shaved his face clean. Then, just to see if it would work, he pushed the razor against his scalp. The little appliance clattered and complained, but it left a neat swath, clean to the skull – so he continued.

When he was through, he collected his hair and flushed it down the toilet, then stuffed his shirt in the suitcase. He looked at himself in the mirror one last time, wondering what Bethany would think of his bowling ball head – Reverend Gideon – that is, if she ever saw him again.

Indeed, if he expected to live long enough to prove his innocence, then he knew he was going to have to shuffle around some rights and wrongs in the process. For the moment, he prayed that he lived to make amends. Then he went out the front door in his vestments, looking for a car to steal.

Little more than an hour south of Richmond, Sergeant Biff Bullens lay back in his lounge chair beside the motel swimming pool, decked out in a Hawaiian shirt and white cotton trousers, straw hat and wraparound shades, sipping a tall Planters Punch and watching a young girl trying to summon the courage to dive head-first into the water, while he punched in the phone number.

Warden Dale Shivers answered on first ring.

'What's the good word?' Bullens said.

'I've been trying to reach you all day,' Shivers said.

'Funny. I was trying to reach you all night.'

'I was indisposed. Where are you?'

'Where am I? Taking my vacation.'

'Biff, the stolen vehicle – the Cadillac from Georgia – it had GPS, and they tracked it—'

'I'm sorry. GPS?'

'Global Positioning Satellite. Were you in Savannah last night?'

'What's that, Savannah, Georgia?'

'You found him—?' Shivers said hopefully.

'I take it you're referring to Officer Gideon.' The girl sprang out and slapped the surface hard, splashing chlorinated water up from her legs. A drop hit Bullens on the mouth and he dabbed it with his tongue. 'No, I haven't located him. Have you?'

Shivers didn't speak for a few seconds. 'Biff, a hotel clerk was found dead in Savannah, in Gideon's room, they got his prints. When the police got there, the body was still warm.'

'Savannah, you say. Well, I'm a long ways from Georgia. Actually, not too far from a little hole-in-the-wall called Deepwater, NC, where our Indian friend had a run-in with a couple of the local yokels last night. See that?'

'The GPS company, when the police called them for tracking

coordinates, said that the owner of the Savannah vehicle had already reported the vehicle stolen an hour earlier, and they already supplied him with the tracking information.'

'So he knew where his car had got to. Why, that is an outstanding invention.'

'Except the vehicle's owner was probably dead at the time that first request was logged. And the police say they sure didn't make the initial call.'

'Huh,' said Bullens.

Shivers' voice softened. 'Biff, I got some people down here who want to speak with you.'

Bullens chuckled. 'Yeah, I heard about that on the news. Why you suppose they'd be looking for me?'

'Well,' Shivers said, 'for whatever pertinent information you might be able to furnish.'

'I see.' The young diver was up on the apron again, examining her tan line against the red sting on her belly. 'Like I said, I'm vacationing this week. Out of touch, so to speak. Tell 'em I'll be back in commission next Monday, if I feel better.'

'Biff . . .' Bullens heard the sigh in the warden's voice. 'Officer Gideon will be in custody soon. We just had a positive ID in Richmond. A college librarian ID'd him. Which is why I've been trying to call you.'

'A college in Richmond, you say.'

'Virginia Commonwealth University. They think they might have him boxed in.'

Bullens drained the drink, then pushed himself off the lounge chair. 'You know,' he said as he headed to his room, 'I've always wondered how my life woulda been different, if I'd got myself some higher education.'

CHAPTER TEN

'You look great,' Squeaky said, when he let Jacob in the back door.

Walking past him and on down the stairs, Jacob went behind the bar and grabbed the box of napkins, the cans of knives, forks, and spoons, then sat on a barstool and started putting together setups for the night.

'Whadda you, got a week to live?'

'I'll be fine.'

'Don't wanna talk, no sweat off my brow,' Squeaky said, and headed out to the back room.

Jacob tried to engage his mind in the quiet rhythm of rolling silverware in the cloth napkins, but it did little good. As much as he tried not to add up everything that was wrong with his life, all the elements had become lead weights in his limbs and his gut. His novel was lost, not a word had been spared. He was homeless, for God's sake, up on assault charges, and a suspect in Alix Callahan's death. Max was gone from his life, that much was certain. Under the circumstances, what settlement judge would consider granting him even visitation rights, let alone custody? The only bright spot in his life was the fact that he was finally free of July.

'Did you want to say something?' he said, aware that Squeaky was lingering behind him.

Squeaky fluttered his lips. 'To you, nope.' Walking away, the old man added, 'Except it's your last day.'

Jacob turned on his barstool. 'You're firing me again.'

'Nope, I've decided to sell the place. It's my last day too.'

'Wait a minute—' Jacob slid off the stool.

'He heard that, didn't he?'

'You're selling it . . . to Price Ashworth?'

'Kinda tough to do that,' Squeaky said, 'since I stuck a "No gold-diggers" stipulation in the deed.'

Jacob studied him, the way Squeaky liked to dangle information just out of reach. 'Not to mention that him and Laura went their separate ways.'

Jacob's heart leapt, and he followed Squeaky into the back room. 'Just tell me.'

'Tell you what, she quit her job?'

The words sank into a curious corner of Jacob's brain. Squeaky pushed past him and returned to the front, dealing glass ashtrays down the length of the bar.

'Squeaky, don't screw around.'

The old man smirked. 'Laura and Dr Asswipe had a little beef,' he said, obviously delighted. 'So she gave her notice, effective immediately. Done-ski. Unemployed. And this idiot thinks all he has to do is up the ante and I'll cave. He called this morning, up to a million now.'

Jacob examined the old man long enough to know he wasn't kidding.

'You gonna stand there all day with your thumb up your ass?' Squeaky said. 'Get the setups done.'

Jacob returned to his barstool, head spinning. Over the next minute or so, silverware seemed to find its own way into the napkins. Amazingly, even though he'd just lost his novel – and now his part-time job – life suddenly didn't seem half so cloudy. So, his novel was gone. Judging from past experience, the world wouldn't miss it.

'You want a few hours, come by tomorrow,' Squeaky said, carrying two cases of beer into the bar. 'I'm gonna need some help gettin the Spite House ready for the new owners.'

'Okay,' Jacob said. 'What are you going to do with yourself?' he said when the old man walked past him.

'You didn't think I planned on slingin beer the rest of my life,' Squeaky answered, squeezing behind the bar. 'You're lookin at Jeff Dakota's new crew chief. I hit the road day after tomorrow. Pennsylvania Five Hundred coming up, in Pocono. Then off to Indianapolis, for the Brickyard Four Hundred.'

Jacob couldn't help but admire the old man, who bent down to stock the beer cooler, acting as if the career change were nothing, loading in bottles four at a time. When he stood, he said to Jacob, 'Wanna hear a doozy?'

'What?'

'Just between you and me. Laura don't know this.'

Jacob nodded.

'Her mother came back. Ten years after the fact. She shit-canned the other guy. Laura was off at college. I'm here, everything sailin along, closin up one night. Bang, she shows up.' Squeaky chuckled. 'We had a long talk. That little table over there. I opened a bottle of good wine. We actually had a few laughs. Then she asked.'

'Asked,' Jacob said, 'if you'd take her back?'

Squeaky chuckled again, as he shook his head in a regretful way. 'I said no.'

He pulled a rag out of his back pocket and wiped the bar as he walked away. 'And that, my friend, was a doozy.'

CHAPTER ELEVEN

G ideon walked briskly from the church in his vestments and crisp collar, carrying his suitcase and trying to keep a pleasant expression on his face – pretending to be a college chaplain looking for a ride home to Baltimore. In fact, he was looking for a car with keys left in the ignition.

The afternoon was too hot, the sun too bright, and he wished he'd waited inside the church till dark. Suddenly he heard the whoop of a siren behind him. He froze, then spotted a police cruiser pushing its way through the clogged traffic, heading for the university. Another patrol car followed close behind, then another. Their blue lights were flashing, but they seemed to be careful about laying off the sirens. Gideon knew they were looking for him.

Suddenly aware of a car engine idling behind him, Gideon turned slowly to see a black woman behind the wheel of a bright red Sebring convertible, waiting patiently for traffic to move. She smiled at him and said, 'Reverend, you look positively lost.'

'Lost?' He laughed heartily. 'An hour ago I called for a taxi cab to the train station, and here I stand, still waiting.' He laughed again, in a forbearing way.

The woman shook her head sympathetically. 'Do you need to get to the train station?'

'I do, Ma'am. Desperately.'

She smiled again, and cleared her bag off the front seat. 'I'll be happy to take you there.'

Outside the station, the parking lot was divided in two sections: SHORT TERM and LONG TERM. The young man inside the booth – he looked like a college kid – was collecting money from a car leaving the lot. Made it easy for the Reverend to snatch a parking ticket from the machine and walk in under the raised barrier arm. The kid never noticed.

He knew enough to look for an older vehicle, one without alarms and ignition guards, and he found one, a big blue station wagon, probably 80s vintage.

He walked around to the passenger side of the car and set his suitcase down, pretended to search his pockets for his keys while he looked around to make sure no one was watching. Then he crouched down and opened the suitcase, retrieved the slim jim and the wires Bethany had left for him. Standing again, it took only seconds before he caught the rod with the tool. He gave a pull, and the doorlock popped up.

He threw his suitcase into the rear, then pushed the driver's seat back as far as it would go, and closed the door. He looked around again, knowing he must look guilty as hell, but as far as he could tell, no one was watching. So he squeezed his head under the dash and found what he believed was the 12-volt power source, then clipped one wire to it. Locating the back of the ignition switch, he touched the other end of the wire to one of the posts.

A man shouted: 'Robert E. Lee Round-the-Clock News!'

Gideon whacked his head on the dash, then reached up and hit the radio off. Then he clipped the second wire to the 12-volt wire and touched the other end to the unused ignition post. The engine started effortlessly. He removed the ignition wire, then rose up in the seat, pulling his legs in the car. Looked around again with a big, embarrassed smile. Damn fool temperamental car.

Adjusting the seat so he was comfortable, he was glad to see the gas gauge showed a full tank. He took the white ticket out of his pocket, pulled the gearshift into drive and followed the exit signs to the booth with a big Baptist smile. As far as Gideon could remember, he hadn't smiled this much all year.

'Baby, where are you?' Bethany blurted, as soon as she answered the phone. 'Is that an airplane?'

In fact, the station wagon's muffler was blown, and Gideon felt like he was trying to steal out of Richmond in a smoke-screen.

'As a matter of fact,' he said, 'I'm stealing somebody's car.'

He could hear Bethany catch her breath. 'What do you mean?'

'A little while ago I stole from a church of God. Now I'm a two-time car thief.'

Landry came on. 'Hey, Jasper, you wanna hear about one fishy sum'bitch of a court case?'

'I don't know,' Gideon said.

'I've been doing some research . . . You inside a tank, or what?'

'What's fishy?'

'Sereno's trial, the whole damn thing,' Landry said. 'You do know that the jury found him guilty of first-degree murder of the drug dealer and attempted murder of his wife, right?'

'He found out she was two-timing, and he went berserk. Happens all the time,' Gideon said, 'even with white people.'

'Yeah, yeah,' Landry said. 'But in this case, the white judge wouldn't permit the jury's decision.'

'What do you mean?'

'I mean, Sereno refused to speak, even to his court-appointed attorney. He refused to defend himself. The judge himself called the trial a travesty, and ended up throwing out the murder conviction, throwing out drug trafficking, and reducing the attempted murder on his wife to aggravated assault.'

'How come?'

'Lack of evidence.'

Gideon lifted his foot off the accelerator, to quiet the car. He pressed the phone to his ear.

'Prosecutors couldn't produce one witness who would testify to having any drug contact with Sereno,' Landry said. 'Not only that, the morning that the drug dealer was murdered Sereno was five miles out to sea. His lawyer subpoenaed five independent witnesses – other fishermen – who swore to that.'

'Uh-huh.' Gideon scowled out at the road, the setting sun slicing across his left eye.

'Uh-huh,' Landry said. 'When Kiefer's body was discovered, no cash was found among his belongings – kind of unusual, seeing as how the DEA figures he moved no less than a hundred pounds of product at a whack. We're talking in excess of a million dollars missing, which was never found among Sereno's possessions or on his property. The FBI figures the money is in Juliette's possession – wherever she is – and they assume that's what you and Sereno are going after.'

'But you know better,' Gideon said, half sarcastic.

'I'm learning as I go,' Landry said. 'Now pay attention. Sereno's murder attempt on his wife – know why the judge reduced the charge to aggravated assault?'

'Why?'

'Investigators found the blood of a third person at the scene.'

'Right,' said Gideon. 'Sereno, Juliette, and Kiefer, the drug dealer.'

'No, Kiefer was murdered in his hotel. I'm talking about the house where Sereno and Juliette lived, on Plantation Key. Someone else's blood was on the carpet along with Sereno's and Juliette's. Not the drug dealer's.'

'Whose?'

'Who knows? Most likely, by the number of wounds on Sereno, it was someone in cahoots with Juliette.'

Suddenly, and for the first time, Gideon got an inkling of the man he was hunting. And the woman he had vowed to protect.

'A good lawyer,' Landry continued. '*Any lawyer* – would've gotten the case kicked before it ever got to trial. But down in Monroe County, you got a Colombian Indian accused of various and sundry offenses, including he bit off his wife's finger? They couldn't wait to lock him up.'

'And set *her* free,' Gideon uttered.

'Worse,' said Landry. 'They lost her.'

CHAPTER TWELVE

‘Oh, stop!’ Price said, when dessert came, a thick Belgian waffle topped with strawberries for July, and for himself a chocolate flourless torte, layered with ganache and finished with butter crème frosting. ‘Talk about decadence,’ he moaned.

They sat across from one another at Aquiline Gardens, Price’s favorite breakup restaurant, coincidentally no more than a mile from July’s house – in the event that she ended up walking home. He knew this wouldn’t be easy. They’d had sex together, off and on, for most of twenty-four hours. With the moon rising over the river, and the water slapping at the wharf outside their window, he raised his glass of Sangiovege and gazed across the table at her.

‘Not only are you stunningly gorgeous,’ he said, ‘but you are also the most uncannily perceptive woman I have ever known.’

July returned a tentative glance, candlelight flickering in her face, as she drank her mudslide through a straw. She’d already finished one mudslide, and two glasses of champagne.

‘And your eyes,’ Price said, as though amazed at their beauty. ‘So incredibly passionate.’

‘I’m afraid,’ she said, pouring some of the thick drink on her dessert.

He watched for a moment, as the cream ran over the edge of the waffle. ‘I think I’d better slow down on the port,’ he said, which was intended as advice for her.

‘I’m afraid for you,’ July told him.

He pushed his wine away as though he hadn’t heard what she’d said. ‘I have someone coming to my house tonight, a potential receptionist for my practice. I want to be clear-headed.’

July’s eyes sharpened. ‘Who?’

‘Actually, one of my former patients. The woman is incredibly competent, your textbook A-type personality. Also incredibly blocked with psychic pain from her divorce. We're going to work on those issues tonight.'

'Jacob is very jealous,' July said.

'What is jealousy but fear with a romantic name?' He took a bite of his torte and his face melted in rapture. 'Oh, you have to try this,' he said as he chewed. She reached across the table and sliced off a corner as large as her fork, and sucked it into her mouth.

Price smiled lovingly. 'We're such complex creatures, we humans. Do you know we're the only species that attempts to separate love from life's other negotiations?'

July stared at him while she poured the rest of her mudslide onto her waffle.

'In other words—'

'I don't need other words.'

'Of course not.'

'I want another drink.'

'They're very rich, aren't they? I mean, after that lobster pie . . .'

'Hey—' July showed the waitress her empty glass.

Price made a small gesture to the waitress, pointed to himself and mouthed the word: '*Cappuccino.*'

Then he returned his attention to July. 'I love rich things myself, more than they love me,' he said, patting his stomach. 'You obviously don't have that problem.'

'Why is she coming to your house?'

'The receptionist? Oh, it's a less threatening space than the office. Anyway, what I was articulating was that love, even in the most idealistic circumstances, such as the two of us – unencumbered, independent – is, in reality, a series of negotiations. You give yourself to me, I give myself to you. Except . . .' Price raised a finger, along with a sagacious smile. 'What is it we withhold?'

He held the smile, as the waitress arrived with their drinks. 'Thank you, we'll take the check when you're ready,' he said, then continued with his discourse. 'Interestingly, many studies point out that the inability in humans to commit to a longstanding relationship has to do with their difficulty in negotiating the materialistic stuff of love.'

Staring at him, July took a big bite of her Belgian waffle and washed it down with her mudslide. Price had a taste of his torte and worked it around his mouth, as he moaned, 'God must be a French pastry chef.'

'Jacob has a gun,' July replied.

'Uh-huh.' Price looked around in hopes that she hadn't been overheard.

'I think he shot Alix on the bridge,' she continued.

'Speaking of confidential,' he said in a hushed voice as he leaned toward her.

Her gaze darkened. 'He's going to do something to you next. I don't know what, but it'll look like an accident.'

Price set his elbows on the table, rested his chin in his hands. 'I'll keep an eye on him,' he replied, in a patronizing way.

July's eyes dropped to her plate. She pressed her fork flat on her waffle until the cream from her drink ran out the edges, then sliced off a triangular bite and put it in her mouth. Chewed a little, washed it down with more mudslide.

Price raised his brow in a professional way. 'As I was saying, negotiations of love—'

'Jacob could also have an accident.'

Price's mouth opened, presumably to reply, which July did not see. She was busy carving another sodden hunk out of her waffle, this one larger than before.

'July, I need you to hear this in the right way,' he went on. 'See, I'm not sure if you're aware that Alix used to see me.'

July glanced up.

'Professionally,' he said. 'But, outside of our sessions together, Alix and I had entered into a business arrangement wherein she agreed to become the principal investor in a business venture of mine.'

July's eyes narrowed.

'How to put this so it doesn't sound . . . Well, I have tape-recorded testimony from Alix – a confession, if you will – detailing the events concerning your husband Sereno and a Mr Kiefer and how you came to acquire a considerable amount of . . .' Price looked around the dining room again, then softened to a whisper . . . '*money*.'

Watching July take another drink of her mudslide, he looked around for the waitress. 'Maybe we should . . . I was going to say, would you like to take a walk on the beach so we could digest all this food?' He looked at his watch. 'I only have ten minutes or so – although, frankly, there's not much to negotiate. I know you'd like certain information to remain confidential – your identity, along with the aforementioned incidents. Alix felt that way too.' He turned one hand upright, then the other. 'And I deserve compensation for the drain that harboring such negativity has placed on my Karmic store.'

July poured the rest of her drink on the waffle.

'Not to mention the legal jeopardy that accrues to me for withholding knowledge of a felony. Of course, I'm not the demanding type, but perhaps a business investment, I do think something along the lines of' – he showed her six fingers – '*hundred thousand*.' He smiled again, sympathetically. 'Which, incidentally, was the same figure that Alix had agreed to invest.'

July sliced off another sponge of the waffle, stabbed it through the middle, then brought the whole dripping hunk to her lips.

'Of course, as a primary shareholder, you will begin earning dividends once the business becomes profitable.'

Before she had swallowed what she was chewing, July speared the rest of her waffle and stuffed it into her mouth, cheeks bulging and cream running thickly down both sides of her chin.

Price gave a low whistle of amazement, then glanced around for the waitress.

Glaring at him, July forced the food down her throat. He offered his napkin.

'I probably don't have to mention,' he said, 'that I've documented details of my offer in a sealed affidavit, to be opened by my attorney in the event of . . . an accident.'

He smiled again, as if July might share the humor. But her eyes lowered in a half-closed gloom, as though deep in thought.

He said, 'Honey, are you all right?'

When her eyes returned to his, they were lit with a peculiar intensity.

Her back lurched up to her ears, and with no sound but a long splash, she emptied her stomach on the table.

In the Speedway Tavern, the night barely crawled. By eleven o'clock, business didn't show any signs of picking up. A few couples and foursomes had drifted in for drinks during the course of the night, but they never stayed long. The four or five regulars sat at the near end of the bar and watched a car race on TV – as always – but because it was the Tavern's last night, they were prepared to stay until the bitter end. Jacob rinsed beer glasses in the back room, wishing that Squeaky would just say his goodbyes and send the stragglers home, so he could go find a place to sleep.

Tomorrow, first thing in the morning, he'd start looking for a steady job. To hell with writing, anyway, as though he'd ever had anything to say that people would be interested in. There were scores of restaurants up and down the coast, and they were always looking for line cooks, while he found something more to his liking. Maybe he'd go to work for a cabinetmaker or house builder, put his carpentry skills to use. Actually, the more he thought about the possibilities, Jacob began to feel a profound relief at not having a novel to toil over, always agonizing over words and images and trying to force some kind of story on the structure. Life was not a plot. Life was unstructured tedium. There was no balance, no ironic twists of any particular significance, no redemption, no happy ending.

When he was nearly finished rinsing glasses, Squeaky stuck his head in the doorway and said, 'You wanna feel better about your life? Get a load of the poor bastard in the corner.'

Jacob stepped to the door, looked toward the far end of the bar and saw the thin, young man holding a coffee cup in both hands, as if warming them. The guy wore a baseball cap low on his face, which was turned toward the television, yet he appeared to be ignoring the race that was on.

'Go see if he wants any more coffee,' Squeaky muttered, squeezing past Jacob, 'and get a load of the mug.'

'What do you mean?'

'The face. Try not to gawk.'

Jacob picked up the coffee pot and walked down the end of the bar. 'Warm it up for you?'

'Don't make a scene,' whispered the guy, eyes flashing out from the shadow of the brim.

Jacob jumped back and an arc of coffee jumped from the pot. It was Alix Callahan.

'We need to talk,' she said quietly.

Jacob only stared. She had shaved her head to a dark stubble and wore a green lumberjack shirt with the collar raised.

Knowing that Squeaky was watching their conversation, Jacob leaned on the bar and spoke casually. 'She's all yours,' he said. 'I never wanted her in the first place.'

Alix tossed a couple of dollars on the bar. 'I'll wait in your car.'

'Wait anywhere you want,' he said. And he'd head straight to the telephone and call Evangeline.

Alix reached into her shirt pocket and pulled a yellow floppy disk far enough for him to see it.

'What's that?'

She dropped the disk back in her pocket as she swung off her stool. 'I made you a backup.'

'My novel?'

'We need to talk,' she said.

'I know it was you,' he whispered. 'You tried to poison my son.'

Her eyes, serious as ever, bored into his. 'That was *not* me.'

Jacob leaned closer. 'You didn't try to run me off the bridge?'

'No.'

They matched glares. 'I've got all the trouble I need because of you,' he said. 'Why don't you go back where you came from?'

'You have no idea how much trouble you're in,' she said, and walked out the door.

Heart hammering, Jacob walked the length of the bar, trying to avoid Squeaky, who stood there nodding his head. 'You must be a helluva writer, don't know the meaning of the word "gawk." '

Jacob took off his apron, heading for the back room. 'I need to take a break, okay?'

'I mighta figured, some weirdo comes in, you'd be involved. Cripes, it looks like a dog tried to take his cheek off.'

Jacob tossed his apron in the corner. 'Okay?'

Squeaky raised his hands. 'By all means. You need any money from the cash drawer?'

'I'll be right back.'

Jacob went through the storage room and out the back door. The parking lot was dark, illuminated only by a light above the door and a single yellow bulb that hung on the porch of Squeaky's Spite House. He approached his car cautiously, seeing her shadow inside. When the passenger door popped open, he stopped.

'Hurry up,' she told him, sitting low in the seat, keeping her eyes on the road below.

Jacob watched her closely, ready to run if he saw anything in her hand. He did. His diskette.

'If I wanted to hurt you,' she told him, 'I've had a thousand opportunities.'

'If you wanted to hurt me—?'

'You can't go back there tonight.'

'I wasn't planning to,' Jacob told her. 'I already palmed her off on your old friend Price Ashworth. You know how that goes.'

Alix kept watching the road. 'Unfortunately, July isn't totally imperceptive. Get in.'

Steeling himself, Jacob walked around the car, opened his door and slid in behind the wheel. She handed him the diskette. He closed the door.

'When did you get this?'

'Before July came home.'

'So that was you last night.' He peered across the darkness, trying to see her face. 'Why come back?'

'I sobered up.'

He kept his eye on her. Indeed, it was the first time he'd talked to her when she didn't seem numbed with alcohol or yagé. 'And you're the one who sent that note in the restaurant.'

'Get down,' she said, peering off at the dark street, where a pair of brake lights glowed.

'Is that her?'

The reverse lights lit, the boxy station wagon backed up, its headlight off.

Alix lunged at him. '*Down.*'

Slumped together across the seats, they could hear the Volvo quietly climbing the driveway. 'What's she doing?' Jacob whispered.

'*Shh*. She can't help herself.'

The car stopped beside them, its engine purring. Jacob could feel the pounding of Alix's heart through her back. Her leg trembled against his. Then the engine sound diminished, as the Volvo moved away. Jacob peeked up over the dash, saw its brake lights again, down at the street. Then the dark wagon drove off.

Alix took hold of the door handle, seeming genuinely frightened. 'I've got to go.'

'She didn't see us.'

'Where's your son?'

The five-second stare.

'Out of state,' Jacob answered, not about to give her any information.

'Does July know where?'

He balked again. 'No.'

She opened the door. 'When you leave here tonight, don't go back to her,' she said. 'Don't let her find you.' The way she surveyed the darkness when she stepped out of the car reminded Jacob of a cat.

'Alix, I know what happened in Florida,' he said.

She stopped short. 'You don't know,' she said, not looking back. Neither did she walk away.

'Her real name is Juliette Whitestone.' Jacob spoke softly. 'In Florida her husband tried to murder her, but you came to her rescue. Sereno was sent to prison. July turned in some drug contacts and went into witness protection.'

She glanced back at him disdainfully. 'You don't know a thing,' she said, and walked off into the darkness.

Jacob knew she'd be back.

CHAPTER THIRTEEN

I t was eleven thirty by the time the agents and detectives had finished questioning the librarian. She hadn't gotten along very well with them, which didn't surprise her, considering they were so all-fired intent on pursuing a man who was clearly innocent, and she told them it was nothing but racism. Even so, they wanted to know everything that he said, and everything she'd said to him, what he was wearing down to the color of his socks – and especially what he was looking for in the library. She lied at first, about his appearance and even where he had sat, but when they told her that fingerprints lifted from the desk and computer keys proved to be a match, she had to admit that perhaps her memory for personal detail wasn't all that sharp.

So they asked again what Gideon had been searching for in the library, and she told them that she wasn't in the habit of spying on library patrons. Then the library's director came through the door and, knowing he could access computer records of past searches, she told them the man they were so hellbent on hunting was looking up islands of Lake Michigan. The truth was, she had done several searches herself after Gideon had left, to cover his tracks. Islands of Lake Michigan was the first one that came to mind.

It was a risk, but she figured that when the man was eventually exonerated, she'd be able to tell her family how she had helped. Now, as she walked to the parking lot and got in her car, all she wanted was to go home and have a big glass of wine and a bath. She opened her windows to let some air in, and as she started the engine, a voice came through the passenger window: 'You must be so tired of answering questions.' A rather soothing and very southern voice.

She turned to the window, feeling the blood rush to her face.

'Do I look especially tired?' she said, which in no way was an invitation, but neither did she drive away. There was something about the man – maybe the broken arm, maybe his boyish, dimpled smile. He had a magnificent jaw.

'I certainly didn't mean to suggest you look anything but spry,' he said in a playful way, while he flashed a policeman's badge at the window. He seemed to have trouble opening and closing the wallet.

'Oh, honestly,' she said, 'I have spent the past four hours talking to you people. I'm starting to feel like a suspect myself.' She had a winsome whine to her voice that had bought her way out of many a speeding ticket.

He tried her car door. 'May I?'

After a moment's hesitancy, she unlocked it, and he ducked inside, heavy with cologne.

'Is this going to take long?' she asked.

He shut the door awkwardly. 'Would you like it to?' He gave her that smile again, the kind of teasing grin that begs for approval.

'Now that's awfully forward,' she told him. 'How do you know I'm not waiting for someone?'

'Ma'am, if you were, he'd have to be a plain lunatic letting you walk to a dark parking lot by yourself.'

He patted down his cowlick, holding his broken arm tight to his chest.

'Wounded in the line of duty,' he explained, the way she regarded him. 'The truth is, I'd like to confide something in you, Miss, but first I need to make sure that we're on the same page. I gather you believe that the black African-American gentleman who was in your library this afternoon is an innocent, wrongfully-accused man.'

'I know for a fact,' said Chardonnay.

The smile returned to the stranger's face. 'See, I knew I had a good feeling about you.'

She leaned back, to study him.

'I've been told I'm an excellent judge of character,' she told him. 'But I don't know exactly what to make of you.'

'I guess you can tell I'm biased,' he said. 'After all these years it's hard to hide it. As a plain and simple matter of fact, I'm the acting vice-president of the Florida chapter of the N-Double-ACP, and an old and dear friend of Mr Gideon. I don't need to tell you how important it is that I find my friend before the police do. What with the way things are in this country, with prejudice and profiling, I'm afraid they're going to kill him before he has a chance to prove his innocence, and all because of the color of his skin.'

Chardonnay nodded. 'What did you say your name was again?'

'Well, that was rude of me,' he said. 'Steve Bennett, DSP. That's

Detective, Special Police. Now, from what I gather, you told my comrades that the man you saw in the library was doing research on what, some islands in the Great Lakes—?'

She gave him a skeptical look. 'How did you say you knew Mr Gideon?'

'Oh, we played ball together, didn't I mention?'

Her eyes lit. 'College?'

'You sound like a fan.'

'You can tell I used to cheer.'

'No kidding.'

'Don't you ask me what years, because I won't tell you.'

The man grinned again, his eyes sparkled. 'Actually, Terry and I – that's Officer Gideon – we played together in high school. I was the quarterback, and Terry was my favorite receiver. When I broke my arm and had to miss the All-State game, do you know what that boy did?'

She gave him a look.

'Boy, kid, youngster – we're talking about an era that predates political correctness. Anyway, I shattered every bone in my arm, and what do you think Terry did? He gave me his All-State trophy.'

She studied him some more, then drummed her fists on her steering wheel. 'I can't tell if you're being honest,' she said with that whine.

'Swear to Baby Jesus,' he said, crossing his heart below his broken arm. 'To this very day, I keep that trophy on top of my television. My wife thinks I'm crazy, but I'm more proud of that trophy than all the others put together. Because of what it means to me, that I had a bond. So now, when I heard that Terry was in trouble, I told my wife that I've got to help my friend, no matter what the personal risk to myself.'

Chardonnay's eyes grew glassy with tears.

'Ma'am, will you help me find my friend?'

She pressed her lips together. Her chest expanded.

'Please,' he said.

She breathed a thoughtful sigh. 'Okay. What if I told you he wasn't really researching islands in the Great Lakes?' She grimaced, as if half-expecting him to arrest her.

He gave her a big smile. 'See, I had a hunch about you.'

Her lips turned up in a sinful smile. 'He's looking for bridges.'

'Bridges.'

'Not any old bridge,' she said, as if it were a sexual thing. 'Trussed-arch steel bridges that span tidal waterways.'

The man closed his eyes, and a heavenly smile came over him.

'Thank you, thank you, thank you,' he said. 'And what bridges, may I ask, might they be?'

'Compendex showed three matches,' she explained. 'One in Baltimore – that's the Francis Scott Key Bridge. Another one in Massachusetts.'

A telephone chirped, and the man flinched. 'Mine or yours?' he asked.

'I don't have a cell phone,' she said.

He patted his jacket pocket. 'Must be mine,' he said, but he ignored the ringing. 'Massachusetts is a big state.'

'There are two of them going over Cape Cod Canal,' she replied. 'You can answer that, if you want. I can wait.'

'If it's important, they'll call back.' The phone rang again.

'It might be about your friend.'

'They'll call back,' he said. 'Now how about that third bridge.'

The phone kept ringing.

'Further north,' she told him. 'Between the states of New Hampshire and Maine.'

'Outstanding,' he said.

She eyed him more carefully now, the surreptitious way he was looking around the parking lot, the way he was letting that phone ring and ring.

'You've been such a big help,' he said, and he reached his good hand inside his sling. 'I'd like to give you a little token of my appreciation.'

A pair of headlights swung around, a car pulling out of the lot. The way the man turned his face away from the light, the way his hand stayed awkwardly inside the sling . . .

She opened her door.

'Hold on,' he said, and reached for her, but she pulled sharply out of his grasp and went walking briskly toward the lights of the street while, behind her, the phone kept ringing. Then his door opened. 'Hey now, where you off to?'

She started to run.

Bullens pulled the phone out of his pocket, turned it on and barked, 'Christ almighty, what?'

'Biff, we've got a complication down here.' It was Shivers again.

'Now, there's a word,' Bullens said. As he watched the woman climb a short guardrail and run off among the darkened buildings, he hurried across the lot to his own car.

'They're quite persistent about you coming back,' Shivers said. 'You know, so you can help with the investigation down here.'

'I wouldn't worry too much. I just got a solid lead.'

'About a package that was found on your doorstep.'

Bullens stopped. 'About what?'

'A package. The Bomb Squad picked it up. Addressed to you.'

Bullens got in his car, but before starting the engine, he pulled his pistol out of his sling, a suppressed Russian Makarov 9mm, and set it in his lap. 'Now who wants me blown up?'

'It wasn't explosives,' Shivers said. 'Vegetation: bark, leaf, dried flower petals . . .'

'Uh-huh.' Bullens turned the key, put on his bright lights, and drove slowly through the lot.

'I don't have to tell you, this looks bad,' Shivers said. 'The package was mailed from Trenton, New Jersey, probably through a re-mailing service. The feds think it came from Sereno's wife.'

'Mr Gloom and Doom,' Bullens said. 'Obviously Gideon sent the stuff, to frame me.'

'Biff, they found trace amounts of the same substance *inside* your house.'

'Of course it's in my house! Gideon put it there!' Bullens buried the weapon under his leg as he approached the street. He looked to his left, looked across, looked to the right. Too many buildings, too many streets. No sign of the woman.

'Officer Gideon will be in custody soon,' Shivers said.

Bullens listened in the earpiece. 'You heard what I said. That black bastard's out to frame me. It's his only way out. Isn't that right?'

Shivers didn't speak for a second or two, and it put Bullens on edge. Then the warden said, 'Biff, are you in Richmond now?'

Now Bullens hesitated. 'Son of a bitch, don't you turn on me.'

'They just want to talk to you about this vegetation.'

'I'll take care of this,' Bullens said. 'You just keep me apprized.'

'Officer Bullens, I don't know what you mean.'

Bullens held his breath, while the extent of Shivers' betrayal came clear. 'Turncoat prick,' he said, then hung up and pulled out of the lot, tires screeching, heading north, to Baltimore.

As it happened, Gideon was already there, inside a Baltimore parking garage that had closed for the night. Lying in the dark in the back of his station wagon, alone in the building, as far as he knew, he dialed his cell phone. The instant the ringing started, Bethany answered, sounding like she'd been crying. 'Baby, where are you?'

'I'm okay,' he answered. 'Where are you?'

'Trying to find you.'

'Baby, wherever I am isn't safe for you. Please go home.'

316

'Terrence, Mr Landry has some new information.'

'Information doesn't matter,' Gideon said, but Landry was already talking.

'. . . suspicious package shipped from Trenton, New Jersey, to a Mr Bullens, which is Sergeant Buford Bullens, the same prison guard who's out hunting for you right now. The bomb squad confiscated the package, thinking maybe it came from you – like maybe a surprise from someone who wanted to blow him up again.'

'Do you believe I'd mail that man anything?'

'Are you listening to me?' Landry said. 'It wasn't a bomb. But it did contain a bunch of tree bark and leaves, which apparently is some ritual drug the Indians take in Colombia. Not only that, but a few jungle darts – sharp little pieces of bamboo with frog poison on the tips – remember our discussion about that stuff?'

Gideon stared up at the ceiling of the station wagon, too closed in for his liking. With the doors locked and the windows shut, the lack of air felt suffocating.

'Sweetie, it's *evidence*.' Bethany again. 'Don't you see? Now they know Sergeant Bullens was taking a bribe.'

'How do they know that?' Gideon shot back – then softened his voice. 'Baby, how do they know it wasn't me who sent it to him? How do they know I wasn't in on it with him from the start – and then double-crossed him? How do they know it wasn't me who shot Cecil in the back – or killed those folks in Delta City? That package doesn't prove a thing.'

Before she could answer – if she intended to – Landry came back on the phone.

'Nothing in this life's a guarantee, Jasper,' he said. 'Sometimes you gotta have faith in people.'

'My faith in Florida people doesn't extend too far,' he said. 'You don't seem to grasp the simple fact: I'm a black man running from the white man's law – and I'm running out of time. Sereno knows where his wife is hiding. I don't know *how* he knows, but he's on her trail.'

'So are we,' Landry replied.

Gideon rolled onto his side. 'What do you mean?'

'Want to hear the reason Sereno's wife was kicked out of Witness Security?'

'How are you on her trail?'

'I'll tell you. First listen. Three years ago she got caught trying to smuggle the same kind of leaf and twigs into prison, tried to bribe a prison guard with sexual favors. You remember that incident?'

'Not at all.'

'That's what I thought you'd say.'

'What do you mean?'

'There wasn't anything illegal about the stuff, no coca leaf or anything. Apparently, back then she wasn't sending her husband frog poison. When she got caught, she told the feds it was just some tea from his home country, and it went to the lab and checked out okay. But she got booted out of Witness Security anyway, for trying to make contact.'

'I don't have any knowledge of that incident,' Gideon said.

Landry paused. 'Funny,' he said. 'Prison records say you were the go-between.'

'Me?' said Gideon, sitting up hunched in the back. 'Me?'

'I got a fax that says the warden questioned you, but because the stuff technically wasn't drugs, no disciplinary action was taken.'

'Mr Landry, I was never questioned.'

'You didn't get caught with Sereno's wife and a bag of stuff she was trying to smuggle in to her husband?'

'I never met the woman.' Gideon waited for Landry to say what he had just realized himself: The setup began years ago.

When Landry did speak, his voice sounded different, maybe a little frightened. 'Here's the thing, Jasper – and you listen closely. The stuff in those packages, leaves and twigs and so forth? The whole kit and caboodle's been shipped to a place called Polygon Analysis, in North Carolina. It's a lab that can analyze a stem, a speck of leaf, a flower petal – you name it – then identify precisely where in the world it was grown. Which means, Officer Gideon, that in the next day or two the authorities are going to locate Little Miss Juliette. So you might just as well let us come get you.'

Gideon peered over the front seats. The garage spread out around him dark and still. But he couldn't shake the feeling that he was not alone.

'Why was she sending Sereno that stuff?' he whispered. 'He killed her boyfriend, tried to murder her too, bit off her finger – then she wants to break him free?'

'That's exactly what I'm saying. The same woman you're risking your life to protect.'

'And now she's sending stuff to Bullens' house? Why?'

'Whys and wherefores,' Landry said.

'Whys and wherefores are why I'm not coming in,' Gideon told him. He wondered if Landry could detect the equivocation in his voice.

'My friend, I'm afraid you don't know half the whys and wherefores.'

CHAPTER FOURTEEN

A t one thirty, when Squeaky closed the bar, Jacob walked to his car with a liter of bottled water and a bag of pretzels – his bedroom, his breakfast. And his novel on a disk in his shirt pocket. He planned on finding a logging road up by Mount Agamenticus, in York, and sleeping in his backseat till the sun came up. Then he'd get cleaned up at the Information Bureau on the highway, and go looking for a job. Or maybe bring the disk to the Copy Shop and have them print out the novel. The things Alix had told him about July being dangerous . . . what could he do about it, really? He wasn't about to leave the state. Besides, who was to say that Alix wasn't the crazy one?

Despite her denial that she'd tried to poison Max, he still believed she was the one who had mutilated his car seat, tried to run him and Evangeline off the bridge that night. What motivation would July have had? Unless she'd been jealous of his visiting Laura, or talking to Evangeline . . . but jealous of Max?

Whatever was going on, he was too tired to figure it out now. After a few hours' sleep, he'd be able to put things in better perspective. Maybe he'd telephone Max and see if he wanted to spend the day at the beach riding waves. Maybe if he got Laura on the phone, he'd see if she wanted to come along. Maybe she'd pack a picnic lunch. Maybe she'd call Evangeline, let her know that Price lied about the radio incident.

Right now, all he wanted was sleep.

He got in his car and stuck his key in the ignition—

—and her voice whispered in his ear: 'Don't jump.'

'*Jesus!*'

In the backseat. Alix again.

'I've got to tell you something,' she said. 'July's husband—'

'I already know. The shaman.'

'He escaped from prison.'

319

Jacob's stomach clenched. For a second or two, he thought he was going to be sick. He turned around to face her.

'So that's why you disappeared,' he said. 'To get away from him. Dumping July on me was just an added bonus.'

She shook her head. 'All I did was invite you to dinner. You did the rest.'

'Yeah.'

'And that's not why I disappeared,' Alix told him. 'Portsmouth. Go to the salt pile.'

'Look—'

'Jacob, drive.'

Heading over the Old Route One lift bridge, Alix stayed low in the backseat, though every now and then Jacob would see her in his mirror, peeking out the rear window. 'We're not being followed, if that's what you're worried about,' he told her.

'You wouldn't know if we were,' she said, as he left the bridge and started wending his way through the sleepy, narrow streets of old Portsmouth. 'July's father was an American missionary in Colombia,' she began. 'Reverend Arthur Whitestone. He and his wife lived in a walled-in compound. They had a maid, a gardener, and a cook – all young native women the Reverend had converted to Christianity – and with whom he had sex routinely. I heard the stories from other Kogis when I was there doing research. Eventually, one of the women got pregnant: the cook.'

'July's mother. I know the story.'

'After she gave birth,' Alix said, undeterred, 'it became obvious to the villagers that her baby was part white. Reverend Whitestone, being the only gringo around, eventually confessed his sin to his American wife. Because Mrs Whitestone couldn't have children of her own, the Christian couple ended up adopting the baby and firing the cook – who was subsequently banished from Kogi society. The American couple named their little girl Juliette.'

'July already told me,' Jacob said.

'There's more.'

He worked his way over to Market Square, where a few late night stragglers were shadowing the sidewalks. Other than that, the town was deserted.

'To Mrs Whitestone's credit, she forgave her husband and raised the little girl as though she were her own,' Alix continued. 'Showered her with affection, bought her American clothes and toys and dolls, brought in Irish tutors to home-school her. They watched American

TV and movies, listened to American music. But little Juliette preferred the company of the Kogi servants, and by the time the girl was ten, she was running away and painting her face and doing yagé. When she was twelve, she snuck off and married one of her cousins. He was fourteen.'

'Alix, I've had a very long day—'

'Pay attention,' Alix said. 'The Reverend and Mrs Whitestone, who refused to recognize the marriage, decided that drastic steps were needed. They sent Juliette to a private school in Arkansas. Three months later she got kicked out.'

'Why?'

'She never told me. Slow down.'

He did. A huge bulker was docked on his right beside the salt pile, a snow-white, conical mountain set on the pier. Jacob pulled over, waited for a milk truck to pass him.

Alix looked around nervously. 'Turn your lights off and drive around back.'

He did as she'd instructed, drove around the salt pile, where he spotted a new white Taurus.

'Where'd you get that?' he asked.

'Borrowed it from a friend.'

He pulled close to the Taurus, hidden from the road by the salt pile. 'Okay,' he said, 'July left private school and returned to her family in Colombia.'

'Not her family. Her cousin.'

'That's right. Husband number one, who was killed by a jaguar.'

'Not by a jaguar,' Alix said, her eyes in his rear-view. 'When July returned, she insisted on moving into his hut. Kogi wives do not do that. They stay with the other women and their children. The men live separately. But July didn't like that arrangement. She wouldn't let him out of her sight. She would follow him to the nuhue – the men's lodge – and flirt with all the other guys. She insisted on going on hunts, chewed coca with the boys. A month after she returned, the boy went to the shaman and asked for a divorce. That's when he disappeared.'

Jacob turned to look at her.

'By the time he was found, there wasn't much left but bone and hair. The men who found him said it must have been a jaguar.' Alix stopped talking and peered out the window, watching a car in the distance, traversing the high bridge. 'The boy's family suspected the shaman.'

'Sereno,' Jacob said.

Alix gave him a look. 'What do you know about him?'

'Enough,' Jacob said. 'Raised in darkness, communicates with animal spirits, has sex with twelve-year-old girls. That's quite a religion.'

'Yeah, nothing like a missionary screwing the natives.'

Jacob shut up.

'Apparently, July and Sereno made quite an impression on one another,' Alix continued. 'After the boy's death, they began spending a lot of time together – too much time, for some tribespeople. Don't forget, July was the daughter of a white man many Kogis never trusted. Factions developed. When Sereno eventually took July for his bride, the *Comisario* – he's the secular leader of the tribe – met with the *Mayores*, the village elders, and they excommunicated them both.'

'And they came north, to Florida,' Jacob said.

'July was technically an American citizen, so she was able to get Sereno a green card. July's dad set them up in Plantation Key with a house and a three-lot parcel that was subdivided from a failed 1975 key lime grove. Sereno started fishing. July started raising native plants.'

'Where'd her father get all this money?' Jacob asked. 'I thought he was a missionary.'

'Oh, yes, the *missionaries*, with their hillside palace overlooking Santa Marta and the ocean, their swimming pool and satellite dish and eight-foot walls and security cameras. They used the Kogis for servants. When they weren't entertaining corporate executives and government bigwigs, they'd send candy and blankets and Polaroid cameras to the tribe, trying to win them over with gifts.'

'Win them over to Christianity?'

Alix smirked. 'You don't believe the Reverend Whitestone was really there to promote Christ.'

'I thought that was the idea.'

Alix spoke slowly: 'Oil. Cattle. Mining. Timber.'

Jacob turned his head to look at her in the harsh light of the moon.

'Making another part of the world safe for profit-taking,' she said, then got out of the car and looked in at him. 'Do you understand now?'

'Understand?'

'The danger you're in.'

Jacob shrugged. 'Isn't it possible the kid was killed by a jaguar?'

'Jesus,' Alix said. 'Do you think I jumped off that bridge because I wanted a thrill?'

She opened the door and got out of the car. 'If you were so afraid of this Sereno,' he said, 'why didn't you call the police?'

She turned back to him. 'It wasn't Sereno who killed that boy.'

'You're saying it was July—?'

322

She walked around the Taurus and got in, and he leaned over to his passenger window.

'Come on, July's no murderer. She's a screwed-up kid with a jealousy problem.'

Alix looked out at him. 'You're right, she's very jealous.' Alix started the car. 'Unfortunately, it's not her problem.'

CHAPTER FIFTEEN

The minister drove north, the sleeve of his vestments blown back by the wind. The sky was just beginning to lighten in the east, and he felt good. Maybe because he had finally eaten a good meal, a bunch of scrambled eggs, grits, and sausages from a fast-food drive-through; and because he'd had a few hours' sleep in the parking garage; but mostly because he finally had an inkling of where Sereno might be headed. His library search – before it had been interrupted – had yielded two trussed-arch bridges over tidal waterways: one in Baltimore, the other in Massachusetts. Right now, Gideon was heading for the first, in Baltimore Harbor, when his cell phone rang.

'Top of the mornin to you,' B.J. Landry told him. 'Been listenin to the news?'

'Where are you?' Gideon asked.

'Probably not far from you,' Landry answered, but his voice faded in and out. 'Hey, pretty big Colombian population here in the nation's capital.' The man was obviously fishing, but he wasn't far off. 'Shouldn't be that difficult to find a flower shop that specializes in South American plants, which is why I'm calling . . .' Landry's voice breaking up again. 'Your damsel-in-distress. I got some more . . .'

Gideon gave his phone a shake. 'I'm having a hard time hearing.'

'Juliette Whitestone,' Landry came on again. 'Her parents were missionaries in Colombia. When she was thirteen, they sent her off to a private school in Arkansas, where she got herself arrested . . .'

'I lost you. What?'

'Accessory . . .'

'Arrested for what?'

'Accessory,' Landry's voice crackled. 'Murder.'

The phone went silent.

324

'Wait,' Gideon said. 'Who got murdered in Arkansas?'

Landry's voice only sputtered, then it was gone. Gideon listened for another two minutes while he drove. When he finally disconnected, he stared out at the morning stars while the single word echoed in the highway racing under his wheels.

Murder.

CHAPTER SIXTEEN

A pair of Jasmine candles flickered on Price Ashworth's night table. From his CD player came the sound of aeolian wind chimes ringing softly against the babbling of a brook. The only other source of illumination in the bedroom came from deck light shining through the stained-glass window he had created, a butterfly feeding on ferns, the image that Laura had said – as she told him to go to hell – reminded her of a kite tangled in a tree.

Price wore a hooded linen robe and sat half-lotus on his Persian rug. The woman, who was in her early forties, sat facing him, half-lotus in her peasant dress. Patchouli-scented incense wafted up between them.

While the woman droned on in somnolent tones about visualizing her emotional pain shrinking to the size of dandelion seeds and blowing away on a breeze, Price's mind stalked across more practical territory – whether to phone Squeaky Frenetti in the morning and raise his offer on the property, or wait till afternoon when the old man would have had his first beer. And July. Would she come through with the money – or pull some harebrained stunt, as Alix had? With July, you couldn't tell. He'd started negotiations high, naturally, prepared to be talked down – but she'd left without saying a word. Which may have meant she was frightened enough to go the whole nut. She was not an easy read.

And what about Jacob? Price was pretty certain that July was just feeling the booze when she'd told him about Jacob's having a gun. And shooting Alix Callahan on the bridge? Didn't sound like Jacob, but with what he'd been through, maybe he'd snapped.

The wall clock interrupted his thoughts. The little wooden door sprang open and the Buddha popped out – two oms. The woman stopped talking. When the Buddha went back in his hut, Price took a deep, audible breath and let it out slowly. That's when he spotted the frog enter his bedroom. At first he thought it was a vision: tiny, bright,

326

and yellow, a most remarkable creature. He took a calming breath and gave his temples a light massage. When he opened his eyes again, it was still there, leaping onto his carpet.

He thought about getting up and putting it into a jar, but then he'd have to find a hammer and nail, to poke holes in the lid. He knew a woman, a very attractive biology professor, to whom he could bring the frog in the morning. Last he knew, she was married, but not happily. He wondered if he could even find a nail, then decided the woman wasn't worth the trouble. The frog stared at him.

'I think we've made excellent progress tonight,' he said to the woman in a hushed voice. 'You have created for yourself a deeper, safer place from which to begin exploring all the pleasures your mind and body have to offer, and to open yourself to new possibilities. Now I'm going to begin counting backwards, from five—'

'Excuse me?' The woman was scowling. 'Did you say, "body?" '

'Yes, I did,' Price said. 'Five . . . You feel a slight rising in your—'

The gunshot sprayed the room with colored glass and sent Price leaping straight into the air, so high he almost touched the ceiling. A second shot blew the rest of the butterfly window apart and pierced the hypnotherapist's kidney. When he came down again, he landed flat, arms and legs spread. A car went speeding away, but outside on the road there was nothing but darkness.

Inside the bedroom, shards of stained glass glittered on the carpet, reflecting the deck light that glared in through the broken window. Dogs were barking in the neighborhood.

The woman was still sitting on the floor, in a modified lotus position, her eyes closed and her face drained of color. 'Dr Ashworth?' she said. 'Are you going to keep counting?'

Unfortunately, the doctor could not answer.

CHAPTER SEVENTEEN

The farmer walked through his kitchen in the early morning. Four forty-five, the eastern horizon shining like chrome, more than enough light to start his chores. He'd done it this way for sixty years and would probably do it the same till the day he dropped. He drank a glass of water to get his system going, then sat in the kitchen chair to pull on his boots. The air felt dry through the screen, which meant the day would be sunny, probably get up in the 80s by noon. Maybe if he finished work early enough, he'd have time for a nap with Marjorie down by the river.

He took his cap and jacket off the hook, put them on. Opened the shed door. Stepped down to the spongy floor, felt his hip complain. Stomped his foot a couple of times to work out the creaks. Yes sir. Farm wasn't nearly as big as it once was, down to four acres and that little plot down on the river. Half acre in kidney beans, an acre in corn, two in timothy. Plus Marjorie's little vegetable garden out back and her tidy lawn in front, the way she'd always kept it. Maybe he'd get around to mowing it today. Maybe, instead of sleeping, he'd bring the pole down to the river and catch a fat catfish for supper. She used to love catfish.

He opened the door to the barn. Tina and Beauty rustled when he walked inside and picked the shovel off the hook. Four cows milking, two beef critters on the hoof, four hogs getting fat. About all he could manage at his age. Truth was, he felt damn lucky to still get around, still do his chores. Lucky the old John Deere still ran for him. Lucky the pickup started every morning, which was nothing short of a miracle, considering how old she was and how hard he'd worked her over the years.

Yup. Some kind of luck, when you think about it. Here you got a billion people in China. A billion people in India. He shook his head and laughed to himself. 'And here we are,' he said, patting Beauty on the rump.

He went to the back and pulled up the latch, pushed the old door out. Swallows were flitting about through the sky, picking at their breakfast. Himself, he'd boil up some grits and have a cup of tea. He propped the door open with a two-by-four and went to get the pickup—

'Now there you go,' he said.

Sitting under the old apple tree, where his old Dodge should have been, sat the most eye-popping two-toned Ford, turquoise-blue and white, probably '64 or '65 vintage, thick whitewall tires – and damned if that body didn't look like it just came out of the showroom, polished up shiny as could be. He went up to the window and saw the key in the ignition, penknife dangling from a chain.

The farmer took a big, comfortable breath of the morning air, leaned on the pickup's rail and bowed his head. People starving in Africa, people uprooted all over the world, plague, famine, earthquakes, war. He prayed to God with a laugh, said, 'Now why am I the lucky one?'

PART FIVE

CHAPTER ONE

The sun was high and hot when Jacob woke up, disoriented, drenched in sweat, and panting like a dog. His car was an oven. He unlocked the door and stumbled outside, where he urinated against a tree and was attacked by mosquitoes. By the position of the sun, he figured it must have been noon.

He felt as if he hadn't slept at all. Between the stuffiness in his car with his windows closed, and the mosquitoes when he opened them, he'd spent most of the predawn hours in a state of nightmarish delirium, thinking of everything Alix had told him – about July, about Sereno – as he watched shadows move through the woods, from trunk to trunk. Then the eastern sky brightened over the trees, and the crows had started. That's when he finally fell asleep.

He started his car and headed down to Route One, then south to Kittery and the Tavern, hoping to find Squeaky. He'd wash up, grab a cup of coffee, then help the old man clean the place out. Maybe he'd meet the new owners and talk them into hiring him to get the Spite House ready for guests. As he approached the Tavern, he saw the moving truck in the back. A bunch of balloons had been stuck to the front of the Tavern, with a long banner hung over the door: 'CLOSED TILL FURTHER NOTICE. COMING SOON: SEAVIEW INN.'

Jacob pulled up the drive to the back parking lot, where a pair of men were carrying a bed up the stairs of the old inn. But the bed, with a rectangular hole in the headboard . . .

'What are you doing here?' Laura practically stammered, emerging from the back of the truck. She was wearing jeans and her gray T-shirt with the little hole in the shoulder, and work gloves – and carrying one of his square-back dining-room chairs. He looked in the back of the truck: the bureau, the hutch, the armoire, and dozens of cardboard boxes. Yes, and that was his old bed that the movers were carrying. The stained glass was missing from the headboard.

'You?' Jacob's understanding broke through the haze. 'You bought the place? Or Price—?'

She was standing inches away from him, those same dark eyes searching his face. And, God, how he wanted to hold her. Just to touch her, to feel the warmth of her hand. But there was something fearful in her look.

'Don't you know?' she said.

'Know what?'

'He's dead,' she told him.

'Who?'

Jacob pulled back, far enough to see that she was serious. Indeed, she looked dazed. 'He was shot last night, in his house.'

Jacob caught his breath. 'Price . . ?'

'Evangeline is looking for you,' she said. 'So are the police.'

'Wait, you don't think—' he began. 'Laura, you know I wouldn't.'

'Someone who claimed to be our ex-neighbor told her you used to take target practice in the gravel pit behind your house.'

'What target practice?'

'Anonymous tip,' Laura said. 'Anyway, Evangeline went out there with a couple of detectives and they found some bullets that match the bullet found on the bridge, and' – she stopped to breathe a sigh – 'the one from last night.'

'Laura, last night I was here, working . . .' Until Alix Callahan showed up. 'What time was he shot?'

'The woman who was with him said it was around two.' Where was he at two? Either with Alix, at the salt pile . . . or parked alone at the mountain.

'The shots came through his bedroom window,' she said. 'They found a bullet in his bedpost. It matched—'

'Hey—'

Jacob looked back and saw Max standing on the porch. His heart froze.

'He doesn't know what happened,' Laura told him. 'Jake?'

Something in her voice . . . Jacob met her eyes.

'It was only that once,' she said, then she turned and walked away.

'Hey, Champ,' Jacob said, trying not to let his voice betray the panic in his heart as Max came down the steps.

'Cool, huh?' Max said, running over. He was wearing one of Jeff Dakota's T-shirts, autographed, and a leather tool belt with a claw hammer hanging down to his knee. 'Owner financing, zero interest rate,' he said nonchalantly. 'All we have to do is replace about thirty windows and sand ten thousand feet of hardwood floors, then start painting.'

'Very cool,' Jacob said, and gave Laura another look as she walked up the ramp into the back of the truck.

'It's called the Seaview Inn now,' Max said. 'Mom and I are gonna sleep up in the widow's walk tonight.'

'Up there?' Jacob said, looking up at the glass turret, but with his thoughts colliding, he could barely listen. He put his hand on Max's baseball cap. 'Where's Gramp?' he said. 'I just stopped to tell everyone good luck.'

Max turned to the porch, Jacob did too. Squeaky was standing in the front door, looking out at them.

Laura stuck her head out of the truck. 'Maxie, help me carry the coffee table. Daddy needs to talk with Grandpa.'

Jacob hurried up the steps, and Squeaky backed into the musty foyer, making room for him. The room was big, dark and brown-hued. From the high ceiling, twin unlit chandeliers hung on either side of a wide oak staircase.

'What the hell's going on?' Squeaky said, his face seeming wrinkled and old.

'I don't know,' Jacob said, looking out. Laura and Max had gone inside the moving truck. 'Do you have a gun?'

'Not for you, I don't.'

'Keep it with you,' Jacob said. 'Whatever you do, don't let Laura or Max out of your sight.' He turned to leave.

'Hey—' Squeaky pounded the door jamb. 'What the frick's goin on?'

'Take care of them,' Jacob said, then he turned and walked down the steps, passing the moving truck without saying goodbye. As he drove down the driveway, he saw Laura and Max in his mirror, walking down the truck ramp carrying a rectangular coffee table he had made, both of them watching him in return. He wondered if it was the last they'd ever see of him.

The drive took less than five minutes. He left his car on the dirt road that bordered the little duck pond, then ran past the new houses. Even though it was daylight, he didn't care who might be watching out their windows this time, as he hopped over the chain and continued running down the old trolley bed into the woods.

Though he had buried the weapon in the dark, he knew exactly where it was – at the head of Whale Rock, in the grassy spot where he and Laura had first made love. When he got there, he found he didn't even have to dig. Someone had beaten him to it.

Staring at the vacant ground, Jacob began to understand . . . Somehow July had followed him that night. But how? As he recalled, he was alone in the pitch black. There were no lights, and no one had followed his car. The cool, dark hole stared up at him, making irrelevant his denial. However she knew where he had hidden the revolver – had he talked in his sleep? – it was obvious that she had the weapon now, with his fingerprints on it. And she'd eventually plant it for Evangeline to find.

As he ran back to his car, a more frightening thought occurred to him . . . that she would claim another victim first.

CHAPTER TWO

July's car was parked at Green Girls when Jacob pulled up. Caution was no longer an issue. He walked directly to the front door and let himself in. The door had been left unlocked. As soon as he stepped into the shop he was aware of the strangeness. The place was wrapped in silence. Flowers and hanging plants in the shop were withered and dry. The glass doors leading into the garden were closed.

He had a sudden, terrible thought: What if Sereno had caught up with her? He let the chill wash through him before he called her name.

'July?'

What if Sereno was still here?

He went upstairs and called her again, but she didn't answer. He looked in each of the rooms and didn't find her, so he concentrated on finding the revolver. In the bedroom, he tore through the closet and bureau, searched under the mattress and through the clothes on the floor. But no gun. Not for the first time, he thought of simply turning himself in to Evangeline and telling her the truth about Alix – the truth about everything. But he was afraid of whatever evidence might rise up against him once he was in custody. He was more afraid of what might happen to Max and Laura.

So he proceeded into the kitchen, searching through the cupboards and refrigerator. The gun could have been anywhere – if it was here at all.

Or maybe it was time to get on the highway, pick up Max and Laura and head to Canada . . . except he knew if the police were looking for him he wouldn't get far. He looked out the glass doors to the rainforest. Too quiet, too still. He went through the pantry and down the stairs, then opened the door to the garden.

'July, we need to talk,' he called into the greenery. No one answered, so he made his way onto the main path and ducked into the thick of the humid forest, thinking that the garden hut would be a good place

337

to stash a revolver – better still, the room with the grasshoppers. But when he reached the hut, he was suddenly afraid to go in. Was she waiting inside, lying in the bed he'd made for her, with the revolver aimed at the door? No. She couldn't use the gun on him. She'd have a knife – and the perfect alibi. The twice spurned lover, on a rampage of vengeance. She'd plant the gun on his body.

He took hold of the latch, braced for an attack—

– and heard a noise behind him, actually some distance away. The sound, a shushing, had come from the direction of the house. Jacob sidled up against the hut and moved quietly to the corner. Peering through the foliage toward the house, he could see the open glass doors upstairs, but nothing suspicious, no movement inside. So he left the relative safety of the hut and moved stealthily through the flora, until more of the house was visible. . .

The shop door was closed.

Had he closed it himself? He couldn't remember. Why would he?

Hearing another sound – this a furtive metallic creak from the trees above him, Jacob looked up into the thick green canopy. Suddenly a shadow moved across the leaves. He heard a crack, the leaves rustled sharply, and something came whickering down, slicing down through the foliage and crashing into the earth two feet away from him – a guillotine of safety glass, embedded deep in the ground. Severed leaves fluttered down around him.

Hearing another crack overhead, Jacob jumped backward as the flash of another pane came slamming down. Through a clean break in the trees, he saw July standing on top of the greenhouse in her white sun dress, straddling the frame. With her bare heel, she stomped on the glass, and another crystal blade tore through the canopy. Jacob leaped back into a spiny bush, and the eighty-pound sheet crashed in the spot where he'd been standing. Scrambling out of the thorns, he ran for the house, while more glass shattered, cascading out of the trees behind him, brilliant, icy shrapnel. Covering his head, suddenly exposed to the open sky, Jacob slammed into the door, grabbed the handle. Locked.

Above him, he heard the clap of a pistol shot, and the pane came down in jagged halves, shattering on the ground behind him. So much for finding the gun. He looked up, saw her balanced on the frame, aiming down. The shot rang out, the glass exploded, and now Jacob was racing back under cover of greenery, followed by two more gunshots and raining glass.

Trapped inside the garden, he had little choice. He made his way to the hut and ran inside, hoping for a few seconds to collect his thoughts. Maybe . . . he looked around . . . pull the mattress off the bed and use it to crash through the greenhouse wall, then make a run for his car.

He heard another crack, then the thatched roof jerked as a thick pane tore through, slicing through the mattress and shattering on the bed. Jacob jumped aside, as the small inner door flew open and a man reached for him, swarming with crickets—

Jacob spun for the door, but he was hauled backwards to the floor as another glass pane exploded in the doorway, thatch bulging down, and he realized who had saved him.

'Out!' Alix shouted, pulling him out from under the hole in the roof. Jacob looked up, saw a gleam of daylight – and July, balanced on the frame, aiming down with both hands. He sprang to his feet and pushed through the door, just as the pistol shot cracked and glass rained down.

'This way,' Alix said, and pulled him against the trunk of a palm, where the overhead growth was thicker. A small backpack was slung over her arm. Grasshoppers clung to her cap and clothing.

'I told you to stay away from her!' she whispered harshly.

'What are you doing here?' he whispered back.

'Shh.'

Above, they watched July's shadow over the treetops, moving slowly toward them. Alix gave him a tug, then pointed beside his foot, where a tiny yellow frog climbed out of a bromeliad. He gave Alix a look, as if to say, *Now what?*

Though they'd made barely a sound, Jacob watched in horror as July's shadow stopped, changed direction, and came toward them.

Jacob pointed to the barbecue grill behind the hut, made a swinging motion – meaning they could break the glass and make a run for it.

Alix shook her head. 'We'd be out in the open.'

He gave Alix a confounded look. Then the shadow stopped. They heard a soft tapping, almost like rain. Behind them, brass casings came falling out of the leaves.

'She's reloading,' Alix mouthed.

They left the tree and headed stealthily for the grill, when a crack rang out above them, then the vicious swipe of vegetation, and they were running again, crashing through the garden, while the overhead shadow cut across their path.

They broke into the clearing behind the hut, and Jacob grabbed the grill by a leg, then they went running through the middle of the thicket, with vines and branches grabbing at them. Jacob slammed into the wall unexpectedly. Glass broke against his shoulder. He stepped back, grabbed two legs of the grill and swung. A pane blew apart, simultaneous with a loud hissing of leaves above them. Daylight flickering, the big shadow crashing down. Then July was draped across the crook of the tree, hair hanging down, her eyes open but dazed.

'Go!' Jacob yelled, pushing Alix toward the break. Instead, she spun around and dived to the ground, coming up with the revolver July had dropped.

Jacob froze.

Alix took a step toward her. She raised the weapon, aimed at July's head.

'Don't,' Jacob said, but he knew he couldn't stop her.

He saw July blinking slowly, a glimmer of light returning to her eyes. Her nose was bleeding.

'She'll kill us if I don't,' Alix said. She held the revolver with both hands, trembling.

July's arm moved. Her leg bent. Slowly she gathered her body together and crouched onto the limb. Staring defiantly at Alix, she reached up and wrapped both hands around the trunk, then began pulling herself up into the green ceiling.

Alix followed her with the revolver. Jacob reached out, put his hand on the barrel and gently deflected her aim, then took the weapon from her, as they watched the girl disappear above the greenery.

'Come on,' he said, and they were ducking through the broken pane, running for the road. But seeing his car – his tires were flat – Jacob turned to the Green Girls wagon parked behind it. 'Do you have keys?'

'No. Give me that.' She grabbed the gun from him, turned to the Volvo's front tire, and fired. The hubcap rang and flew off the wheel. She steadied her wrist with her other hand. Fired again. The car sank.

Another car came around the corner, fast. Alix froze. Jacob recognized the black Saab too late, then it stopped beside them.

Susan Evangeline stared out at Alix for only a second or two, but Jacob knew it was longer than she wanted to. It was the first time he'd seen anything in her face that resembled human emotion.

She turned to Jacob. 'Mr Winter, you can come with me and answer some questions, or you can wait for the police,' she said, back in character. 'Neighbors heard shooting, there are four cars on the way.'

Without hesitation, Jacob opened the back door and got in. 'Let's go,' he said, and left the door open for Alix – who stood there. 'Come on.'

Evangeline turned to Jacob. 'Is that yours?' she asked in an unruffled way, referring to the gun in Alix's hand.

Abruptly, Alix came to the door. 'Move over,' she said to Jacob, and tossed her backpack in.

'Hand me the weapon, please.'

It was obvious to him that Alix was not going to surrender the revolver or even look at Evangeline.

'We need a ride to Kittery,' Alix replied, slamming the door. 'Take the Memorial Bridge.'

'Is this a hostage situation?' Evangeline asked dispassionately.

'I don't think so,' Jacob replied, then looked at Alix.

'Just drive,' Alix said, keeping her head turned toward the side window. And Jacob realized: She was hiding her scar.

Evangeline started down the road. Jacob watched her eyes in the mirror, the way she stared out her windshield as she turned onto Market Street. Then she put her sunglasses on, despite the lack of sunlight. He couldn't recall a more nerve-wracking silence.

'As you can see, I never shot her,' he said to Evangeline. 'I didn't shoot Price Ashworth. I never shot anybody. And that's not my gun.'

'Shut up,' Alix told him.

Jacob looked over at her, but she kept her face turned away, as Evangeline negotiated through traffic at Market Square, turned down State Street, and drove onto the Memorial Bridge. The floor of the car vibrated as they passed over the grating, the green arched bridge off to their left against the open sky.

'Maybe I don't deserve an explanation,' Evangeline said.

Jacob knew she was talking to Alix, but Alix didn't respond.

'Was it for my benefit?'

Alix smirked, but kept her face to the window. 'Your father must be proud,' she said.

'He passed away last October.'

'I'm sorry to hear it,' Alix said. 'Stop here.'

'What are we doing?' Jacob asked her. Evangeline pulled her car toward the rail at the midpoint of the bridge, under the STATE LINE MAINE sign.

'We need your car,' Alix said.

Evangeline shifted into neutral, stepped on the parking brake. She turned around in her seat. 'Do you want me to tell you how much I hate this job?' she said. 'Do you want another apology?'

'No.' Alix turned to face her, held her sunglass-shielded eyes for several seconds. 'I want you to walk.'

Evangeline opened her door, but as she was about to step out of the car, her radio came alive. 'All units, 10-17,' a male voice said. 'We're looking for a 10-24, Jacob Winter, six-one, two hundred pounds, wearing blue work shirt, khaki pants, brown moccasins, caution, armed and dangerous, armed with ten-thirty-two, handgun. Last seen in vicinity of the I-95 overpass, Portsmouth bank of the Piscataqua, possibly on foot. All units, acknowledge.'

'What's a ten-seventeen?' Jacob asked.

'Shots fired,' Evangeline explained.

'The girl was shooting at us,' he said.

'I said shut up,' Alix snapped.

'What's a ten-twenty-four?' he persisted.

'Wanted person,' Evangeline answered. 'July was firing at you?'

'Alix, you're a witness,' Jacob said.

'I didn't see a thing,' she said.

Jacob gaped at her.

'Mr Winter, if you didn't murder Dr Ashworth, don't blow it by acting guilty,' Evangeline said. 'The reason I knew you didn't fire the revolver on the bridge was that the entrance and exit holes in the sweatshirt were identical – which means, the bullet did not pass through a body. Someone planted the shirt after the fact, possibly to frame you.'

The radio squawked: 'DA One, do you copy? Over.'

'They're waiting for me to respond,' Evangeline said. 'Let me get on my radio and have them pick up July.'

Jacob looked at Alix.

'You may also be interested to know,' Evangeline went on, 'your wife admitted to me that your assault on Dr Ashworth occurred in your bedroom, as you've stated.'

He looked up at her, trying to detect sincerity in her face.

'How does any of that clear me in Price Ashworth's death?' he asked.

'Did you kill him?'

'No.'

'For Christ's sake, do you believe her?' Alix snapped.

Jacob looked from one woman to the other.

'How do you usually acknowledge?' Alix said.

Evangeline hesitated.

'Do it.'

Evangeline picked up the microphone, thumbed it on, and said, 'DA One, ten-four, copied.'

'Now get out,' Alix told her.

Evangeline stepped out onto the road, and a car shot around her. Alix got out the other side, revolver hidden from the passing traffic. She stepped over the curbstone onto the sidewalk. Evangeline did the same, cool as could be in her shades.

'You're stealing my car,' she said. 'Aiding and abetting a murder suspect. Accomplice to deadly assault. What do you expect me to do?'

Alix extended the revolver toward her, butt first. Evangeline regarded her tentatively, then slowly reached out and took the weapon.

'Forget you saw me,' Alix answered, then turned away, walked around the car and got in the driver's seat, leaving Evangeline standing like a mannequin, the weapon in her hand. The wind didn't even ruffle her hair. And now Jacob knew something else about the women. They were still in love.

Alix shifted, kicked the gas, and they shot ahead. 'Don't say anything,' she said, as she negotiated Evangeline's car through a pair of intersections and around a rotary, then headed up Route One, a six-lane boulevard of malls and outlet stores and lobster restaurants. Pulling into a parking lot, she stopped the car with a jerk beside the same white Taurus he'd seen at the salt pile the night before. She got out, grabbed her pack from the backseat. 'Pull around back,' she said. 'I'll pick you up.'

Then they were driving south again. Neither said another word until Alix turned onto I-95 heading south. 'By the way,' she said, looking over at him, 'nice bed.'

In the distance the high bridge poked up above the trees, then they began climbing and the sky opened up. 'It was July's idea,' he told her.

'I'm touched.'

As they sailed under the web of green steel, Jacob pressed back against his seat. Down on the Portsmouth pier he saw the rusty salt bulker flying Panamanian and American flags. Dump trucks drove on and off the deck, loading Maine gravel to bring south.

'What's your problem with heights?' Alix said.

He didn't answer.

She gave him a look. 'Ever fly?'

'Twice.'

'Were you afraid then?'

He closed his eyes. 'First time no. Second time, petrified.'

'What happened?'

'I don't know.'

'Why were you flying?'

'First time? My parents split up. My mother and I flew to California to find a place to live.'

'Second time?'

'My mother's funeral.' What he chose not to say was that he remembered almost none of it, except he was told later that he had to be subdued during the flight, and the pilot made an emergency landing in Chicago. He'd taken the train the rest of the way.

343

'So, now we know,' Alix said, the skeletal steel racing past her face. 'It's not a fear of heights.'

He gave her a look.

'It's a fear of losing your family.'

He didn't respond, but looked out his window. Watching the tree-tops passing their windows, as the bridge retreated in the distance, he felt he could breathe again. He sat up in the seat, relaxed his shoulders. 'Can I ask you a question?' he asked.

'What?'

'What's in the backpack?'

Alix replied, 'Something to make sure she can't escape.'

'Okay, you don't want her to escape,' he said, tired of her cryptic answers. 'So why wouldn't you let me tell Evangeline about her?' Of course he knew that if July's identity were disclosed, Alix herself would be exposed to retribution from the drug underworld. But at this point exposure seemed inevitable. 'If what you say is true, and Sereno is on his way . . .'

The way Alix's eyes narrowed as she stared out at the road, Jacob's question was answered.

'You don't want her arrested,' he said. 'You want Sereno to kill her.'

'He's coming,' Alix answered. 'That's all I know. She knows it too. That's why she's coming apart.'

'And you're just going to let it happen.'

Alix gave him a look as she reached under her car seat and pulled out a black laptop computer – the one that had disappeared the night she jumped off the bridge. 'Turn it on,' she told him.

He took it from her, flipped open the lid and hit the start button. When it had powered up, Alix turned it toward her and worked the thumb pad as she drove, then turned the computer back toward Jacob. An email was on the display, only two sentences long, and written in Spanish . . . ' "*Hemos trabajado mucho. Tus primos dicen hola,*" ' Jacob read, and he translated: ' "We have been working hard. Your cousins say hello." ' Similar to the message July had written on his own computer when he'd first moved in with her. 'What's wrong with that?'

'Not a thing,' Alix replied. She scrolled to the bottom of the screen and pointed to about twenty lines of alphanumerical code, under the centered word HEADERS. 'Third line down,' she said. 'It's written in Kogi, a derivation of a primitive tongue called Chibchan. No one in the world, other than Kogi Indians, knows the language.'

Jacob looked up at her. 'What does it say?'

She pointed to the text. 'A date, a time, a location on the Florida coast.'

He stared down at the computer. 'So . . . July orchestrated the prison break,' he said. 'Does she *want* Sereno to find her?'

Alix shook her head. 'I don't know what's on her mind – or his,' she said. 'Even if you thought you had some vague idea about what makes these people tick, you'd be wrong. All I know is, anyone who ever got close to July is either dead – or about to be.'

Jacob turned off the computer and closed the lid. 'So what are we doing?'

Alix gave him an obvious look.

'Hiding.'

CHAPTER THREE

———

The minister stood inside a phone booth outside Fort Howard, but he had made the call on his cell phone.

'Yeah, Sereno's wife, this girl Juliette Whitestone,' he said, when B.J. Landry answered. 'You say she was arrested for accessory to murder in Arkansas?'

'That's right.'

'Who got murdered?'

'A girl from town, not a student,' Landry explained. 'She was run over. Juliette was charged with the crime, along with a local boy – also a townie – who claimed to be Juliette's boyfriend. The car that ran over the girl belonged to him. Because Romeo was twenty-two, he was tried as an adult and got twenty-five years.'

'What about Juliette?'

'Her father hired some hotshot legal team who won her an acquittal – even though the prosecution all but proved she was the driver. Her fingerprints were all over the wheel.'

'So how come the young man got convicted and Juliette didn't?'

'He tried to claim self-defense,' explained Landry, 'testified that the other girl, the dead girl, was insanely jealous and had been plotting to murder them both.'

'Sounds like Juliette stole the other girl's boyfriend.'

'Except it was the other way around,' Landry said. 'It was Romeo who moved in.'

'What do you mean?'

'The other girl had been Juliette's girlfriend.'

'We're talking about the same Juliette? Sereno's wife?'

'One and the same. Romeo testified that as soon as Juliette started dating him, the other girl began stalking him – put a rattlesnake under his car seat, set fire to the woods behind his house, sent him and Juliette anonymous death threats, things like that. He confessed to the

346

court that he and Juliette lured the girl out to the woods on the promise of three-way sex. And they all got to drinking and smoking pot, and he ended up running over her.'

'What about Juliette's prints on the steering wheel?'

'Southern chivalry at its finest: Romeo took the blame, testified that after he killed the girl, Juliette drove herself back to the campus because he was too drunk to drive – and didn't want to lose his license – which is how her prints were on the wheel.'

'I see,' Gideon said.

'I don't think you do, Jasper. The dead girl had been run over eight times when they found her – back and forth – pretty much ground into the dirt . . . like I said, with Juliette's prints on the steering wheel. Not only that, but the dead girl's mother testified that her daughter couldn't possibly have been jealous, because she was the one who broke off the relationship with Juliette – not the other way around.'

Too much information suddenly. Gideon stared out at the Patapsco River, where the trussed arch of the Francis Scott Key Bridge stood silhouetted against the Baltimore skyline. He had spent the better part of an hour in the phone booth looking through the Yellow Pages – under Flowers, Greenhouses, Nurseries, Plants, and he'd called every number that seemed even a remote possibility, but the most exotic plants he'd found were gardenias.

'You said you knew a lab where they're analyzing the vegetation that was sent to Bullens,' Gideon said. 'Has the whereabouts of the greenhouse been determined?'

'When they find out, I'll be the first one to know,' Landry told him. 'Fishin buddy of mine's got a brother-in-law that works there. He promised to give me a heads-up before they make it official.'

Gideon let the phone book close. If Juliette really was the one who'd sent the package . . .

'Something I still don't understand,' Gideon said. 'You're saying this girl Juliette set up Sereno down in Florida, got him sent to prison. Why on earth would she be trying to help him escape?'

'That's easy,' Landry said.

'What do you mean?'

'To set him up again.'

Gideon paused.

'She was in cahoots with Bullens,' Landry explained, 'who wanted revenge on Sereno for killing his drug business.'

A sharp breath came out of Gideon's lips. It might have sounded like a laugh.

'You know the real funny part?' Landry asked. 'Sending that package to Bullens' house.'

'What's funny about that?'

'Think about it, man. She set him up too.'

Gideon shivered.

Then Bethany was in his ear. 'Sweetie, okay now? Please let us come take you home,' she pleaded. 'Your children need you.'

'They need you,' he told her. 'I'll be home when I finish my business.'

'What business? Terrence, it's over. This woman is not worth protecting.'

'Baby, my chest is full,' he said.

'I don't think I heard you.'

'It's not over,' he said. 'In the eyes of the law, I'm still a wanted man.'

'But you're innocent.'

'And maybe so is the man I'm looking for,' he said, 'the only one who can clear my name.'

'He's not going to surrender to you,' she snapped. 'For what? To be sent back to prison and get killed? To be sent home and get killed?'

'Bethany, I've got an obligation,' he told her.

'Obligation?' she said sharply. 'Obligation, as what?'

'Obligation,' he repeated, losing patience too. 'As a man.'

CHAPTER FOUR

The sensation was intense, like a nap interrupted by a fall. Jacob lurched up, opening his eyes. Sleep left him in a flurry, glaring reality swarmed in its place. Except... He pulled himself upright, gazing out the windows.

The old house looked the same as when he'd last seen it, when he was Maxie's age. Shade trees larger certainly, some gone; a deck added on the side, the driveway hard-topped. He thought maybe he was still dreaming, but the door opened and his father was standing there.

Alix turned the engine off and got out of the car. Jacob opened his door and stepped out too, thinking that, last his father had heard, Alix was dead. But the old man gave her a casual smile.

'Maybe we should move the car away from the house, so it doesn't attract attention,' Jacob said to Alix.

'It belongs here,' his father said.

'What do you mean?'

'It's my car.'

Jacob turned to Alix. She stepped inside. Then back to his father.

'Come in, Jake,' the old man said, opening the door wider.

Jacob stepped into the living room, and his memory expanded. The place actually smelled the same. Books still piled everywhere, stacked beside the couch and the old Boston rocker.

'Make yourself at home,' said his father, with a stiff, upright stance. He did not step forward to shake hands, and Jacob was glad of it.

'You told me you didn't pay my legal fees,' he said.

The old man shrugged. 'I didn't think you'd accept.'

'I'll pay you back as soon as I can,' Jacob said.

'Which means, "Thank you," ' Alix said.

His father gave him a long look, then clasped his hands. 'I certainly hope you two can stay for dinner.'

Jacob chuckled. The old man's sense of humor hadn't changed. 'I don't know,' he answered, then said to Alix, 'Honey, do you have any plans?'

She sneered. 'Not for you.'

CHAPTER FIVE

E ven at nine at night, the traffic pours steadily over the Bourne Bridge onto Cape Cod. From the rocky bank of the canal, where the diminutive Indian stands in a heavy trance, the stream of taillights means nothing. In fact, he is no longer conscious of the deep, dark water rushing past him. With a New England road map opened in his hands, he has risen above it all, above the land and water, high over the top of the skeletal arched bridge, and he is soaring northward, following the coastline. Below him, headlights traverse highways, neighborhoods lie quietly. The wind rushes all around. He passes over Plymouth Harbor and Massachusetts Bay, the jagged, sparkling crown of Boston, where a single boat trails a soft wake in the water. He looks down on Salem Harbor, the peninsulas at Marblehead, Gloucester, and Cape Ann. He sees the river emptying at Newburyport, then glides over miles and miles of sandy beach and an ocean that's soft as velvet.

In the distance, Sereno can already see the wide Piscataqua flowing out to the ocean and the three bridges connecting the banks, New Hampshire to Maine.

And there in his vision the great arched bridge rises up over the river, cars and trucks coming and going, utterly unaware of what is hovering above them . . . or down below: the glass house on the bank, filled with flowers and plants and trees that he hasn't seen in years . . . and will never see again.

CAPE COD CHARLIE'S BAIT & TACKLE, the sign said. Gideon watched the silhouetted arch poke up above the trees. He cut to the right and slowed down, hoping to find a phone booth, where he could look for greenhouses or nurseries . . . and that's when he spotted the old farm truck. It was parked alone in a deserted rest area. Even in the dark, Gideon had a bad feeling, so he turned in. The place was a public

351

park, he saw by the signs, with marked trails and scenic overlooks of Cape Cod Canal.

He pulled closer to the truck and read the license plate – Virginia 1967 – then he knew. Stepping furtively out of his car, he went over and touched the hood. Still warm. Realizing that Sereno was near, jitters were already swarming through Gideon, as though he'd drunk too much coffee. He was alone now, and suddenly he felt a powerful resistance to continuing. No Landry on the telephone, to dissuade him; no Bethany, begging him to come home. Although cars passed steadily in both directions, by the looks of the place, nobody else was about to turn in. Across the highway was a small, boarded up Baptist church.

He went down a few wooden stairs to a grassy picnic area. A sign sat in the middle of the lawn, lit by three small floodlights. Gideon went close enough to read that he was at the widest sea-level canal in the world. Then he stepped out of the light. Off to the side he noticed a fairly wide trail cut into the trees, so he went over – and found himself looking at a rustic set of steps laid down the side of a long, wooded, and very dark hill.

Much too dark. After all, what did he know about the New England woods – or any woods, for that matter? What little he knew about Sereno – that his home had been the forest and mountains of Colombia – it was all too clear to Gideon that once he started down that trail, he would be at the Indian's mercy.

A wind whispered through the trees. So what else could he do, go home? Come all this way, find his man, then turn tail? If he did that, he'd never be able to face himself – never mind Bethany or the children – without recalling this night, and how he had shrunk from adversity.

He started down the trail as quietly as he could, which wasn't quiet at all. The steps were crooked and unevenly placed, and three times before he'd descended the first few steps he tripped noisily. What did it matter? If Sereno were anywhere nearby, he'd probably been aware of Gideon's presence since the moment he drove into the parking lot.

At the bottom of the steps, Gideon reached a plateau where there was a small clearing. From here he could see the canal out ahead of him, a wide, silvery glimmer under the full moon. At his feet was yet another set of stairs to negotiate, these more uniformly constructed, with square lumber and a proper railing – but much steeper. Gideon thought he could see a paved road at the bottom, probably a service road alongside the canal.

Taking the wooden rail in his hand, he started down. With every step, he watched the trees rise up in front of the arched bridge, with all the car lights streaming across . . .

Then Gideon stopped.

Across the service road, standing amongst the pile of boulders that made up the canal's bank, he spotted Sereno. The Indian was turned away from him, his face raised to the stars.

As quietly as he could, Gideon came down the rest of the stairs, then started across the road, his minister's robes ruffling in a gusty, salty wind. Despite the steady slapping of water off the boulders, he knew his approach had not gone undetected.

Stopping at the edge of the road, Gideon said in a gentle voice, 'I'm here to help you,' much the way he might speak to his son.

The Indian lowered his head, but he did not turn.

Gideon walked two steps onto the grass, stopping at the edge of the bank. 'I have a friend,' he said, 'an *amigo*, who will bring us back safely. He knows we are innocent. He knows about your wife, Juliette, and what she did.'

The Indian began to turn. Gideon began to shiver.

'Sereno, man, they know what happened in Florida, with Kiefer and Juliette. They know now.'

When the Indian came fully around, it looked to Gideon as if he was grinning.

'I can't tell if you understand me,' Gideon said. 'I'm telling you the truth, they know you did nothing wrong.'

Now the Indian started to laugh. It was not a sarcastic, bitter sound, but actual laughter, full-bellied and helpless. Gideon got the joke. He held out his arms. 'I know, I feel ridiculous.'

Sereno tossed back his head and laughed some more.

'Man, do you *comprendo*? Bullens – *Toro* – he's looking for us both.' He took a step onto the top boulder, and the Indian stopped smiling.

'You need to come back with me,' Gideon told him. 'If Bullens doesn't find you, then the police will. Either way, we're both dead if you don't come with me.' He could see something shiny clipped to Sereno's T-shirt pocket – the garage-door opener, he hoped. 'Please, let me call my friend.'

Slowly he reached in the pocket of his robe. Just as slowly, Sereno brought his hand to his mouth.

'Easy,' Gideon said. '*Telephono*.' He showed Sereno the phone. 'My friend will come get us, both of us. I give you my word, you will be safe. *Seguro*.'

Giving the Indian another uncertain glance, Gideon began entering the number, when a car suddenly roared out of the blackness, its lights flashing bright. Blinded, Gideon raised his hands, expecting to be arrested.

But a shot rang out, and Sereno dropped heavily to the rocks.

'He's unarmed!' Gideon cried.

'If you're talking to me, OIC Gideon, you oughta know I don't hear so good.' The car door shut, and a one-armed silhouette stepped between the headlights.

On the rocks, Sereno had gotten to his knees. Darkness soaked his orange T-shirt between his collar bone and shoulder.

'Or is it Reverend Gideon now?' Bullens said with a laugh.

No hiding place. Gideon kept his hands raised, though he wondered why bother, knowing he was about to be killed anyway. In other circumstances, he might have tried to think of a way out, something he could say to Bullens to buy time, or win his trust – or he might even threaten him. But he knew that Bullens had only one option if he expected to claim innocence – by silencing the two men in front of him. And what were Gideon's options? one: run down the rocks and dive in the canal; two: run at Bullens and disarm him; three: run out of range of the headlights. But, already balancing among the boulders, Gideon knew he'd be dead before his second step.

'You know, I got a stereo system that was made in Denmark,' Bullens said, wanting to talk first. Not that he would have felt any hesitancy about killing them – he was simply savoring his power. 'Over ten thousand dollars I paid. Six grand for the speakers alone.'

Gideon waited for the gunshot, hoped the first bullet would do it, quick and painless.

'Whistling,' Bullens said. 'That's all I hear now, in both ears: Whistling.'

'Do you see any other course?' Gideon asked him.

The black silhouette stood motionless in the headlights. 'I don't think you understand, Officer Gideon,' he said loudly. 'This little prick stole from me – nearly a million dollars – and then all but blew me off the face of the earth . . . just so you don't think this is all pleasure.'

Gideon kept quiet.

'See where I'm comin from?' Bullens said. 'Criminals nowadays get free college education, free rehabilitation, free room and board, TV, medical, dental. Does anyone in this great fucking country give two shits about the victims?'

Gideon saw Bullens straighten his arm, his weapon aimed at Sereno. 'Maybe you could translate something for me,' he said. 'Where's my fucking money?'

'He doesn't have your money,' Gideon said.

He heard Bullens chuckle. 'Like I said, Officer Gideon—' He fired the gun again. A vicious spark leapt from the rock to the left of the

Indian. 'This is about victims' rights.'

'He doesn't have your money!' Gideon shouted.

'Oh, I know who's got it,' Bullens said calmly, 'what's left of it. His half-breed wife. And now Mr Sereno is going to tell me where she's at, isn't that right?' The pistol fired again. Another spark flew up, this time to Sereno's right.

'He doesn't know! He's been looking for her too.'

'No kidding? I'll bet he'll show me exactly where she is on that map, when he sees how serious I am.' Bullens turned the weapon toward Gideon.

'Drop your weapon!' The voice rang out from the darkness behind Bullens' car. 'Police!' the voice shouted. 'Drop it!'

'Very good,' Bullens replied, keeping his pistol trained on Gideon. 'These two men are wanted criminals. I'm with the FBI, dispatched out of Macon, Georgia.'

Staring past Bullens' headlights, Gideon could barely make out the lone figure standing to the right of the car. 'You need to drop your weapon – now!' the voice commanded.

'Stand down, officer!' Bullens shouted back. 'This is Federal!'

'Drop your weapon!'

Bull turned toward the darkness, and the cop retreated into the trees.

'We're on the same team, son,' Bullens said, squinting off to the darkness while he moved out of his headlights. 'I've been tracking this pair of renegades for a thousand miles.'

'Sir! I need you to drop—'

'Are you seriously going to shoot a federal marshal? I just want to get on my radio.'

All of a sudden the car engine roared. Wheels screaming, the headlights swung across the bank, as the door shut and the car sped off down the narrow road, Bullens escaping.

The cop jumped out from behind the tree. 'Don't anyone move!' he cried as he took aim at the car with both hands, but the taillights disappeared in the distance. Then, wheeling to the rocks again, he shouted, 'Get down, both of you!'

Gideon lowered to his knees, saying, 'Sir, this man is shot.'

'Get down!'

'I am down.'

'On your face! Hands behind your head!'

The man's voice shook with fear. Gideon did as he was ordered.

Pulling his radio off his belt, the policeman stepped down onto the rocks above Sereno, who lay sprawled, facing him.

'The man who shot him is going to come back,' Gideon warned. 'He wants us dead. He may be on foot this time.'

'You let me worry about that,' the cop said, keeping his weapon trained on Gideon. He brought the radio to his mouth. Before he had a chance to speak, Sereno made his move. It sounded like he'd spat a seed, and the policeman flinched as though he'd been stung by a wasp – then held his hand up to the moonlight, trying to make sense of the bamboo sliver hanging from his skin. He turned toward Gideon, as though he might have been responsible, then back to Sereno, positioning his feet on two rocks at the top of the bank, where he could keep both men in sight.

'If either of you makes a move,' he warned, 'I'll start shooting.' As he swung his pistol from one to the other, he staggered. Bringing the radio to his mouth again, he stumbled drunkenly, trying to keep his balance, but he fell heavily forward, pitching down a long granite slab.

Hearing the splash, Gideon crawled down to the bank, where he saw Sereno tangled with the officer.

'No—'

The Indian looked up at Gideon, holding the pistol in his hand. The young policeman slipped slowly down the rock, his legs pulled sideways with the current.

'I didn't know,' Gideon said, kneeling at the top of the bank. 'I swear – *Jurar* – I did not know.'

Sereno stared up at him, black eyes blazing.

'Please.' Gideon began lowering himself down the rocks. 'I cannot let this man die.' When he reached them, he caught hold of the officer's collar. Sereno lay perfectly still, watching, as Gideon pulled the paralyzed man back onto the rocks. Then, slowly, the Indian raised the pistol.

Gideon froze.

But Sereno didn't fire. He flipped the pistol into the canal.

Gideon took a deep breath. 'Lie back,' he said. 'Let me call for help.'

But the Indian pulled himself to his feet. Gideon watched, amazed. He could make out two solid splotches of darkness on the rock where Sereno had lain, and darkness on the back of his jersey. By the time he had reached the top of the bank, he moved as though he wasn't hurt at all. Then he was gone.

Gideon got his arms under the unconscious cop and hoisted him up and over his shoulder, and he started climbing too. As he crossed the service road, he heard a car engine roar. He looked to his right and saw, in the darkness, the police cruiser pulling away, Sereno at the wheel.

CHAPTER SIX

They had a macaroni and cheddar casserole and steamed broccoli. Jacob's father baked a fresh raspberry pie for dessert and opened a bottle of red wine, but ended up drinking alone. When he raised his glass and said, 'To the author,' Alix lifted her glass. Jacob didn't join them.

'Don't deride yourself,' his father told him. 'The world's too full of people eager to help.'

Jacob resumed eating. He could feel Alix's eyes on him.

'This was Jacob's favorite dinner when he was a boy,' his father said. 'Remember I used to make this when Mom was working?'

'I appreciate it,' Jacob said, not taking his own eyes off his plate. 'She was teaching a couple of night classes, wasn't she?'

'Four nights a week,' his father said. 'Graduate writing classes.'

'I never asked either of you,' Jacob said, 'why she got home from work some nights at nine, other nights at midnight or later. She used to come in my bedroom to say goodnight, and she'd talk to me. Most of the time I could tell she'd been drinking, and I figured she'd stopped at a restaurant or bar after class. I worried about her driving. But one night when she hugged me, her hair was wet, it was in the winter, and it mystified me. I was only ten.' Jacob looked up at his father, who picked up his glass uncomfortably.

'Your mother and I had an understanding,' was all he said and, by his tone, all he intended to say. Then he drained his wine.

Jacob said, 'An understanding.'

His father gave him a steadfast look. 'We were adults,' he said, and he shook his head sadly, 'doing the best we could with an impossible situation.' He poured himself another glass. 'So, Alix,' he said, 'why don't you tell us about the culinary delights of the Colombian mountains.'

'I ate well,' she said, eager to comply. 'Everything was fresh.

357

Potatoes, beans, corn, plantains, sugarcane, pineapples. Sweet manioc.'

'Jake, you should go before it all disappears,' his father said. 'The Kogi are God's people. Industrious, spiritual, ethical to a fault.'

'So I've heard,' Jacob said. 'And they chew coca all day.'

'Coca-chewing is a privilege of the men,' Alix replied.

'We're not talking about processed cocaine,' his father explained. 'The coca leaves aren't much stronger than caffeine, just enough to suppress the appetite and deaden pain – so the men can work longer and travel farther.' He took another drink and said to Alix, 'Tell him.'

'Jacob, you'd fit right in,' Alix said. 'It's a highly structured society. Everyone knows exactly what's expected of them.'

'Uh-huh.'

'Women spin cotton, men weave it. Men break the ground, women sow and harvest. Men do the woodworking and tool-making. Women collect wild foods, they care for the coca bushes, they do the cooking and make nets and bags. Roles for men and women are clearly delineated.'

'Speaking of fitting in,' Jacob said, and gave his father a sideward look.

'Jacob, shut up,' Alix said.

He put down his fork, pushed back his chair. 'I'm gonna let you guys get caught up,' he said. 'Mind if I take a shower?'

'Not at all, Jake,' his father said. 'You know where everything is. Make yourself at home.'

Ignoring Alix's glare, Jacob brought his dinnerware to the dishwasher, then walked down the hall. Before going into the bathroom, he peeked in at his old bedroom, an office now, with wall-to-wall bookcases, books stacked on the floor, and a cheap pine desk. The only thing familiar was his old closet door with the half-moon scar, where he had once pitched a fastball from the end of the hall.

He took a shower. Brushed his teeth with his finger. He didn't shave. When he was through, he went into the living room and lay down on the floor in front of the couch. He took the remote control off the coffee table, and found a news channel on TV, where he saw his face.

CHAPTER SEVEN

T he hospital security guard, sitting in a chair between potted palms, looked up from his magazine. The black minister, carrying a backpack under his arm, gave a gentle smile, and the guard returned to his reading.

Gideon went up to the information desk on the other side of the lobby and said quietly, 'There is a policeman lying in an old station wagon parked on the next block. He may look dead, but he's only frog-poisoned.'

Before the woman could respond, he turned and walked briskly through a set of double doors and up the stairs. On the second floor, he passed the nurses' station, and when the women looked up, he winked confidently. 'I can find it.'

Proceeding down the corridor, he turned a corner and ducked into the first room he came to, where a man was sleeping soundly. Gideon closed the door. Opened the closet.

Ten minutes later, the hospital had filled with so many uniforms – state police, town police, sheriff's department, hospital security guards – all of them embroiled in a frantic room-by-room search for a black man dressed in a minister's robe, that one more uniform hustling down the stairs did not raise suspicion, even if it was different from them all: tan shirt, with dark brown trousers and trim, and an insignia that read FLORIDA STATE POLICE.

Despite the commotion inside the hospital, the four parking lots outside remained relatively quiet – except for a peculiar white Caravan that seemed to have a life of its own. Parked among a sea of vehicles in the patients' lot, its doors kept locking and unlocking, its lights coming on and going off again. Someone watching might have believed the van haunted. But no one was watching, except one man – and he was walking to the van as fast as he could, with its keys in his hand.

In the morning, a woman would open the closet in her husband's hospital room, to get his clothes. Tucked inside the leg of his trousers, she'd find a minister's robe, with a note that read: 'Your vehicle has been appropriated by the Florida State Police. It will be returned. Thank you for your cooperation. Sgt Terrence Gideon, Alligator Alley Correctional Institute.'

CHAPTER EIGHT

Jacob stared dazedly at the silent TV, a great white shark patrolling a reef. His neck ached.

He'd been sleeping again, slouched on his father's living-room floor with his head propped against the couch, the television remote on his chest. He could hear his father's fitful snoring from another part of the house. He sat up and flexed his neck.

'Mind if I sleep a little now?' Alix asked. She lay on the couch behind him, reading a textbook. A carving knife and hammer lay on the coffee table.

'Was I snoring?'

'No, but one of us needs to stay awake,' Alix said. The blinds were drawn and shut tight, and it looked like every light in the house was lit.

'If the police find us here, we're caught,' he said. 'I'm not running any more.'

'It's not the police I'm afraid of,' she said.

'You're not talking about July—?'

'I'm talking about a level of perception that's beyond anything you can imagine.'

'Wait a minute. I thought you said Sereno was the shaman.'

'Jacob,' she said.

He turned to look at her.

'Sereno trained her.'

He scowled, as things began making sense. 'Are you telling me that July somehow *knew* where I buried that gun?'

'Not somehow. She followed you.'

Now more segments of his memory assembled. The car without headlights that ran the white Caravan into Fecto's Explorer. Was it July – targeting Evangeline, for talking to him? Or the night at the beach, when he hadn't seen her car pull up behind him . . .

'The first time you kissed her,' Alix said, 'she began to despise you.

361

She's been watching you ever since.'

Alix turned off the room light, then lay her head back down. 'Give me two hours.'

His father's snoring filled the house. While Jacob sat against the couch, flipping through channels, looking for a news report, outside a car passed slowly on the road, its radio booming as it went by. Then the snoring stopped. Now Jacob listened to every sound, highway traffic in the distance, wondering if he'd even be able to hear footsteps on the lawn, or a window sliding open in the dark.

Above him, Alix stirred.

'Does this bother you?' he asked.

She gasped, 'What?'

'The light from the TV,' he said. 'Did it wake you?'

'No, someone asked me a question,' she said.

He smiled. 'Sorry.'

He switched channels again, stopped on a man kneeling amongst a pile of rocks, pulling a rattlesnake out of its lair. 'My father doesn't know very much about July, does he?'

'No,' Alix said.

'I didn't think so.'

He lay there for a moment or two. The highway in the distance sounded like the ocean. Despite everything, he couldn't help feeling sad for July.

'So what are you going to do, if we ever get out of this,' he said to Alix, 'now that you're no longer dead?'

'Seriously?'

He turned his head to see her. She was quiet for a moment. Then she propped herself on her elbow. 'I think I'd like to teach.'

'Really?'

'Yeah.'

'College?'

'Elementary school. First grade. Apple on my desk, a vase of fresh flowers. I want an old farmhouse on the ocean, with lots of land, lots of privacy. A cat and dog, a clothesline.'

'Family?'

'Why not?' He looked at her again and saw a glimmer in her eyes. 'How about you?'

He said, 'I suppose I'll claw my way to the top of the writing world, you know, sell movie rights to Disney, that sort of thing.'

'Reasonable plan,' she said.

Jacob chuckled. He laid his head back against her leg, and was glad

she didn't move it. 'You know what I really want?' he said. 'All I want?'
'What?'

'Someday,' he said, 'I want to be able to face my son without shame.'

He didn't see her foot coming until it walloped him in the shoulder, hard enough to knock him to the floor.

'What was that for?'

She rolled onto her other side. 'So you'll shut up and let me sleep.'

Jacob lay there in the dark for several minutes, attending to the pain radiating from his arm. Then he sat up and retrieved the remote, started surfing channels till he came to fireworks – a station going off the air for the night.

While he watched, he remembered when he was a boy, lying on a blanket with his father in Boston Common, watching the fireworks display over the Charles River, while the Boston Pops performed the *1812 Overture*. Jacob and his dad were playing a game, naming each of the fireworks after friends and relatives. While he was coming up with names, his father was coming up with the words to leave him.

Jacob turned off the television, then got up and went into the kitchen, found his father's car keys on the counter.

'What are you doing?' said Alix, standing in the doorway.

'Going to protect my family.'

'It's not safe,' she told him, but he went out anyway, looking all around the darkness as he got in the car and quietly shut the door, careful not to wake his father.

When he started the engine, Alix came outside with her backpack slung over her shoulder and got in beside him.

'You don't have to do this,' he told her.

'Just drive,' she said.

He backed down the driveway, then started off through the quiet town, past the Brandeis campus. As he merged onto the highway, he tried again. 'I know what happened in Florida.'

'You don't know a thing,' she said

'Sereno tried to murder July,' he said. 'You came to her rescue. That's called self-defense.'

She stared out at the road racing under his headlights.

'Alix, I know you stabbed him. I heard the tape.'

'I lied,' she snapped.

He looked over at her. 'Under hypnosis?'

'Just shut up about it,' she said. 'Drive.'

CHAPTER NINE

From Boston to Hyannis, the police cars prowled, searching for their missing patrol car and the Indian driving it. The Virginia farm truck had been impounded at the State Police garage in Bourne, along with Gideon's station wagon, where both vehicles would be torn apart, fingerprinted and blood-tested.

Despite the Massachusetts State Police having been placed on alert, it would be another hour before the stolen patrol car would be discovered, sunk to its axles in a cranberry bog, and another few minutes after that, that the man who owned the cranberries would realize that, yup, he was missing his old stake-body flatbed dump truck. Which, at that moment, was loaded with empty crates, cruising unsteadily across the Merrimack River on I-95, entering New Hampshire.

While the white Caravan negotiated the back roads of Plymouth, Gideon watched the road signs for a secondary route back toward Cape Cod, so he could continue his search for Sereno. With the Indian's bullet wound, he knew they were both running out of time – not to mention the fact that every minute or so, another police car sped past with lights flashing, which meant they were either heading to the hospital or they'd caught up with Sereno. When his cell phone went off, he answered without hesitation.

'Thought you might want to know, I just heard an APB,' Landry said. 'There's a missing cop down off Cape Cod. People heard shots fired. They found a truck with Virginia tags and a station wagon from Georgia.'

Hearing Bethany's voice in the background, Gideon said, 'Put my wife on, please.'

'Gideon, did you find that Indian or not?'

'May I speak with Bethany?'

'Hey, these Massachusetts drivers are crazy, ain't they?' Landry said, fishing now for Gideon's whereabouts.

'I wouldn't know.'

'They're onto you, Jasper. Use your head. You don't know where this girl is. Right now I'm the only one that does. And probably so does Bull Bullens – which means that from here on, we're gonna do this my way.'

'What do you mean, you know where she is—?'

'Oh, didn't I tell you? My fishing buddy called me. The lab that analyzed those plants, they know where they were grown.'

'You'd be saving the life of an innocent man if you'd share that information with me,' Gideon said.

'Well, maybe we can work out some kind of arrangement.'

'The police will kill him,' Gideon said.

'Right now the police don't know about this. The lab ain't finished double-checking their tests, so the information won't be released to the authorities till morning – but they're ninety-nine percent sure. And I'm heading there now.'

Gideon made another turn, following the signs south. 'Arrangement like what?'

'I'm thinking something along these lines: You tell me where you're at, I come get you, then we go together and bring this crazy Indian home.'

Gideon paused for a few moments, only to make Landry think he was considering the offer. 'Mr Landry, I appreciate all you've tried to do. But I don't believe Sereno's going to trust me if I have you along.'

'Hey!' Landry snapped. 'In case you haven't thought about it, if you get yourself killed you're never gonna be able to prove your innocence. And I'm gonna look bad for trying to save your ass back in Jacksonville – which means I'm out of a pension! Do you comprehend any of this, Gideon?'

'Yes, sir, I comprehend that I've got about six hours to find him.'

'I used to think you were smart!' Landry yelled. He lowered his voice. 'All right, see how this grabs you. I talked to the people at WITSEC. The agent who interviewed Juliette Whitestone back when she got caught trying to smuggle that jungle vegetation in to her husband; he remembers the interview. According to his notes, he questioned the two parties separately: Juliette, and one junior officer by the name of Terrence Gideon.'

'You already told me, and I told you, I was never interviewed. I don't know a thing about that.'

'I recalled you saying that,' Landry said, 'so I faxed them your photograph, along with Biff Bullens' photo. Guess what? The agent remembered Bullens, not you.'

Gideon paused, trying to grasp the ramifications.

'Which means,' Landry said, 'whoever set up the interview – Warden Shivers in this case – was perpetrating a cover-up.'

'Hold on.' Gideon came to a fork in the road and went left, staying southward. 'You're saying the Warden knew that Bullens was the one funneling drugs through the system – and he protected him?'

'Protected himself, more like it. I'm saying that Warden Shivers was probably on the take from the get-go. Which means that Biff Bullens isn't the only one determined to keep you and Sereno quiet – and that means you've got no choice, Jasper. You've got to let me take you in.'

'And end up in court, me and Sereno against the state of Florida? I don't think so.'

'You cannot stay out there,' Landry said. 'I don't care if you got a hundred garage door openers. If the warden's mixed up in this, you can bet some other powerful people in Florida are too.'

'Then you tell me: How do I get a fair trial?'

'We'll take it out of state.'

'Where, to the *Supreme Court*?'

'They are going to kill you if you don't come in!' Landry yelled again.

'I'd rather be killed than made a fool of!' Gideon yelled back.

Then Bethany came on the phone, soft and warm in his ear. 'Baby, I love you,' she said, and Gideon breathed a sigh.

In the background Landry said, 'You talk some sense into him.'

Gideon said, 'You understand what I'm saying, don't you?'

'I do, baby.'

'Then you aren't mad at me?'

Bethany said nothing for a moment. Then, in her sweetest voice: 'Portsmouth, New Hampshire.'

'Aw, Jesus,' Landry cursed.

'I love you, baby,' Gideon said, and turned the Caravan around.

CHAPTER TEN

For the better part of an hour, from Lexington to Salisbury, neither Alix nor Jacob spoke a word. As the Taurus crossed the state line into New Hampshire, Alix said, 'I take it you're one of those people who think it's a choice.'

'One of those people?'

'You actually believe your father woke up one day and made the decision to start preferring men—?'

'No one made it for him,' Jacob said.

'Like you made the choice to prefer women.'

'Women happen to be my preference, my orientation, that's right.'

'But you could just as easily have chosen to prefer guys,' she said, and he saw the trap he'd stumbled into. 'Let's say one guy in particular,' she continued. 'You *choose* to think about him day and night, the way he looks, the way he looks at you, the way it would be to kiss him.'

'We're not talking about me,' Jacob said. 'I never passed judgement.'

'And here's the other choice you make in the bargain,' she went on, not about to stop. 'From now on, you won't be attracted to women. It will mean nothing to have a woman kiss you on the mouth, to hear her lose her breath when you kiss her. Nothing. To undress her, Jacob. To fall asleep in her arms. To want nothing in your life so much as her love . . .'

She stopped talking for a moment, and he thought she was inviting him to respond – until he looked over and saw her wipe her eye.

'Because you've made a *choice.*'

Jacob didn't say a word. Instead, he returned his attention to the highway, watching the night continue to swallow them both.

'Sereno was not trying to murder July in Florida,' Alix told him.

He rolled his head toward her.

She said, 'We were trying to murder *him.*'

Jacob stared across the darkness that separated them.

367

'Watch the road,' she said.

He did, dazed.

'We waited for Sereno to come home,' she explained. 'When he walked into the bedroom, July shot him, and shot him again. But he kept coming, so I came out of the closet . . .with the knife.'

Jacob waited for her to continue; she didn't.

'You were protecting yourself,' he said. 'You knew Sereno had murdered the drug dealer. It was only a matter of time before he came after July.'

'Sereno never killed Kiefer,' Alix told him. 'He never killed anyone. He's a *shaman*.'

Jacob looked over at her, and a fierce shiver climbed his back. 'You're saying July murdered the drug dealer—?'

Alix met his gaze, then turned away. 'Kiefer probably tried to break off the affair with her,' she said, her voice distant. 'So she paralyzed him with poison, then mutilated him . . . while he watched.'

'Then took his money,' Jacob said, 'and convinced you that Sereno was coming after her next.'

'Because Sereno was also getting ready to leave her,' Alix said.

Jacob pulled up to the toll plaza at Hampton, dropped four quarters in the basket, then drove on. After a minute he said, 'So now we know.'

'Know what?'

'The reason you won't go to the cops. Not because you want Sereno to find July.'

She gave him a look.

'You want him to find you.'

CHAPTER ELEVEN

T he stake-bodied farm truck stopped at the midpoint of the High-Level bridge, tight against the curb, and the flatbed went up, dumping crates all over the roadway. A trailer truck sounded its horn as it drove past, shattering a number of crates to splinters. Then the Indian stepped down from the cab and began walking across the lanes, oblivious to another eighteen-wheeler rushing past, obliterating more crates, oblivious to the blare of its horn. The driver got on his radio.

About the only reason a man would stop here – which is why there was a law against it – was if he wanted to jump. But this crazy Indian, the driver would report, kind of hunched over and hobbling, was not jumping, not by the looks, not yet anyway.

He was straddling the median curbstone, looked like he was sniffing the air, then he crossed the southbound lanes to the railing. Christ, it's two thirty in the morning and the guy's wearing shades, he's operating a commercial rig without running lights or even headlights – *Miles Standish Cranberry Farm* stenciled on his door – dumping the load all over the highway. Whatever the hell's in them cranberries must be some potent.

In fact, the Indian was entranced, surfeited with a woman he hadn't seen nor heard nor touched since she was a girl. He was filled with every aspect of her. Drunk on sensations, he leaned on the southbound railing, staring out over the river.

Even with the salt wind whistling through the hollow columns, he could detect her scent in the wet wind from below. In fact, he could sense her all around him. He could smell the flowers she had touched, he could see the house in which she slept.

Ignoring another truck rushing past, ignoring the pain in his shoulder, ignoring a weakness so strong that it felt like sleep was riding on his back, he crawled over the railing and grabbed hold of the steel rungs, climbing down into the sweet black wind.

369

PART SIX

CHAPTER ONE

I t was three in the morning when Jacob and Alix arrived at the Tavern. The place was dark. So was the old inn up above, the Spite House. But Laura's car was parked in the lot, and so was Squeaky's – which meant they were there. But . . .

'Porch lights are usually on,' he whispered, and wished Alix had returned a more confident expression.

They stepped out of the car. The night was quiet, disturbed only by the breath of the tide spilling into the harbor and their footsteps on the gravel lot.

Jacob climbed the porch steps as softly as he could, and tried the door. He was relieved to find it locked. The boarded-up windows on the ground floor were intact, another fact that eased his mind.

Suddenly the porch light came on – in Alix's hand. Jacob squinted into the brightness. 'It was loose,' she whispered – then unscrewed the bulb again and everything went dark, much darker than before.

Jacob backed down the steps, staring up at the building.

'Where are they sleeping?' Alix whispered, coming close.

Jacob whispered back: 'Max and Laura are up top, in the widow's walk. I don't know where her father is.'

They backed farther into the parking lot, far enough to see the glassed-in widow's walk poised silently against the silver sky. Jacob shivered, imagining that July might have gotten inside – or that she might be up there still.

Alix grabbed his shirt – and pointed up. The window above the front porch was open – only two or three inches – but open.

He took in as much of the building as he could, trying to see if anything was moving behind the windows on the second floor. All he could see were reflections of pine boughs swaying. Then a whisper:

'*Jacob—*'

It was Alix, crouched at the corner of the building. 'Phone line,' she said, holding the severed wire in her hand.

Jacob's heart surged. His mind flew in a thousand directions, as Alix returned to him. 'Do you have a key?' she said aloud, seeming to sense how frightened he was.

'No.' He bent and picked up a couple of small rocks sturdy enough to reach the second floor windows. Targeting a window in the corner nearest him, he flung the stone and it hit the wooden shutter. A slat broke and hung down. His second shot was on the mark. Glass shattered, and Jacob stared up at the massive house, watching for a light to come on. Every second that passed frightened him more.

Then Alix grabbed him, and pointed to the opposite corner of the house. Up in the window, a movement contrary to the swaying branches. Yes, a head. Then a flashlight beam shot out of the window, caught Jacob's eyes. The window opened.

'What the frick are you doing?'

'Squeaky, where's Max?'

'What time is it?'

'Where is he?' Jacob repeated.

'They're asleep,' he answered, 'upstairs, in the widow's walk. I'm camped out at the bottom of the stairs.' He showed him his pistol. 'Nobody went up or down, okay? Everything's copasetic.'

'There's a window open,' Jacob said.

'What window?'

'Over the porch. Did you open it?'

Squeaky pulled his head back inside. The flashlight rippled off the sheer curtains. Then Squeaky returned. 'The lights don't work. We got power out?'

'Go up and check on them,' Jacob called. 'Squeaky, hurry!'

As the light dimmed on the window curtain, the window to its right began to glow. Jacob paced in the same direction. Then the house fell dark again. He stopped pacing. 'Please,' he whispered. He felt Alix's calming hand on his back.

Then the light appeared in the center window, the one that was open. And a silhouetted figure approached the curtain. The window went up.

'Somebody opened all the doors,' Squeaky said, then turned away. The light went out.

'Jesus,' Jacob whispered.

'Shh,' said Alix.

Suddenly two windows blazed with light. Squeaky came to the window. 'They unscrewed the frickin bulbs.'

'Squeaky, go up and check!'

As they watched, a window on the third floor lit – the stairway light,

Jacob assumed. He could hear Squeaky's footsteps now, clocking upward. A door slammed. The light went out.

Then the glass turret on top of the roof took on a glow. Jacob's legs shook. He heard a murmur of voices.

Then Laura's scream. '*Maxie?*'

The turret lit up like a lighthouse. Squeaky threw open a window, pushed back the curtains. 'He's not here!'

'He might be in one of the rooms,' Alix suggested.

Laura came to the window and cried desperately. 'Jacob?'

'Get to a phone,' Jacob yelled. 'Call Evangeline!'

CHAPTER TWO

The white Taurus sped past the dark woods, then slowed within sight of Green Girls. Jacob's Mazda was still parked in the street, tires flat. July's Volvo was in the small driveway.

'Light's on upstairs,' Alix whispered, her voice as soft as the rainfall inside the greenhouse. 'She must be expecting us.'

He stared hard at the place, trying to think of a strategy, but his brain was short-circuiting. 'Cover your face,' he said, hitting the gas as he cut the wheel, and the car plowed across the lawn.

'*Jacob—?*'

'Duck!' He pulled her down as he crashed through the glass. The impact was stronger than he expected. The greenhouse frame buckled the car hood before it gave way, and glass fell like a waterfall over the car, sending spiderweb cracks all over the windshield. The Taurus stopped with a jolt against a sapling palm, and the rear window blew in.

So much for a sneak attack.

Jacob picked himself off of Alix, ignoring the pain in his shoulder. 'Okay?' he asked.

She studied him in the dark.

He got out of his car and started walking into the garden.

'Wait—' Alix grabbed her backpack and ran after him, caught hold of his shirt. 'You're in the dark,' she whispered. 'She can see and hear everything we do.'

'She's got Maxie,' he said and pulled away, but she grabbed him again with both hands.

'She wants you dead,' Alix said. 'That's all she wants. You. And you're walking right into her arms.'

Jacob looked around. Raindrops fell all over them, washing down his face. 'Leave if you want,' he said, and pushed through the wet foliage toward the house.

376

Alix sighed. 'We'll stay together,' she said, and followed close behind, holding his arm. The scant light drifting down from the kitchen was little help through the rainfall.

'Smell it?' Alix whispered.

'What?'

She pointed up toward the kitchen.

He recognized the stench. Yagé.

'*Wait—*'

Alix grabbed him. She stood petrified, gaping through the darkness behind them. He could feel her hand tremble. He turned.

A pair of eyes shone back at them in animal iridescence, low to the ground.

'Maxie?'

'No.' Alix pulled him back.

Jacob stiffened.

'Not July, either,' she breathed.

With the dark and the rainfall, they could see nothing but the shining eyes that tracked their approach. In fact, Jacob did not see the body until they were almost on top of it, glistening among the foliage about twenty feet behind the Taurus and close to the glass wall. They stopped there.

The Indian lay in the downpour, draped over the wet leaves.

'He's hurt,' Alix said, and freed herself from Jacob's grasp. But when the Indian raised his hand, Jacob caught her arm.

However, Sereno didn't even seem to be aware of them. His head had turned toward the glass wall behind him. In fact, he seemed to be pointing at something outside.

Alix crouched lower, and looked out. Then she caught her breath.

'What is it?' Jacob said, pushing to the glass and peering out at the bridge, the tiny yellow beacon flaring at the very top of the arch, illuminating . . . the glass fogged. He wiped it with his shirt sleeve; then felt Alix's hands on his shoulders, as if trying to prevent him from seeing.

The beacon came on, then went dark again. Something was moving up there.

'Wait for the police,' she said.

When the beacon light flared again, his heart stopped. He fell to his knees, his legs given out.

'Jacob?'

He looked helplessly at her.

'She's got Maxie up there.'

★ ★ ★

Clutching her arm, he pulled himself to his feet.

'You can't go.'

'I have to,' he said, making his way to the car. 'If the cops go up there, she'll push him off.'

He opened the door and got in.

'Wait,' she said, looking over at Sereno, who was once again reaching out his hand, this time toward Jacob. She ventured closer.

'Be careful,' Jacob cautioned, as she crouched beside the Indian. But he couldn't stay to protect her. He turned the key, kicking a roar of power through the engine, then threw it in reverse and backed outside, tearing more glass from the greenhouse.

'Jacob, wait—' Alix ran out to him and grabbed onto his open window. 'It's for you,' she said, handing him the thing.

Jacob frowned. 'A pen?'

'A dart. It's poison.'

Covering the end with her thumb, she tried to transfer the weapon to Jacob. He gave her a look.

'If you go up there,' she said, 'you have to kill her.'

He took the pen and stuffed it in his pants pocket, then kicked the accelerator and tore across the lawn.

The Taurus shot onto Woodbury, tires screeching, Jacob flying underneath the overpass, then swerving left onto the approach ramp. He was doing seventy when he joined the highway, eighty-five when he hit the brakes, the car shrieking to a stop beside the curb. Ahead of him he could see highway flares blocking the right lane where a flatbed truck was broken down. Blue lights of a police car were flashing – which prevented him from climbing the ladder rungs.

He left the car and made it to the railing before he realized what he was doing, looking out over the river and the lights of the sleeping town, the cranes downriver stretching up into the predawn sky. As though shaken from a dream, his legs buckled beneath him, and he sat down hard on the curbstone. Trying to ignore the dizziness, he grabbed onto the railing and struggled to his feet again.

On the other side of the railing, level with the roadway, was the top of the upper chord that arched up over the entire structure. It was a hollow rectangular steel, four feet deep but only eighteen inches wide. It was what July and Max were standing on high above him, and what Jacob would have to climb. He looked up as far as he could but, because of the curve, was unable to see its top. Then dizziness took hold, and he closed his eyes. Clutching the railing under his arm, finding his breath, he looked up again.

The bridge architects, to aid maintenance workers, had thoughtfully strung a cable handhold along the outside of the chord, about waist-high, attached to stanchions positioned every eight feet. But, to discourage daredevils, the cable did not begin until the chord had already risen about twenty-five feet off the roadway. Which meant that, for the first 100 feet of his climb, Jacob would have to balance on the chord, with nothing to hold onto but the wind. The rail threatened to pull out of his arm, his legs weakened. But Maxie was up there, he told himself . . .

And he remembered what Alix told him – that his fear of heights is actually a fear of losing his family. If she's right, then perhaps it follows that his determination to save his family might quell his fears. And that's how he proceeds.

Setting his mind to the single purpose – saving his family – he steps onto the curbstone and throws his leg over the top railing. As he stretches his foot to the outside curb, his moccasin feels loose, so he kicks it off and it goes fluttering away in the wind. He kicks off the other moccasin too, before he swings his back leg over. Then, keeping his left hand on the railing, he steps carefully out onto the narrow chord – and regrets losing his shoes. The steel is cold and wet with dew. It doesn't matter. He is in control of his fears.

He looks ahead of him. The chord rises up like a greased water slide, and the cable handhold is far out ahead of him, but Jacob thinks only of Max. Saving Max. There is no thought of danger, no weakening of the limbs, only strength and purpose. Steadying himself on the railing, Jacob starts climbing. Simple as that. A trailer truck blows and blasts its air horn, as though to warn him.

As the chord rises, the steel railing under his left hand falls away, and now he must let go. This is when he first notices the wind, gusting, then slowing, tugging and pushing at him, but Jacob is spurred on by an image – he and Laura and Max sitting together at dinner. Arms outstretched, he does not even need to watch his feet. The strain in the calves tells him he's climbing.

Another eighteen-wheeler rushes past, then a couple of cars, and they all signal with their headlights or horns that they're aware of him. But they're well below him now, further and further distant. Of course, Jacob is aware of the open air on his right side, and the deep river way below. None of it frightens him. He is saving his family, he tells himself over and over.

About ten feet ahead of him, the cable handhold begins. Anchor-bolted to the outside of the chord, it rises diagonally to the top of the first stanchion, four feet high. Seeing the cable reminds Jacob of his precarious position, and suddenly he starts wobbling, arms outstretched, up in the dark, up in the crosswinds, telling himself over and over he is saving his family.

But his legs won't listen. As they give out beneath him, he makes a desperate lunge for the cable, and his bare foot slips off the steel. His leg follows, pulling his hip, then the rest of his body, then he's hanging by his hands.

And not falling.

Jacob opens his eyes – and sees that his right hand has managed to grab the cable at its base. His left hand clutches at the edge of the chord, but it's a useless grip. The wind whips at his legs and dangles him like a marionette. The cold steel under his face energizes him. *Max*, he thinks. Throwing his left arm over the top of the chord, he gets a better grip on the opposite edge, then swings his leg over. Transforming his quivering muscles into energy, he hoists himself up until he's stretched out flat, his cheek pressed against the icy steel.

Off to the east, he sees a deep red line appear on the flat horizon. He can feel the hum of traffic through his face. The cable clenched in his fist, he pulls himself to his knees. *Breathe*, he tells himself, and sucks in a deep breath of ocean air.

Now climb.

CHAPTER THREE

A lix knelt beside the Indian in the wet garden, nursing him from a steaming cup of yagé. Sereno was covered with a wool blanket, with his head propped on her backpack. He drank greedily, though his breathing was shallow and his eyes were closed.

She had tried to call for an ambulance but found the telephones dead. So now she waited, knowing that the police would arrive eventually. At least she'd been able to turn off the sprinkler system.

She was not aware of footsteps behind her until she felt Sereno stiffen. Then a flashlight beam swept across the greenery beside them.

'Well, outstanding,' the man said, a rather tall, well-built man. 'But is this the same Mrs Sereno I remember? I don't think so.'

The flashlight beam moved over Alix's face.

'He needs an ambulance,' she said, believing him a cop.

'I'm sorry, you'll have to speak up.'

'He needs help!'

'Didn't you already call for help?' Bullens asked.

'The phones aren't working,' she said.

'You say the phones are dead,' he replied with a smile in his voice, and a gunshot fired. Sereno jerked. Alix fell back, screaming, 'What are you doing?'

She could see that he held a pistol in his hand that was slung across his chest. 'This man is a dangerous killer,' he explained. 'He stole money from an orphanage, and I'm here to return it to its rightful owners.'

'He doesn't have your money!' Alix cried, throwing a handful of dirt at Bullens and stuffing her backpack under Sereno's head again.

'Now, that I heard.' Bullens smiled, leaned in closer, aiming his light at Sereno's face. The Indian squinted, dazed, while Alix felt his fingers moving against her palm, surreptitiously handing her something. She took it, concealed it.

Bullens swung his flashlight and weapon together at her.

'Do you know where my money is?'

She glared into the light. 'Yes, I do.'

Bullens grinned. 'Well, outstanding.'

'I'll take you to it,' she said. 'But call an ambulance for him.'

'Ma'am, I'm trying to show restraint, but this is a personal issue,' he said. 'You know this little son of a gun raped and murdered a Girl Scout?' While he shone the flashlight on the blanket that covered Sereno's legs, the dark spot his blood soaked through, Alix checked her hand . . . A cigarette lighter?

'Okay, who's driving?' Bullens said. 'Probably you.'

'The money's here,' Alix said.

'Here?' He shone his light in her face. 'Well, that's even better. Let's get it and I'll be on my merry way.'

'Call first,' she told him.

'Ma'am, who's got the gun?' Bullens gave her such a smile that even in the dark she could see his dimples. 'As soon as I'm on the road, I'll radio the ambulance from my car.' With the pistol sticking out of his sling, he gestured toward the house.

Alix stood up, surreptitiously slipping the lighter into the pocket of her pants. 'It's not in the house,' she said, and she turned toward the garden, knowing full well that, money or not, he was not going to leave either of them alive. But what was she supposed to do with a cigarette lighter, set him on fire?

'I guess you know if you do anything sneaky,' Bullens said, walking so close behind her that she could smell beef jerky on his breath, 'I'll be forced to stick this piece up that high hiney of yours – what some folks call a lead suppository.'

'I'm taking you to the money,' she said, as she pushed a branch aside . . . and there was the hut, dark and misshapen.

'Don't snap that,' Bullens told her.

She held the branch and he caught it with his shoulder. A pane of greenhouse glass crunched under his foot, but he seemed not to hear it, shining the flashlight on the caved-in roof.

'You sayin my money's in here?'

'Yup.'

'What, ain't no one ever told you about offshore banks?'

Alix pulled the door open. Inside, a slab of the thatched roof hung down. She felt his pistol poke between her shoulder blades, and she stepped inside.

'You got a light in this place?'

'Nope.'

Green Girls

While he shone his flashlight around the small room, Alix stuck her hand in her pocket and retrieved the lighter. 'Quite a bed,' he remarked. The light beam reflected off the green arched headboard, the broken glass on the mattress, down to the thatch-littered floor, then swung up the wall and through the hole in the roof, illuminating a severed palm frond. 'What in hell happened here?'

'Thunderstorm.'

Bullens chuckled. 'You got some attitude, lady. Take money that don't belong to you, then act all sullen when you gotta return it.' He shone the flashlight on her face again. 'Kind of a hard-assed type, aren't you?'

'It's in there,' she told him.

'Speak up.'

'Move,' she said and, pushing past him, swung the outside door closed, revealing the smaller, green door on the side wall.

'In there?'

'Yup.' What did Sereno expect her to do, torch the hut and hold the door closed?

He tapped the narrow door with his pistol. 'I hate to dilly-dally. Come on, help me out.'

She gave the wooden lock a twist, and the door popped free. Then she stepped aside, to let him in.

'Go get it,' he told her.

'It's your money, get it yourself,' she said, and his flashlight smashed her face.

She dropped to her knees, pain radiating through her skull with such intensity – her cheekbones, her sinuses, even her teeth – she had to hold onto the floor to keep from passing out. Bullens tapped her arm with the light. 'I'm used to men,' he said . . . 'by way of apology. Now let's get this over with, so I can leave you two in peace. Go ahead and have a seat while I check.' He directed his flashlight to the bed.

'I'll sit here,' she whispered. But she didn't sit, exactly. She leaned forward on one knee, lowering her head, while blood seeped from her nose and ear. She felt the glass under her hands.

'Come on, I didn't hit you that hard,' he said, and turned to the door. The instant he pulled it open, the grasshoppers sprang at him. Bullens stumbled back, swiping his flashlight at them, protecting his face with his broken arm and pistol, growling, '*You fucking—*'

'*Bitch*' caught in his throat, sliced by the ragged glass in Alix's hands. He reeled backwards and fell on the bed. Alix tore open the door and ran. Bullens, his cheek pressed to his shoulder, bounded after her—

—and was blindsided by two hundred sixty pounds. Both men hit the ground so hard, with Terrence Gideon landing on top, that Bullens easily could have lost consciousness. But here, with his fortune at stake, he did not allow it. Dazed though he was, with his throat cut and his arm broken again, he grabbed his pistol in his good hand and swung it like a hammer, connecting with the black man's face and sending his glasses flying. Then he got his finger on the trigger, but Gideon knocked his wrist upward. The pistol fired twice, answered by the chime of breaking glass, then the fierce hissing of leaves – and Gideon spun out of the way.

As the crystalline sheet slammed down between them with a ground-jarring crack, Bullens' arm swung to the side, point-blank at the black man's chest. But the shot never sounded.

'Fucking misfire,' Bullens cursed. 'Worthless Russian piece of—'

In fact, his arm was no longer attached to his shoulder – a fact that Bullens was at that very moment trying to comprehend.

Gideon, putting his glasses back on his face, stared in amazement at the sight in front of him. The arm lay on the ground with the pistol still clutched in the hand, Bullens' white finger pointing stiffly through the trigger guard. Bullens himself, lying on the other side of the sheet of glass, looked like a baby who had opened his mouth to scream but couldn't catch his breath. Then the softest sound came out, a shuddering 'Ahhh.'

Carefully, Gideon removed the pistol from the disembodied hand, as though he feared that Bullens could somehow will it to fire. He stuck the weapon in his pocket, then picked up the arm and laid it across Bullens' chest, to keep it from touching the ground.

'Are you hurt?' a woman asked.

Alix touched Gideon's shoulder, standing over him.

'No, Ma'am, I don't think,' he said in a shaking voice, even though he could feel a jagged hole in his teeth, where a molar should have been. 'You?'

Although her hand and wrist glistened with blood, and her mouth and cheek were streaked, she said, 'I'm okay.'

She stepped over to where Sereno lay, and gently removed the backpack from under his head. Slinging it over her shoulder, she walked around Bullens and went to the hut. Grasshoppers continued pouring out the door. 'Still want your money?' she said, no sympathy in her voice.

His gaping eyes followed her as she opened the backpack and poured its contents into the hut, a seemingly endless flurry of hundred-dollar bills, some in banded stacks, some loose. She tossed the backpack in after it, then picked up a fistful of dried thatch from the floor and snapped a flame from the cigarette lighter.

'Ahhh,' Bullens objected. The blood flowed from his opened shoulder like oil from a pipeline.

Turning back to the garden, she showed Sereno the flame. Though the Indian was barely visible in the darkness, she could see the sparkle of his eyes. Touching the flame to the thatch, the fire took hold, and she tossed it inside the hut. Grasshoppers sprang over Bullens, who shivered silently in the firelight. His mouth seemed to be moving, but he wasn't making a sound.

The thatch made good fuel. Flames swept across the floor. Windows cracked, and the front wall blossomed into light and heat.

'Ma'am,' Gideon said, 'we'd better move him back.'

Bullens, head turned toward the fire, lay flat and glaze-eyed, motionless.

'I'm not touching him,' Alix said.

Above their heads, the trees began to squeal. Then a voice rang out. 'Freeze!'

Susan Evangeline, wielding a small service revolver, pushed through the brush, talking into a hand-held radio. Seeing Gideon dragging Bullens across the broken glass, she trained her weapon on him while she moved carefully toward Alix.

'What's going on?' she said. 'Where's Jacob Winter?'

'I don't know,' Alix replied unconvincingly, after a moment's hesitation.

'The police are on the way, you can talk to them,' Evangeline said, then turned to Gideon. 'Are you Officer Gideon?'

Kneeling beside Bullens' body, he looked up at her.

'This man saved me,' Alix said.

'I need you to stay put,' Evangeline told him. 'There are people coming to get you.'

The black man tensed.

'It's your wife and friend,' Evangeline told him, holstering her weapon. 'They asked me to give you a message. A Warden Shivers was arrested in Florida. He's made a confession, and you're free to go home.'

Gideon studied the woman who was telling him this, as if afraid to believe her. She did not attempt further persuading, but turned back to Alix, reaching behind her and taking a handkerchief from her pocket. 'What did you do?'

'I'm okay,' Alix said, closing her hand on the blood. When Evangeline reached to wipe her face, Alix pulled away. 'I'm okay,' she repeated. 'The man back there needs an ambulance.'

Michael Kimball

'He's dead,' Evangeline told her, stuffing the handkerchief in her hand. 'Wrap this around it.'

'Not him,' Alix said, and pointed off where Sereno lay.

But only the blanket was there.

Evangeline directed her flashlight to the bloody spot, the tiny bullet hole. She lifted the blanket, and her beam illuminated something else. She picked it up and turned it over in her hand. 'A garage-door opener?'

'*Max!*'

Two people broke out of the trees, a woman and an older man, both hurrying through the darkness toward the burning hut.

'He's not here,' Alix told them.

'Where is he?'

Evangeline said, 'Mr Frenetti, the police are aware of the situation—'

Squeaky shouted, 'Someone better tell me where my grandson is!'

Outside, a car engine roared to life.

Squeaky's head snapped around.

Then, with a squeal of burning rubber, his Impala was gone.

CHAPTER FOUR

High above the rest of the world, Jacob Winter climbs, right hand clutching the cable. Although he is almost to the top, and his ascent has begun to level off, he still cannot see the beacon or his son out ahead of him, only the chord under his feet as it rises ahead of him. But he seems to have gathered strength as the world has slipped away – the traffic, the river, the awakening town. Far below he sees red lights down on the salt bulker. The ship is also flying a red flag, which means it's fueling – Jacob wonders why he knows this, and why he bothers to think of it now – perhaps because it's preparing to leave, and the crew members might be heading home to loved ones. Up here there is only the sky to embrace him, big and rose-colored.

'*Dad!*'

Jacob stops, terrified. Suddenly he can see two heads atop the structure – now bright from the airplane beacon – now silhouetted against the sky.

'*Dad!*'

He wants the cry to be a seagull's, because he's never heard such fear in his son's voice. And so it happens, that a seagull swoops up from below him, balances on the breeze, then dives away.

'*Dad, don't come up here!*'

July stands behind Max with her arm wrapped around his chest. Beside them the airplane beacon flares again, and Jacob can make out the flash of a knife blade in her hand.

'*July, let him go!*' Jacob's poor voice, sliced with fear, barely comes out of his mouth.

Then he sees a small movement ahead of him. At first he thinks it's a loose bolt rolling on the chord. Then it takes a timid hop. Yellow and glistening, a tiny frog. And another one, about two feet away, crawling up from the bottom of the cable. Then he sees them everywhere, like dandelions, inching along the chord, clinging to the cable.

387

Michael Kimball

'She told me you were up here!' Max cries out. 'That's why I came!'

'Hang on, Max!' Jacob yells.

Max stares down at him, terrified.

'We were afraid you'd desert him,' July calls.

Jacob watches a frog clinging to the cable. Wide-eyed, the tiny creature crawls purposefully toward his hand, leaving a glistening trail where it has been. Knowing he must let go of the cable to let the frog pass, Jacob lowers himself to the chord, gripping the edges in both hands. He feels himself pushed by a gust of wind, but he crawls ahead, shivering uncontrollably. When he tries to stand again, he is not able. The muscles will not return to his legs.

She yells across the wind. 'You're deserting him right now.'

Jacob gets up to one knee and lunges toward the cable, catches it in both hands, then pulls himself back up on his poor legs, thinking that if he can get close enough, if he plays the wind right, he can get a shot with his dart.

She swings around to him. 'Stop coming!'

'July, you're out of danger,' says Jacob, within twenty feet of them now. 'Your husband is in custody.'

'Oh, are you here to rescue me?'

'I'm only saying, there's no reason for this,' he answers, stepping ahead. 'You're safe now.'

Suddenly July grabs Max by the arm, swings him so violently against the cable that his foot slips off the chord. 'You think I won't?'

'*Max!*'

'Stop where you are,' she warns, angling the blade toward Max's ribs, 'or the boy will fly.' Max clutches the cable with both arms.

Jacob hangs on too. 'Please,' he says to her. 'What do you want from me?'

'What makes you think I want anything?' She smiles. 'But I think your boy wants to see you jump.'

Maxie shakes his head. 'Uh-uh.'

'Okay, then. You,' she says to Max. 'You jump – and your dad won't have to.'

'Max, no!'

July nods her head up and down, like a little girl. 'One of you has to.'

'Please,' Jacob says.

'Oh, look at the baby,' she says. 'I bet Max is a brave boy, not a big coward like you.'

'Max, don't!'

He sees Max lean out over the cable, looking down at the river.

388

'*Maxie, no!*' Far below them, sirens sound like music, distant and disconnected. 'Max, I mean it,' Jacob says to his son. 'Promise me.'

July laughs. 'Oh, like you promise him? You're such a liar.'

'July, tell me what you want. I'll do anything.'

She stares at him. With each flare of the beacon, he can see the oily glisten of her eyes, and he knows she's been drinking yagé.

'I want you to jump,' she says lightly.

'Jump why?'

She wraps her arm tighter around Max, her knife angled up by his ear. 'I'm going to count to five,' she says. 'And if you don't jump, then your boy is going to. *One.*'

'Stop it! Why?'

She prods the back of Max's hand with the blade. A tear blows out from under his glasses, across his cheek. 'Let go, baby,' she teases, but he squeezes the cable tighter. So she touches the blade to his side.

'July—' He moves toward her.

'Come closer, Jacob, I'll stick him now. *Two.*'

'What do you want me to say?'

'It doesn't matter what you say,' she replies. 'You're a liar. *Three.*'

'Okay, I'll jump!'

'*Four.*'

'*Will you wait!*' he shouts. 'I told you, I'll jump!'

'Dad, no!'

'Don't worry, Max, I know how to do it,' he says. 'Feet first, body straight as an arrow, I'll be fine.' Jacob nods at his son with all the bravura he can muster, but he's actually just instructed him. 'Something I never told you – I used to do cliff diving.'

July wrinkles her nose, but he can tell that his confidence has begun to undermine hers.

'Do it,' she says, and she studies him intently, the way she had when they made love. He sees a helicopter rising up above the Portsmouth horizon. July tightens her grip on Max.

'No problem,' Jacob says, as he pushes and pulls on the cable like a diver testing the springboard, but his legs weaken beneath him. 'Does it count extra if I do a couple of back-flips?' He tries smiling at her.

But July's eyes move to her right, aware of the man crouched on the opposite, southbound side of the bridge – while Jacob furtively pulls the pen from his pocket.

'Maxie, hold onto that cable,' he says. 'No matter what happens, don't let go.'

July snaps back to him, glaring suspiciously.

'It's a sniper,' he tells her, concealing the pen behind his leg, thumb covering the end hole so he doesn't lose the dart. The helicopter hovers about a hundred feet out from them, turning slowly to the side, revealing another man kneeling inside the open door, aiming a rifle.

'That's another one,' Jacob says. 'If anything happens to Max, you know they're going to shoot you.'

'Stupid, they're aiming at you,' July says, waving the knife out at him. 'I'm protecting Max from you, because you've lost your mind. Everybody knows. As soon as you jump, I'll drop the knife and let him go.'

'Okay,' Jacob whispers. He can only whisper. He lets go of the cable. Stares straight out across the red sky.

'*Now.*' The word oozes from her lips.

He looks back at his son, tries not to let on how hard he's shaking.

'July, would you take off his hat?'

'*Stop it!*' She squeezes Max's shoulder. The pain makes him bend his back.

'Just, please, let me have one last look at him – without the hat. July, please. Then I'll go.'

'There,' she says, and whips off Maxie's cap, revealing the friar's head.

In the instant of her distraction, Jacob goes, '*Twooo!*'

The hollow pen pops from his lips, bounces off the steel, and is gone . . .

July turns back toward him, betrayed. Seeing the dart stuck in his teeth, she almost laughs, then looks as if she's going to be sick. 'I hate this,' she says, and turns her knife to Max.

A booming horn stops her, the departing blast from the salt bulker leaving port, and the ship is answered by a startled squeal of seagulls, as the birds scatter from the understructure of the bridge, hundreds of seabirds exploding upward as though bursting out of the river itself, rising up in a furious flutter of wings, higher and higher and suddenly they're attacking the arch, picking tiny frogs off the cable and chord, screeching and bickering over the bounty, while July swipes her knife in the air, screeching back at them . . .

Then stops.

Jacob sees it too.

Coming straight at them through the barrage, its wingspan spread four feet wide. July lets go of Max, as the yellow-headed bird swoops in at her, wings beating hard, July slashing fearfully with her blade.

At the same instant, Jacob leaves his feet – *I'm doing it,* he thinks, *actually doing it* – and tackles her.

Green Girls

The moment expands . . .

Jacob watches the yellow diskette fall from his shirt pocket and go fluttering away. He swings out over the river, hanging onto July's waist. She stands at the edge of the chord, having caught the cable under her arms, straining against the pull of his weight. His knees bang up against the side of the chord. If he can swing a leg up—

But her own knee knocks at his ribs, and he slips lower.

'Dad!' Max drops to his stomach, trying to reach his father.

'Max, no!' he gasps.

Looking up at July hanging over the cable, beaming down at him. She rears back with her knee . . . and drives hard into his chest.

The impact loosens his grip. He slips down, catches her waistband with his thumb, wraps his other arm around her hip, hanging helplessly with the red river waiting silently below.

He hears machine gun fire – no, it's the helicopter coming closer. Wind from its rotors beats at his back. Cheek pressed against July's bare stomach, her warmth is an odd comfort to him. . . until he hears her chiming laughter above him. She simply wiggles her hips, and he slips further.

'Dad!'

'Maxie!' he cries, wanting to tell his son to get away from her, but he can't talk with the dart stuck in his teeth. He tries to spit it out—

Then it hits him.

It must hit her too, the way she suddenly starts trying to shake him free.

Jacob looks up, watches her black eyes flare as he lets the bamboo point touch the smooth, stretched skin below her navel. She hardens her muscles. He pecks at her, and she gives a fierce, throaty objection. Her arms tighten around the cable; her knees strike his shoulders in tandem, once, twice—

Then he lunges. The tip pierces her skin.

She lets out an enraged shriek, and he forces the shank in further. Her knees struggle against him.

Above him, a cop grabs onto Max, pulling him back. 'You can't help, they'll pull you off,' he says to the boy.

July's knees stop. A drop of blood forms around the bamboo. She gives two more feeble kicks. Jacob looks up, sees the helpless fear in her eyes. The knife falls from her fingers, hits Jacob's back and falls. Then her heel slips off the chord. Jacob swings to the side . . .

They fall.

Yes, metabolism rises and time slows down, but not much. Jacob is reeling his arms furiously as he falls, trying to keep his upright alignment.

The green steel whispers past him. Traffic on the roadway appears stationary. In fact, it is stationary. Roadblocks barricade both ends of the bridge. The roadway rises.

He sees July above him, arms outstretched, a placid look on her face, both of them silent, weightless, floating like fairies—

—actually, like the pair of fairies depicted on the headboard of Jacob's marriage bed, Price Ashworth's stained-glass lovers balanced in the air, wings spread blissfully against the stars and crescent moon.

Jacob envisions his radio, black and streamlined, as it floats silently over the bed, at the end of its power cord, flying toward the stained glass, when Price's arm leaps up to intercept the radio, which swings around his arm . . .

Jacob hears a whooshing sound, then a loud ring of steel, as a green column flashes past his eyes, leaving him with the revelation: He was only trying to smash Price's stained glass.

He reels his arms. The bridge disappears. July is no longer with him.

Out in the middle of the river, he sees the salt bulker going away, pulled along by three small tugs. On the Portsmouth riverbank, he sees a crowd of people – not watching the ship depart, they're watching him fall. He sees police cars, emergency vehicles, fire trucks, searchlights . . .

In his imagination he sees his bed being carried by the movers, his fine mahogany bed with a rectangular opening where Price's stained glass had been – and he realizes: Laura smashed it for him.

Below him he sees seaweed floating.

His reflection rises up.

Yes, indeed, a beautiful time to figure things out.

CHAPTER FIVE

The Piscataqua is deep, its current is strong, and in summer the river is filled with striped bass and bluefish and mackerel. But the water is much too salty to drink. When Jacob had drunk enough, somebody pulled him up.

He choked, then he vomited, and someone said, 'Boredom.'

Jacob felt more hands on him, then something slid forcefully under his back.

'Is he boarded? Strap him. Watch his arm. One, two—'

Jacob felt the river wash over him as he rose into the air. Then someone put a blanket over him and tucked it under his shoulders. He coughed up more water, turned his head sideways to spit it out. A motor was chugging behind his head.

'My son,' he gasped, 'Max.'

'Max is fine,' someone said, holding his shoulder. 'They're flying him down.'

Jacob looked up at the underside of the bridge; all the structural steel above; a helicopter hovered over the arch. A man wearing bifocals looked into his face and asked, 'Do you hurt anywhere?'

Jacob had to think about it, then the pain started. That's when he knew for sure that he was still alive. His stomach ached. And his legs. His arm seemed to radiate pain all over his body.

'Are you sure?' he said. 'Maxie's okay?'

'Perfectly fine,' the man said. 'He's coming down to see you.'

Jacob watched the helicopter fly slowly overhead, thought of Max inside, and he tensed. Then he saw the concrete bridge pier rocking beside them, covered with barnacles to the high water mark, and it occurred to him that he had probably never appreciated anything as much as the sight of those barnacles.

'Can you wiggle your toes?' the man said.

Jacob did.

'Easy,' the man said, holding his knee. 'We'll be there in a minute.'

The motor revved. They started to move. A woman knelt beside him and gently folded the blanket down from his shoulder. 'I'm going to splint your arm,' she said. 'Try not to move.'

She had a thin face and frizzy hair, and a wonderful smile. He felt her warm fingers on the back of his wrist.

'What about the girl?' Jacob said. 'There was a girl up there.'

The woman's smile turned sympathetic, and she strapped his arm to a stiff plastic board.

Jacob coughed some more, then looked back toward the bridge, where divers were dragging a body into a police boat.

The woman patted his hand. 'All set,' she said, and pulled the blanket to his shoulders again.

'How about inside?' said the bifocaled man, probing him gently, running his fingers along the back of his neck. 'Ribs, belly, chest?'

His arm sent another throbbing message to his brain. 'Starting to feel this.'

'You will,' the woman told him.

Jacob looked off downriver, where the three small tugs were hauling the salt bulker out to sea. Then the rescue boat made a turn, heading for the Portsmouth dock, and suddenly Jacob could hear some cheering over the sound of the motor. He looked up and saw an ambulance parked on the pier, its red lights flashing, and a small crowd of onlookers being kept back by yellow tape. He could see Squeaky's red Impala parked on the other side of the salt pile. He tried to sit up, to see if Laura was there with her father.

'Take it easy,' said the guy with bifocals, keeping his hand on him.

Behind the fire trucks, he saw the helicopter land, its rotor slowing as it sliced the morning air. Laura and Squeaky were pushing through the crowd on the pier, then Max came running out of the chopper. Laura dropped to her knees and took him in her arms. Squeaky held them both.

Tears blurred Jacob's vision. He wiped his eyes. Then all other sounds disappeared.

'Dad! Hey, Dad!'

Max was standing at the edge of the gangplank, looking like he wanted to dive into the river. He probably would have, if two paramedics weren't holding him back.

'Dad!'

Max broke away from them and ran down the gangplank to the

lower dock. Jacob pulled his good arm out of the strap, found the catch and freed his chest.

'Mr Winter, you need to wait for the stretcher,' the man said.

'That's my son,' he said, and reached down for the middle strap. The boat bumped the dock.

'Mr Winter—'

'I can walk,' Jacob said.

'He'll be okay,' the woman said, freeing Jacob's feet. 'Just be careful of your arm.'

As the man stepped onto the dock and tied the boat to the cleat, Jacob climbed stiffly out and went immediately to Max, hoisting him up in his good arm. Max hugged him back with both arms and legs. Jacob tried to stop shivering.

'Mr Winter, you need to come to the hospital,' said a paramedic in a blue jumpsuit. There were two of them. Close by, Laura stood arm in arm with her father.

Jacob ignored them both, holding his son, savoring the warmth of Max's warm breath on his face.

'Then I'd like a word,' said a familiar voice.

Jacob looked up to see Susan Evangeline coming down the gang-plank, flanked by two Portsmouth policemen.

Laura headed them off, saying, 'Can I have a minute?'

'Ma'am, he needs to be treated,' said a cop.

Evangeline studied Jacob for a moment or two, then turned back to the cops. 'Give them some privacy,' she said. 'Emergency's over.'

Jacob looked up to the pier, where he saw Squeaky holding onto the barrier, watching.

'Mom said somebody stole Gramp's car,' Max said.

'His car? It's right over there,' Jacob said – but the Impala was hidden from view, on the other side of the salt. 'Squeaky, your car,' Jacob called, but the old man couldn't hear him over the commotion. Besides, the way Max was holding onto Jacob. He had never known the boy to be frightened, until now, with his face buried in the crook of his father's jaw. 'It's okay, Champ,' Jacob said. 'Everything's gonna be okay.'

'Everything?' Max replied in a small voice.

Jacob felt a blanket drape over him. Laura tucked one corner around his chest and the other gently over his injured arm.

'I've been trying to come up with an apology,' she said quietly, keeping her hands on him.

He took a breath, deep enough that it hurt his ribs, trying to swallow his injury. 'What you said yesterday.' He gave her a cryptic look. 'Once?'

She nodded. 'I couldn't go through with it.'

He met her eyes, so full and beautiful, and she lowered her head onto his chest. It was a tentative gesture, but he didn't pull away.

'Jake, I'm so sorry I hurt you,' she whispered, and got her arms around them both, so solid and warm that he almost forgot they were ever apart. 'If you can ever forgive me,' she said, 'I'm going to need someone to make furniture for the Inn. A desk man too. Part time, it wouldn't pay much, but you'd have free room and board. And all the time in the world to write.'

Jacob looked away, at the crowd of watchers, all the faces, and he saw a couple in love, an African-American police officer and a woman who must have been his wife, holding each other tightly. They both looked like they'd been crying. A tall, brawny white man wearing a cowboy hat and handlebar mustache stood nearby, smoking a pipe while he watched them. Then Jacob saw Squeaky, standing off by himself behind the barrier, watching him intently.

He looked back to the bridge, and he breathed in the salt air off the river. Then he put his mouth close to Laura's ear. 'I don't think I'm ready,' he said, soft enough so Max wouldn't hear.

She slipped her arm out from under his, and stared up at him with regretful, liquid eyes.

'I'm sorry,' she whispered.

'We need you to lie on the stretcher, Mr Winter,' one of the paramedics said, reaching to take Max from Jacob, but the boy hung tightly to his father.

'Can he ride with me?' Jacob asked.

'I don't see why not,' said the man. 'There's a jump seat back there.'

'Mr Winter, when you're up to it,' Susan Evangeline said, moving in, 'I'll need to ask you some questions.'

'Can it wait till he gets to the hospital?' said the paramedic.

'Also,' she said, showing Jacob a yellow diskette, 'one of the officers found this on the bridge. Your name's on it.' She tried to hand it to him.

'Throw it in the river,' Jacob said. 'I never knew what to write about, anyway.'

'Don't—'

Jacob looked to his left, where Alix was pushing to the front of the crowd. 'It's a good book,' she told him. 'Don't throw it away.'

Max reached out for the diskette. Evangeline gave it to him.

'Sir, we've got to move,' the paramedic said, lifting Max out of Jacob's arm, his diskette tight in the boy's fist. Then, catching sight of the bloody handkerchief wrapped around Alix's hand, he added,

'While we're at it, Miss, you'd better come along too.'

'I'll take her.'

Alix looked over.

'She can fill me in on the way,' Evangeline added.

Alix stood with a foot on the rung, staring at the ambulance floor, uncommitted.

'Please,' Evangeline said to her. 'I need to talk to you.'

Alix backed down, gave her a long look, then said to the paramedic, 'I'll go with her.'

'You can follow us,' the driver said, as he helped Jacob to lie back on the stretcher, then strapped him down and covered him with the blanket. As they jacked the stretcher in the air, Jacob caught Alix's eye.

'Would you call my father for me?' he said.

'For what?'

'Tell him I'm sorry about his car,' he said. 'I'll pay whatever his insurance doesn't cover. The legal help too. I'll reimburse him.'

'What about dinner?'

'What dinner?'

'You owe him dinner,' Alix said.

Jacob's chest jumped with a laugh, and the pain shot up to his shoulder. 'By any chance, do you have a brother you used to torment?'

Alix smirked. 'I'm an only child.'

'Me too.'

'Can you two finish this up at the hospital?' one of the paramedics said, as they wheeled him into the ambulance.

'Would you like one?' Jacob said.

'Wait.' Alix stopped the other door from closing. 'Would I like one what?'

He looked out at her. 'A brother.'

The way she smiled at him – as bright as the big sun rising over the river – he realized that he'd never seen her happy before. She took hold of his foot – and her eyes welled with tears. First time he'd ever seen her cry too. 'I think that would be nice,' she told him.

From far downriver came another departing blast from the salt bulker. It was a 16,000-ton ship, once American, now Panamanian, with a crew that included Panamanians, Croats, Filipinos, and a Norwegian captain and chief engineer. Below decks were hundreds of places, cargo holds and cubbyholes, where a stowaway could hide during the day, and lots of room to roam at night, when most of the crew was asleep. There were caches of food and water, and even medicines, if a man were in need.

In a few days the bulker would reach Great Inagua Island in the

Bahamas, where it would pick up another load from the salt distillery. First, however, there was a load of Maine gravel destined for Peru. Who would ever know, in the dead of night as the ship made its ponderous way through the Panama Canal, if someone were to climb down to land? A man used to mountains and night travel might have no problem traversing the *Cordillera de San Blas* and making his way to the archipelago just offshore, a chain of tiny islands inhabited by the Kuna Indians, a small-statured but proud and primitive tribe, among whom another small-statured man, knowledgeable in the ancient ways of healing and spirit flight and magic in the world, might find a home.

THANKSGIVING

'**D**ad,' Maxie said, 'we're supposed to be there. Now.'
With a frosty wind gusting out of the north, he carried the last chair out of the shop, the seat balanced on his head. There were eight in all, Windsor chairs made of ash, with ornate cockleshells carved in the top rails. Although Windsor chairs did not traditionally have top rails, these chairs did, and they were curved to conform to the human back, with rounded seats and a single length of ash bent completely around, to form the back.

Jacob, standing on the rear bumper of his car, wearing his wool hat and a winter coat, took the chair from Max and set it, with the others, atop the butterfly table he had also made, its own ornamental legs pointing up at the ice blue sky. The table had rounded drop-leaves, and cockleshells carved in the drawers. He had bought the wood for the dining room set with some of his thousand-dollar advance on *Bridge*, which a small Boston publisher was going to bring out in the spring. 'Here comes,' he called, and threw the rope over the top of the load.

Alix caught it, and pulled it tight. The furniture creaked.

'Mom's all worried,' Maxie said. 'She's afraid Gramp Frenetti and Gramp Winter are gonna be the first ones there.' Laura had dropped Max off the afternoon before, so she could get everything ready for the dinner.

'What's she worried about?' Jacob asked.

'No one's ever met Gramp Winter!' Max said, steam pouring from his mouth.

Alix tossed the rope back to Jacob. He had spent the past four months living at Green Girls, while Alix had rejuvenated her flower business – and her poetry. In payment for his room and board, Jacob had built her a birch bed and bookshelves for her bedroom.

'She's also worried about the food,' Max told him. 'Let's see. We're having shrimp panzanella.'

'Mmm,' Jacob said. 'That reminds me, did you put your pies in the car?'

'Yeah, only an hour ago,' Max said. He took the rope from his father, carried it around the side of the car and threw it over to Alix. He had baked the pies the night before, with Alix's help: lemon-cranberry meringue and pumpkin-peanut butter. 'She's making diavolillo stuffing for the turkey,' Max went on. 'And your favorite – serpentone – special for Thanksgiving, with cranberries, apples, and butternut squash.'

'Sounds good, what is it?' Alix said.

'Stuffed pastry,' Jacob told her.

'I know what she's really worried about,' Max said. 'You know, she had her hair done twice yesterday? I thought she was gonna bust a gasket. Then she went out and bought three white shirts, and she kept trying on jeans, like, ten different stores. Oh, yeah, don't forget to tell her how beautiful her fingernails look.' He rolled his eyes.

Jacob gave Alix a look. 'Sounds like your day yesterday.'

'Look who's talking.' Alix was wearing a green wool sweater she had knitted, with orange and red markings around the collar and cuffs, and loose-fitting chocolate-colored corduroy jeans. Her hair was shingle cut and tinged with a shade of red that matched the highlights in her sweater. In the backseat she had set the floral centerpiece she had created, along with individual orchid sprays she had made for each dinner guest. Susan Evangeline would be at dinner too, celebrating her first month in private practice. 'Hey, Maxie, ever seen your dad in a necktie?' she said.

'Are you kidding? I never saw his hair combed, either.'

Alix laughed. 'I feel like we're going to the prom.' She tossed the rope over the load, back to Jacob. 'How nervous are you?'

'Not very.'

'Not much.'

'Just remember what you tell me,' Max said to his father. 'Head, not heart.'

Jacob pulled down on the rope and knotted it. 'I'm not so sure about that, Maxie. I don't think that works any more.'

'What do you mean?'

'He means don't think so much,' Alix said. 'Word for the day: Bend.'

Max looked up at his father. 'So, Dad,' he said. 'What does work?'

Jacob tugged at the load to make sure it was secure. 'Maybe you should tell me,' he answered, then slapped the car roof. 'Let's go, everyone, over the river and through the woods.'

'Are you sure that's enough rope?' Max said. 'It's pretty windy.'

'It'll do,' Jacob said.

Max gave him a quizzical look. And a minute later he gave his father the same look when Jacob steered the overloaded car onto the I-95 ramp, heading up over the High-Level bridge.

'What's the matter?' Jacob asked him.

Max shrugged his shoulders. As soon as they merged with the traffic going over the bridge, the wind buffeted the car, and the load shifted to the left. Jacob let the gust carry them into the passing lane.

'Don't worry,' he said to his son, even though he knew that, with the strength of the wind, the whole thing might let go and come crashing down on the bridge.

But it didn't.

And as late as they were already, Laura's turkey might be cold by the time they got there, or overcooked.

But it wasn't.

With all the dining-room furniture stacked on top of the car, the guests might be standing in the empty room, Squeaky Frenetti and Susan Evangeline and J. William Winter III, none of them speaking.

But that wasn't the case, either. In fact, they were all in the kitchen, Squeaky carving the turkey, Jacob's dad mashing potatoes, Laura putting the finishing touches on her shrimp panzanella, and Susan Evangeline tossing the smoked mussel salad she had brought while Squeaky told them all about the Pennzoil 400, which Jeff Dakota had won.

'Dad,' Max said, as they crossed over the bridge into Maine.

'What?'

'I think I know what works.'

'I'm listening.'

He gave Max a look, which Max wouldn't return.

'Tell me,' Jacob said again. 'What works?'

Max kept his eyes focused on his knees. 'You and Mom,' he said. 'And me.'

Jacob saw Alix's eyes in the rear-view mirror, watching him.

He touched Max's knee. Max still refused to look up.

'Hey, Maxie.'

He took hold of the boy's sticky hand.

'What?'

Jacob said, 'It works for me, too.'